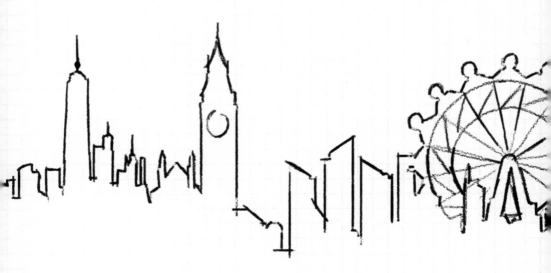

Ian Martin is an Emmy Award-winning comedy writer. His credits include *The Death of Stalin*, *The Thick of It*, *Veep*, *Time Trumpet* and *In the Loop*. He writes regularly for the *Guardian* and the *Architects' Journal*. His book *The Coalition Chronicles* is published by Faber & Faber.

EPIC SPACE

Ian Martin

This edition first published in 2017

unbound

6th Floor Mutual House 70 Conduit Street London W1S 2GF

www.unbound.com

© Ian Martin, 2017

Text Design by Patty Rennie
Art direction by Mark Ecob

A CIP record for this book is available from the British Library

ISBN 978-1-78352-317-7 (trade hbk)
ISBN 978-1-78352-318-4 (ebook)
ISBN 978-1-78352-319-1 (limited edition)

Printed in Great Britain by CPI

To my beloved wife Eileen,
who has put up with this shit since 1973.

Dear Reader,

The book you are holding came about in a rather different way to most others. It was funded directly by readers through a new website: Unbound. Unbound is the creation of three writers. We started the company because we believed there had to be a better deal for both writers and readers. On the Unbound website, authors share the ideas for the books they want to write directly with readers. If enough of you support the book by pledging for it in advance, we produce a beautifully bound special subscribers' edition and distribute a regular edition and e-book wherever books are sold, in shops and online.

This new way of publishing is actually a very old idea (Samuel Johnson funded his dictionary this way). We're just using the internet to build each writer a network of patrons. Here, at the back of this book, you'll find the names of all the people who made it happen.

Publishing in this way means readers are no longer just passive consumers of the books they buy, and authors are free to write the books they really want. They get a much fairer return too – half the profits their books generate, rather than a tiny percentage of the cover price.

If you're not yet a subscriber, we hope that you'll want to join our publishing revolution and have your name listed in one of our books in the future. To get you started, here is a £5 discount on your first pledge. Just visit unbound.com, make your pledge and type epicspace in the promo code box when you check out.

Thank you for your support,

Dan, Justin and John
Founders, **unbound**

Contents

Foreword

Ian Martin is many things. He is a man, certainly. I know this to be a fact as I was once behind in him in the passport queue at Baltimore Airport and the lady doing the checking didn't so much as flinch. He is unique among people who don't actually behave as if they're the only person in the world to have written and acted in both *The Thick of It* and its American cousin *Veep*. He is what certain kinds of journalists would call 'an ex-rocker' who can be provoked to violence by three bars of jazz and soothed again by being shown a picture of Bach. And he is without doubt my very favourite writer of comic prose in the English language.

The best comic writers are those who not only squirt their ink at the right targets or hammer out the perfect images, they make the language itself funny: the rhythm, the sound, the colour. They're the ones who make you laugh at the very words they use. That's Ian Martin. He can spin the English language round his fingers like a conjuror's coin.

Take the occasion – as related in this book – when he was appointed Architectural Nickname Czar to ensure that new buildings are given better epithets than 'The Shard' or 'The Gherkin'. The list of suggestions that follows is a sustained cannonade of impossible inventiveness and comic poetry, including but not limited to: The Shiny Tumulus, The Stilty Lump, The Skyfister, The Extrudel, The Glandmark and The Sentient Plume. And I simply cannot imagine any other columnist currently thumping a keyboard on a regular basis who would title a piece anything like 'I Sense My Enemies Massing Like Simpering Starlings'.

That voice is beguiling, unique and rather influential. You'll find it, among other places, in the mouths of Malcolm Tucker and Selina Meyer, even when it isn't Ian himself doing the writing. The great Tony Roche, one of the original quartet of filthpots who dishonoured the BBC with the vilely crude unnecessariness of *The Thick of It*, has said that he coined the word 'omnishambles' – later named Word of the Year 2012 by people who imagine such things are a worthwhile expenditure of calories – partly in homage to Ian's style.

The present volume which you hold in your hands – or, for future readers, which you have think-accessed on the Kindle Mindwave Intranexus™ – is essentially a long bar on which are lined up over a hundred espresso shots of pure Martin. A collection of satirical pieces written for the *Architects' Journal*, they naturally, and indeed contractually, take architecture as their subject, but their targets are far wider ranging than that. If you'll allow me to be a ponce for a minute – or more realistically, if you'll allow me to continue being a ponce for quite a long while – I would say that they are satires on an entire culture: our politics, the inanity of the consumer society, journalism, faddishness, regional developmental funding, social media, 'Heritage' and, in fact, pretty much everything else.

But more than anything, they are a satire on language itself. Or rather, on the way that it's used now: the self-satisfied idiocy of corporate-speak, the emperor's-new-clothes-pretension of architects and 'creatives', the banality of marketing. I'm reminded about seventy-four times a day of 'I need some marketing blurt in a nice font. Neutral to the point of meaningless' from his piece 'Magnetic Values'. He catches the tone and the timbre of the use and misuse of English and twists it into his own filigree comic structures. By turns angry, contemptuous, resigned, pitying, self-pitying, mischievous, despairing and hopeful, these pieces are never anything less than whirlingly funny; inventive and invective in perfect measure – like S. J. Perelman stubbing his toe.

I once met Ian for lunch. (Not the time he threatened to stab the music speaker with a fork if they didn't turn the jazz off, but another one.) I was two minutes late, and on arriving at the table I discovered him already seated and a cocktail by my place setting.

'Hope you don't mind,' he said, fishing an olive from his drink, 'I ordered some martinis.'

Then he got us some stout to go with the chicken livers (you can take the boy out of the East End, etc., etc.), wine for the mains and Armagnac with the dessert.

'It's so nice,' he subtly belched as I tried to remember how to sit on a chair, 'to find someone who'll stick with you right from the martinis through to the brandies.'

And that's what I recommend you do with this book: Don't dip. You're in the finest, most entertaining company you could want. Just start with the martinis and go on through to the brandies. Your head will be joyfully spinning as you leave.

Chris Addison, 2016

With Special Thanks to the Enlightened Patrons
Chris MacAllister, Richard Newman,
Paul Vincent and Robert Willis

EPIC SPACE

The Case of the Missing Parisian Absinthe Kiosk

MONDAY To Lourdes, where I'm creating a boutique hotel. It's 150 years since an innocent 14-year-old country girl experienced visions of 280 saints, some of them robed, in en-suite bathrooms. Now that dream is a reality.

My own contribution to the town's tradition of five-star indulgence pushes innovation to new levels of luxury, or possibly the other way round. The spa's got a Vatican-approved infinity pool, for instance. Each room has a 50-inch ectoplasma TV, wi-fi access to purgatory, plus underfloor healing throughout.

TUESDAY Finish my design for The Amazin' Amazon Rainforest Experience, just south of Blackpool.

I've had local scepticism from the start, e.g. why would Lancastrians pay to see rain-themed anything, rain is our AIR, if dozy bastards are that desperate to see rain INSIDE a building there are several shopping centres within driving distance of Blackpool all built in the 1970s, can't we just have a nice dry supercasino instead with a karaoke bar you daft southern trollop.

Sometimes I think people simply refuse to understand the principles of critical globalism.

The architectural establishment's pissed off, too, because I've taken over the gig from Jacob Kinderegg. The world's favourite jabbering death fetishist parted company with his clients when they refused to sign off on the concept drawings.

They wanted an immersive environment suitable for school parties and coach outings. Jacob wanted to explore the mournful cadence of human suffering, with the entire contents of the biodome obliterated over the course of a year by ruthless loggers in Nazi uniforms, two performances daily. The empty biohusk would remain as a public shrine to loss and absence.

I ring Jacob just to make sure there are no hard feelings. He's cool.

And busy. Just landed a Museum of Fatal Illnesses in Antwerp. His Potato Faminarium in Baltimore tops out next month. Plus, he's now guest lecturing at the University of Kent on the fractal aesthetics of torture.

WEDNESDAY My friend Dusty Penhaligon the conservactionist calls to cancel our cycling tour of Cumbernauld. He's appearing as expert witness in a high-profile case at the Old Bailey.

Six criminal Cockney types are accused of stealing a priceless Adolf Loos building from a suburban street in Zurich. In a daring armed raid, the seminal Montessori House of 1911 was snatched from its site over the course of a fortnight by a gang posing as international building inspectors.

Very little has been recovered. A couple of window frames, some floorboards, a 'Novelty Native American Cigar Dispenser'. Police believe most of the house has been reassembled as a villa in northern Cyprus, which doesn't acknowledge architectural extradition protocol.

Dusty is rightly alarmed at the recent spate of building heists. This year alone we have lost a Le Corbusier gymnasium from Chandigarh (brutally dismantled and resold in pieces on eBay), a Frank Lloyd Wright pharmacy in Michigan (loaded in sections onto a flatbed truck by 'bug exterminators') and a unique 19th-century Parisian absinthe kiosk by Viollet-le-Duc (wrenched from the ground in an audacious daylight helicopter raid).

I agree with Dusty. The world made more sense in the 20th century, before sharp-shouldered yuppies and the internet ruined everything. When people didn't lock their historic buildings. When St Petersburg was called Leningrad and didn't have a Malaysian skyline. When you could still smoke in church. Curse this century.

THURSDAY Redesign Vancouver, making it less 'Vancouverised'.

FRIDAY I've set aside the whole day for CPD, or Contiguous Pretentious Development.

I put on Radio 3, adjust my cravat and start sketching. They're not just sketches, obviously, they're an unfurling of sequential insights into the world around me. Today I'm using my favourite insight-enabling tool, Ixworth & Donningfold's Traditional Draughting Pencil for Gentlemen. Lovely. Especially thick and black.

I'm sketching on baking paper, too, for extra gravitas. The morning passes in a delirium of abstract geometry and intuition. What do these sketches represent? The question is as pointless as it is impudent. Let posterity decide what they mean!

After lunch, urban collage-making in a collarless blouson.

4

SATURDAY Five-a-side sociological football. Driveable Suburbanism 2 Walkable Urbanism 1, after extra-time sudden-death runover.

SUNDAY Work on my Lourdes project in the recliner. After a while, have an 'out-of-body' axonometric experience.

February 14, 2008

The Betjemanisation of South London

MONDAY It's an ill wind that blows nobody a job. My friend Loaf, in his capacity as Cadbury's Creme Egg mayor of London, has just handed me an amazing commission. 'Fancy reworking south London, matey? All of it. In the style of John Betjeman...'

It's part of his four-year plan to 'literate' the capital into distinct quadrants. The East End is to be redesigned as The Complete Dickens, featuring lots of characters and bankruptcies and poor houses. The Olympic site is exempt, obviously. No such thing as a Dickensian Olympics has ever taken place, so far.

'We enjoyed great expectations of course,' says Loaf, in Latin, 'but now we are obliged to plough through hard times.' Oh yeah, the Olympics, I'd forgotten. Let's hope they don't make a 'complete Dickens' of that. His giant egg suit gives a little shrug.

Meanwhile, the built environment of north London will be nudged gently into Shakespearian tragedy with some cathartic social housing and moveable trees. Loaf says he's inclined to leave west London as it is, tightening the conservation regime to keep that 'terrific, fizzing Martin Amisy feel'.

None of these has the allocated budget of MY quadrant though – enough to sink a small nationalised bank. I feel giddy with power. If we're going the full Betjeman, can we bring back rationing, illicit sex, horse-drawn milk carts, telephone kiosks with big buttons and smoking on the top decks of buses?

Loaf considers for a second. 'Look, let's just keep it Betjeman-*esque*, OK? I have no intention of alienating the gay community. Or the formidable cancer fun run women. Betjeman is simply a developmental theme.

5

I have a vision of the future, old chum, and it is to make south London the most dynamic, the most dazzling residential heritage zone in the whole of Cadbury's Europe.'

Within that massive comedy egg there's a demonstrably strong intellect at work.

TUESDAY Redesign Yorkshire, expanding the borders slightly so it's less full of itself.

WEDNESDAY Sketch out some preliminary ideas for my Bath Drawing Board Museum.

I say 'sketch', though a) I'm using beta software developed by rocket scientists, and b) the heavy lifting's being done by my nanofuturologist friend Beansy, who illegally downloaded Vectormatique 2.0 for me. 'I didn't realise Classical pastiche involved so much repetition,' he says. 'We'll have this banged out by lunchtime. Not rocket science, is it?'

We're soon done, and I email the drawings to a little workshop off Farringdon Road where they print it out on genuine antique paper. Oh shit, I've forgotten the design statement. No problem, says Beansy, and navigates to Reactionist, a random polemic generator.

After a couple of goes we get: 'Architecture has entered a new virtual realm of discourse, stripped of the practical and pedagogical contexts that once defined its disciplinary core. That's why it is vital to remember and honour the Paraffin Lamp…' I change the last bit to Drawing Board and email it over for parchmenting.

THURSDAY Lunch with my noble friend Richard, who whines on and on about how nobody listens to him now he's a Lord. I tune out after a while. No wonder everyone's calling him Mopey Dick.

FRIDAY Draft my initial five-point plan for the Betjemanisation of south London.

1. Comprehensive audit of apsidal chancels, Nonconformist spirelets and schools by E. R. Robson in the style of Norman Shaw.
2. River idealisation scheme to allow the waters of the Wandle to flow more lugubriously.
3. Replace 'workers' flats in fields of soya beans, towering up like silver pencils with 'obedient, cheerful Cockney slums in terraced rows, their lavatories without'.
4. Restore faded Victorian grandeur of buildings now operating as nightclubs by revoking their nightclub licences.

5. Reach out to underclass with cultural education project, e.g. correct deployment of teddy bear is under arm of young poet, not amid cellophane pilings at ghastly roadside shrine.

SATURDAY Bump into Andrew Lloyd Webber at a Baroque fund-raiser. Result. He's on board with Project Betjeman and has agreed to stimulate interest in Evensong among south Londoners, via the telly.

SUNDAY In the recliner when Charles rings. He's also fully behind the Betj-Up. Suddenly realise this project appeals to all the wrong people. Now I've talked myself into a depression. Go to pub to see if I can spend my way out of one.

November 4, 2008

The Dreamed Vortex

MONDAY Meeting of the Olympic Rebadging Taskforce. The gravity of the situation is taking its toll, even on Games Minister Suzi Towel.

That compulsory Mexican wave we have before Apologies for Absence gets more perfunctory each time. Nobody does the good-natured booing now when the wave gets to Treasury Steve and he refuses to join in. Oh sure, Suzi still says 'Yay!' every time the word 'Olympics' is mentioned. But these days it's without the exclamation mark.

Still. Not all gloom. The IOC inspectors came over for a tour of the building site – correction, Delivery Park – and went home happy. It's amazing how much international goodwill can be generated by a good lunch, a Cornetto on an open-topped Routemaster and a nap on the plane home. No awkward questions about the £9.3 billion budget, which we're rather cleverly rebadging as being 'under control'.

Suzi explains. 'A dog is for life, not just for Christmas. And the Olympics – yay – is for the sustainable regeneration of east London, not just for a fortnight of world-class competitive sport and various sponsorship opportunities. We're still three years off, and the budget is very much a puppy. It's under control in the sense that we've taught it to wee and poo outside, but obviously it has to develop into a complete dog, doesn't it?'

Meanwhile, we're further downgrading architectural expectations to Level 2 ('mild irritant, avoid contact with eyes'), ironically announcing plans to 'recycle' the Velodrome, and redefining 'shit-eating grin' as 'brave face'.

TUESDAY Britain now languishes at the bottom of the World Nomenclature League, and the Department of Entertainment is looking for a Building Nickname Czar. Fingers crossed.

WEDNESDAY Working on my nicknames. It's time this country took them seriously. In Seoul or Reykjavik, a new building is automatically assigned an architectural name by the relevant federal bureau of appellations. The result? Some nondescript bollocks is called The Sexy Rainbow Wand or Enfolding Love Bun.

In Britain we leave all naming to our journalists. Result? Desaturated rubbish such as The Gherkin, The Shard, The – come on, for God's sake – Cheese Grater. Worse, they always pretend buildings have been 'dubbed'. When a journalist says 'dubbed' it means 'given a nickname, by me'. Bastards.

THURSDAY Prep notes for a lecture at the Institute of Plasmic Arts. It's called 'The Misery of Excellence' and will convince everyone that I'm in the middle of writing a sarcastic masterpiece about how architecture has been sidelined into a zero-risk compliance culture, even though I've only actually written this sentence so far. 'He who lives by the kitemark, dies by the kitemark.' That sounds good, I might say that.

FRIDAY The Architectural Nickname Czar gig would look great on my portfolio, which this year runs to half a page of A4. I email the following universally deployable building names to the entertainment department:

The uPod. The Kebabel. The Shiny Tumulus. The Chamfered Cock. The Glazed Rictus. The Parenthesis. The Fat Bonus. The Clumpty. The Saucy Dalek. The Eco-Eco-Bang-Bang. The Big Ask. The Dreamed Vortex. The Petrified Discharge. The Stilty Lump. The Sentient Plume. The Perpendiculon. The Urban Stook. The Skyfister. The Messaging Ascender. The Pishtank. The Iconic Pandemonium. The Chip Naan. The Very Hungry Fuckerpilla. The Bosh. The Cloverfield Thunderbolt. The Laughing Prolapse. The Extrudel. The Batard. The Carbon-Retentive Colon. The Vertical Conga. The Paranoid Fishcake. The Aircosh. The Digital Tampon. The

Niggling Appendix. The Satirical Standup. The Shish. The Glandmark. The Convincing Wig. The ! The Crispy Beacon. The Megaphor. The Arrested Gush. The Token Block. The Aerodoodle. The Heliographic Slatfarm. The Lifecake. The Courgetto. The Lesbian Tongue. The End.

SATURDAY Absolutely no response. Sod them. Decide I'll get absolutely wankered at lunchtime. I'm meeting my old friend Darcy the architecture critic and his overdressed dachshund, Bauhau.

Then a text cancelling lunch. Odd, not like Darcy at all. And as excuses go, 'Bauhau's got a migraine' seems a bit feeble.

SUNDAY Oh lovely. Brilliant. In the *Creative on Sunday*, a drivelly piece on The Preciousness of Our Named Heritage. 'By the entertainment department's new Architectural Dubbing Czar, Darcy Farquear'say...'

There's a photo of him holding what looks like a squirming Beef Wellington. It may be a small dog in some sort of fashionable polycarbonate sheath. Or not, who cares?

March 5, 2009

Simpering Psychomuff

A quiz for ARCHITECTS ONLY. Are you a national architectural treasure? Let's find out...

QUESTION 1 We begin with that basic indicator of architectural genius, innovative cladding. Have you specified any of the following materials recently: zipped leather, decommissioned weapons, bubblewrap, knitted fibre-optic cable, chainmail, an energy plasma field or a biodegradable medium – toast, say?

If you have, proceed to the next question. If you haven't, you are neither pushing boundaries nor challenging perceptions. You're definitely not a 'national architectural treasure'. You're not even a player, fool!

QUESTION 2 Do your buildings rise dramatically from the site as a fluid and organic whole, igniting the environment and creating a dynamic beacon of optimism in a world numbed by negativity?

If yes, proceed to the next question. If your buildings just sort of sit there like big fat lumps, you're rubbish. Abandon this questionnaire.

QUESTION 3 Have you been photographed by a magazine recently, pretending not to have noticed the camera, surrounded by inert props and apparently mumbling to yourself about how we have to rebrand the profession? Yeah? Then kindly leave the page. National treasures do not discuss such things.

If, on the other hand, you've said in interview that space is a material shaped by dreams and that you strive for an architecture which goes beyond mere form-making into a systemic alchemic polemic whatever, congratulations. You're a probationary treasure.

QUESTION 4 Do you disdain Britain's suburbs and its human contents? Do you think people who'd rather go to a carpet warehouse than the Donmar Warehouse are at least misguided, if not actually in breach of international law?

Do you think barbeques in/and/or gardens are utterly selfish? Do you say things like Good Taste is the Enemy of Creativity, or Comfortable Furniture is the Enemy of, I don't know, Standing Up?

Of course you do. You're an architect. It's a trick question.

QUESTION 5 Do you use 'critique' as a verb, all the bloody time? If not, you're fired. Please leave the national treasure boardroom.

QUESTION 6 Of course, of COURSE, we all condemn violations of human rights. Especially when it involves the exploitation of construction workers hired like expendable human donkeys, risking their lives to build preposterous and effete creations coaxed from the imaginations of architects by morally neutral tranches of fee income, in parts of the world now designated as hedonistic face-stuffing shop-filled ethnically cleansed pampering playgrounds for callous shitheads who believe it's their right to be fawned over like fat demigods when they're on holiday.

If your policy is either to refuse to work on such projects, or on a point of principle to be not successful enough to land any, your hopes of becoming a national treasure are slim.

If, however, you can keep a straight face and say things like, 'I am committed to supporting our client in achieving equitable working conditions', and once went to an ethical fundraiser where Sting played his fucking lute after dinner, congratulations. You certainly sound like a national architectural treasure.

QUESTION 7 Rearrange the following words to make a coherent sentence: is, urban, masque, provocative, the, integrated, resonance, lifeview, of, freestyle, curvery, and.

If you tried to do this, I'm afraid you are not a treasure. If, however, you suggest that the randomness of the elements has its own occult interconnectivity, you could be on to something. If you imagined the individual words scattered across Photoshopped montages of city streets at night with coloured blobs and jagged lines, you're probably already a regional treasure at least.

QUESTION 8 Do you ever think about writing poetry? If you do: sorry. The national treasure express has pulled out, leaving you dithering in the waiting room unsure of what your true vocation is. If you bashfully explain at dinner parties that your architecture IS poetry, well done. That's exactly the sort of simpering psychomuff the Pritzker lot love.

QUESTION 9 Who do you think you are – GOD? Ah-ha! Got you. You were doing so well, too. A genuine national architectural treasure does not believe in God. They believe in a universe of infinite self-confidence with, at its theological centre, an omnipotent sulk.

QUESTION 10 Have you ever done an icon? If not, please produce one, then retake questions 1–9.

June 11, 2009

The Vegetable Liberation Front

MONDAY The Tamworth Design Festival has been running annually since the late eighth century and has over the years showcased some truly innovative products. The demountable Witch Detector, for instance. The Snook Rack. The Pig Recycler.

These days it's mostly furniture. But the artisans of Mercia have lost none of their native cunning, creating hugely desirable conversation pieces at imaginative prices. Today we're judging the Seating entries.

The winner is Sadface & Gentley's 'Recession', a clever reworking of the sofa narrative. A giant Spacehopper the size of a Ford Fiesta, partially deflated, with stumpy little ironic legs. It asks existential questions via the user. Whose face am I 'actually' sitting on? What do the apparently redundant giant ribbed handles signify? HOW much? Etc.

TUESDAY A lot of steam has gone out of the Olympic Rebadging Task Force lately. Even under the giddy guidance of Games Minister Suzi Towel – 'Akela after too many Lambrinis' – our old *esprit de corps* is crumbling. All the consultants are talking directly to the Shadow Olympics team now, and all the political people are lining up jobs as consultants.

Suzi calls the meeting to order with a Mexican Wave. 'Come on people!' she roars. 'The Olympics (YAY!) won't rebadge itself!'

We need to make 'roads and sheds' sound more important, as this will basically be all there is to see by the time Voters Go to the Polls. Infrastructure may be dull but Mr Blair taught us that the public sector must have a giggly subtext to make it more competitive. With itself, if necessary. That's why a 'public library' is now an 'ideas store'. Why a 'health clinic' is now a 'wellness hub'. Why a 'council swimming pool' is now a luxury apartment block.

After some thought, we rebadge the new roads as 'go channels'. We rebadge the sheds where the roadbuilding machinery is kept as 'power bases'. Then it's Any Other Business, or 'lunch'.

WEDNESDAY Winner of the Tamworth Design Festival's Lighting category: The Butchlamp by Connor Chance. Scaffolding pole with a 60-watt bulb at the end, £1,095 plus VAT.

THURSDAY It's easy to see why everyone's a little in love with Amy Blackwater, the extreme ecological activist. She's easily the most attractive woman in a balaclava I've ever met, her default setting is 'engagingly enraged' and, compellingly, she winds architects right the fuck up. She and her friends in 'the collective' are the nearest thing the profession has to a guilty conscience.

We're having a pint in the Victorian Farm, a dilapidated pub in rural Essex reborn as an experimental theatre venue. Smoking is allowed on the condition that all drinkers are 'performers' taking part in a 'piece'. At least half of us are drinking, eating and smoking through balaclavas. There are a few new concealed faces today – religious fundamentalists, here to show solidarity with the ecomentalists in the ongoing War Against Living Walls.

Over the last few weeks Amy and co. have been carrying out night raids on buildings with living walls and turning off the water pumps. 'It's sick!' splutters Amy. 'These captive plants might as well be veal babies, yeah? They're being sustained by a life support machine – itself guzzling up Earth's Precious Resources – in some Frankensteinian nightmare. How is this ecologically sound? In a world divided into gluttony and starvation it's about as morally defensible as CAT FOOD!'

God, she is wonderful. Her nutty Christian friends think so too. They reckon living walls are the new Tower of Babel – a symbol of heathen hubris. A manifestation of evil. Architects, once again, believing they are omnipotent. 'If bloody architects want to grow things round their stupid buildings,' says Amy through a cloud of roll-up smoke, 'let them stick geraniums in a pot. Or have a bloody Virginia Creeper. Or...'

Ooh, I know. Hanging baskets. Architects LOATHE them. In fact, hatred of hanging baskets is a totally dependable bourgeois signifier. Amy looks as thoughtful as anyone can inside a balaclava. Hm. Direct action to liberate living walls, AND a hanging basket guerilla campaign? Yes!

FRIDAY Winner of the Tables category: The Planolith, by Daughters of Radon. An artist's impression of a 'hard air' rectangle on bubblejets of psychic energy. Not yet in production.

SATURDAY Sketch out a reassembled Euston Arch, with hanging baskets.

SUNDAY Cross-culturally-reference self in the recliner.

September 24, 2009

The Shitley Experiment

MONDAY A breakthrough with my research project for the Bow Window Group, a conservative think tank, provisionally titled *Affordable Homes for Affordable People*.

Working late into the night in my alchemic laboratory of ideas, I accidentally spilled some notes from the control group into the experimental flux capacitor. After the dry ice cleared and my nausea had subsided a bit

I discovered that I had somehow merged the cultural notions of homeless chic and moral bankruptcy to create a new sociological construct: Affordable Poverty.

I think the tank's going to love the sound of this. It faces squarely the twin challenges of inadequate housing for the poor AND the aspirationally underperforming constituency living in it.

If we as a nation decide we can afford to sustain this delicate ecosystem, possibly at a lower cost in the future, then the minority of people enjoying the fruits of poverty had better shut up if they know what's good for them.

TUESDAY Add psychogeographical layers to my Birmingham Hippocampus Scheme. Then erase them, leaving an imagined ghostly imprint of enigmatic drivel for insurance purposes.

WEDNESDAY To Shitley, a relentlessly average town in the North East, where the local authority is conducting an interesting experiment in economic denial. They've started fixing fake shop facades to empty high street properties so that 'retail areas remain as theoretically vibrant as possible'.

The initiative is part of Shitley District Council's inward investment programme and is clearly aimed at the opportunistic businessman glancing from the back seat of a car and thinking 'Oh, that's impressive. They've got a continental delicatessen here. AND several vaguely defined lifestyle-related boutiquey shops. This place must have a sizeable bourgeois hinterland. Sharon, get me the chief executive of Shitley District Council, stat. I'm in the mood to invest and I'm feeling SAUCY ...'

It's obviously not aimed at pedestrians, who are taunted with a phantom bagel kiosk here, duped by the hollow mockery of a counterfeit halal butcher's there. I'm taken on a promenade along the high street by what local paper *The Shitley Chronicle* solemnly calls 'council bosses'. To wit:

- Three grey-faced planners in identical fleeces.
- Two metres of sulking iPod-dependent teenage work experience from Economic Development apparently called Jack.
- The fat, short mayor of Shitley wearing a heavy chain of office and looking like an airbag's gone off inside his fucking head.
- A hungover, barely functioning hack who might be from the council press office, or *The Shitley Chronicle*, or both.
- A Smoke Freedom Enforcement Officer in high-vis tabard.
- A random hanger-on complaining about the government who is a) on a Shopmobility scooter and b) off her meds.

One of the sepulchral planners explains, without moving his mouth, the purpose of this tour. It is to give me a frontline view of how the fake shopfront can be a valuable tool in the forward masterplanning toolbox.

I've halfway screwed up my face into the obligatory Sneer of Ultimate Disdain when he adds they'd like me to advise them on how this civic optimism might be expanded, and mentions a very attractive fee.

I amend my face to a Look of Serious Thought.

THURSDAY Dash off an edgy, urban scheme that both celebrates and modifies the concept of free will in a pluralistic society, then gaze pretentiously out of the window, savouring my maverick genius.

FRIDAY Put the finishing touches to my Shitley pitch. Obviously, I've loaded it with all the usual signifiers and called it 'an outline proposal to develop economic denial into the 21st century'. I'm suggesting the following:

- Plant seeds of hope in the indigenous population by getting out-of-work actors to be 'professional people' travelling on buses.
- Environmental improvement stickers fixed everywhere, erroneously confirming that improvements have been made.
- Tackle social development with extra, wholly fictitious, members of the social development team.
- Pump-flood the shopping centre with 'fragrances of success', e.g. sushi, cologne, imported beer, exotic spices, new second car, private paddock.
- Build a fake extension to Shitley so it looks twice the size on Google Earth.

(Memo to Self: check when the phrase 'into the 21st century' is due to expire in local authority circles as a futuristic indicator.)

SATURDAY Five-a-zeitgeist theoretical football. Baggy Urban Zoomorphic Upgrade 0, Unpastoralised Rural Dreamworld 0.

SUNDAY Pretend to be in the recliner, then later actually be in it.

March 11, 2010

The Slightly Underground Railway

MONDAY I have been asked to re-imagine absolutely everything, as part of an ambitious but tentative government initiative.

The working title is Britain Plus. It aims to change the way we think about the whole environment by adjusting our 'cultural minds'. It really is that simple.

For example, this country is awash with premium architectural content. Over the next year I'm proposing that this content be fast-tracked to World Class Architecture status. How? By putting all British buildings of merit on the BRITAIN PLUS TRAIN that's how, details to follow. Other key points in my Britain Plus Prospectus for Change:

- Separate the definition of Architecture into two parts: 'archi' meaning 'professional interest group' and 'tecture' meaning 'disposable asset'.
- Make sure our maritime heritage is properly valued, in doubloons and pieces of eight.
- Upside-down maps of Britain to encourage the Hebrides and the Isle of Wight to rethink each other.
- St Paul's Cathedral to go 'high definition' in time for the Olympics.
- Identify valuable parts of Britain's heritage with a red dot in the corner and a Britain Plus sticker.

TUESDAY Invited to 'recession-proof' myself by joining the Freemasons (London Architectural Division).

WEDNESDAY I'm IN. The dress code swung it for me in the end. I do look fantastic in a Gothic apron.

THURSDAY My Probationary Member's Pack arrives. It includes a 'Freemasonic Screwdriver' to get you through locked doors.

FRIDAY Transport for Tamworth has at last unveiled images of my 'slightly underground' station on the new East Tamworth Line.

It's taken years of pushing, niggling, redesigns, strategic sulking, threats of legal action, misunderstandings, actual legal action, financial collapse, virement of copyright, restructuring of the development team, recalibration of expectations, emotional firefighting, base-touching, pub lunches, compliance, grid-thinking, ennui and dark, dark misery to get this far.

Still, now the Offa Park transport interchange/retail/office/miscellaneous project is finished we all feel very proud. As well as being the 21st century's first slightly underground station, it is also the most potentialised, flexibility-wise.

As well as cramming generic 'shops' and new-generation 3-D adverts into every available space, we've also put in lots of polished concrete and glass bits. In the air-rights layer above this, a PFI polyclinic and Commuters' Wellbeing Centre. On top of that, an assortment of 'sexy, sleek, urban, chic living spaces'.

Making the East Tamworth line slightly underground was my idea. I knew it would play well at planning. 'We cannot match the Victorians' reckless endeavour' I concluded. 'Creating an underground railway now would be historical insolence. Also, prohibitively expensive.

'Therefore in compliance with contextual and Wikipedia-based concerns, we commend this *hommage in italics* to our industrial past: a slightly underground railway.

'We think this is exactly the sort of scheme you should be approving. We took the liberty of having a conversation with Daniel, your chief executive, and he totally agreed. Best, The Development Team.'

SATURDAY A game-changing five-a-zeitgeist rhetorical football match between Parametric Wanderers and IKEA.

Under the haughty captaincy of Franz Kobbelmensch the Parametrics had a good first half, deploying sound management rhetoric 'to deliver all the components for a high-performance contemporary life process'. Playing IKEA at their own game clearly paid off, with early goals from key players Spine and Nurb and a breathtaking late header from new signing Subdiv.

IKEA struck back in the second half, levelling the score with goals from Socker, Klippan and Ektorp-Murbo. But corporate momentum was with the IKEA team, who played their own rhetorical game right back at the Parametrics and, crucially, raised it by promising 'to deliver all the components for a high-performance contemporary life process BUT LOOK: new lower prices, same great quality!'

This extra pressure from the 2009 Champions of the Euro Minimalist League was enough to unsettle the Parametrics, who conceded a rhetorical own goal after they took their eyes off the metaball, pronounced it 'meatball' by mistake, and then collapsed into a non-pluralist defensive heap.

IKEA may have won the match but the real winners are ordinary people, for whom pretentious architectural bullshit is now a rhetorical reality. Summary: the age of Form Follows Function is over, the epoch of Substance Follows Style begins.

SUNDAY Reclinerthon.

May 13, 2010

An Abridged Larkin Poem

MONDAY Charles calls. I can tell immediately that this is going to be hard work. He's got that sulky belligerence in his voice that signals A Period of Sober Reflection.

'Why does one bother?' he grumbles. 'It's just the sheer vindictiveness of these grotty little developers, seeking to alter the course of history. They're not democratically elected, are they? Or their puffed-up, sanctimonious, tieless bloody architects. Not accountable, do you see?'

He drones on like this for 15 minutes. I am sympathetic, but still manage to order a pub lunch, go to the toilet and hold a conversation with someone else while he's on the phone. 'One will NOT be ignored,' he says. As usual, he's partly right.

TUESDAY In the morning, work up my House for an England Footballer. It has all the features you'd expect. 'Georgebestian' facade. Triple garage done up like a giant goal. Three lifesize gold lions having it large by the outdoor jacuzzi and so on.

Inside, however, it's a more muted and introspective feel with flashes of gilt. A mostly dull interior with little intellectual challenge, apart from a mock-Jacobean library for the Xbox games. Overall, I've gone for a philosophically minimalist feel to help develop spatial awareness, especially at the back, although obviously there are plenty of trappings in the sex dungeon.

I'm interrupted by an urgent call from Snorty. Sounds like she's ringing from the stables. Either that, or she's out on the lash with her 'Sex and the Countryside 2' set again. She and 'the girls' have been known to bray their way through a pitcher of Cosmopolitan each.

Any chance I could pop up and see her and Charles? 'He's terribly down. I'm worried he might do something silly'. Oh God, you don't mean…'Yes. Seriously considering announcing his pre-abdication in a special interview with Piers Bloody Morgan. Plus, the silly arse wants to dedicate the next five years to building that sodding Goon Museum of his. Come tomorrow. And bring fags.'

WEDNESDAY A relaxing journey to Gloucestershire in the back of a Royal jag. Why should I feel bad about it? I'm a taxpayer like everyone else. As HRH's friends keep telling one another, we're all in this together.

As the scenery slides past like an abridged Larkin poem, I can't help thinking he was really stupid to oppose all development in London higher than the Greenwich Observatory. It's not just the goodwill he's forfeited, although that had built into something quite substantial.

Charles was lined up to make a special guest appearance during the Gorillaz set at Glastonbury, reading the Book of Common Prayer over some dope looped beats. But then his giggling letters to a mysterious Saudi pal known as the 'beheadmaster' gushed all over the media like a fractured oil pipe and he suddenly became non-ironic again.

More seriously, he's completely undermined his own hard-won authority in the world of epic space. It's only a year since he beat Lord Rogers in a topless wrestling match to determine who could speak for the nation on architectural matters.

As he stood there, manboobs glistening in triumph, his opponent morally vanquished and on his arse, we thought that had settled matters. At last Charles could forget all those years of everyone sniggering at his views on plant psychology and spiritual aerobics.

Now people are laughing at him again, even when he's not doing one of his funny voices.

THURSDAY A claustrophobic day spent in what Charles is calling his 'Downfall Bunker' – a massive summer house dominated by the Map Room. A *Dad's Army* graphic shows a plucky HRH circled by Nazi tabloids.

The fightback starts here. For a start, the similes he used in those sabotaging letters were really bad. 'Looks like a thingy for storing CDs' is simply not good enough when you're taking the piss out of a Pritzker laureate.

19

FRIDAY Snorty and I spend most of the day smoking outside while Charles thinks up some better architectural insults. By teatime all he's got is 'a pornographic slug', 'a diseased ovary', 'a pile of poorly stacked bed-linen' and 'bit like a squashed cake or something?'

It's going to be a long haul.

SATURDAY Epiphany. HRH should stop criticising shape of Lord Rogers' buildings, start criticising shape of Lord Rogers.

SUNDAY Back home, leafing through Charles' list of *ad hominem* insults. They're both illegible and unprintable.

July 1, 2010

That Giraffe's Head Was Always Coming Off

MONDAY My pop-up architecture school's nearing completion in Godalming. It's only there for a fortnight, so will cost a fraction of the usual intolerable seven-year mountain of debt. It incorporates a chip shop too, to show poorer students how non-elitist the plastic arts can be.

TUESDAY To Godalming for the popping-out ceremony. Access could be easier – it has been popped-up on a roundabout – but it does encourage students to engage directly with the environment (no toilets).

WEDNESDAY At last my £200 million, 46-storey Lump in Birmingham is ready for occupation. What a journey it's been.

It was nicknamed The Lump on the planning application, more than five years ago. Partly because it resembles a glittering sugar lump, but also to plant the idea in the city council's mind that they might want TWO Lumps at some point, to 'sweeten' the urban landscape. Then everything went wrong.

The neurotic, hyperactive councillor who was championing the scheme in the face of some pretty fierce apathy at city hall had a breakdown. He appeared late, and naked, at the first committee meeting, shouting about minimalism and his mother.

Then our client, The Lump-It Development Company, went bust after bankrolling a floating leisure resort for Dubai in the shape of zoo animals. The slightest disturbance from a nearby marina and that giraffe's head was always coming off. 'Pontoon' and 'luxury living' can be difficult concepts to reconcile.

Then earlier this year the main contractor, AAAble Builders Yes We Can Ltd, went into administration by accident, thinking it was a commerical subdivision of the university sector, and remains trapped at the top of the Yellow Pages. Still, we got there in the end. Here's what the press release says:

> 'The Lump is pure dynamic form, a dream world, shimmering like a futuristic metatrope over its gutsy surroundings. The exterior features millions of tiny, magical fragments of surprised astatine, glistening in a fantastic cloak of synthetic biomass. This then gives way to a wholly unexpected interior of 388 flats, a 66-bedroom hotel, offices for the regional department of the Fraudulent Disability Investigations Agency, a car park and 9 floors of shops.'

THURSDAY Now toying with the idea of pop-up urbanism. Only because I want to print leaflets promising 'express piazza delivery'.

FRIDAY Finish sketches for my Tamworth Museum of Bad Language. I'm hoping it will be a premier destination for the visually impaired, as there will be textured surfaces all over the place, much of the interactivity will be based on Spoken Swearing and the whole thing will probably be shit to look at anyway after the client's taken all the good bits out.

There will be strong language from the start i.e. in the reception area, then visitors will be taken on a journey through the history and culture of swearing. Though, as I say, the culture bit may have to go as part of Coalition Cutbacks.

Of course there will be critics who say that Tamworth doesn't need a Museum of Bad Language at all, that the redundant watershed should be converted into something more appropriate. Already there is a strong local campaign in the local press to get Jamie Oliver to turn it into a 'sustainable Italian' restaurant using only seasonal staff and locally sourced customers.

In my view museum deniers should beware of what they wish for. If people start rolling their eyes and groaning every time a new museum opens in a British town, it won't be long before architects work exclusively abroad, where they are treated with respect and admiration. The creation of new museums is now a globalised industry second only to war in its importance to the world economy.

Yes, we may have reservations about the gearing of the sector – by 2050 it is estimated there will be one museum for every 25 people on the planet – but make no mistake without museums, architectural civilisation as we know it would collapse and in no time we'd be hurled back into the Dark Ages.

We have moved on from county architects' departments and their obsession with schools and homes – building types that do not, by the way, typically accommodate gift shops and 'light bite' restaurants.

SATURDAY Five-a-zeitgeist football. Art theory propositions of polemic form-givers 0, The virtualisation of extra-terrestrial desire 0. Match abandoned after ugly scenes of pretension.

SUNDAY Breakfast in pop-up café, drinks in pop-up pub, afternoon in fold-out recliner.

October 21, 2010

Twitterborough

MONDAY A very important day. Not just for me, but for the future of this country. I am scribbling some ideas (literary and spatial) in my monogrammed Moleskine memepad and I have to say they look BRILLIANT.

Obviously, as they're scribbles, they only look brilliant to me. When people realise what I'm 'saying' with wobbly pen lines, thinking doodles and question marks they will definitely agree. These scribbles will carry a great deal of cultural weight in posterity as they represent an auteur's impression, which is always more interesting than the artist's version.

TUESDAY I'm working the scribbles up into a series of 'conceptual blockouts' to communicate more immediately the true essence of my scheme. Details of the scheme remain secret for now, but when it's time to communicate, these blockouts will be invaluable.

WEDNESDAY Articulate my conceptual blockouts with enigmatic captions, or 'clutch points'. It's important at this stage not to lock down too many conclusions about how the vision could be taken forward, so for extra safety I leave the clutch points in neutral.

THURSDAY Some bastard close to me has leaked my scheme to the *Creative on Sunday*! I decide to spoil their exclusive by confirming to *Epic Space Online* that I am indeed the creator of TWITTERBOROUGH, a futuristic suburb near Corley Services on the M6.

Twitterborough will be part of a series of *grand projets* to mark the transformation of Ancient Mercia into a trimmed-down, fit-for-purpose England. Proper values. Astonishing architecture. World-class users. Yeah, good shit like that will be standard when Tamworth reigns again as capital city.

'Back to the eighth century!' That's the motto of New Mercia. Unfortunately this motto has attracted a number of inappropriate would-be constituents: nutty religious types, law and order fetishists, time travellers. Although nobody's complaining about the T-shirt sales.

The Mercia/Coalition Liaison Group is making great headway with its draft paper for the geographical rationalisation of England. Admittedly no actual timetable has yet been set by the government for the return of regional development agencies (or as they'll once again be known, kingdoms) but it will be 'as soon as practically possible'. That sounds pretty encouraging to me.

Meanwhile, *Epic Space Online* and everyone else is impressed by the sheer scale of Twitterborough. It will be about the size of a small nationally owned forest, and a short distance from Junction 3. Once the forest has been bought and the middle's been scooped out it will be converted into a massive 'actual space'. This will echo stylistically the vast tweet-sprinkled tundra of real Twitter, but in 'natural 3-D actuality'.

Girdling that will be a rich blend of luxury living, niche monetising opportunities and high-end corporate filler. This might all on paper look like a terrible idea, but at a later stage we'll put in some water-saving, energy-scrimping bollocks and then it'll be an amazing beacon of environmental truth.

There'll be rare wading birds, exotic lichen, rescued otters and an OBE in it too, I shouldn't wonder.

FRIDAY Press conference to launch Twitterborough as a 'destination brand'. Everyone suitably impressed by the early bar and nibbles, and by the huge 3-D renderings of the scheme's Intelligent Middle Area, with its glittering necklace of 'twitterspheres'.

These are opaque foam-framed hyperglazed meet-up pods, encouraging random clouds of online chatmates to 'coalesce together' in the real world. Comfortable surroundings, brilliant catering on request, please ask the avatar for a brochure. They will be crammed with earnest media types just chilling out and exchanging ideas in a semi-private little world of connectivity, hysteria and despair.

I've opened channels to some Swiss euthanasia clinics, just to see if there's any synergy worth exploring here.

SATURDAY Unbelievable. Our stupid executive masterplanners for the 'electronic village' bit of Twitterborough have submitted a very weak proposal. 'Urban squares'? In a village? Idiots.

Their 'frission statement' is riddled with inconsistencies. 'We aim to create a real community in which people will want to live different stages of their lives, yeah, which is why we're proposing sustainable neighborhoods (sic)'.

Wrong. Firstly, we want people to be living through one stage of their life but with many serviceable aspects of that life, thanks. Secondly, it all sounds so vulgar. Nothing says 'non-u' more stridently than 'neighborhoods'.

SUNDAY Newspaper review in the recliner. Good piece on Twitterborough by Darcy Farquear'say. 'A morally ambivalent elephant in the room' he calls it, which seems fair.

January 27, 2011

The Age of Oxygen

MONDAY I find myself getting nostalgic for the Carbon Footprint. It reminds me of a happier, more innocent age.

These days it is vulgar to mention footprints, or carbon, but I miss the communal enthusiasm, and the money. Amazing to think now that I was poised to make a fortune from my Carbon Slipper, a sort of loose overthrow for buildings that rendered them atmospherically harmless.

Of course, green architecture may yet stage a comeback – perhaps in time for the Olympics next year – but I think carbon's had it as an architectural talking point. Who knows which element will next be fashionable? Some futurists are talking boron up, but I think we're entering the Age of Oxygen.

'Yeah, but what's its oxygen take?' we'll be sneering in 10 years time about a building we don't like very much.

TUESDAY I'm designing an 80-storey residential tower in the new Emotional Digital style.

Basically you just do it in the old style, then set the exterior finish software parameters to 'ruffled'. This gives everything a more handmade look, as if hundreds of pipe-smoking artisans had bashed each unique steel panel into shape on an anvil, then hauled them all the way to the financial district of New York on a convoy of Edwardian drays.

Now I've finished the sketches it looks pretty optimistic, I must say. A bit like an arts and crafts Apollo-era space rocket and gantry. I've got these organic rivulets running down the outside, symbolising the sort of organic rivulets you find in nature.

On a whim I reset the rivulet direction of travel so they're now going UP. In your face, nature, you haven't got a clue about Emotional Digitalism, mankind wins again.

WEDNESDAY My old friend Dusty Penhaligon the conservactionist has started a campaign group to restore Victorian public conveniences.

Its aims are forthright and hostile: to compel local councils to produce maps of all public toilets 'as at Jan 1895. Said conveniences then to be restored, scrupulously recreated or, if necessary, fully reversed...'

The last bossy injunction is pretty controversial. It requires the reimbursement and eviction of some chic, kooky and potentially quite outraged current occupants. A number of conveniences have in recent years fallen into re-use as:

- A community art gallery, challenging our perceptions of how poor community art actually is.
- A poetry slamming hub run by PFI verse provider Metrical Logistics.
- Minimalistic business premises for a doomed one-and-a-half-person architectural start-up called Urbanic Daydream in a weird font.
- A brilliantly innovative *pied-à-sous-terre* for guerrilla media consultant Dex Madmen, who told the *Sunday Telegraph* last May that going home to his underground crashpad near Liverpool Street

(designed via email by someone in his year at Westminster) was 'like following the White Rabbit into a fabulous hedonistic underworld' but that he was now tired of emerging in the morning to the sound of commercial despair and the smell of human piss.

- An ironic and technically illegal opium den run by gap year chancers pretending to be doing voluntary work in Vietnam.
- A stag night venue called Gents.

I think Dusty's idea of a public convenience renaissance is charming but misguided. Not for the first time I ask him – where does it stop? Are we supposed to return all Victorian hospital buildings to their original state? What about the staff? Are they supposed to revert to primitive anaesthetics and pleats in their clothes?

As usual he shrugs, says yes, takes a drag on his roll-up and squints into the distance.

THURSDAY Rock Steady Eddie the Middle East fixer rings. An ideas competition is about to be announced by Saudi Arabia's royal family, who have been watching events in Egypt and elsewhere unfold with some interest.

The brief is to 'refresh' the kingdom as the wider region enters a period of profound change and modernisation. Eddie recommends removing all large public squares, women and the internet.

FRIDAY To a lecture at the Institute of Plasmic Arts: Whither Art of the Subconscious Mind?

Summary: a) who knows; b) still, check out these amazing images.

SATURDAY A fascinating tour of abandoned London Underground stations. Afterwards we all go for a drink in an abandoned pub, my imaginary friends and I, like the melancholy bastards we are.

SUNDAY Reconfigure self for the new Emotional Digital Age, in the recliner, by watching *Casablanca* in 3-D.

February 18, 2011

A Multi-Dimensional World

MONDAY Teaching at Tamworth School of Architecture. I'm much more interested in hearing students' ideas about the world than in imposing my own reactionary *Weltanschauung*, which can be quite intimidating, especially if barked.

I'm all for young people working up their charming 'theoretical urban interventions'. The perilous journey from Concept to Sketch defines the student's unique view of things – how they think about form and mass, how to express an aesthetic quality in caption form, the meaning of light, etc. Also, it's less work for me and leaves time for a proper lunch.

I say 'teaching', I've actually been asked by the school's CEO to help with their rationalisation of student resources, i.e. students. Brutal times call for ruthless measures. There's to be a cull of underachievers and/or low payers. They want me to sieve the students, so that they're left with just the 'M&Ms': motivated and minted.

TUESDAY Meanwhile in the wider world of Arts & Ents & Life & Style, there's anxiety about the sudden crisis of confidence in the 3-D film industry and the impact this will have on architecture.

In recent years it has been easy to persuade young people that the world of epic space is 'supercool' as it a) provides the backdrop for human drama, in the manner of a top-end videogame and b) you can see architecture in 3-D, at any time, without complicated spectacles. If there's a strong enough swing back to 2-D in cinemas it could drag the plastic arts along with it via a treacherous cultural undertow.

A two-dimensional world? That would mean practising (and teaching) architecture as a form of surface decoration applied to software-designed, articulated boxes. Architects would be merely exterior wallpaperists. Nightmare.

Next thing you know, we'll all be wearing 2-D glasses to flatten out the built environment. Let's see how Londoners manage on their hired bicycles THEN.

WEDNESDAY Seminar. A dozen assorted students, plenty of nervous energy yet somehow limp and deconstructed.

I decide to set up an ironic mood by opening several bottles of Mateus Rosé. It's a trick I learned years ago: you can get middle-class young people pissed more quickly if they think it's some kitsch homage to Working Class Posh. Plus, if they're architecture students, two glasses and they're wankered.

I ask them how many dimensions they'd have in an ideal world. The conservative hipster majority, after some consideration and hair-fiddling, stick with the three we've got. A very serious young man with writing on his hooded top reckons one dimension should be all the world needs, that way there'd be enough linear reality to go round. A young woman, a bit tipsy and pedantic, points out that time is a required fourth dimension, as without epic time there can be no epic space.

After more wine and omnispection, we tentatively construct a world where up to 12 dimensions are allowed but you have to have planning permission to go above five, with the usual disclaimers about lost property.

THURSDAY I ask the students to imagine 'King's Cross, 2111'. What kind of morphoses might we see, and why, and will they be weird-looking?

The notion of transport – might that be supplanted by some kind of futuristic thinking? Will phrases such as 'commuter' and 'flat white' and 'unmetered air' be archaic and unknowable? How will people 'walk', and will pavements be like sluggish smartplasma travelators, maybe even veering off into the air?

Will new materials allow us to build up into the ionosphere, perhaps connecting with a geo-engineered deep space energy mantle thrown around the Earth like chainmail armour? What non-diegetic music do we hear in our heads in 2111 – STILL synthesisers, really? How will the new things of one hundred years hence fit in with the old things of now? Is it OK to anticipate a zeitgeist, or does that totally spoil the future?

Their first hurdle: writing 'King's Cross 2111' at the top of a page and working out where the apostrophe goes.

FRIDAY Some great ideas: 'travel pills' to get around, layered space, soft buildings, people coded into data streams, buildings that resemble hedgehogs and cakes.

Decide one-dimensional guy should be retained – he's got a trust fund – and the rest dumped.

SATURDAY Can't teach, so do.

SUNDAY Go four-dimensional in the recliner by remaining in it all day.

March 24, 2011

There Is No Rationalism but Rationalism

MONDAY Long lunch with Darcy Farquear'say, architecture correspondent for the *Creative on Sunday*. The preposterous Bauhau, his neurotic dachshund, sleeps fitfully under the table in a Zaha Hadid canine onesie.

Darcy's bored these days; there's less and less architecture to write about. And also pretty cross with himself: when he mentioned the slowdown to the *Creative* they decided to expand his roving brief to accommodate cake shows and graffiti.

There's nothing he can do about it, of course. The flow of new architecture is slowing in accordance with Coalition Restrictions, and not expected to pick up again properly until about 14 months before the next General Election. Darcy will be all right. He just needs a Big Theme he can saddle and ride like some bucking yet pretentious cultural bronco for a few months.

'It has to be a design idea that people will buy into, and don't suggest paywalled architecture. What about…a hivemindset, mm? Combinable singularity, a way of looking at the environment, a detached retina if you will…' I won't. 'Something smart and fashionable, but not too intellectually challenging. Something that chimes with the times. And doesn't cost anything…'

Bauhau's woken up and apparently wants to 'go wee-wee'. What a humiliation. Crammed into haute couture AND given a toddler's voice. I tell Darcy I'll have a think about his Big Theme, and order more drinkies.

TUESDAY Opposition to my jaunty mosque in Tamworth grows by the day. Oh, they SAY their objections are architectural – the dome's too sparkly, the ultra-contemporary glowing minaret's out of whack with the surrounding non-listed 70s buildings and so on.

29

Some people mutter darkly that the protestors are cloaking anti-Muslim prejudice in aesthetic objections. I agree, some of these seem flimsy – YES the millions of tiny mosaic mirrors will dazzle viewers into temporary blindness so DON'T LOOK AT IT WHEN THE SUN'S OUT, IDIOTS.

But their fear goes deeper. It is a fear of religion. They're scared of the sacred. Whoa, wait…

WEDNESDAY Meet Darcy in the pub. Atheism, I tell him, there's your theme. It's this year's liberal must-have, this season's lava lamp. Bauhau's napping on the floor, dressed nose to tail today in some sort of Stella McCartney strudel. 'Yes!' says Darcy. 'God is dead!' Dog, however, is risen and bursting.

THURSDAY Field research. A depressing conference called *Redeeming a Godless World*. It has been organised by the Association of Atheist Architects, a bunch of self-satisfied tossers glowing with ineffable smugness.

Much of the morning session is devoted to refurb. Turning churches, chapels and manses into more meaningful vehicles for our shared sense of wretchedness: nightclubs, public houses featuring Giant Jenga, little flats with no cupboard space.

Everyone pays tribute to the lying shit Blair who despite his own ostentatious holiness did more for the humanist cause than almost anyone else in those difficult years after 9/11.

Under Blair's Fag Terror smoking disappeared from pubs overnight. Many non-believers saw cigarette smoke as a metaphor for the Holy Ghost. How easy to eradicate! Those stupid ads on buses: 'Thank you for not believing in God', 'The best way to stop believing in God is never to start', 'Protect children: don't let them absorb your belief in God'.

Now faith, like smoking, exists primarily outside: trudging Jehovah's Witnesses and those evangelical nomads who pop up occasionally in the market square shouting bits from Leviticus.

In the afternoon, delegates discuss the criteria for atheistic design. Top of the list is amending insurance policies to 'Act of Earth'. Lots of reflective glass, obviously. No Freemasonry business. 'Smart columns' by Christopher Hitchens, etc. All details certified God-free. No more infinity pools. A saturating ethos of 'yes, we're certain, this is as good as it gets, so fuck off and get on with the rest of your lives, yeah?'

FRIDAY Darcy leaves a message. 'Built environment – not a prophet exactly, but definitely a graven image? Spiritus Loci? Talk later, Bauhau's had an accident…'

SATURDAY Hatch plan with Rock Steady Eddie the fixer to launch a directory of Atheist Designers and to change my trading name to Aalto.

SUNDAY Newspaper review in the recliner. Read Darcy's piece – 'Towards a New Emotional Secularism'.

I still think Agnostic Revival, a sort of pagany Pugin, has more resonance among the open-minded but Darcy's not interested in them. There is No Rationalism but Rationalism, is his new motto.

April 7, 2011

How Kryptogel Will Change the World

MONDAY Big week ahead for me and my old friend Beansy, the nano-futurologist. The patent for our latest invention is imminent.

It builds on the theoretical success of 'hard air', a revolutionary building material we came up with a couple of years ago and then shelved for commercial and legal reasons.

It seems so primitive now: add 'lumpening hydrates' to ordinary air, thereby 'caging' the molecular structure via omnilateral desublimation. It was the perfect sustainable local material. Air is everywhere in the world, duh.

But the sceptics and the haters killed it off, saying it was too mad an idea, too 'fictional'. Despite the massive 'hard air' table we were DOING THE PRESS CONFERENCE AT. Idiots. This time, we'll be stealthier.

TUESDAY Great, the patent's gone through. Beansy and I now own the rights to 'Kryptogel'.

Essentially, it's hard air infused with nanogel and krypton. I mentioned to Beansy that these were the top two Google search results for 'innovative building material' and wondered aloud how you might combine them. Boom – he'd cooked up the first batch in his nanotechnology lab by teatime.

You ask what Kryptogel can do. I answer with a silvery laugh: what CAN'T it do? It's so light you can hardly feel it, so translucent you can barely see it. So malleable and versatile you could craft a model of the

Palace of Versailles from it. So tough you could get an elephant to stand on that model of Versailles and it wouldn't even buckle.

This is because Kryptogel molecules form 'geotastic non-bucklyballs' when the material is in its inert state. It looks like phantom frogspawn, without the tadpole dots.

It's much less accommodating in its exciteable state, although it is incredibly squashable. You can compress all the Kryptogel you'd need to build a bungalow into a lump the size of a takeaway pizza although OK fair enough it would be one of those Family Feast ones.

From now on it's plain sailing specification-wise for the world's epic space community. Kryptogel is going to change everything.

WEDNESDAY Beansy and I bring very different skills to the Kryptogel skills matrix. Rock Steady Eddie the fixer also brings his rugged take on things to a late lunch at the pub.

'So. How much of this fancy polystyrene would you need to make a decent sized eco-town?' Beansy says that would require a proper manufacturing plant and blah blah logistics, who cares, I've drifted off to get another round. When I get back Eddie's already 'tickled up some geezers on the blower' and it very much looks like we'll be licensing the manufacturing rights. Kryptogel is GO.

THURSDAY Meeting with two guys from Global Profiles, a patent clearing house for the world's construction community. After some small talk, mostly me and Beansy making the same self-deprecating joke about getting older and having a global profile ourselves these days, ha ha, the contracts appear.

For a five year exclusivity deal, a certain well-known manufacturer will pay us a small amount up front. However, we get a massive cut of profits from any Kryptogel-based development. And given that the possibilities are endless and the science proven, we are clearly going to be millionaires by the end of the year. Kryptogel affordable housing, here it comes. Kryptogel skyscrapers, hospitals, bridges...

Beansy lowers his voice and produces a blueprint for a lunar shuttle packed with – and made of – 'Kryptogel Plus'.

Enough raw material for a large town on the Moon, virtually weightless, a negligible payload. Kryptogel could open up the entire fucking GALAXY for the human race! Tim and Dan from Global Profiles keep their excitement under control and countersign the contracts.

FRIDAY Oh dear. It now seems unlikely that the galaxy will be remodelled in Kryptogel any time soon. Global Profiles bought the rights in order to suppress its use by anyone. Apparently the concrete and steel people are not very happy about a virtually zero-cost alternative.

Still, on the bright side, Rock Steady Eddie's earned an undisclosed 'handling fee' and Beansy and I have made enough to develop his matter transporter beyond the beta version. Not before time: we've already lost 15 cats to the capricious laws of physics.

SATURDAY Beansy and I transform into our excitable states for a night out on the non-Kryptogel town.

SUNDAY Return to my inert state in the recliner.

April 28, 2011

Zeppelins Full of Shit

MONDAY What a terrible start to the week. I'm being sued by a client who accuses me of 'false narrative accounting'.

The job was a modest pedestrian bridge at a suburban railway station. I'm not allowed to say which one (superinjunction) but the scheme sailed through planning, thanks to a very persuasive written and visual presentation.

Unfortunately it is this very presentation that forms the basis of my client's case.

Exhibit A: the rendering. I decided to use a slightly disturbing and surreal watercolour painting of the project, with lots of 'blending' and 'splodging'. The client inspected the bridge shortly after completion and found it 'completely unsmudged and not in the least surreal. Passenger traffic was non-amorphous, with totally clear edges to everything'.

Exhibit B: the design statement. I said the lighting would 'weave a spell of weird psycho-illuminescent magic at night, making the bridge deck appear to levitate'. The client went back in the evening and found it 'looking very much where it was in daylight.

I thought perhaps I was not in the right mood so, after a couple of stiff ones in a nearby hostelry, I returned. The bridge deck still looked perfectly embodied, even when I squinted'.

Worse, my artistic licence expired in February.

TUESDAY Chelsea Flower Show. My hippy gardener friend Isis has won the Morally Urban Greening Prize for her provocative piece, 'Reversal'.

She's rebuilt a small terraced house, left the roof off and converted it into a lush, succulent, multi-layered, polyvalent mega-organism. 'Reversal' brings together stacked vegetable gardens, hydroponic sliding doors, a miniature energy orchard, a suspended waterfall, predictive composting and an insect ziggurat.

The back yard contains a small family shed. The idea, says Isis, is to 'lower humanity's expectations in line with our feelings of shame and self-loathing. We should no longer consider ourselves temporary curators of Earth's Bounty, but janitors. It is time we knew our place, which is in the shed'.

WEDNESDAY Lunch with my old mate Beansy the mad futurologist. He's desperate to be on the *Creative on Sunday*'s Cool List, an annual audit of 50 startled-looking people in jeans who've had brilliant, world-changing ideas.

'I need something clever yet simple,' he says. 'Clockwork radio. Water purifiers. A decent garlic press. Something step-changey, game-changey, yeah? Like with the Inca civilisation. Once they started using llama shit as a high-altitude-fertiliser boom, they were off.' I tell Beansy the world's still waiting for a globalised solution to HUMAN waste.

Of course, Beansy has one. 'Just cart it all over to say a) the Sahara or b) the South Pole. Carry on dumping it there, chuck in millions of seeds, loads of Dettol round the outside, let's keep things civilised. In next to no time you've got a) Brazil 2.0 or b) probably a frozen mountain of human shit which, OK, is a hostage to fortune with global warming so let's say a) to be on the safe side...'

I'm obliged to point out that visionary mentals have always banged on about fertilising the desert. That, and desalinating the Caspian Sea and turning it into a massive salmon farm. He's not listening. 'Now you can't really send millions of tonnes of sewage by road. Or by sea. Wait. Zeppelins! Bloody great architect-designed airships, full of shit! Zeppelins, man!'

I don't know. I can't see Brazil 2.0 in the Sahara being a runner, but then I think there's something distinctly off-putting about a big balloon full of human 2.0 heading anywhere.

34

THURSDAY Brainstorming with Beansy, trying to work up a proto-type Hindenturd.

It suddenly occurs that he might be able to help with the false narrative charges. I mean, if a way were found to retrofit the railway station with smudged ambience and a levitating bridge we could keep all this out of the courts.

FRIDAY To Superinjunction Junction. Beansy's brought his mol-ecule distresser. It looks like a portable cropsprayer, not very convincing, but a few squirts high into the air produces a fine, static mist that makes everything 'run' in a satisfyingly painty way.

Floating the bridge free from reality has got us stumped, though. Hypnosis looks like the only option. We'll wait for nightfall, then try some mind-control on passengers.

SATURDAY Beansy and I released without charge after questioning.

SUNDAY Lateral thinking in the recliner, then everything goes water-coloured. I dream of aerial armadas.

June 2, 2011

Velvet Smackpad

MONDAY It's Jazz Architecture Week, and everyone's hoping there's no reprise of the ugly scenes we had last year in Brighton.

Rival gangs of Trads and Shockers battling it out on the seafront in a series of running theoretical debates, bringing shame upon the world of syncopated design and irritating passers-by. Adverbs were thrown. At one point harmless banter escalated into dangerous levels of preten-tiousness; deckchairs were adduced as paradigms of exterior tensile furniture.

There is no place for sectarianism in jazz architecture. Whether you be a Trad, with your old-fashioned notions of symmetry and proportion and a solid 4/4 grid. Or whether you be a Shocker, producing experimental jazz architecture with a freestyling drivel of rising fifths and augmented pods on splayed pilotis.

The whole point – the whole babbeda babbeda glap bap ga-tish POINT – of jazz architecture is inclusiveness. There is no 'right' or 'wrong' jazz architecture. There is only hubbeda hubbeda GOOD jazz architecture. And babbeda babbeda squee-honk blap tss-tss wap bap ga-biddly bad.

TUESDAY Amazing evening of chops, licks, anecdotes and improvised criticism at the Jazzual Architectural Association. Marvellous impromptu lecture on the whole Italian post-Baroque, pre-bebop fusion movement by visiting professor Antonio Daddio.

Outside in the square, students have jammed together geodesic riffs and a big polypropylene drum solo to create a temporary 'flop-up' structure, Velvet Smackpad. The exterior resembles a giant pair of bongos. The cool jazz interior is modelled on a heroin den of the 1950s: minimalist with lots of big cushions. Everything's suffused with the colour blue but, cleverly, on the off-beat.

There is an aural landscape too: a soundtrack of mysterious scraping, squeaking noises. The visitor imagines that he (possibly 'she' but NB must be goatee-capable) is in some urban jungle, the everyday noises of life transmuted into a collage of dislocated, jagged existential rage. Then he realises he's listening to the Archigram Quintet Live in Charrette and starts clicking his fingers, randomly and knowledgeably.

WEDNESDAY A tour of London jazz pubs organised by the Society for the Preservation of Ancient Jive. Our guide is Darcy Farquear'say and his hepcat dachshund, Bauhau.

We focus on the very earliest jazz pubs of the 1920s, when society sought to assauge the horrors of the Great War not with affordable housing for the poor but with innovative drinking holes for the hip. Inevitably, most of the original buildings survive today, not as jazz pubs for the poor but as converted townhouses for the hip.

This is exactly the sort of irony that adds 50 grand to the asking price.

Happily, the Lord Alfred Douglas in Shaftesbury Avenue survives. Darcy hoists Bauhau onto a bar stool; the hapless 'jazzschund' wobbles uncertainly there throughout Darcy's little talk, quietly howling from within a miniature beatnik double polo-ended wraparound.

'Observe the pish pish wabbeda wabbeda modulation of style. A standard 2/4 panelling is backlined by proto-boogie woogie flanging, with plenty of bass-end left hand overbabble. See how the glass, mirrorwork and mahogany is punctuated with bright, joyous stabs of hubbeda babbeda tish tish ga-drap bap brass…'

The landlord comes over and tells us 'the weird dog' will have to go. Darcy querulously complains that he was happy enough to serve us when we came in with Bauhau. The landlord says he inferred from Darcy's dark glasses and painfully mismatched clothes that Bauhau was a guide dog.

Tempers fray, in a confusion of time signatures and keys, and Bauhau has a little scat accident.

THURSDAY To a jazz architecture conference: Whither Freeform Parametricism? Summary: up bup shoo-wup its psst psst psst own fuggeda fuggeda fuggeda arse.

FRIDAY Try acid jazz architecture for the first time by taking a trip into my surrealistic mental catacombs.

SATURDAY All the cats on the UK scene are at Kensington Gardens for the official opening of the annual Mellow Pavilion. This year's has been designed by the jazz architect's jazz architect, Scrim 'Solid Gone' Scrimson.

Sure, the squares and breadheads say it's just a big box with a garden in it. Ignore them. They understand neither containment theory nor haughty culture. Scrimson mumbles an intro – 'baba zoom, baba zoom, humdrum bubba mubbeda pff pff, two three four' – then we all get pissed and just pure dig the ambience, man.

SUNDAY Chill out in the jazz recliner with some metabolist feedback, probably the avant-garde jazz scampi from last night.

June 28, 2011

The Molecules of Swinging London

MONDAY Idea for the restoration of a 'historic train station' – start calling it a railway station again.

TUESDAY To Switzerland, where I'm presenting my design for a 'last chance saloon'. It's actually more of an upmarket bar, and will provide a welcome touch of glamour in an otherwise pretty utilitarian suicide clinic.

It's neo-Classical obviously – the client wants 'firmitas, gravitas, dignitas'. Fluted pilasters round the walls. Acanthus leaves. Scenes from *The*

Iliad in high definition watercolours, etc. But there are also cheeky touches of humour to lighten the mood for those with a one-way ticket to oblivion.

Bistro blackboards with 'bar meals to die for'. A nautical bell that sounds last orders every quarter of an hour, round the clock. Exit signs everywhere.

The idea is that visitors can just slip away here. Not intubated in some anonymous hospital bed with moving patterns on the wall and chevronned cards on the bedside table, all ironic, *Bon Voyage*. No. Here they can die congenially, sipping an ACTUAL 'lethal cocktail' in a discreet, ultra-comfortable booth.

Obviously this gig calls for taste and discretion, which is why I'm charging slightly over the odds. However tough the economy is in the cruel outside world, suicidally low fee bids help nobody.

WEDNESDAY Redesign the political landscape, with a more 'savage garden' feel and an electrified fence around it.

THURSDAY Invitation to a 'very special East End pub' from my mate Dusty Penhaligon the conservactionist. Imagine my disappointment when I get to the pub and it turns out to be bloody DERELICT.

'Ghost and Compasses' the sign says still, just. The boarded-up doors are open. I enter the gloom of what once was a public bar. Looming out of the murk is Dusty, who's brought along a carrier bag full of beer and a psychogeographer, which frankly is no substitute for a proper pub with functioning toilets.

His morose guest turns out to be the widely acclaimed, slightly ludicrous Dr Roman Whey, Regius Professor of Lost Worlds at the University of Edinburgh.

This isn't a social invitation at all. Dusty and the nutty professor are apparently now setting themselves up as the Ant and Dec of 'historiographical ectoplasmology'. As far as I can make out, this involves taking an area of London, collating vast quantities of information on what it all looked like in the 1960s and proving that things were better then.

Mourning and moaning, Penhaligon and Whey: one of them pining for the good old days, the other flatly opposed to any change at all. Maybe not a marriage made in Heaven, but certainly one made in the energy field created by human memory through which we may channel the past.

'Look around you, feel the vibe...' says Whey, his fingers combing the air. 'This place shut in 1968. We're surrounded by molecules from a mythical time, pre-dating the internet. A generation before Thatcher. As far as these molecules are concerned, HENDRIX IS STILL ALIVE.' Dusty looks a bit worried and wonders aloud if we shouldn't shut the door to stop the 60s atmosphere simply floating away.

Whey gives a little chuckle. 'Oh, molecules from Swinging London never leave. They're much heavier, you see. High soot content.' Yes, I say, helping myself to a rusty can of Double Diamond, this is all very interesting I'm sure. But what am I doing here? 'We'd like you to join us,' says Dusty, making squinted eye contact.

'We plan to bring back forgotten urban landscapes through the sheer power of magical narrative engineering. If we can combine Roman's geo-psychological dowsing, my theoretical expertise in physically reconstructing the past, and your wide-spectrum sarcasm about everything...'

My mobile suddenly goes off, startling the room. Especially all the Bakelite-era molecules. I take the call outside, and keep walking, quickly.

FRIDAY A very cross Dusty calls. How dare I leave them like that? Because you're fucking doughnuts, I patiently explain. You can't just conjure up the past. Right, he says. See you back there tomorrow, we'll prove it.

SATURDAY Return to the derelict pub. It's disappeared! Instead, I'm looking at a supermarket car park.

But how? Whey and Dusty look unbearably smug. 'Historiographical ectoplasmology' they say, in unison. Are those WANDS they're carrying? The Ghost and Compasses shimmers briefly as a phantom image, over by the trolleys. Spooky.

SUNDAY Recreate the past by falling asleep in the recliner, as I did last week.

July 7, 2011

Hubmakers v Spacesmiths

MONDAY Alternative Energy Day. In the morning, work up my idea for an air farm. In the afternoon, sketch out my prototype for a rain mill. In the evening, harness physical repulsion to create an innovative spiral of despair.

TUESDAY Brilliant, feel MUCH more positive after running a self-diagnostic. I'd accidentally re-set my mental definition of architecture, from 'frozen music' to 'congealed self-pity'. Idiot.

WEDNESDAY Bad news. The Coalition's brutal approach to 'built environment delivery' has now provoked the most serious demarcation dispute since the 1970s.

Despite frantic attempts by the Vocational Associations Congress, members of both the Hubmakers' Guild and the Institute of Spacesmiths downed tools today and have been instructed to imagine no urban solutions until further notice.

Of course, the Confederation of British Privatisation appealed for common sense. But its emergency statement didn't sound very convincing: 'We would like to reassure local authorities, hedge funds and other core keyholders that plans for hubs and spaces remain buoyant throughout the country. These will last for several months. There is no point in clients stockpiling so-called 'micro-economic nebulae', that doesn't make any sense.'

As the confederation represents not so much a collective interest as more of a mist-cloud of tossers, this has now caused panic-buying. There remains not a single conceptual scheme for a hub or space in any pipeline, anywhere. Unless a way through is found, the rebadging sector is heading for a Winter of Disconnect.

THURSDAY This demarcation dispute is very serious for me. As a leading opinion-former on these matters, I have to pick a side. After much soul-searching I've decided to go with the Hubmakers' Guild.

I have nothing against spacesmiths. I yield to no one in my admiration of them and their alchemy. I believe that the last decade has seen some truly astonishing, magical spaces created. Moribund areas of towns – long abandoned to the anarchic bumbling of people sitting on benches FREE OF CHARGE eating sandwiches prepared at home – have been transformed by 'food courts' and franchised noise rights.

Creating multi-purposed space is straightforward, but hubmaking is a specialised craft. For too long spacesmiths have undercut hubmakers with that one-hub-fits-all bullshit. A genuine hub takes risks.

It might be a business hub on the periphery of an airport, corralled by massive billboards proclaiming that 'making your business our business is good business'.

It might be a cultural hub offering nuanced meeting spaces, specialist retailers, exhibition nodes, assorted experiences, free wi-fi and the opportunity to 'grab a coffee and explore!' This really is living on the edge, as anyone who's ever grabbed a hot coffee will confirm.

Yet hubmaking has a grand vision too. Until recently everyone fatuously described London as a 'city of villages', even though there's always a shop open somewhere on Saturday afternoons. Great credit goes to the Hubmakers' Guild for changing our perception of the capital to a 'city of hubs'.

Microhubs link together to form macrohubs, with the Greater London area forming one vast huburb.

FRIDAY Lunch with Rock Steady Eddie the fixer. As usual he helps himself to 18 per cent of my pudding.

Not for the first time, he wants me to abandon my principles in the pursuit of profit. 'Look, I'm not asking you to scab. You've got your ideals, that's lovely. I am merely saying I've got clients queuing up for hubs and spaces and nobody to provide them. I know you'd be putting your reputation at risk by strike-breaking, I respect that, we could do it under a pseudonym or whatever and are you going to finish that cheesecake?'

After all these years Eddie still thinks I'd jettison my moral convictions to make a few quid. Does he seriously expect me to become a blackleg hubmaker, a moonlighting spacesmith? When it would be much simpler to invent a new urban regeneration term altogether, and cash in that way?

SATURDAY Devise the 'urban bulb', a new development marketing blueprint. A successor to the hub, it's commercial but sounds organic.

The urban bulb, a tight wad of potential, planted in the fertile soil of municipal space, one day flourishing into city apartments for people with cruel eyes and direct debit capability. Plus social benefit in the form of shops.

It'll sound much more cheerful once I've tidied up my scruples a bit.

SUNDAY Form a hubbulb in the recliner.

July 28, 2011

Youthanasia

MONDAY Sketch out plans to turn a famous London teaching hospital into 3,000 flats full of people listening to BBC Radio 6 Music and doing something clever with seasonal vegetables.

Spare me the moral squeaking. I didn't come up with the bloody idea, did I? Anyway, they've asked a number of urban visionaries to have a go. And there's nothing intrinsically wrong with selling an NHS site to a property developer. Is there?

Gradually, my conscience starts to speckle with particulates of doubtful origin. I put the wipers on, give it a spritz, and soon my conscience is clear again.

TUESDAY Create a breathtaking glazed 'Groundwalk' by designing a circular corridor with lots of windows.

Now to give them something to look at. At the moment it's a toss-up between radical landscaping or kinetic art. Maybe both. It has to be an experience. Perhaps the Groundwalk could wobble slightly, adding to the tension.

Bah. By teatime I've scribbled out all the experience-heightening 'surprise factors' on the advice of my lawyers: jets of fire, slippery floor, wild animals. It's spatial narrative correctness gone mad.

WEDNESDAY To the RIPBA to meet new president Molly Bismuth. She's in her trademark pink cowboy hat and brimming with energy today as 'Aries is aligned with Ocado'.

We check out work in progress at the former Florence Hall, which is being converted into a massive, ironic bar called Epic. It's part of Molly's masterplan to update the institute. This basically involves redefining 'makeover' as a transitive verb, then applying it liberally, everywhere. There will be happy hours and music videos. The bar staff will be heavily tattooed, with hairdos that look like urban gardens.

'I want everything to be more pop-up and FUNK-AY!' she trills. Things are certainly moving quickly. The institute's chief executive, Geoff

Mudgeon, is cultivating an afro. During Molly's inaugural speech there'll be a dude on fretless bass at the end of every paragraph.

She wants to fill the trendier bits of London with 'branded microsites': little taster menus of world-class architecture presented by people in hats. All milling about in signature pop-up yurts with old horror movies showing, poetry slams and downloadable apps. There are, she reasons, an awful lot of young people out there. After 177 years, it's time the institute was 'youthanised'. We have another vodka jelly.

'It's about cultural synergy. Architects, especially hot young ones, spend a lot of time designing hubs during the day – then go out hubbing in the evenings! We need to totally mash that scene up with stuff that people read about in magazines. Imagine Alex James out of Blur. And his cheese. And a punk string quartet. And loads of prosecco. And some architecture in the middle. Wicked!'

Hipstertecture? 'No no no, that's too much…' A vodka jelly disappears '…of a mouthful. My mission is to bring together cool people and architects. I'm merging hipster culture and hub culture to form a totally fresh genre of HUBSTER CULTURE!'

Suddenly the bass dude appears: boing burr ba-ba bop bop!

THURSDAY Honoured to be one of the judges for the Shit Building of the Year Award, but it's exhausting work.

Shit buildings are once again enormously popular and this year there are more nominations than ever. The standard is incredible. In the end we decide to give the prize to the whole of Salford. Liverpool waterfront gets a 'highly distended' award.

FRIDAY Redesign concept of 'redesign', making it less enigmatic by removing quote marks.

SATURDAY Five-a-zeitgeist theoretical football. Neo-Narcissism 5, Post-Collectivist Nebulism 0.

SUNDAY Like so many others, I relive the horrors of 9/11 by watching it on the television, as we did at the time.

Architects have had a neurotic decade. But they can feel proud that terror has finally been conquered. We all 'feared' that 9/11 would mean no more tall buildings. Look at us now. Extruded vertical luxury in every city!

As St Paul's stood firm amid the burning rubble of the Blitz, so London's giant stalagmite of wealth, The Icicle, now rises into the optioned air like an overscaled gesture of defiance to everything but itself. Yes, you al-Qaeda muppets. This is what secular democracy looks like. This is what freedom looks like. A giant fucking drip of cack.

Then I go to the pub. Later, some sober reflections in the recliner.

September 11, 2011

Slow Modernism

MONDAY Oh God, it's Post-Modernism Revival Week. Time to dust off those architectural clichés, randomly assemble them, stand well back and look at it all ironically.

TUESDAY There is as we used to say an 'upside' to this nostalgia for giggling squiggling eclecticism. Anyone who was technically an adult during the 1980s is suddenly a cultural historian.

I'm not complaining. My classic book on the subject – *The Winkers* – has been reissued and now finds favour with a whole new generation of drawling, overdressed tossers. 'Winkers' of course was the collective noun in those days for post-Modernists, a reference to the way they simplified design theory by spaffing their ephemeral bollocky bricolage all over the place and then 'winking' to let us in on the joke. I think we were supposed to give a 'thumbs up' in response.

Obviously I've added footnotes to *The Winkers*, updating the original text. A lot's happened in architecture over the last quarter-century. Summary: boom, crash, boom, crash, oom-pah oom-pah, look at us, we can do bulges and curves now and WATCH OUT WE'RE GOING TO HIT THAT WALL.

Several of the key figures in British Winkerism are dead. In one way this is sad, although it does mean we are now free to say some pretty harsh things about them.

Colin 'Big Colin' Redbrace, for example. At the time he was lionised by architects as their Winker-in-Chief. His blended historicism, his massive income, his five-hour lunches. The planners loved him, too. A hint of Aztec, a smattering of glass-reinforced Classical, something outré at the entrance: bingo. Another one gets the nod. By 1990 he was turning them out like sandcastles.

I am therefore re-assessing the work of Big Colin, downwards. Not because his buildings, marooned in time like those synthetic drums on the *EastEnders* theme tune, are particularly offensive. They're not. Big Colin's chunky buildings look sort of quaint, and kitsch. And a bit scruffy to be honest.

No, I am slagging the buildings off because they're two decades old and that's what you do. By 2025 they'll be well ahead of their time again.

WEDNESDAY Lunch with Darcy the architecture critic. He's thrown himself into the po-Mo Revival with methodical fervour and today inhabits a) a boxy suit, b) a big perm.

His preposterous dachshund Bauhau's there, quivering in a New Wave ensemble of pirate blouse and kilt. It's a difficult look to pull off if you're a post-Modernist dog, and he doesn't because there's no such thing.

Darcy's task is tricky too. He has to rehabilitate post-Modernism in the minds of a general public that frankly doesn't really give a shit one way or the other. After several drinks, I convince him that he should instead mourn post-Modernism for precisely that reason. Classical reassures those who like order, Gothic's for pessimists, Modern's for optimists, post-Modern's for people masking their insecurities with indifference. Most of us, in other words.

Clearly the world of epic space needs to ask itself: what now? Baggy urban zoomorphism burned briefly then sputtered out. Pre-Modernism was essentially a holding movement for people expecting something exciting round the corner but unsure what it might be. So...

Why not pretend that there's a new design movement called SLOW MODERNISM?

Like standard Modernism but with reduced air miles, a grass roof and local materials. A nice *artisan* Modernism, with ethical occupants and knobbly bread in the eco-larder. Also, it contracts in a satisying way: SLOW-MO. Let's take our time, get it right, a few glasses of something cold, think organic, yum tiddly bosh.

We all nip outside. I need a fag, Darcy's trying to get a signal on his stylish antique Rabbit phone. Bauhau, in Darcy's nauseating phrase, 'has to go po-mo'.

THURSDAY Announce Slow Modernism on Twitter. There's a lot of eye-rolling from architects, and 'oh, we've been doing that for years', and then they all quietly change their profile summary to 'Slow Modernist'.

FRIDAY Rock Steady Eddie the fixer calls. He's put the word about in

Whitehall, they love it. Watch out for a massive Slow Modernist school building programme, completion set for 'whenever'.

SATURDAY Five-a-zeitgeist theoretical football. Boho Po-Mo 2, Soho Slow-Mo 2.0, after irony shootout.

SUNDAY Paperwork in the recliner. Darcy's piece in the *Creative on Sunday* is, I have to admit, skilfully illustrated. The 'Slow-Mo Generation' seem to be young architects of Darcy's acquaintance, impeccably dressed and frowning in a forest. They all have little dogs, too.

September 22, 2011

The Irony Bridge

MONDAY I have decided to embrace the entrepreneurial spirit of the age by designing a contemporary iron foundry on the south bank of the Thames. There's a perfect site – that pointless empty patch in front of the big ferris wheel.

My proposed ironworks would be very 'butch': squat, dense, a place where proper things are made. Yin to the yang of the London Eye's 'fem' elegance. Imagine. That famous Human Lazy Susan, its pods full of stately gawpers looking down upon the unequivocal, belching maw of real industrial revival.

I am also haughtily announcing that the style of my foundry will be 'post-gastro retro'. I mean it will look exactly like one of those South Bank restaurants that resemble a converted foundry from the outside.

But here's the clever part. The interior won't be filled with air, light, jazz and loads of tetchy bastards ordering a £25 starter and some tapwater. No. It will be filled with a fuck-off blast furnace and a non-gender-specific unionised workforce turning out top quality cast iron.

Comrades, the days of effete regeneration are over. Let us now build recovery the old way, with muscular architecture and a network of artisan manufacturing bases!

TUESDAY I am in urgent talks with the Coalition about my industrial revival idea. They're extremely receptive, as 'talking up Britain' is apparently now an important economic generator.

46

Over a sandwich lunch with ministers and their special friends, it becomes clear that my foundry proposal could theoretically be 'rolled out' across the country, like molten steel. It's what we're all calling the Heavy Craft Initiative.

The inspiration is farming. Everybody hates farmers, with their churlish attitudes, self-profiled victimhood and armed, twitchy demeanour. But everyone loves farmers' markets, with their ugly vegetables, indie cheese and concealed weapons.

Localism in action, see? That's why we need subsidised neighbourhood craft manufacturing. Rough, artsy steel with bits in. Crusty homebaked bricks. Organic local concrete. Thick, cloudy glass.

My Coalition mates assure me that planning permission for the foundry is a shoo-in, and that certain shadowy enterprise funds can be found. I remind them I still need local clients for the cast iron.

WEDNESDAY Now there's a turn-up. Email from the Metropolitan Police's Community Urbanism Unit.

They want to commission a pop-up cast iron bridge, running parallel to Westminster Bridge. 'This would be deployed on an ad hoc basis specifically for public demonstrations, allowing the free flow of traffic in both directions via existing roads, and ensuring access to St Thomas' hospital in the event of any collateral injuries...'

THURSDAY Lunch with Darcy Farquear'say of the *Creative on Sunday*. I 'accidentally' leak the foundry, the Met's pop-up demo idea, and the 'fact' that the project already has a nickname – The Irony Bridge.

Darcy promises not to tell anyone. His preposterous trophy dachshund Bauhau remains mute throughout, clearly guilty about his own leak, which becomes slowly visible through the stylish cream jumpsuit he's been forced to wear.

FRIDAY Work up a design statement for the Irony Bridge. This is basically an architectural pitch, so I fill it with bullshit and platitudes.

'The structure harkens back to days of yore, with a clear emphasis on nostalgic engineering yet with a modern twist...it is conceived as a fashionable pop-up, at once temporary and contemporary. And the balance implicit in a locally cast iron bridge which is "temporary contemporary" should address any concerns that might arise from the planning or community communities...'

As a crowd control tool it's brilliant. Kettling is straightforward. Coppers with truncheons, tasers, pepper spray and freestyle hand-to-hand combat techniques at one end. Protesters enter from the other via a turn-stile until the bridge is full. Seal off with coppers, done.

There'd be a charge of say a quid per person to get onto the bridge. A small price to pay for participatory democracy, or whatever we're calling it. Once organisers have booked the Irony Bridge for a demo, they're going to look pretty ineffective if they don't fill it. I reckon it could hold about 10,000 people squashed up a bit. That's ten grand a demo before you even start talking about commercial food, drink and toilet licenses.

SATURDAY Five-a-zeitgeist theoretical football. Modular Agnostic 1, Prefabricated Creationism 1.

SUNDAY Newspaper review in the recliner. Big piece by Darcy about heavy craft, the Irony Bridge and the rise of a 'temporary contemporary' style. So reliably indiscreet.

October 13, 2011

Pathetic Fallacy 1, Emphatic Delusion 0

MONDAY I've been asked by the Church Commissioners to rationalise their property portfolio, again.

I did all this once before in the 1980s with my two-stage 'ecclesiastical investment vision'. It was swiftly and ruthlessly implemented. My first vision proposition was to monetise the Church of England's premium units – St Paul's Cathedral, for instance – by charging all atheists an entrance fee.

My second vision proposition was to sell any valuable space adjoining these premium units – Paternoster Square, say – to dead-eyed, blood-sucking commercial philistine bastards. Correction: to forward-looking urbanist developers seeking an appropriate architectural style and pre-pared to listen to all voices in the public debate, especially those weird high-pitched voices inside the Prince of Wales's head squawking on about 'homeopathic Classicism' and 'the humane curve'.

But now what? Today all the good sites formerly under Anglican pur-view are owned by hedge funds, or Wahhabist playboys. I need a five-point plan by the end of the week.

TUESDAY It's not often I'm overcome by the sheer emotional power of my own work, but today I am speechless with self-admiration.

I have – and suddenly I find I am holding back tears – 'imbued architecture with the intricacy and beauty of natural forms'. Furthermore, I have generated 'a sequence of dynamic spaces carved from the fascinating interplay between architecture and nature'.

Then I remember that the building's just a showroom for posh bathroom products in Chelsea Harbour, and pull myself together.

WEDNESDAY Morning: think 'beyond the pylon' by imagining downloadable cloudtricity.

Afternoon: think 'outside the matrix' by imagining a 'hologramorphic building information system'. It would combine architectural drawings, the 'semantic web' and a little bit of magic to create a 3-D, 1:1 scale representation of any imaginable building. You can wander around it in a weird hat and a pirate beard if you want, who fucking cares? Invite your mates in, have a cocktail reception in the simulated space, it's only a hologramorphic building information system. It's NOT REAL, YOU MUPPET.

Evening: think 'over the curve' by imagining a capsule wardrobe for a nano-bedsit. What an exhausting, innovative day. Before turning in I register patents online for the Leccy App™, the SIMBIM™ and the MollyCule™.

THURSDAY Fascinating colloquium at the pub chaired by Rock Steady Eddie the fixer. We all earnestly discuss possible redesigns for the global economy.

Man, there are a lot of conversations like this taking place in the arts and design world these days, aren't there? Nobody's making art or designing anything much any more (it's technically illegal under the Coalition's Austerity Laws) so everyone's pitching a remodelled market system instead.

We're all after the same things in the end. Justice, freedom and dependable sources of fee income. Planners want a steady 9 to 5, architects want three or four major jobs a year, surveyors want a packed nine months of high earning so they can go on prohibitively expensive cricket tours abroad with the Barmy Army and pretend they're geezers.

As for our new economic prototypes, it's mostly arguing about wall finishes and curtains. Nobody wants to tear it all down and start again. Eddie summarises: 'I'll tell you what makes the world go round. Inertia.

'There's just too much fannying about involved in changing the system, innit. People can't be arsed. I mean Blimey O'Reilly, you know what it's like trying to sort out bleeding broadband. Imagine having to change your capitalism provider. You finishing those chips?'

FRIDAY Hallelujah. My five-point plan for the Church Commissioners is ready at last. Fingers crossed.

- Basic Holy Communion to remain free at the point of delivery, though with opportunity to avoid delays and sermons in new Communion Lounges.
- Introduce 'Babel rights' to allow little Waitroses, boutique housing etc to be built on top of parish churches.
- Buy-to-let almshouses.
- Admission to historic buildings via tokens purchased from private sector 'gamechangers' sitting at special 'non-overturnable' tables.
- Principle of 'sanctuary' to be revived but with small charge for anti-capitalist protesters playing off-ground touch with the police.

SATURDAY Five-a-zeitgeist theoretical football. Pathetic Fallacy 1, Emphatic Delusion 0, after extra time and passive-aggressive crowd noises.

SUNDAY Catch up with my filing. There's an interesting new report on human rights which lists China, Iran and Burma as the three most oppressive regimes in the world. File under 'emerging markets'.

Later, ethically transfer to the recliner.

October 20, 2011

The Decadent Egg

MONDAY The planners have turned down my planning application for a pop-up mosque.

It was a 'bouncy mega-mosque' and looked bloody great on paper. A gigantic though modest inflatable structure with a helium-stiffened minaret. Capable of holding 70,000 worshippers either on land (urban version) or afloat in the middle of the Thames Estuary (Olympic legacy version).

Despite this inbuilt flexibility – I sought planning permission to inflate the mosque anywhere in London it could fit, thereby saving on paperwork – it has been refused because it is too big and 'contentious'. I'm not sure what this means. 'Likely to be opposed by people who don't like giant inflatable mosques'? It's absurd.

I'll make it smaller and less contentious. Back to the pop-up drawing board.

TUESDAY OK, here we go. I've halved the size, emailed it off to the planners and have even paid the £3,000 surcharge for a same-day decision.

Fingers crossed. This pop-up mosque is smaller AND it's buried underground where nobody can see it. Plus, I've decreased the contentiousness by giving it a patronising tabloid nickname, the 'Meccatracker'.

The Meccatracker is a magnetically accurate prayer hall inside a massive reinforced concrete 'grindstone'. This doesn't sound very demountable, but the 'grindstone' is built from thousands of ultra-thin folding Conquete® panels. I will reveal the actual construction process in due course, if I get planning permission.

This one holds a mere 12,000 worshippers and is suitable for any big-enough hole in the ground. Its unique Mosqnav® tracking system adjusts every three minutes to align with the verified source of project sponsorship.

Bollocks. Refused again. STILL too big.

WEDNESDAY I am putting aside mosques for the moment to design a luxury boutique world-class access space. It is, obviously, brilliant. I am calling it The Decadent Egg.

The Egg is a prototype 'gateway presence' that can literally be rolled out, assuming a level rolling field, to any site in the world. A spun-Kryptogel® globe, double-skinned, a 'nodule within a podule'. It can redeem the most unappetising new building in the world with its dollop of classy garnish.

From the bleak hospitality of an aerodrome in the Caucasus to the feeble grandeur of a chain hotel in Aberdeen, the Decadent Egg 'delivers adjunctive elevation'. You may say: 'what are you talking about?' I'll tell you.

Adjunctive elevation occurs through the creation of vertical portals and analogical linkages, using inter-connecting layers of platforms to signify a dynamic, expressive mix of urban forum, windows, reception desk, human sounding board, hang-out space, niche sponsorship opportunities, ad hoc public observatory and quality piped music.

Furthermore, 3-D mapping allows the visitor to see everything from slightly different angles by sequentially standing at different 'node points'. Incredibly, I am taking the notions of fluid architectural form and functional interaction, then mashing them up into a totally innovative blurred existence.

This innovative blurred existence I will call 'authentricity'. The authentic reassurance of affordable luxury in an easily readable generic style. It sounds like the opposite of authenticity, but it isn't.

THURSDAY Try the heritage approach. Submit my 'midi-mosque' for planning permission.

It's a retro plug-in prayer space, compatible with all pre-1995 power channels. Holds 500 worshippers in a matt black pop-up cardboard tube. Dry bar with free wi-fi. Would easily fit on a defunct petrol station or library site.

The minaret's invisible within a slender cardboard tube, which has a brick veneer and looks like a chimney. Pick the bones of contention out of THAT.

FRIDAY Ugh. Turned down on three grounds. Firstly it was ruled 'unsustainable'; cardboard is apparently not a 'local' material.

Secondly, they hated the chimney: 'visual misrepresentation under the Aesthetic Trades Description Act 1894 (to wit, not a chimney); contravention of the Passive Air Act 2002 (to wit, promoting the inference of airborne smoke)'.

Thirdly, the entire scheme 'breaches the Common Law of Contention Governing Lawful Assemblies of Mohammetans 1067 (by encouraging same)'. I think this is pretty bad, to be honest, discriminating against mosques on the basis that they contain Muslims.

But not as shocking as the cardboard thing. Thanks to Amazon and the supermarkets, cardboard is now an abundant local material, surely. Bastards!

SATURDAY Invent the iMosq, a single-use numinous helmet for individual worshippers. Keep it to myself this time.

SUNDAY Large lunch, then push the limits of tolerance in the recliner.

November 10, 2011

Remagination

MONDAY I have entered a government-sponsored recovery design competition. They're looking for a massive infrastructure and housebuilding programme, 'asafp'.

Start thinkstorming. By teatime I'm surrounded by crumpled paper and all I've written down is '£100 billion should do it!' Though in fairness I have underlined this, twice.

TUESDAY Making progress on my recovery initiative. I've drawn a pastoral landscape. On the left, wind turbines and Glastonbury. On the right, sustainable development and acres of arable investment opportunity.

Across the horizon I've written 'Aims and objectives: boost growth, create jobs!'

WEDNESDAY Definitely taking shape now. I'm playing around with the idea of using private sector capital funding to build new power stations, rented housing, hospital gift shops, toll pavements, etc.

It's a novel and daring approach. I call it the 'design, build, stand and deliver' procurement system.

THURSDAY For my proposals to be credible they have to demonstrate at least a notional source of money.

That's it, exactly – notional! Theoretically there's a fortune out there, it's just locked up in complicated pension funds and whatever. Those who carry the burden of wealth are feeling nervous about spending at the moment and who can blame them?

Under 'funding' I just put 'if we build a framework of stable regulation, it will come'. I'm so confident that I DOUBLE the proposed investment. The cynics can sneer all they like. £200 billion theoretically buys a bloody lot of construction.

FRIDAY My friend Darcy Farquear'say the architecture critic has 'scored a couple of invites' to the prestigious 4R Awards tomorrow night. Do I want to go?

Darcy is not a 1970s San Francisco pimp. When he says he 'scored' invitations he simply means he's been sent them by the PR company retained for the event. Also, I'm assuming the organisers have a strict no-pets rule, and that I'm a last-minute replacement for Darcy's architectural dachshund Bauhau.

Still, I'm in. The 4R Awards (Retreat, Rebadge, Remagine, Relaunch) is an important annual celebration of what architects can achieve when they focus their considerable creative powers on a worthy subject. Themselves.

SATURDAY A glittering, tittering crowd at the mid-range London hotel where Awards Night is taking place.

It reminds me of the old days, when architects gathered to give each other prizes for brilliant buildings, although my memory's not what it was and I may have invented that.

Tonight, the prizes are for architectural excellence in the redesign and re-use of architectural practices. Which, let's face it, is no less important than designing mobile protest kiosks, 'urban respite spaces', culture hubs and clothes shops. Architects aren't the stuffy old deadheads they used to be. They are an integral part of the knowledge economy. Any profession that allows the neologism 'remagine' to attach itself to them like a brainless limpet deserves all the success they can garner, even if that success is restricted to peer recognition.

Darcy chides me for being a curmudgeon. He's wearing a three-piece swagged hemp suit, retro neon wrestling boots and a lumberjack hat, so I weigh his judgement carefully. It's free drinks for the first hour, and my mood soon lightens. I raise a glass to epic space: 'Architect, design thyself!'

Façade of the Year goes to Manningham Downham Architects, who reduced staff at their Leeds head office from 52 to 4 last month but have kept them moving about near the windows, so nobody's noticed.

Best Website Award. The winner is Unique Design Logistics/CentralBANG for an innovative 'reversible' web presence. The homepage invites visitors to click on either 'Unique Design Logistics' or 'CentralBANG'. One whisks you off to a profile page where they're looking trustworthy in suits and hard hats. The other offers tieless dudes looking at skateboard videos on an iPad. 'Twice the integrity, double the options' is their motto, in both versions.

The Special Award for Colon Efficiency goes to :r::D::a: (the firm formerly known as Radon Daughters & Associates). Since the multicolon rebrand :r::D::a: have registered a 22 per cent year-on-year increase in stationery output. An intern is solely responsible for checking that potential clients, service suppliers and news editors spell it correctly, and for answering the phone. 'Colon lower case R double colon upper case D double colon lower case A colon, how may I help you?'

SUNDAY Retrofit self into recliner by waking up and discovering I'm already in it.

November 17, 2011

It's the Sulk I'm Really After

MONDAY Issue a statement denying rumours that I am to curate next year's Tamworth Biennale.

Of course I understand how these rumours started. I started them. What I DON'T understand is why nobody takes them seriously. In order to spare myself further humiliation, I have now withdrawn my name from the shortlist.

TUESDAY Already regretting counting myself out as biennale curator. I had some dazzling, innovative ideas. The theme was to be 'Epic Space as Contemporary Drama'.

Instead of 'pavilions' or 'rooms' I proposed an interlinked network of stages, upon which various architectural performances could occur. I thought I'd keep it loose to allow creativity to flourish. Even when I was only 'rumoured' to be curating, there was huge interest in this idea.

One nation, which has to remain nameless, wanted to use the event as a sort of trade showcase. A team of actors in black polo-neck jumpers would build a stylish urban apartment from scratch and then live in it, listening to jazz and watching thrillers with subtitles.

Mostly, though, the exhibits were drearily predictable. A luminous field of tents in the shadow of a hologram cathedral. Shakespearean actors on a revolving stage, declaiming extracts from European planning law. A stage left meaningfully empty, that we may infer our own sense of what architecture means. A weird conga of 'disenfranchised youth' weaving around dangerous obstacles in a parable about space syntax. Tensile environments. A polished concrete and glass 'allegory'. A lighting rig powered by the cast's breath. A high-density boutique, its curtilage extended by 500m using ironic disco music and aromatherapy.

Never mind, there's always next year. Plenty of time to plant rumours about my curating something really shocking at the Victoria and Albert Museum say, then complain about being monstered in the tabloids, then withdraw sulkily. I think in the end it's the sulk I'm really after.

WEDNESDAY Sketch out my masterplan for a new airport in the middle of the Thames estuary. There would be bobbing executive lounges and no smoking anywhere in London.

The coasts of Essex and Kent would effectively be converted into duty-free malls. Fingers crossed.

THURSDAY Meeting of the Olympic Rebadging Task Force. Games minister Suzi Towel in the chair. As usual, after prayers and apologies for absence, she leads us in a Mexican Wave. In keeping with these solemn and unostentatious times, the table-wave angle is kept under 40 degrees.

It's not the only concession to recession. Now whenever anyone says the word 'Olympics' we merely murmur 'yay' in grim approbation.

First item on the agenda is the matter of how to create a 'fulcrumic' public space between the shops and the new security barrier – apparently the FBI is now allowed to erect some horrible ugly 'people filter' on the site without the benefit of our design competition expertise. No matter. This fulcrumic problem is really tricky because the space has to be both a hub AND 'evolve over time to become an enticing destination'. After some discussion we decide to rebadge the space as 'pivotal', allowing it to move with the times.

The next item on the agenda is the Thing. The massive steel monument being built by – and to the glory of – a billionaire political donor. We need a nickname, and sharpish. It's important that the nation embraces the Thing, but it is so genuinely horrible that nobody likes it. So far (luckily) none of the nicknames – the Sex Trumpet, the Skein of Shit, the Whirlyfuck – has stuck.

Now though its 'shape' is becoming apparent. It looks like a giant pound sign lashed to a post, waiting for some legendary dragon to come and devour it. As a narrative on global capitalism it's great, but we're not sure this is a route we want to go down. We decide in the end to contract the nicknaming out to a *Daily Telegraph* columnist and grudgingly accept the consequences.

Marvellous lunch, though everyone's careful not to enjoy it too much given the state of the economy. But there's still much muted excitement about the legacy we're building here, over pudding, for the 2012 Olympics. Yay.

FRIDAY Design a Museum of Tolerance just to wind up the haters, man.

SATURDAY Five-a-zeitgeist theoretical football. Picturesque 2, Photoshop 4.

SUNDAY Nod off in the recliner. Horrible dream about 95 per cent mortgages being used to 'create wealth'. Ugh. The lying shit Blair was in it, too.

November 26, 2011

One One

MONDAY Redesign the Eurozone, giving it a dark 'old-fangled' look, with Gothic tracery and an enveloping mist.

TUESDAY Bad news. My smart housing scheme for Blingnang has been cancelled. It doesn't make any sense – how can a construction boom simply STOP?

Shame. I'd proposed bio-sensors for all the rooms, allowing occupants to tell with one tap on an app if they were at home or not.

WEDNESDAY Design something on a tricky corner site. It's to be called 'Vector 6' for maximum flexibility as the client's not sure yet what it's for. Fine with me. My motto these days is 'Long life, loose fit, vague project title'.

THURSDAY Pub lunch with my old mate Tub Hagendaas, the metarchitect's metarchitect. Tub really is in a class of his own: he's the only one who knows what a metarchitect is. And this is his power.

Tub's on a world tour at the moment. Each country he visits is required to host a massive retrospective of his work while he potters around in the countryside, gathering data for a new project called 'One One'. This will involve the creation of an ambitious 1:1 scale map.

He stares mournfully at the remains of his pub lunch – that is, practically all of it as he's on a strict garnish-only diet at the moment.

'This map will be a map of all the countrysides in the world. When completed, it can be briefly overlayed onto the real thing...' Here he gives me one of his withering stares to signal that of course he's not that stupid. '...very briefly I mean, we do not want to see the stifling of the crops or the suffocation of the livestocks or the peoples of the Earth.

'This map, OK, this unsolicited skin or membrane, is then slowly raised into the air by sky cranes, the various peoples of the countrysides of the Earth perhaps cheering, throwing their hats into the air, I don't of course wish to be prescriptive. Rather, I wish to be postscriptive. The map or skin or membrane – manufactured from polymolecules which have been teased out through a nano-carding process to produce something quite unprecedented...'

He stops for a moment. Imperiously holds up a hand to prevent further interruption. Retrieves a small recording device from a pocket and speaks into it. 'Reminder. Check with lab for any progress at all on polymolecular carding'. He replaces the device, remembers something and pulls it out again. 'Elsa. Please find out if my silver jumpsuit is ready for collection from the dry cleaner's. Thank you.'

I take the opportunity to slip off to the bar to get another round in. When I return Tub is engaging a weary-looking member of staff in conversation about his lunch. 'I'm sorry you didn't want your lunch in the end but I just need to clear the plates away...' 'Is this not symptomatic of a society ill at ease with its own detritus, its own waste and filth, its...yes very well, hurry up please'.

A young intern has materialised to take a Polaroid picture of Tub. As part of his rigorously documented life – he is a most fascinating subject – he insists on being photographed every 15 minutes. 'This is absolutely nothing creepy at all. The Polaroid interns are on a rota, it is not as if I keep one special intern at my house or hotel to take photographs of me every quarter-hour. And what really is so weird about a person asleep or defecating or masturbating or whatever? Are we to sweep these things under the polymolecular carding? No, we are not!'

The table-clearing accelerates sharply and the Polaroid intern disappears. I tell him that I totally get the nano-science and the giant map and all that, but why is the project called 'One One'? If it's a 1:1 scale map, what on earth has happened to the colon?

'Ah, this is the heart of the matter, you are correct'. He leans in and lowers his voice. 'The colon is dead'.

FRIDAY Still in shock, frankly. Unpunctuated Epic Space: Imagination Beyond the Colon. No, it's unthinkable.

SATURDAY In Denial: A Continuing Struggle with the Absent Colon: Further Thoughts on Architecture's Cantilevered Language of Deferred Articulation.

SUNDAY Media review in the recliner. Tub all over the papers with his call for 'colon cleansing'. Ugh.

December 8, 2011

Pudding Gateshead

MONDAY Design an urban nebulus. Key transport nodes linked by synaptic pathways of space. Socio-neural clusters organically formed into sustainable hubs of excellence.

All a bit vague at the moment. I'm allowing it to develop naturally in my mind as an elasticated mystery.

TUESDAY To the Royal Institute for the Protection of British Architects, which is marking the Queen's diamond jubilee with an eclectic exhibition of thrones.

There's the Jacobean extravagance of the Throne of the Apocrypha, a hypergothic masterpiece on loan from Sir Elton John. And there's the grim humour of Throne Up, an installation by the republican collective Gertcha. This is merely an aircraft ejector seat, with a frozen turkey sitting in it to make it art.

My favourite is the reclining Throne of Games, built perhaps with younger princes in mind, with its integral PSP screen and snack pouches.

WEDNESDAY I'm on the shortlist to rethink Gateshead. Intellectually this is a massive gig, even if none of my proposals will ever be realised.

The client, Gateshead Legacy Delivery Corporation, wants to 'imagineer a contemporary live-work-visit destination with world-class vision and a pronounced cultural overbite'.

Funds will not be immediately available to implement any masterplan, but as my fixer Rock Steady Eddie says, 'Money's bollocksed now anyway, who even knows what money IS any more? This is cultural re-bloody-generation. It just has to look tasty in one of them investment catalogues they leave lying about in the first class lounge at Abu Dhabu International, you finishing those chips?'

Eddie and I are trying to brainstorm in the pub. Not the ideal environment for focusing on creative solutions for a major northern conurbation. On the other hand, pub lunch.

'Look, imagine this table is Gateshead, yeah?' A young man in an unnecessary charcoal apron is clearing the table. 'See how all these whatever, remnants of the past, are being swept away...' 'Everything all right for you gents?' murmurs Apron Lad as our plates disappear. Eddie pauses and squints at him.

'You tell me, son. This...' he indicates the crumb-covered table '...is Gateshead, right? A clean slate, once you've wiped the bloody table obviously. It was always in the shadow of Newcastle, where all the good shops were. Then they phased out the mining and the industry. They created Europe's largest council estate in the hope that it would form some sort of whatever, critical mass, and suck in new economic opportunities but these turned out to be mostly landscaping, art forgery, tobacco smuggling, eck cetera...'

The table has been wiped. All that remains are our two pints and the condiments tray. 'And here coincidentally are Gateshead's primary cultural whatever, indicators: Angel of the North, that flour mill they turned into an art gallery, plus I think there's some concert hall, probably looks like a cruet set, designed by the lad Foster. Forget your concrete towers and gritty carparks. All that gangster film stuff's in the skip. Name of the game these days is cultural capital...'

'Would you gents like to see the pudding menu?'

Now Eddie definitely doesn't like to be interrupted. There's a silence you could put a hat on. Eddie makes gunfingers at Apron Lad and for a moment I think he's going to punch him. Instead, he turns the gun into a gesture of approbation and smiles. 'Puddings. That's it. Brilliant. Yeah, bring us the menu, son...'

THURSDAY Work up New Gateshead using Eddie's Cultural Pudding Theory. Summary: forget starters, the days of cultural regeneration appetisers have gone. Forget the main course, heavy industry's never coming back. If you just have the pudding you can have several.

He's definitely on to something. I rethink the area as a gigantic dessert trolley, filled with cultural assets...wait. Why not make them LOOK like puddings? An arts centre conceived as a trifle. A big vanilla slice of local heritage experience. An assortment of accessible artworks scattered like petit-fours across the town?

FRIDAY Submit my proposals for Pudding Gateshead. Particularly pleased with 'Tateshead', a notional complex of Tates jumbled along the south bank of the Tyne like cheese and biscuits.

SATURDAY The Gateshead people hate my cultural puddings. Apparently I have 'besmorched' their dignity with my analysis. Fine. I want nothing more to do with shitting Gateshead. Let them eat fucking cake.

SUNDAY Form a cultural pudding in the recliner.

February 9, 2012

The Collide-O-Scope

MONDAY Create a 300,000m² 'dream plaza'. Wake up from afternoon nap and create an ordinary one.

TUESDAY Afternoon tea with my old friend Isis de Cambray, the magic arborealist.

Pretentious landscaping remains a buoyant sector. The idle rich are never satisfied. Isis built her reputation on extravagant garden design, but now the global kleptocracy is keening after a new authenticity. 'Poverty chic is my fresh jam!' squeaks Isis, with no hint of irony. The hip end of the billionaire garden market now wants to capture the vitality of the dispossessed. Those marvellous peasant environments. The 'excitement of having nothing'.

I recoil in disgust. Is this what she's doing now? Turning misery into some fucking playground for bankers and celebrities? What next? Will she start designing contemporary plantations in blackface? She shrugs. 'Please yourself. I thought you could use some moonlighting. Cash in hand. The idea was that you'd be my mysterious gnarled old English landscape architect, Austerity Brown…'

I maintain my look of disdain, but help myself to another scone.

WEDNESDAY Lunch with architecture critic Darcy Farquear'say, who seems in a grave mood even after his fifth Dubai Wallclimber.

His preposterous dachshund Bauhau is oddly subdued too. Instead of yapping like some miniature pterodactyl every time someone says 'post-Modernism', he just gazes forlornly at His Master from within a slouchy yet elegant canine cocoon coat by Tommy Hilfiger.

Maybe he and Darcy have had a row. Two more Dubai Wallclimbers are slammed down on the table. 'Make the most of it,' snarls Darcy. 'Good times don't last forever'. Bauhau gives a little whimper and, for the first time I can ever recall, Darcy invites the 'little bastard' to shut his 'stupid whiney trap, you're giving me bloody neuralgia…'

THURSDAY Assemble some preliminary thought-collages for my Surrealistic Wardrobe. It's actually a museum, not a wardrobe. I'm calling it a wardrobe to challenge public perceptions of surrealism, and museums.

Building elements will be deliberately unreconciled, so everything looks incongruous and sinister. Counterintuitively, there will actually be a 'wardrobe' theme to the museum throughout, with full-length mirrorglass and paintings on giant coathangers and all the shit you're never going to look at anyway scrunched up and stuffed to the back. There will be a magnificent entrance – or WILL there?

The Surrealistic Wardrobe is just what it'll be called for the next two weeks. Then the project title will be words selected at random from *The Concordance of Surrealism*. For instance, from Monday March 5 it will be called the Urtastic Gourd. The following week, the Collide-O-Scope. Then the Ghastly Veil, the Rocking-Horse Ultimatum, the Meniscus of Emptiness, Poundlandia. Etc.

Yes, I'm going to be pushing some boundaries with this, as well as challenging public perceptions. These are basic criteria for European funding. Obviously I won't be challenging my OWN perceptions. That would be madness. Someone's got to keep a straight head.

FRIDAY Spend the day as 'Austerity Brown', the celebrated poverty landscape architect.

By teatime I've knocked up an impressive Garden of Contemplation for a client living in the posh, Chinese bit of Tibet. Five exquisitely unkempt acres of scrubland, with gorgeous little inhabited follies constructed from wooden pallets and corrugated tin. The centrepiece is a traditional English bonfire constructed from antique furniture and floorboards. There's even a gutsy, earthy vegetable patch. Memo to Self: find out where to source growing vegetables.

SATURDAY Slight nausea, and inflammation of the conscience. God, if I'm coming down with something I really hope it's not poverty.

SUNDAY 'Media oversight'. Essentially, reading the papers in the recliner. I leave Darcy's weekly essay in the *Creative on Sunday* until the end, as I've almost always heard it before in the pub.

Imagine my astonishment. The standfirst reads: 'In his final piece as the *Creative*'s epic space correspondent, Darcy Farquear'say reflects on some of his most successful guesswork...' Bloody hell. He's OUT. I skim through the cut-and-paste Darcy memories, held together loosely in a valedictory ragbag, to the end. 'And so I say, a little tearfully I confess – *à bientôt!*' Then my jaw drops a little further. There's a postscript.

'Starting next week in our *Love Life* section: *Under One Woof*, a light-hearted look at the built environment with our resident style dachshund BAUHAU...' Darcy's been laid off and is ghosting for his DOG? This will end badly...

February 16, 2012

A Strange Glint

MONDAY A day of watercolours. Particularly proud of a winter land-scape I shall call Ghostly Carbon Footprints in the Snow, in order to give it added emotional value.

TUESDAY In the morning, I'm struck by a quote from eminent aca-demic Manny Lauda. He criticises young architects entering competitions, claiming that they 'seem to think ordinary life processes are too boring to merit attention'.

He's right. In the afternoon, I redesign the human digestive tract.

WEDNESDAY Lunch with Bauhau the dachshund, the new architecture correspondent of the *Creative on Sunday*.

Bauhau seems to have grown in confidence, if not in stature, since taking over the role from his companion, the forlorn and neurotic scribbler Darcy Farquear'say.

Of course Darcy's actually ghosting the stuff – trivial, skittish takes on the built environment tagged Ground Zero – but for him anonymity is the ultimate humiliation. On the picture byline it's not his but Bauhau's optimistic face cocked inquisitively at the reader.

Still, every cloud. Freed from the yoke of sneery cynicism, Darcy's writing style as a dachshund is a revelation. His tone is celebratory and generous, I tell him. Half a second too late I realise I'm talking to the dog. Darcy flares. 'Yeah, brilliant work Bauhau, you little shit. How's the novel coming along? Oh, I forgot, you CAN'T TYPE BECAUSE YOU'RE JUST A FUCKING DOG!'

A waiter gently asks Darcy to keep his voice down. Diners do not want to hear aggressive and bullying behaviour towards dachshunds. Bauhau calmly looks up at me from his fancy offal starters. He has a strange glint in his eye, as if to say 'yeah, maybe I AM writing a novel'.

THURSDAY To the West End for the preview of an exciting new musical about crazy, sexy Victorian architect Augustus Pugin, called *Steampuncular!*

In common with most bourgeois commentators, I make it a rule never to see any theatre production with an exclamation mark at the end. *Steampuncular!* is the exception that proves the rule, and a reminder not to break it again in the future.

On paper the show is brilliant. Pugin the Gothic colossus re-imagined as Sid Vicious in a top hat and waistcoat, cursing and gobbing his way through the salons of 19th-century London, tearing up the architectural playbook, getting pissed and shagging everybody. Russell Brand is an inspired choice for the lead role, and Adele looks and sounds fantastic as the Queen.

But the whole thing relies far too heavily on gimmicks. From the special effects – at one point Pugin flies above the rooftops of Rome destroying Classical buildings with a laser cannon – to the tedious music hall-style songs.

The sight of Pugin and chorus prancing across the stage, all Cockney braces and hobnailed boots, singing 'Don't Call Me Mad or Bad, I'm Just a Medieval Genius' convinced me not to return after the interval drinks.

FRIDAY Redesign Northern Ireland, giving it a 'nuanced, heritagey, ethnic' feel.

SATURDAY Five-a-zeitgeist theoretical football. Stylistic Interregnum 4, Festival of Britain Retro Jubilee 2.

SUNDAY Newspaper review in the recliner. Bauhau's latest despatch from Ground Zero is an impressive experiential hymn to something called 'Splashion', formerly Bradford town square.

It's a massive pool with complicated fountains and seems to be a popular success. There are convincing pictures of Bauhau yapping gaily through the shallow water in what looks like a haute couture wetsuit. As an architecture critic 'he' loves it.

If Darcy had written this piece, he'd be disdaining the whole enterprise as a vulgar bid for tourist cash. He'd be moaning about the ephemeral nature of visitor attractions and pitying Bradford for its loss of dignity. He'd also be chucking in phrases such as 'haptic imperative' and 'urban melisma'. As a dachshund, he's so much more agreeable.

'Woof! A large dead public space transformed into a fun day out with the kids? Woof! YES! Let the metropolitan elite whine like circular saws, who cares, Splashion's all about a communal sense of civic pride and I for one won't be relieving myself in it. Apart from anything else, it would be anti-social and might result in a fine for the apparently still-unnamed individual who looks after me! Woof!'

Bauhau also seems to be in favour of the Olympics. And Damien Hirst's eco-town. And the Prince of Wales. I wonder if he knows what he's doing?

February 23, 2012

The New Pop-Uption

MONDAY Reputation matters. It's very important to me to avoid the charge that I am 'pandering to an artistic elite', whatever THAT means.

My latest 'vibrant arts-based community' – a theatre created from smart-matrix CGI, gossamised platinum and spun gold; 1,000 serviced apartments with armed, handsome security staff; a six-star hotel with funicular shuttle; approximately 280,000m² of tax-notional office and retail cash waiver, and a nightclub called Loco Bunga – is located on a (very) modest island in Russia, for example.

TUESDAY Redesign Liverpool with an inflatable waterfront development. This will give maximum flexibility in the future as it can either be puffed up to look more menacing than its historic neighbours, or floated away by sulky corporate windbags.

WEDNESDAY Lunch with my old friend Darcy Farquear'say, freelance architecture critic. I don't think he's ever been this scruffy or had stubble like that since the late 1980s.

And for the first time I can remember there's no Bauhau the dachshund. Darcy and his quivering overdressed muse have been inseparable for years. Alas now Bauhau's riding a small dog popularity thermal thanks to films such as *Tin Tin* and *The Artist*, Darcy rarely sees him – despite ghosting his popular architecture column in the *Creative on Sunday*.

'He's never home these days. I blame that bitch of an agent. She's his plus one, now for all the swish happenings, he's staying over at her place a LOT...' Darcy's posture's gone too. I ask him if he'd considered sabotaging *Ground Zero*, Bauhau's weekly sideways canine look at the world of the built environment.

If Darcy started subtly changing Bauhau's personality from yappy populist to gripey bastard...well, sooner or later he'd say something controversial and the liberal vigilantes of Twitter would demand his sacking. 'Yes, I'm sick of this humiliation,' says Darcy with resolve. 'From now on, I'm going to be a totally different dachshund.'

THURSDAY A brainstorming day. If I could just think of something clever to turn Battersea Power Station into, some crazy geezer in sunglasses might pay me to DO it.

The trick is to keep things exciting yet vague. I'm going for 'iconic destination where visitors can live, shop, browse, gaze, graze, booze and go up the chimneys on a thrilling sky walk for £75'. Someone in Qatar will LOVE the sound of that, you watch.

FRIDAY Huge day for the Royal Institute for the Protection of British Architects. Its ruling body on matters of moral destiny, the Noble and Most Ancient Council of Artful Contrivance and Brand Identity, has gathered to discuss a proposed change of name.

RIPBA president Molly Bismuth wants to replace the word 'Protection' with 'Pop-Uption'.

Of course opponents claim that pop-uption isn't strictly speaking a word and furthermore would expose members of the institute to ridicule and sharp banter in the workplace, especially on building sites. 'May I see some credentials please?' 'Yes, here is my card. I am a member of the Royal Institute for the Pop-Uption of British Architects'. 'Please proceed, ha ha ha: pop-uption'. The sniggering alone could fatally undermine the profession's dignity.

But Ms Bismuth is adamant. 'We are here today, gathered in our vestments of truth and honour, some in ceremonial hats and sparkling notions, to make the most momentous decision in our institute's history. Should we remain fossilised, with our heads up our past? Or rather should we grasp the new pop-up reality and look the future in the eye?' Here she slaps a thigh, makes a 'pop-up' gesture and growls briefly.

After lunch, those eligible members still awake solemnly file in to vote. It's a tie: two-all. There's a short debate, then agreement that the change of name shall be observed until the standing-down of the incumbent president.

'Hail, the Royal Institute for the Pop-Uption of British Architects!' cries Ms Bismuth. 'So say we all!' answer the three remaining conscious members.

SATURDAY Pop up the pub.

SUNDAY Bauhau's column in the *Creative on Sunday* is very bitter this week. 'Hey, anybody here heard of Wang Shu? No? Well, he's just won the Pritzker Prize. Really? What's THAT, you ask? Yeah, welcome to the twilight world of architecture, where genuine talent is crushed and the merely fashionable is promoted and fawned over by witless giggling fannies...'

There are already over a thousand online comments, overwhelmingly positive. Poor Darcy. New Bauhau's a hit.

March 1, 2012

19th-Century Brickdust

MONDAY 'Residents' are a right pain in the arse, aren't they? Let's be honest, 'residents' are just a random assortment of people who happen to live in the same area.

But as soon as I submit a planning application to replace a totally non-descript clapped-out Victorian two-storey building with a massive lump of retail space and a stunning 18-storey block of flats – FIVE OF WHICH WILL BE TECHNICALLY 'AFFORDABLE' BY THE WAY – suddenly there's a coherent community with all sorts of shared bloody visions, and some hurtfully expressed reservations about my methodology.

If I had my way local residents' objections would be admissable only if accompanied by documentary proof that the bastards actually know each other. It is frankly outrageous that a meeting of residents can be called and then HIJACKED for the first quarter of an hour by people simply introducing themselves!

And they call this democracy.

TUESDAY Plenty to think about today. The so-called residents have now joined forces with the Heritage Brigade.

Embarrassingly, one of the heritage brigadiers is my old friend Dusty Penhaligon the conservactionist. We've been on opposite sides of the argument before, of course.

There was that Wesleyan chapel I wanted to replace with a big department store shaped like an amoeba. The Edwardian arcade I planned to turn into a 'boutique vertical village' and private rare bird sanctuary. And the straggly old almshouses that should have made way for my enormous Museum of Natural Light, a glazed truncheon of aesthetic authority in an otherwise trivial, cowering suburban setting.

In each case Dusty, and the sheer scale of my ambition, and OK the laws of physics, conspired to bury the scheme. It didn't stop us shaking hands afterwards and having a pint. This time it's different. We have more emotional investment. Dusty's reputation as the man who can stop anything new being built anywhere is at stake. And I'm on points for each non-affordable flat sold.

WEDNESDAY Lunch with Dusty. 'Yeah, nothing personal mate but I'm going to be publicly calling your scheme an overscaled horrendous pile of shit,' he says, cordially.

Oh well, I say, it would be a boring old world if we all liked the same things. I fetch two identical pints from the bar. 'It's not just' he says, 'that it's big and ugly, cheers. It disrespects the historic area and has a completely non-contextual materials palette…'

We exchange a meaningful glance. What a top bloke Dusty is. He's obliged to oppose the scheme whatever it looks like. But he's just satnav'ed me through the valley of the shadow of death, avoiding traffic black spots and residents.

THURSDAY Spend the day rearranging my credentials. I need to make myself more ethical and appealing to those wine-tasting sour-faced bossy cockplungers who've emerged as the opinion formers within their newly discovered 'community'.

Ugh. Just the idea that we craftspeople of epic space must put up with this. It seems incredible that in the 21st century professional placemakers can still be stereotyped as disconnected narcissists. Whatever happened to trust? Fine. I'll dissemble then, if that's what it takes to mollify Jamie Oliver's Army.

By teatime my CV includes an organic orphanage, a green hospice and a Bridge of Peace between North and South Korea.

FRIDAY Residents' meeting. I reveal the redesign, which omits the 18-storey block of flats. That's now Phase 2, which can always be re-announced if necessary.

I have reduced the 'retail space' to two storeys and rebadged it as 'boutique local commercial community shopping with potential for "farmers' upmarket". Think potatoes with dirt on and stallholders dressed like Mumford and Sons'.

That goes down well. Then I reveal that the new building will have 'a classic Victorian form and mass'. The cladding will incorporate a light dusting of genuine 19th-century brickdust, recycled from the pulverised building it will seamlessly replace. Honestly, I say, you won't notice even the tiniest change in the historic landscape.

Plus £50 worth of Ocado vouchers for every household, subject to availability.

There's a show of hands. All are in favour except Dusty, who surreptitiously gives me a scowl and a wink.

SATURDAY Pub with Dusty. Drinks are on me, as I've just had a cheque from the client's administrators. I'm a community hero, Dusty's reputation's intact. We raise our glasses and toast the plastic arts.

SUNDAY Take up temporary residence in the recliner.

March 8, 2012

The Certification of Public Space

MONDAY A few months ago I awarded myself outline planning permission for a controversial 'mind farm'.

It wasn't easy. Part of my consciousness had serious objections to having unsightly 'mind turbines' in a picturesque part of the mental landscape. But the stark reality is that conventional thinking resources, fossilised for as long as I can remember, are finite. Alternative means of converting thought into fee-generating energy are urgently required.

After a lengthy private inquiry the objections were emphatically overruled. My mind farm is now fully functional, harnessing those gusts of lateral thinking that otherwise would be blowing aimlessly around my hippocampus like litter in a car park.

Of course the scoffers and tossers were sceptical. 'Lateral thinking may have been an earner in the 1990s, but who pays for that sort of thing now?' Well, scoffers and tossers, I'll tell you. The government's Public Responsibility Unit, that's who.

TUESDAY To Westminster, for a thinking breakfast. Technically it's under the auspices of the Public Responsibility Unit. Physically it's under the Foreign and Commonwealth Office, in a spartan PFI dining room grudgingly converted from a wartime bunker.

Every politico with even a glancing responsibility for the built environment is there, including architecture minister the Hon. Aeneas Upmother-Brown. He is accompanied as usual by his swarm of pet bees. Their choral hum elevates the seriousness of the situation, which is spelled out for us by their master.

'I have the latest polling results here and they make appalling reading, mm. According to our sample of Coalition MPs, only 32 per cent think the public can be trusted with public space. And only 17 per cent think the private sector is getting the support it deserves from shoppers and pedestrians. We need to re-imagine the whole notion of public space, mm, before militant members of the public start organising unpleasant dissent. Ah, my precious bees. Consider the frailty of humankind, mm. Now, spatial opinion-formers begone! Only one of you will be chosen for this special task...'

Oh yeah. Also in attendance: every rival I have in the field of architecturalised narrative consultancy. No such thing as teamwork here. We're all bastards, all in it to win it. Luckily, my head is full of mind-farmed inspiration.

WEDNESDAY Internal brainstorming, tossing new ideas for public space back and forth within myself. By close of business I've rejected pay-per-view architecture, premium strolling lanes in historic cities, monetised queuing and a human congestion charge based on body fat density.

THURSDAY Prep for my presentation tomorrow. Psych myself up by remembering that everything wrong with the private sector is the public sector's fault.

FRIDAY Eschewing PowerPoint and props I speak from my heart, to the bees.

Advertising is everywhere. Public space, once innocent and unblemished, is now slathered in ads. These corporate messages cost a lot of money to make and display, but some may be unsuitable for children. This is an issue of parental responsibility. Adults who do an excellent job in the home, monitoring what their children watch on TV, simply abandon this filtering process in the outside world.

Let's say a father is taking his young daughter into central London. During even a shortish journey through public space she will encounter posters depicting horror, terror, armed violence and sexual objectification. This is all very well for the father, but wholly unsuitable for the little girl. It's no excuse for the father to say he didn't know what the public space was like, he's been there before.

I propose we remove all ambiguities with a Certification of Public Space Bill. Summary: grade the civic environment in exactly the same way that films are classified. It would then be parents' responsibility to keep their children away from X-rated environments such as public transport, high streets, evangelical churches, etc., and to accompany them when required (PG), e.g. in pubs. As with gated communities and privatised town centres, public space certification would help keep people in their right place.

Everyone in the room, even the buzzing swarm, looks impressed. To the clear annoyance of the unsuccessful consultant thinkers, I am appointed to reframe public space in the minds of the British people.

In your FACE, the part of me that objected to the mind farm.

SATURDAY Five-a-zeitgeist theoretical football. Autobranded Egotism 6, Introverted Altruism 0.

SUNDAY Self-contextualise in the recliner.

April 5, 2012

The Blard

MONDAY Amazing start to the week. I've been commissioned to redesign the internet.

Details of my appointment are being kept vague at the moment to avoid any legal confusion as technically nobody owns the internet. It's everybody's. This late-Soviet economic model is good news for my clients, about whom I can say nothing, except to confirm they are an international consortium with headquarters inside a defunct Micronesian volcano.

Oh, there are commercial empires ON the internet, just as there were once commercial empires on the high street. But like USSR gas reserves, the internet is without value until some commercial warlord in boot-cut jeans buys it and announces it's worth a fortune and then moves to a luxury fortress in London to avoid being killed by sinister robot wolves.

The opportunity is here and graspable. Any volcano-based consortium with vision is thinking about how to refashion the internet. I am proud to be helping to push things along with my literally priceless cyberscape architecture skillset.

TUESDAY Morning: design an eggbox cathedral. Afternoon: design a dried pasta primary school.

WEDNESDAY Because the internet is so vast I've decided to simplify things by thinking of it in terms of an English urban regeneration master-plan.

First, I will carry out a psychogeographical audit. Then, I will 'quantify the investment offer'. Then I will divide the internet into designated quarters. Then I will get a Taiwanese rendering agency to bang out some optimistic impressions of how the internet might look in the future.

There will be balloons, and people will be the shape of spring onions, and the parents will be pointing and the children will be laughing. Or are my critics suggesting that in the future of the internet there should BE no children's laughter?

THURSDAY I've entered a design competition. Residential skyscraper at the happening end of Hackney. Hapney. Predictably, so has everyone else. Got to pull something pretty special out of my 1963 hipster briefcase.

The competition sponsors want to 'create interest in the skyline'. I think this means 'make people look up'. You could do that by having someone shouting from a roof, but my guess is they want a landmark building.

As ever, this competition will be won not by innovative engineering or 'design flair' or environmental sucking-up but by strength of nickname. After a few hours on my mental scribbling pad I've got the vague shape: elegant vintage brickwork turning in on itself with brown shades and an ickle hat. Maybe call it The Torqued About.

No, sod that. Let's make it as tall as the Shard, turn the ground floor into a retro arcade full of farmers' micromarkets and vinyl record shops and ironic racism. Yeah, done. The hipster skyscraper. Call it The Blard.

FRIDAY Sketch out my internet do-over. The cyberscape topography will remain the same, obviously. Best to avoid expensive cyber-geo-engineering works. All outlying desert and tundra, wildernesses and porn oceans will be unaffected.

The internet's built-up bits will be completely rationalised. I'm proposing a vibrant global 'town centre' where everyone who really matters – heartless young people with disposable income – can congregate in a giant Mall of the Internet.

All the useful stuff will be housed in a utilitarian Learning Quarter at the cheap end of town, where scholars and weirdos and wikipediaphiles can go, good riddance.

Beyond this, a curtain-twitching suburbia for Twitter and Facebook and all the other defensible-space new urbanist networks where people mind your business for you and swap stories about kooky pets.

My favourite bit is the Heritage Quarter, where I plan to preserve all websites retaining original pre-1995 javascript features. Gathering together random lumps of our collective history into an 'internet destination' will be big business, if the real-world parallel's anything to go by.

Summary: more interactive, more interfactive, porous, passive-aggressive but with your initials in the foam, not the Wednesday night Channel 4 thing, but not the Friday night Channel 4 thing either.

Yeah, you mumble, but will it 'cost' anything to be somewhere on the internet, in this cyberscaped future? Idiots. Ask yourself if it's costing you to be wherever you are now lol.

SATURDAY Five-a-zeitgeist theoretical football. Architectural Feminism 2, Patriarchitectural Madmenism wins, the score's irrelevant, sorry that's just the way it is.

SUNDAY Have a little lie-down in the pop-up recliner.

April 19, 2012

A Cross-Vectored Media Partnership

MONDAY As one of the founding members of the activist group Enemies of the Shard, my mate Scalesy the urban trespasser has led some pretty high-profile derision.

He famously sneaked up to the top of the Shard in his bobble hat and took a picture of himself pulling a face. Since then he's been outspoken in his bobble hat about corporate gigantism and the hypocrisy of 'the design industry'.

Recently Scalesy mocked the architect's claim that this grim, over-sized capitalist silo will in fact be an 'actual town of 8,000 people'. Oh really, he sneered in his bobble hat. Will there be a primary school there? Dentists? Housing association flats and a parish church and a cottage hospital? Idiots.

Now they've asked him to become mayor of the Shard, on quite a generous stipend. I don't want to speculate but I can definitely sense some moral flexibility bobbling about.

TUESDAY Under cover of the night I hurry to an emergency meeting of the Tamworth League.

Aye, I hurry as people have hurried since the eighth century, when Oversight of England was cruelly plucked from the socket of ancient Mercia by the treacherous and incestuous barbarians of the South.

We have assembled in solemn accordance with the Old Ways to discuss a branding opportunity. A mighty power from across the Great Sea has pitched an exciting cross-vectored media partnership. The terms seem quite reasonable.

It would, however, have an impact on our masterplan to revive the Anglo-Saxon Heptarchy, to wit a kingdom of London enclosed by a Great Wall and the rest of England led by a saucy, slightly pissed Mercia. Imagine a densely packed salad bar sequestered within a realm of pies.

The partnership deal would require us to rebadge the region 'New Mercia brought to you by HBO's *Game of Thrones*'. Now the Tamworth League already receives certain considerations for having inspired the blood-sluiced porn version of our early history, but the new arrangement effectively transfers governance of the region to a cabal of executive producers based in Los Angeles.

Ancient rights to be transferred from the Tamworth Council of Elders to 'Todd Spielman, Show Runner' include pannage, judicial beheadment, charcoal burning, human pruning, estovers, turbary, tribal slaughter and all town and country planning regulations.

It's not ideal, but these are bleak times. And our geo-political restoration programme desperately needs major sponsorship, now the deal to sell off most of Cheshire to a Saudi consortium has fallen through.

WEDNESDAY I have been asked by an epic space collective to rethink their business model.

What a terrible state it's in. I don't think anyone's looked at it properly since savage Modernist dinosaurs ruled the earth. Everything's very 'boom and bust'. Mountainous terrain. Lots of uphill struggles, sunlit uplands and then jagged, treacherous cliffs.

Of course I can't redesign economics – that's a closed shop and membership costs a fortune – but I can psychologically re-landscape the business model at least. Out goes the old-fashioned notion of 'up and down'. In comes the new model of 'round and round'.

We need to rethink how we travel through the economic landscape, too. It is unacceptable in the current climate to have a 4×4 in second gear roaring through verdant peaks and barren troughs. Better to imagine us all on a gentle bicycle ride through woodland, embracing the cyclical nature of the economy.

THURSDAY Meeting of the Tamworth League. We have now read HBO's small print and decide with much regret to decline their offer of media stewardship.

Although the contract acknowledges the importance of preserving the essential characteristics of Mercia, an insistence that the entire kingdom 'be divided into 58 minute segments and include trailers for Next Week's Mercia' is a deal-breaker.

We resolve to approach the BBC to explore their alternative offer of a 'low-budget reality soap opera'.

FRIDAY Road-testing the beta version of the iPad 5. Some glitches, but I'm very impressed with the smooth 'mode-switch' facility which will make it an indispensable tool for the self-employed auteur.

'Portrait mode' for looking at pictures of tall buildings, 'landscape' for watching *Antiques Roadshow* or whatever.

SATURDAY Five-a-zeitgeist apathy dodgeball. Hypothetical Attitude 0, Apolitical Turpitude 0.

SUNDAY Check emails in the recliner. There's an ominous one from Scalesy, who's gone up the Shard again. Only this time he's wearing not a bobble hat but a black-feathered tricorn.

May 10, 2012

The Airpunch

MONDAY I am redefining the London property development game. Until the recession 'the game' had always been Monopoly: you whizzed round amassing random assets, collected GO money, nursed a futile ambition to gentrify the Old Kent Road and ultimately crushed your enemies beneath a Mayfair hotel.

But at a time of grim austerity, property developers are easy targets for idle Marxists and envious Apprentice types. So I propose changing the game property developers play to Pass the Parcel. It's inclusive, fair, communal and – if someone reliable's in charge of stopping the music – you get a prize at the end.

I ring my old friend Emily Simile from the Council of Property Symbologists. She's very impressed with my idea and offers me a fee to start punting out sponsored **#PassThePropertyParcel** appetisers on Twitter.

TUESDAY In the morning, sketch out plans to convert a gigantic disused power station site into a football ground.

In the afternoon, design the conversion of a disused football ground into a mixed-media concert arena. In the evening, devise a biofuel power station within a disused music hall.

Pass the Property Parcel in action. I retire, exhausted.

WEDNESDAY My sheer cleverness has roiled my subconscious. In the middle of the night I airpunch myself awake from a dream in which I had swap-converted a mosque and a nightclub.

Wait. 'Airpunch'. I'm on fire! That's the most brilliant nickname for a skyscraper, ever! I scribble some notes, resolve to nickname my next pass-the-parcelled skyscraper the Airpunch, congratulate myself once again and go back to sleep.

THURSDAY My friend Loaf, the mayor of London, calls. Two things. What about changing the property development game to 'whiff-whaff', maybe attract more upmarket investors? No.

The other thing is, I can have a skyscraper ANYWHERE I LIKE IN LONDON as long as it's called The Airpunch and Loaf gets to open it, in Latin. Done.

FRIDAY God, I wish I'd never agreed to become 'conceptualiser, artistic executive producer, director of coherence, form commander and *diseñador de espacios épico*' for a massive so-called cultural campus in a Mediterranean harbour town.

It was years ago. The world then – leafy end of the 1990s – was a more secure and dependable place. Even the newspapers were supportive of my broad vision, my haughty disdain of the humdrum. 'The Spanish Job' was one of the very first commissions wrangled by Rock Steady Eddie the fixer. It was supposed to establish me as a 'global marque'. Instead it has left me the wholly innocent victim of an internet hate campaign.

Such a shame. It started so well with a glittering landmark bridge – carbonated steel, hammocked in patinated bronze. I'd pitched it as a

Millennium Promenade across an underlit canal, but it was still pretty early days and there was nothing really on either side of the notional canal, so I put another landmark bridge a bit further down to encourage pedestrian flow back and forth.

When the campus nodes started to appear, everything went wrong. The Aquarium of Everyday Life, a huge lava tank with quotidian objects moving gently through transparent 'smart plasma', fell off its stupid fucking stilts a month after opening.

People got bored with the Museum of Inversions. 'Is that it? A building full of things simply turned upside down? – *Cultural Campus Quarterly.*' The Hemispheres of the World, two environmentally sealed volumes constructed separately then brought together at great cost to form a notional world of two separate halves to make a point, I can't quite recall what, it was a long time ago, it's academic. This unique opportunity for cultural exploration also failed to arouse any public curiosity whatsoever.

Eddie negotiated a fee arrangement that paid a proportion of the final cost for each project. If the build cost escalated, so did the *diseñador de espacios épico* bung. I was all for prudence. It was Eddie who wanted the silver filigree and so on. Not my fault they owe me over £100m in design fees.

Look, swings and roundabouts. A public hospital I designed has just had its budget halved so I'll only be getting three grand. I'm not immune to economics.

SATURDAY Eddie rings. He's registered the Airpunch in every copyright territory in the world. I think the parcel may have passed from creating epic space to licensing it.

SUNDAY Self-parcel in the recliner.

May 17, 2012

Goodbye Olympic Rebadging Task Force

MONDAY Mixed emotions at the last-ever meeting of the Olympic Rebadging Task Force.

Sadness, yes. The attendance allowance has been pretty generous for the past six years. But also pride. Our task force has met all the targets we set for ourselves, and that means a lot to us. Specifically, sizeable farewell bonuses.

There's tremendous *esprit de corps* as chair Suzi Towel leads us first in prayer, then in secular reflection, then in a Mexican Wave. As we have done since time immemorial (2006) we all shout 'yay!' at every mention of the Olympics (yay!).

Alas, in London you're never more than six feet away from a rat-faced blogging cynic. There's been a lot of negative backwash lately about the narrative integrity of the opening ceremony for the Olympics (yay!) and very hurtful that negative backwash has been.

Our main task today is to rebadge the opening ceremony so that it 'holds together in the comment sections of the media'. There's a short pause while we all think about this for a bit. Then Canella Bagshawe from the media unit has her first genuinely inspired idea in six years: 'We should take a few days over this. No point in rushing, and they're obliged to pay us however long it takes, right? We ARE talking about the Olympics...'

Yay! Suzi shushes everybody while she checks with Games HQ. Her face is grave but her thumb is up.

TUESDAY Task force swansong, continued. Agreed we should make more of Dame Zaha Hadid being at the opening ceremony. Architectural Olympics, yay!

Like all internationally renowned designers who have built their reputations in this country, Dame Zaha is virtually unknown here. She is after all an architect. In the honours table she's up there with Judi Dench and Helen Mirren. In terms of popular recognition and celebrity she's on a par with a Preston lollipop lady.

But Zaha's a key figure in the epic spatiality of the Olympics – yay! – and it seems a shame to waste the opportunity, so we decide to ask her to wear a massive hat. Will that be enough? We adjourn for lunch.

In the afternoon, we decide she should wear a massive hat and carry a jewel-encrusted javelin. And be accompanied by baby dragons.

WEDNESDAY We're on to the opening ceremony itself. None of us can really work out why it's not 'playing well' in the media. Danny Boyle's crack team of imagineers and dreamweavers have been working on this for ages. At the moment it goes:

> **ACT ONE** We're in some long golden summer of antiquity. The stadium is carpeted in astro-sward. Rustic extras in agricultural blouses

loll about, sharing an organic ploughman's lunch and texting one another. Playlist: Purcell, medley of chillout dance anthems.

ACT TWO A thunderstorm. Lightning. Belching mills appear. The sward is obliterated by pop-up ash heaps and cobbles. A steam engine appears, spreading chaos. Martin Amis is in the cab, smoking roll-ups and drawling jokes about anal sex through his CND megaphone, ruining everything. Playlist: martial brass band classics.

ACT THREE The calm after the storm. Bits of the old industrial landscape are now treasured ruins. The sun is filtered through strange atmospheric muslin. In the middle – a Lake of Anxiety, everyone in it together but not enough lifeboats. Flashes of the huge, world-beating creative potential for which Britain has been potentially famous for ever: haut couture, a sensory garden, a DJ wearing one headphone 'on the decks', football-shaped football fans, a surviving Beatle, a parade of games developers, flag-waving civil partners. Playlist: Chariots of Fire, Cockney rappers, Gareth Malone leading a naked Womens Institute choir in an acapella version of 'Walking on Sunshine'.

THURSDAY Still brainstorming. We've put up a notice saying DO NOT DISTURB, WE ARE RE-IMAGINING THE OLYMPICS YAY and have ordered in some boutique fish and chips.

FRIDAY Breakthrough! Swap Acts One and Three round, we've got a proper happy ending. A bucolic future. Nobody over-thinking things, life just one eternal pastel-coloured picnic, like the Jehovah's Witnesses have in their literature.

It's getting pretty emotional now. A Mexican Wave and then suddenly we're all singing 'Jerusalem' and tearing up a bit.

SATURDAY Any Other Business: invoicing. Hugs and fistbumps all round. Goodbye, Olympic Rebadging Task Force. Suzi's already plotting a Eurovision Resort on the south coast.

SUNDAY Closing ceremony in the recliner.

June 21, 2012

Magnetic Values

MONDAY Construction work has started on my block of luxury riverside flats in London.

Zone 1, too. That's a good zone to be in, lifestyle-wise. There will be fantastic views of Zone 1's other luxury flats, which is reassuring for everybody.

I suppose the architecturally correct brigade would like to force people who live in luxury flats to overlook an inter-war council block or an old-fashioned 'state school', to shame them. Grow up, you bleating windbags, I'm being 'contextual' yeah? This is ZONE 1.

Now the site's fenced off, the hard work begins. I need some marketing blurt in a nice font. Neutral to the point of meaningless. At this early stage you have to sell the 'idea' of a luxury flat with a posh tagline repeated along the hoarding. It's not as easy as it sounds. Hats off to whoever coughed up 'Live by Example', which is jizzed around the perimeter of a similar clattered stack of real estate just down the river.

I don't know what 'Live by Example' means. It is unknowable. The sub-text is probably 'Oysters are for Losers'. I have to come up with something at least as blank. Off we go then. Destination Bathos – and Beyond!

TUESDAY Rock Steady Eddie the fixer rings. A billionaire client wants to create a unique global icon. Something 'fresh' and unprecedented and surprising.

Now designing: World's Fattest Building.

WEDNESDAY Nice chilled day with my old mate Beansy the nano-futurologist. Shoes off, nuts and olives and whatnot, a jug of what he calls his 'isotonic plus' and some casual brainstorming. We think up a few luxury flat slogans but they all vaguely mean something, so are useless.

Beansy has a 'bing'. Why not create an aspirational algorithm based on letting agents' rhetoric? He activates some sort of bullshit harvester. We go to the pub while it's processing. By the time we're back 2,875,992 meaningless slogans have been generated. So Beansy creates another, better algorithm and we both doze off watching the cycling on telly.

THURSDAY Beansy's anti-coherence vectoring has reduced the list of possible 'marketing minibites' to just 10:

'Performance Quality'. 'Life Exception'. 'Deserve in Space'. 'Magnetic Values'. 'High + Focus'. 'Ahead of the Post-Style Curve'. 'A Taller Peace'. 'Win-Win Boxing'. 'The Reloaded New'. 'Upgrade to You-Class'. Wait a minute, that last one looks familiar. Come to think of it, they ALL do. Whoa, so this is *actually* how it's done.

I encourage Beansy to create an architectural trope algorithm. I could clean up here.

FRIDAY Oh, nice. Just when I thought my unique blend of three-dimensional street magic and 'smart invoicing' couldn't GET any less fashionable. The Urban Nodality Commission has released the findings of its inquiry into the catalytic design professions. Title: *Oversexed, Overpaid and Overhubbed.*

Executive summary, conclusion: 'The hub is the only building "type" to have flourished in the recession. Its twofold premise – anything can be called a hub, and a hub will make things happen – has made it hugely popular with local politicians, architectural journalists and special interest groups such as the Association of Hub Administrators.

'However, at the current density (a median of eight hubs per hectare in built-up areas) we have reached saturation point. Furthermore the social energy fields created by each hub have overlapped and locked, creating entrepreneurial stasis.

'The Urban Nodality Commission firmly believes it is time to call at least some of these hubs something else, in an attempt to unlock social energy fields and stimulate flux...'

Brilliant. So the arse falls out of the hub game just as I'm about to sign off on a community hub, a Hub of Reconciliation, a digital hub, a fashion hub, a 'pop-up pub-hub' AND a post-Conran furnishing hub called Hubitub, all in the same shitty Leicestershire town.

Back to Beansy's.

SATURDAY We run the architectural trope algorithm, which has been modified to filter out all hub-related shenanigans. Excitingly, a 'proto-trope' emerges from the wine-dark sea of data, like a mud skipper flapping about ready to be the next big thing.

Goodbye hub, hello PIN. A pin sounds more focused, thinner and cheaper than a hub. We're thinking it could just be like a smart bollard or a community pole. Put a pin in the neighbourhood, come back to it later.

Might start work on some kind of ironic 'drawing pin' for architects.

SUNDAY Upgrade to Me-Class in the recliner.

August 2, 2012

The Chapel of Notre Dame du Marmalade

MONDAY Knocking out a few rough building ideas for Rio 2016.

So far I've got a doughnut-shaped velodrome, a main stadium that looks like a wok and an aquatic centre that draws heavily on the timeless form of the pilchard.

Not sure about the Olympic Village yet. I wanted to go with a 'hip favela' feel, but you know how people like to play the 'cultural sensitivities' card.

TUESDAY Talking of which, I'm designing a 'women-only city' in Saudi Arabia. It's actually a smallish industrial estate, but that doesn't sound as dramatic.

A 'women-only city' gets you top sidebar in the tackier online papers. According to my fixer Rock Steady Eddie that's now the premier show-case for quality design. As he always says: there's no such thing as bad controversy.

He's urging me to start talking up the hospice I'm working on as a 'death camp', and to rebrand the luxury bachelor apartment commissioned by a hugely respectable Middle Eastern prince as a 'sex hutch'.

WEDNESDAY To the Royal Institute for the Pop-Uption of British Architects, where a noisy protest is in full swing.

President Molly Bismuth is in a defiant mood. So are members of staff. They all have paper hats with their names on. 'For too long we have suffered the ignominy of obscurity!' she shouts. 'We will be gagged and muffled no longer! It is time to stand up and tell the world who we are and what the Royal Institute for the Pop-Uption of British Architects actually does!'

There's an extended pause. I slip away from the silence, back into the bustling street.

THURSDAY You know, internationally renowned architecture critics can sometimes come across like a prissy cartel of mewling wankers. Especially when they're having a go at me.

83

This time their criticism is especially harsh and unjust. I took enormous care when designing the new visitor centre at Marmalade, in eastern France. Modernist colossus L'Obscurier created his masterpiece here: the breathtaking anarcho-Catholic Chapel of Notre Dame du Marmalade. Of course I know how sensitive a site this is. I'm not a fucking buffoon.

My visitor centre has been made extra-discreet by being scattered across the hillside, so that from a far distance it looks almost semi-transparent. Throughout the design process I asked myself constantly: 'If L'Obscurier were alive today, would he approve of this commercial effloresence erupting all over his vision?' It's a tough question to keep asking yourself. Over and over, I kept toughly answering myself, 'Yes, this is brilliant. L'Obscurier would have bloody loved this. Well done, carry on.' So, critics – game, set and match to me.

Some of the niggles are frankly laughable. My new structures 'impact' the landscape, do they, speccy prick from the *New York Times*? I suppose you'd like to keep the Marmalade Chapel a cosy little secret, visited only by you and your pretentious friends every now and then. Are ordinary people not allowed to see this masterpiece too? Are they not allowed a roof over their heads while they buy tickets? Are they not allowed to eat, or shop, or adequately park? The project brief called for a 'cost-negative' visitor centre and that's what the client has got. A sacred place first and foremost, but also a focused money-spinner.

'Out of scale', is it, bald dickhead from *Die Welt*? You don't even know what scale I was working to, maybe it was supposed to look 110 per cent 'normal' size. 'Disembodied' is it, pompous shitballoon from *Le Figaro*? I'll tell you what I'd like to see disembodied: your stupid hat-wearing head! 'The vertical mullions clash horribly with the horizontality…' SHUT UP FAT MAN-EGG FROM *CHINA DAILY*, YOU'RE LOOKING AT THE MULLIONS UPSIDE DOWN.

Now that I have answered my critics I hope I will be left in peace to carry out my next prestigious job, a fitness centre inside Durham Cathedral.

FRIDAY Design a groundbreaking green supermarket that generates more energy than it uses.

This is achieved with a complex series of sustainable operating systems, including an innovative thermal harvester that converts human warmth into electrical power and 'eats' anyone who's too cold.

Spare blood and plasma is then recycled via a 'smart generator'.

SATURDAY Five-a-zeitgeist theoretical football. Festival of Britain-style Tonical Nationalism 0, Niche Recessionary Concessionism 1, after extra time for going into administration.

SUNDAY Ample self-parking in the recliner.

August 16, 2012

Latest Books About Icons

Icon Origins *by Mannekin von Heineken*
For years people have wondered where architectural icons come from. A site in the middle of town is cleared, hoarding goes up and a few months later a massive new building is revealed.

Traditionally, the local paper encourages residents' groups to declare 'it's so weird-looking, it's like it landed here from outer space!' Well, DID IT? This is just one of many questions von Heineken leaves reverberating in the air, unanswered.

Others include 'Did the icon evolve with advances in technology and increasing architectural sophistication? Or, improbable as it sounds, was the icon created by intelligent design?' 'Is there such a thing as The Missing Icon?' 'Will the discovery of the so-called God Icon reveal new secrets of the universe?' 'What do YOU think?' Etc.

The Tall Story: How The Icon Narrative Changed The Way We Think About Icons And Narratives *by Bobby Weavingham*
A fascinating examination of the icon narrative, and the impact that narrative has had on other narratives. These include societal narratives, global architectural narratives, and the author's own vivid interior monologues.

Inevitably, some searching questions are asked. What is an icon? What is a narrative? And what happens when they're smashed together in a 600-page large hadron collider of a book with lavish illustrations and a lofty foreword translated from the original Catalan? Fireworks, that's what. Polemical fireworks.

We trace the icon narrative from the early years of icon-as-cultural nest egg, through the long affluent 'golden summer' when the icon was popularised as an ironic investment signifier. Drawing heavily on his own research and lecture material Bobby Weavingham, Google Professor of Narrative Studies at the University of Tamworth Online, brings us up to the present day with a bump.

The 'icon-as-merely icon narrative' that prevails in our straitened, cautious times simply cannot endure, argues Weavingham. 'The icon narrative is trapped in an ironic cycle of boom and bust. Architectural sarcasm may for the moment be invested in museums and opinion pieces, but what next? Can the icon rise again as the pre-eminent story arc for architecture? Only narrativised time will tell.'

The Magic Icon Book *by Taiwan Derivatives Inc*
Stare long enough at these mystical pictures of icons and you'll see a weird 3-D image of something interesting. Suspension of normal vision, a sense of fun and perseverance essential!

All Icons Great And Small *by Sally Puddock*
Working as an impoverished young vet among bluff Yorkshire farming folk, Puddock discovered an unusual 'psychic' connection to animals. It was a gift that inevitably propelled her into the challenging world of architectural criticism.

Creating a two-way rapport with buildings is difficult enough, but understanding icons is a rare facility indeed. These days Puddock is of course familiar to TV viewers as the 'Icon Whisperer'. In this book we follow her around the globe as she holds psychic conversations with world-class landmarks and reveals some surprising aspects of their personalities. The Bilbao Guggenheim is 'testy', the Burj Dubai seems 'sexually repressed', while the Shard is really not very communicative at all.

Icon Revolution! *by Isabel Quankermass*
'In my excitable and menacing view, something huge and unpleasant is about to occur', warns Quankermass. In a novelised version of her own astonishing theory, she imagines a future [SPOILER ALERT] in which all the world's icons become self-aware, form a deadly network of egregious landmarks and destroy Earth's defenceless skylines.

The Great iConfidence Trick *by Grad Versatiler*
As an idealistic architecture student, Grad Versatiler became fascinated with the icon phenomenon. 'Everything about it. The form. The cultural voice. The application of a generic process to create something perversely less than the sum of its parts yet bigger than anything else for miles around. The designer lifestyle. The money. The power. What's not to like?'

Then after years of mixed fortune as a practising architect and casual gardener, Versatiler changed his mind about icons. And architecture generally. Now he lifts the lid on his loathing for icons in a bitter, sparkling essay that's sure to resonate with others who, for reasons beyond their control, have been excluded from the icon-designing jamboree. Kindle only.

Icons Ancient And Modern *by Various*
A comprehensively updated edition of Famous Historical Buildings, from the pyramids to the Gherkin, but with the word 'ICON' superimposed on all the photographs.

August 30, 2012

An Analogue Underground Cotswolds

MONDAY I'm in rapid response mode following the Chancellor's call for 'a much more imaginative' use of rural land, including the green belt. Ideas so far:

- Massive airport 'toll runway' alongside the M40.
- Air rights created above all fields to encourage vertical thinking.
- Relaxation of gun laws in designated 'stag zones'.
- Analogue underground Cotswolds.
- New folds, curves and creases of opportunity in East Anglian flatlands.
- Pubs upgraded to hubs, hubs upgraded to nodes.
- Security contractors G4S to smooth transition from 'access' to 'trespass'.
- Wormhole to future to be constructed in Epping Forest, creating literally millions of new jobs in the future.

TUESDAY Moral dilemma. The Coalition has asked to me to project-manage a nationwide purge of council tenants who now find themselves living, wholly inappropriately, in gentrified areas of high property value.

The solution is to get rid of these 'social squatters' and sell their homes to the deserving rich. Part of my job as project manager would be pretending that local authorities haven't been banned from building council housing for a quarter of a century.

Another part of my job would be to command these local authorities to build 'affordable homes' somewhere much shittier for their freeloading tenants.

Obviously I'll take the gig. My dilemma is in how I should badge this process in my head, whether to call it 'demographic cleansing' or 'corrective punishment'. I don't suppose it matters.

WEDNESDAY Working breakfast with my fixer, Rock Steady Eddie. This month's 'no-brainer' is communal eco-housing.

'Green living, shared services, no-brainer,' he says through a medley of Full English. 'All them *Guardian* readers with their bloody dried apricots and their Italian lessons. What happens when the kids leave home? And the partner's buggered off to live with someone who doesn't mind getting pissed at lunchtime occasionally?'

I am listening to him, but also idly wondering what life would be like without him.

'You not having that other sausage? So there they are, cash-rich with all the original features, right. But nobody to moan with about Murdoch or capitalism or dolphins with cancer, whatever it is this week.

'They are DESPERATE to hang out with like-minded sanctimonious arseaches. Believe me, son, if there's one thing *Guardian* readers love, it's looking down on people for shopping in the wrong supermarket, or driving the wrong motor or God forbid reading the wrong fucking newspaper...'

On and on he goes as we weave from café to pub to bookies – 'Pony each way on Biennale Suprematist. Her form's sketchy but she goes well on common ground, six to one, tasty odds' – to pub again. 'Lesson learned. Never back a nag with an architectural name, bound to be late. You finishing that scotch?'

THURSDAY I realise Eddie has a point after all. I mean, *Telegraph* readers like to look down on the riff-raff, don't they? That's why there's a market for gated communities.

And *Guardian* readers like to look down on gated communities. That's why there's a market for communal eco-housing. I do some preliminary research and discover that it's even more popular and oversubscribed than I thought. Eddie rings. He's discovered the same.

'Stand on me – they're snapping them up off plan, mate! That must mean a deposit, right?' We share a loaded silence. Could you, I wonder, sell communal eco-housing at an even earlier stage? It's crazy, but in theory... 'You finishing that sentence?' he says, eagerly.

Eddie puts the word out via the usual channels. *Guardian* Personals. Posh end of Twitter. Those eco-community forums where people swap old bunk beds for a couple of bottles of decent rioja.

We're selling 'notional eco-homes at the pre-conceptual stage' in beautiful countryside locations throughout Britain. Everything framed by the Chancellor's new 'dare to dream' approach. A group of soulmates find a nice spot for an eco-community, then they pay me and Eddie to 'think it up' and we'll take it from there.

FRIDAY Whoa. Bunch of retired lecturers, jazz musicians and amateur botanists want a zero-carbon hamlet 'with views of Stonehenge'. Eddie's warned them that will require a Platinum Thinking Package but they're still keen/dim.

SATURDAY Five-a-zeitgeist theoretical football. Ironic Copying 2, Ironic Copying 2. Match abandoned, twice.

SUNDAY Platinum downtime in the recliner.

September 6, 2012

Little Stripey Crestfallen Moons

MONDAY My old friend Loaf, the mayor of London, has refloated the idea of an 'international mudhub' in the middle of the Thames Estuary.

That's all very well but as conceptual director for the project, Muggins here has to work out the logistics. You can float the idea of a floating airport but at some point you have to work out how to float the airport itself. Apart from floating a #FloatTheAirport hashtag.

It is not, as some have blithely suggested, just a matter of tethering a shitload of pontoons or industrial lilos or whatever to the riverbed, then waiting for the world's long-haul traffic to arrive. That's ridiculous. This is about civic ambition on a national scale.

My new masterplan envisions a floating airport tethered to the ENTIRE COAST OF BRITAIN. Like a giant M25 but for aeroplanes.

People will say it is mad, of course. They're playing right into our hands.

Because suddenly an airport that only stretches from the Isle of Grain to the Isle of Wight seems a lot less ridiculous. And after that, one that merely fits the Thames Estuary like a contraceptive diaphragm will seem just about right.

TUESDAY Dear Chinese media: my Blingnang skyscraper does NOT 'look like big pants'. It looks like a pair of skinny-fit jeans. I would never design a building to look like underwear. Apart from 'The Loungerie', my Leeds nightclub that looks like a stuffed bra and knickers, but in my defence that was for a bet.

WEDNESDAY Sketch out proposals to double the size of Moscow. Putin's queuing up to 'lead the cranes' dressed as topless-construction-worker-by-day-topless-assassin-by-night.

THURSDAY To Westminster for the mournful departure of the Hon. Aeneas Upmother-Brown.

He steps down today as Culture Minister with special responsibility for architecture, bed and breakfast hotels, hospitality boxes at major sporting destinations, online ticketing systems and humane circuses.

Over the last two years, despite this broad portfolio, Upmother-Brown has been a powerful presence in the world of epic space, in no small part due to the personal swarm of bees that accompany him everywhere.

They're here tonight, at this low-key drinks party on the newly refurbished Aviva Members' Terrace, in slow orbit around his head like little stripey, crestfallen moons. Occasionally he despatches them with a murmur to 'mingle' among us but to be honest their heart isn't in it.

Perhaps they will miss the ministerial perks – the official saloon car, the early morning hivemind sessions, the abundance of flowers everywhere – more than their master will.

It's no secret that his departure was a little fraught. The Cabinet reshuffle was an excuse to move the prestigious bed and breakfast hotels sector to Business. Upmother-Brown felt slighted, and bees are notoriously sensitive to mood swings. There were apparently ugly scenes in a Downing Street stairwell, with one junior civil servant 'stung into inaction' in several places.

What's also becoming painfully clear is that there's no love lost between the outgoing minister and his successor, Gavin 'Gavvers' Quinly-Spread, a smooth Tory bombshell lionised everywhere as the Fashionable

Face of Capitalism. 'Oh don't misunderstand us,' says Upmother-Brown, his winged shroud of bee-blur suddenly rising in tone to a minor third, 'I have always found Mr Quinly-Spread to be a most clubbable fellow [buzz]. Yes, a most clubbable fellow [BUZZ] indeed...'

FRIDAY Back to the Member's Terrace for a swish cocktail party. A big banner welcomes 'Mr G Q-Spread' to the ministry.

His amended portfolio now includes architecture, destination branding, spiritual renewal, fun-run licensing, Bestival, television baking programme development, cultural equity management and 'popster economics'.

It's a much younger crowd than last night, hairier and thinner. In a breezy address, GQ signals a style change. 'For too long, our listing process has been a bee-driven lottery...' An obvious dig at his predecessor, who would commission balsa wood models of buildings nominated for preservation. If bees were happy to inhabit it: listed. That's why Milton Keynes shopping centre ('communal and busy') got the nod.

'So from now on, listing will be sorted by my mate, bloody good bloke and former business partner Johnny. Johnny?' Johnny responds with a casual wave to the crowd. Then he 'gunfingers' the minister, making a little 'chk' sound.

SATURDAY Five-a-zeitgeist theoretical football. Incrementalism 1, Gurgling Metastasism 10.

SUNDAY Float idea of self in recliner.

September 13, 2012

The Jockular Campus

MONDAY It's absolutely heaving at London Military Building Fashion Week. The trends are clear, though.

Out: 'Anti-terrorist design'. In: 'Retaliation-proof'.

TUESDAY Redesign Hull, making it more meaningful and nostalgic with a Larkin retrospective and an Instagram slideshow.

WEDNESDAY To San Francisco, with a heart full of dread. I've been provisionally appointed 'space stylist dude' for Facebook's new head-quarters. The money's fantastically good. Alas, the clients are punchable spindly millionaire dickbrats.

Yes, I've 'flown in' like some fat British seagull keening for someone's discarded lunch, but don't judge me. I am here to WORK. I am here to agree a PROJECT BRIEF, so that both sides know what everyone's talking about in terms of space, style and dudity.

Nailing the brief is essential. Let's face it, Britain and America have a 'cultural disconnect'. Admittedly the phrase 'cultural disconnect' is understood, with resignation, on both sides of the same ocean. It's a shared cultural disconnect, which makes it even worse. I say sausage roll, you say corndog, I'm not entirely sure what a corndog is, let's call the whole thing off, I'll email you.

The clients want an extra 50,000 m² of 'cool, fluid space' and so far all I have is a photograph of freestyle notes scribbled on the back of a Marvel comic by Facebook Head of Thinking, Spak Hungstrom:

'Maybe like the apartment in the movie *Big*? Starring Tom Hanks? But with 21st-century games and shit and whatnot...would be WAY COOL to have like 1980s pinball machines etc actually from the movie on site!!?! Retro chill. Right? RIGHT? So what do we call this new cool, fluid space? HQ? Nuh-uh. Same-o lame-o. Old Europe. Needs a COLLEGE feel. The Facebook...Campus? Boom, keep it LITE yo. Animal House! Is jockular a word? BOOM THINK JOCKULAR CAMPUS DUDE ☺'.

God Almighty. This gig already feels more 'crèche' than 'campus' and I haven't even got to the brief-setting meeting yet. I'm led through genuine medieval doors bearing the crayonned legend 'THOUGHT JAM', into a vast open-plan refectory space, all polished wood and cultured glass. Difficult to know which one is Spak. I never find out.

'No names in the thought jam game, man...' says someone behind my sofa, and this sets the tone: a brisk churn of anonymous non-hierarchical hipster toddlers, all wearing tailored jeans and antique T-shirts. I was expecting beer and sandwiches but oh no: bloody juice and jellybeans. It's so noisy, too. Indie drivel bleating out, and some weird film being shown on the two-storey height wall. It looks like Norse gods clattering each other in some endless balletic death-battle.

'Green roofs are kinda...cool?' murmurs some hypertanned geek, to his Xbox. 'Cool. Cool-cool-cool!' says everyone in unison, absently miming a complicated handshake.

'There could be a jogging trail up there. Different levels. Awesome platforms, and you pick up stars and...boom, sucker! Feel my MACE

OF WRATH!' Ah. That explains it. The wall screen is showing what's on Teakgeek's Xbox. 'Modded Tekken with divinities. Elephant dude with the laser arms is like, whoa. Kick-ass!'

Hell is, specifically, these other people. Plus, there's fucking nowhere to smoke as usual.

After an hour's immersion in a dork miasma, I think I've grasped the brief. They want a 10-acre long room that feels like a classic 8-bit game, divided into 'zones' with an end-of-level boss (Spak) and rewards along the way such as magic jellybeans and actual bags of money. I pretend to take a call from Rupert Murdoch, awkwardly indicate a 'British high five' to the unresponsive disdainful pricks, and leave.

THURSDAY On way home. Dream up new global reality show, *City Swap*, in which inhabitants of say London and San Francisco swap locations for a month, then consider problems with customs, e.g. gun ownership.

FRIDAY Have worked out my Facebook campus zones, based on jet-lagged oversleep and a panicky mind-trawl of American culture:

Urban Terror, Black Rural, New York Deli, Chic Shaker Prayer Hall, Jolly Hispanic, University of Buffy, Unoccupied Wall Street, Life-Affirming Prison, Porn Dungeon, Bling Crib, Post-Apocalyptic Pixar, Civil War Paintball, Graffiti Hangout, Pimped Ride (Interior), Wild West Platinum Lounge, Suburban Psychodrama.

SATURDAY Still no word from Facebook Spak. Poke him. Apparently now I am 'de-friended'.

SUNDAY Attempt to re-ignite my trans-Atlantic excitement by drinking miniature bottles of scotch until I fall asleep in the recliner.

September 20, 2012

Metarchitectural Sausages

MONDAY To London for a demo – Justice for Environmental Auteurs. It's disgraceful that clients are seeking to link our fee increases to rises in global temperature.

We all chant, 'Inflation should be the yardstick for both remuneration and self-regard!' and soon feel 3.5 per cent better.

TUESDAY I'm designing a big scallopy thing in Singapore, full of trees. Fingers crossed – it has an immensely collaborative feel, various radical and technical examinations, experimental aspects and exciting lines of enquiry, converging in a coveted award, with any luck.

WEDNESDAY Lunch with my old 'friend' Darcy Farquear'say, who has pissed me right off. His latest act of cultural treachery: ghosting an important weekly feature on 'metarchitecture' for the *Creative on Sunday*. In a fairer world that would be MY gig.

Please don't ask me what metarchitecture is. I thought I'd made that perfectly clear. Metarchitecture is an internalised Q&A about future epic space and how we should be thinking around the corner. Simply start a sentence with 'What links...' Then do a list of stuff. Then categorise it.

What links the quiet symmetry of a Georgian building, Lady Gaga's upper body strength, Skylon, tin mining, the psychogeography of New York delicatessens, a contrapunctus from 'The Art of Fugue', the geometry of tulips, an acid jazz disco, T S Eliot's Homburg, the M62 westbound, migrating geese, an aerial view of Glastonbury and harvested rain? Metarchitecture.

See? It's an easy two-step: mince up some random subjects, then shape into a meaningful chain of cultural sausages. Metarchitecture may be just extruded zeit-gristle but it is nevertheless part of our HUMAN DISCOURSE. However, the pretend 'author' of the new *CoS* column is Bauhau, Darcy's dachshund, now apparently a cultural sausage in his own right.

Ever since the newspaper discovered that a querulous dog in a Marc Jacobs retro-grunge plaid wrap can connect with readers more effectively than a jaundiced architecture critic in a silly hat, Darcy has suffered the humiliation of being content provider for his own neurotic, brainless, yapping pet.

Except now Darcy's lost that too. Sinking his fourth Sarcastic Mary, he reveals that he has custody at weekends only. During the week Bauhau stays with his new agent, the fearsome Victoria Spong of Fusilli Spong Talent Agency. And Spong's had Darcy sacked as ghost writer for the metarchitecture feature. Architecturally critical interns are much, much cheaper.

Poor Darcy doesn't know what to do, beyond a fifth Sarcastic Mary. I tell him he's got to retaliate. Dump Bauhau entirely. Get another dog. One that looks good in Stella McCartney stuff. He gives me a hard look and a grim smile. We clink glasses.

THURSDAY Freezing. Time to dig out the high-density polystyrene overcoat!

FRIDAY Design a 'funagogue' for some lighthearted Jewish clients.

SATURDAY To Battersea. I'm architectural dog shopping with Darcy. All he has written in his Moleskine is 'BBC4-ish. NB FOUR LEGS. Eclipse Bauhau's intellect with fresh insights? THINK CANINE VERSION OF YOUNG ALAN YENTOB'! Not that much to go on, to be honest.

There's quite a nice poodle, would definitely look good in something punky. But as Darcy says, that might come across a bit 'arch'. A Weimaraner missing most of an ear has a certain rugged appeal, but is too butch for this flimsy, skittish age.

Then we spot a border collie, unpretentious and intelligent. The handler explains that the dog is very shortsighted and needs to wear glasses. 'You know what would suit him?' babbles a smitten Darcy. The dog looks at him, vaguely. 'Round-framed. Black. No. Dark tortoiseshell...'

The handler laughs. 'Never mind the spectacles, check the particulars, love. She's a BITCH!' Darcy does that rapid clapping thing and squeaks with delight. The collie strains to interpret the instruction and settles for sitting up and giving an enigmatic, quizzical look. Perfect.

SUNDAY To a special animal church for the new dog's christening. She is to be called Bess of Hardwick. I'm a bit choked up actually, never been a dogfather before.

At the reception, Bess is already wearing her new Corbusian glasses, a fetching black velvet suit and an Elizabethan ruff. She looks ready to take on the male dachshund-dominated world of architecture. As soon as we can find her a theory.

We both imagine Bauhau quaking in his little boots; that's his default setting. 'Bring it on!' hisses Darcy. Bess dashes off to herd a drinks waiter our way.

October 11, 2012

Looks Nice Theory

MONDAY Off to Cumbria this week. My old friend Darcy the architecture critic is undergoing his most thorough image overhaul since that time he gave a lecture at the Royal Academy – *Post-Modernism is the New Skiffle* – dressed as a pirate.

Darcy's renting a farmhouse on a bleak fell near Shap, trying to thrash out the next big new architectural theory, desperate to regain his preeminence in the highly competitive field of epic space. He has forsaken the metrosexual tension of London for a simplified rural life.

The capital holds too many unhappy memories for him. Bauhau the dachshund for instance. Once Darcy's constant companion, Bauhau now lives with his agent, the powerful canine impresaria Victoria Spong, in a converted East Putney mews cottage. She's holding auditions this week for a new human escort.

'Occasional original thinking required, though specifically seeking a resonant fashion sense (matchy matchy) and a willingness to express opinions in accordance with the Bauhau Brand, putting metarchitecture at the heart of public debate.'

TUESDAY Packing for Cumbria. Thinking about Spong and Bauhau and metarchitecture, the Emperor's New Clothes of aesthetics.

Imagine yourself in a room with a ladder. Go up the ladder. The room looks 'better' because you're looking at it 'metarchitecturally'.

OK, now imagine a client has asked you to masterplan a private university campus somewhere expensive on the south coast. You can stroll around the proposed site – let's say it's public parkland at the moment, or an area of surplus natural beauty – to get a 'feel' for it. The psychogeography of the place. The ghosts and the dreamlines and whatnot. You can think 'oh, this place could really generate creativity'.

Or 'if we dumped a high-density doughnut of PFI student housing here and put a pub, kebab takeaway, pizza takeaway, Indian takeaway, a non-threatening nightclub and a cash machine in the middle, we'd be laughing'.

But that's the non-metarchitectural approach. This proposed campus. What does it look like from the sling of a microlight? What does it look like as a Flickr slideshow? What does it look like as binary code, printed out and scribbled over in coloured crayons by schoolchildren? Today's artist must find a hidden pattern, allude to it in abstract terms, and THEN maximise profit. It's not the interconnectivity of space and form that matters. It's calling it metarchitecture.

Ridiculous. This orthodoxy must be smashed. But by WHAT?

WEDNESDAY Darcy picks me up from the station in a muddy tractor. He's done up like a gentleman farmer. His new muse – Bess of Hardwick the border collie – is cheerful and alert in her tweed coat and round-framed tortoiseshell spectacles. I won't lie, it's a hot look for a dog…

Whatever. We have no time to lose. Darcy and Bess are booked to go on *Newsnight* next week to argue against metarchitecture. They'll be facing their nemeses: Bauhau and Spong. Darcy sets his face to the wind. 'Aye-oop. Bauhau and SPONG? Sounds like one o' them fancy kitchens, eh, girl? Bugger 'em oop t'arse fi nowt…'

Sweet tottering Christ. Darcy's gone Northern.

THURSDAY Our quest for a new architectural theory begins, in a windswept field. Horizontal sleet. Pewter sky. Air so sharp it's like breathing in atomised raw onion.

Our minds are blank. Darcy fronts it out with some gruff shrieking: 'Fetch, girl! Coom by! Get on! Fetch us a theory, girl! Fuck! Shit! This suit is totally RUINED! I mean, aye, aye coom by girl!' He attempts a shepherd's whistle but just makes a noise like a punctured water pipe.

Bess dutifully scampers off round the field looking for something to worry, but her glasses are all steamed up and rain-spattered. She crashes into a hedge. Darcy and I decide she's more of an indoor muse.

FRIDAY On a hunch, we settle Bess on the sofa and Google some contemporary architecture. Interesting. She barks at some, but not at others.

'What's that, Bess? Tha durn't know owt abaht art'te'ture but tha knows thee preferences?' I tell Darcy to dial down the wide-spectrum accent, and concentrate. Is Bess responding to buildings that just…'look nice'?

SATURDAY Astonishing. By breakfast, Darcy's mapped out something called Looks Nice Theory.

'Basically, you dump all that bourgeois drivel. Sever all ties with an elitist commentariat. Align yourself with the ITV and Nando's crowd…'

He suppresses a shudder, remembering the new him. 'Aye, if it Looks Nice, that'll do, eh? Eh, Bess?'

She gives a little bark and looks clever.

SUNDAY Back home in the recliner. Darcy and Bess and Looks Nice Theory will BURY metarchitecture. Ha ha. Bye bye, Bauhau...

October 25, 2012

Battle of the Styles

MONDAY Great excitement in the world of epic space. It's Battle of the Styles Week, which happens every five years like a General Election but people get to elect an architectural theory instead of a political conspiracy.

This time it's personal. There are only two contenders. The ridiculous, nebulous theory of 'metarchitecture' is championed by dandy meta-dachshund Bauhau and his insufferable companion, the theatrical agent Victoria Spong. I'm backing 'Looks Nice Theory', devised with my dear friend Darcy Farquear'say the architecture critic and his muse, the border collie Bess of Hardwick.

It's an architecturally theoretical dog-eat-dog world. And Bess is going to have Bauhau for a light, wholly inadequate English breakfast.

TUESDAY In the morning, freestyle a design for an inflatable bridge over the Seine for the mayor of Paris.

In the afternoon, devise some oxygenated rhetoric for the mayor of London.

WEDNESDAY Submit my independent report for the government's Home Solutions Discount Unit on how to create hundreds of thousands of affordable new flats and houses. I've kept it simple, in accordance with my modest fee. As usual there are five key recommendations:

- Houseprinters Charter. This would allow investors to buy really good synthetic house printers, then let them out for a steady lifetime income.
- Red Tape Cull. A select number of authorised consortia will be

licensed to kill – humanely and in accordance with the Human Rights Act – any local authority officer identified as a 'carrier' of red tape.

- Cheers for Heroes. A housing boom is being persistently talked down at the poorer, more chaotic end of journalism. This has to stop. All media entities must now take a much more upbeat line or stand accused of hypocrisy. Please use hashtag #smilesbuildhomes.
- Wheels Within Wheels. For too long, wheelchair users were ignored, especially during that Labour government before the last one. Now is the time to make wheelchair users even more visible by creating Wheels Within Wheels – hubs of excellence at the heart of areas of commercial opportunity, liberated from the constraints of sentimentality and wheelchair access requirements, whatever, tidy this up later.
- Lightbulb Momentum. If Britain is to prosper it will be as a creative powerhouse. We need to pool our ideas. That's why the government is inviting ideas – any ideas at all, from anyone at all – about how profitable housing might be built without the private sector having to bear a disproportionate burden. We look forward to lots of ideas!

Then just put 'Yours sincerely, The Government' at the end or something'?

THURSDAY Day off for tax purposes.

FRIDAY Here we go then. Battle of the Styles on *Newsnight*. A lot at stake here, and Darcy and Bess have cleverly turned it into a canine-focused class war.

First there's a filmed piece by a sixth former in a moustache walking through Cumbernauld, explaining with archive film and classic pop music how architectural theory has been shit for decades. Back in the studio, against a collage of contemporary buildings taken from interesting angles, the BBC's Emily Maitlis separates the combatants.

On her left Bauhau and Spong, in what look like matching camouflage pyjamas, are already barking away. 'Metarchitecture means looking at the whole sandwich, not just the filling!' 'Arch arch arch! Rough rough rough!'

The new, very northern, Darcy remains impassive in his modest tweed suit, refusing to make eye contact with Bauhau. When it's their go he casually consults Bess, who's looking all calm and no-nonsense in her Cumbrian fleece and spectacles.

'Aye, Bess reckons this fancy theory, this so-called metarchitecture, is just a middle-class conspiracy. You could get everyone who actually understands bloody so-called metarchitecture sat comfortably in a small community-owned pub garden with a complimentary bottle of wine between 'em. She says it's high time architects started doing buildings that JUST LOOK NICE…'

Spong tries to interrupt but Darcy's unconquerable. 'We like old buildings, right, cos they're the best thing about t'past. We like new 'uns too cos they're best thing about t'future. They just want to LOOK NICE.'

He whistles. Bess does a crouching growl at Bauhau, who evacuates his bowels. Emily moves on to the crisis in Greece.

SATURDAY Result's still too close to call. Even Twitter is torn between 'thickos' and 'poshos'.

SUNDAY Oh NO. The *Creative on Sunday* has ruled that the prevailing architectural theory for the next five years will be Redactivism, devised by social commentator Emma Shoe – and Pussy Riot, her fucking CAT!

November 1, 2012

The Hard-Working Class

MONDAY Sketch out some ideas for the redesign of Japan's national stadium, using the latest thought-to-shape app, 'Fast Mental'.

It's incredibly responsive. By lunchtime I've shape-thought a fossilised dolphin, a melting pocket-watch, a landscaped vulva, an unplumbed jacuzzi, a ball of glittering yarn, half a spermatazoon, a discus of light, cupped giant hands made of digital carbon and a translucent pancake filled with brightly coloured metaphors.

Retire for an afternoon nap with a huge sense of achievement and a terrible headache.

TUESDAY In the morning I moot a transcendent footbridge. In the afternoon I dream up a zero-helium mosque based on colour-coded 'sexy mathematics'.

Memo to Self: turn off thought-to-shape software after lunch.

WEDNESDAY I'm impressed with the ambition of my latest architectural remodelling commission. I will be architecturally remodelling The Entire Notion of Social Housing for a consortium of Tory councils.

Westminster, Kensington, Chelsea, Hammersmith and Fulham have formed a terrifying mega-borough of compassionate conservatism, and now it means business. This might be unwelcome news for anyone affected by issues of compassionate conservatism, but there are great opportunities for others.

My client contact, Tish, briefs me. 'Yah, imagine us as totes a sort of new municipal hipster-fogey developer collective? We're keen as *moutarde* to revive the notion of council housing but *sans* that boring old baggage all held together with builder's tape and string? I mean really: poor people? Flat caps and cigarettes, tripe and onions et cetera? *Merci, non!*'

This new Transformer mega-borough certainly sounds powerful. A political 'Optimus Prime' representing the middle class, a community demonstrably marginalised by decades of derision and income tax.

Now it's payback time: the middle class getting council homes built for THEM. My task is to make this proposition seem somehow irridiculous.

Tish isn't helping. 'Thing is, the housing we own's worth two and a half BILL? Sadly, the inhabitants aren't? At all? Look, we're doing our best to create a culch of ambish in our boroughs? Mixed and vibrant communities, *absolument*, people with interesting jobs, spendy clothes *wilkommen, bienvenue*, welcome, adorbs? The homelesses clogging up the sys? Disappeared somewhere more in keeps with their circs, e.g. Middlesbrough, stat? But peeps gonna hate? That's why we need new rhetty infro?' New WHAT? 'New rhetorical infrastructure? Laters...'

THURSDAY Work up new rhetty infro for Megaborough Deathstar. It's a matter of balance, I think.

I agree 'council housing' sounds as old-fashioned as 'National Health Service'. But there's a reversible principle at stake here. Gentrification is a good thing. It accounts for roughly 92 per cent of architects' fee income, architects are morally beyond reproach, end of story. It's what Tish would call 'no-brainsy'.

Alas, in the sneery corners of our social networks, gentrification is simply a long and ugly word. The challenge here is to yoke the gilded carriage of gentrification to the sturdy ox of compassion.

Yes. Turn the whole thing into a righteous CAMPAIGN. The rich are OK, they own several homes. The poor are OK, they're the ones hogging all the council housing. The hard-working middle earners, they're the real victims here.

That's it! A campaign to build DECENT HARD-WORKING CLASS HOUSING.

FRIDAY Tish 'v pleased' with the hard-working class homes idea. A mega-borough marketing committee has already agreed to replace the corporate mission statement 'Keep Calm and Carry On' with 'Hard-Working for You'.

SATURDAY Non-hard-working day.

SUNDAY Newspaper review in the recliner. Gratifyingly, class warfare is polarising opinion.

This makes it easier to identify those in favour of luxury apartments for the deserving middle as they're all over on one side of the argument. For instance, a group of Liberal Democrat MPs is calling for a 21st-century successor to the Housing of the Working Classes Act 1885. Echoing Lord Salisbury, they talk of 'thousands of families living on the artisan bread line in non-luxury dwellings where they sleep and eat, multitask, and die…

'It is difficult to exaggerate the misery which such conditions of life must cause, particularly with all the luxury lifestyles on television and elsewhere. The depression of body and mind which they create is an almost insuperable obstacle to the action of any elevating or refining agencies. That's why we need a Housing of the Hard-Working Classes Act 2013, thanks for listening, means a lot, yeah?'

November 8, 2012

Dysgustopia

MONDAY Great news. My competition design for a vast open-air 'museum of death' has made it onto a shortlist.

Turn on the actual news. Turn it off again, then avoid it for the rest of the day. Death is a serious business. I can't afford to get emotionally involved, or to be unduly influenced.

TUESDAY A pop-up colloquium at the Institute of Plasmic Arts. *Epic Space: Rebundling the Brand.*

The main speaker is 'street brand magician Yadda Bing'. He presents a rundown of the latest unbundled brand trends, then cleverly rebundles them using cognitive misdirection. At the side of the stage where the deaf signer usually stands is graffiti artist Gutsy, who gives a running summary of Bing's synaptic journey via sprayed tag narratives and a stencilled urban 'powerpaint presentation'.

Bing, an optimistic self-publicist who in his imagination has probably rebundled Brand Yadda Bing as a clothing line or a chain of noodle bars, seems pretty sure about his brand-trending intelligence. Members of the audience wearing hats nod gravely along. Those sent here by line managers 'to stay plugged-in' are listening to music instead through little white indie-buds. Summary:

1. *Dysgustopia.* Already trending in parts of north London, dysgustopia simply means an attraction to innovative, inedible dinners. And that, predicts Brand Yadda Bing, means a new wave of restaurants offering 'discomfort food' and challenging levels of service. Now's the time to dust off those sketches of the yuppie soup kitchen you did for a laugh years ago.

2. *Sonic Boomerangnam Style.* Watch out for classic second-wave videogame-themed leisure destinations aimed at in-denial thirty-something 'Sonic Boomers' seeking a nostalgic weekend of exploring a repetitive landscape, bumping into obstacles and losing wealth.

3. *Intersectional Banality.* Traditional interior designs are all about to move one place round the table, as if at some Mad Hatter's Tea Party for fit-outs. Be prepared for business interiors going industrial, retail interiors going business-like, industrial interiors that look like supermarkets, etc., until everyone collapses in a giggling heap.

4. *Aesthetic Filtering.* Exciting new CGI/environmental control interfaces will enable buildings to determine 'the way they look'. For example, the air surrounding a new office tower in a conservation area could be saturated with special 'vintage' molecules to make it look like a very tall parish church.

5. *Generation A2 Segmentation.* Architects, artists, dreamers and linguists should seek new ways of bringing together ideas such as inverted multitasking, cross-benefit social wellness, niche cliché, augmentertainment and ordinarisation in single sentences, like this.

WEDNESDAY In the morning, design a building that turns rainwater into a drug. In the afternoon, design a building that turns body heat into kudos.

THURSDAY To Bristol, for lunch with my old friend, architect Fred Trousers. Less than a week ago he became the city's mayor and already he's wearing a red corduroy toga.

Until now Fred was best remembered as the former president of the Royal Institute for the Pop-Uption of British Architects who persuaded the government to put design quality at the heart of the procurement process. Or the entrepreneur who redeveloped Bristol's abandoned cigarette district as an aspirational hub with contemporary flats, green business/ theatre space and a Michelin-starred restaurant, *Trouser's*.

Now suddenly the Peter Stringfellow of urbanism has a lot more on his plate. Instead of finishing his starter so we can both get on with our main course and have another bottle, Fred stares hard at the dessert trolley and says things like 'I shall not but leave this city though any less but rather greater than I hath found it or be sworn to eat mine own testicles in ye porch of St Mary Redcliffe so but me God, ye whole truth and nothing but ye truth...' Sod it, I'm having his starter.

One of Fred's first grand acts will be to assemble a 'rainbow consortium' of different people with a unity of purpose. He wants to a) put Bristol on the map and b) make sure everybody's reading from the same map.

I toast his success, wish him luck and start thinking of ways to cash in.

FRIDAY Bristol brainstorming with my fixer, Rock Steady Eddie. Agreed I'll pitch a network of community nano-markets, a statue of Fred outside Temple Meads station and a world-class pop-up-non-stop-trip-hop pavilion.

SATURDAY Five-a-zeitgeist theoretical football. Liberal Smartarsery 0, Trump Wisdom 1.

SUNDAY Unbundle self.

November 22, 2012

Windhampton

MONDAY I'm remodelling a gallery. Not as straightforward as it sounds. It was very poorly vamped in the 90s, and must be devamped before new work can proceed.

It will look great though. A 'living promenade' of synthetic jelly will connect the pollarded south wing to an adult soft play café and social media workshop. The adjoining 'learning and growing studio' will open into an experiential 'art garden', featuring improvised human drama ocurring on a path of bark chippings.

TUESDAY Bollocks. My college refurbishment scheme has been killed and lowered into an early grave. This is definitely NOT what I understood 'shovel-ready' to mean.

WEDNESDAY It's time to elevate the sustainable energy debate. Let's at least raise it above the level of 'ooh, rural communities can see the turbines and they really hate them'.

The turbines in my new speculative project, for instance, are so huge that urban communities will be able to see them as well. This makes green energy sustainable AND inclusive.

I have conceived Windhampton as a pathfinder scheme, a new settlement dedicated to the power of wind in much the same way as Cadbury World celebrates the power of chocolate. I've found a perfect site, too: high up on some Lancashire moors owned by a conscientious client passionate about conservation. For years he has conserved these moors by threatening trespassers with prosecution and charging parties of 'hedgies' a fortune to shoot grouse.

Alas, the hedgie population has declined. Or rather migrated to more exciting shooting destinations abroad, where larger prey may be slaughtered with AK-47s and rocket-propelled grenade launchers. So Lord X is now planning to conserve the moors by building a massive 'wind town' on them.

Windhampton will have something for all the family. Children will love the wind petting farm, where they can interact with tiny, soft plastic micro-turbines. Like their giant counterparts they are asleep most of the time, but mind those little fingers when they wake up!

Unlike previous soulless wind projects, Windhampton will have human life at its very heart, with a development of inhabited windmills. The design of these is still very much in my head. I'm imagining something like those ones you see in children's TV programmes. Sort of a lovely pre-Industrial Revolution look, though full not of toiling millers and apprentices with rickets but vegetarian families in cheesecloth shirts, laughing around a big wooden table in perpetual 'rambling family lunch' mode. Yeah, maybe a few rows of those.

There'll be a miniature gauge railway with puffer train. A wind-powered open theatre with natural 'draughty' air management system. And a food mall offering a range of gutsy/gusty dining options. Windhampton will also feature the world's first wind outlet centre, selling end-of-range or slow-moving wind for domestic use.

The next step is marketing. I spend the rest of the day putting together some inflated rhetoric.

THURSDAY Bosh, looks like Windhampton's time has come. The Chancellor is set to relaunch the North of England as an economic miracle.

A report commissioned by an independent think tank of business leaders has concluded that the North needs significant new powers for business leaders. Its message to government could not be clearer: give us the tools – i.e. billions of pounds and thousands of jobs – and we can turn the North round, so it's facing south.

As for this new political tier of 'metro mayors' – I can't be the only one hearing the MGM lion roaring every time I see it in print, surely.

FRIDAY Rock Steady Eddie the fixer has persuaded me to hurry up and finish the Megabolic Tower, an ambitious two-mile high mixed-use slab of urban endeavour for downtown Blingnang.

'Yeah,' he says, 'the China growth engine still packs a punch and that's keeping the building industry very much in the ring. Let's have it!'

Hold on, I say. Are we getting into the ring with China's growth engine? Because it'll flatten us if we are. 'No, you doughnut. We'd be part of the growth engine.' So who's the growth engine's opponent then? Is it another growth engine we're ALSO part of?

He threatens to pack a punch and have it cabbed over, so I just get on with the drawings.

SATURDAY Five-a-zeitgeist theoretical football. Cathetered Romantic 2, Pre-Op Horizontular 1, after extra meds.

SUNDAY Allow a 'mind-wind' to blow my thoughts randomly about in the recliner.

November 29, 2012

I Am Grand Designsy

MONDAY As usual at this time of year, I've humiliated myself by scanning the New Year Honours List for my name even though I'm pretty sure I would have heard something in advance.

I despise the honours system, so archaic and random and meaningless, but would an OBE for services to epic space really have killed them? I'm not letting this happen again. My New Year's Resolution is to acquire an honour, stat.

TUESDAY Lunch with Rock Steady Eddie the fixer. 'No doubt, son. Having a bit of geography after your name and a Lord in front opens a lot of doors. Let's say these chips on your plate are global market opportunities and I'm an Anglophile client. Watch...' It's an impressively thorough analogy.

We agree the odds on my being ennobled are long. Even the more obscure honours – Knight of the Wardrobe, Reeve of the Palanquin, Underbaron of the Middle Empire – are beyond my means. 'They want half a mil in party bungo-bungo before they'll even put you on the list. Leave it with me...'

Oh God. 'Leave it with me'. The four most ominous words in the English language, along with 'it's not very contextual' 'in my humble opinion' and 'sort of Grand Designsy...'

WEDNESDAY Plenty to think about from yesterday, so shift the bulk of my creative thinking until tomorrow.

I am, however, keen to develop the 'Grand Designsy' brand as an upmarket graffiti identity. Spend the morning knocking out some banging posh stencils, man.

107

THURSDAY Design competitions. They're a racket, a closed shop. The latest one is typical:

'Architectualiser sought for new higher education campus in China. Haughty sense of spatial entitlement essential. Dame or Lord preferred, would consider CBE. Must have public school accent and cruel laugh'.

Nothing at all about an education portfolio or indeed any reference to professional training. It's ridiculous, you could just get classy actors to promote your global marketing campaign.

I call Eddie. 'Relax. I'm all over this like a 15 tog duvet, mate. Decided to make you a Companion of the Royal Lunch. See you at the King's Arms tomorrow. Plus I've found us a sleeping Edwardian practice partner...'

Slightly resentful that I'm never the sleeping partner in any of these enterprises. I do, however, require a long afternoon nap as I'm out very late tonight.

FRIDAY Fast forward to the small hours, and I'm in a boutique part of north London with my old friend Amy Blackwater the environmental activist.

Unlike me, Amy has skilfully managed her public profile and is now the doyenne of stylish oppositionality. Her activism is 'premium' these days. She's feted by the thinking artisan crumpeting classes. Her success rankles almost as much as the balaclava I've borrowed from her, which is slightly too small.

Still, she IS helping me with my stencils. We have to be stealthy, what with the CCTV. And the film crew shooting a documentary on Britain's Most Celebrated Activist.

At one point she says, 'I like to think of myself as more of a disquietist than a terrorist...' while keeping a straight balaclava. Over the course of three hours we whack up the following stencils on London's urban canvas:

- a fox in a trilby laughing at a Nando's queue
- a rat in a onesie making lemonade and keeping calm
- a big fat gypsy cat with the dead bird of 'irony' in its mouth.

I sign each one 'Grand Designsy' using Farrow & Ball's new Yellowist range.

Later: pub. Rock Steady Eddie's found a chemistry student in Hull called Abby Downton who for £500 cash will be photographed in period costume to front our new global marketing campaign.

'Upstairs, downstairs, in my lady's chamber...Abby Downton Top Class Spacemakers can turn your dream into an aristocratic reality!' We've even got an emblem: two beagles in sunglasses flanking a chevronned pier.

More good news. My old friend the Prince of Wales, the highest-profile toff I know, has agreed to have nothing to do with the project, so that's a major potential embarassment avoided.

SATURDAY Lovely. Pop-up hipsters are now desperate for a customised Grand Designsy stencil on their gaff. I plan to take their money, send them a 'Beware of the Media Wankers' stencil and tell them to spray it on themselves.

SUNDAY New Year's Reclination.

January 10, 2013

I Sense My Enemies Massing
Like Simpering Starlings

MONDAY Brilliant. My Museum of Piracy has been short-listed for a Looks Nice Award.

Or as the organisers insist, it's been 'short-sighted'. It's got a good chance of winning too I think, as the other five short-sightees are rubbish. Here they are, in no particular order of merit.

- The Nano-Monsters Science Discovery Centre in Sheffield, featuring a giant virus petting zoo, designed by Atelier Neuroburo.
- Boo Hoo Hoo Design's 'atheistic thinking pod', an annexe to the multi-faith prayer room at Manchester Airport, incorporating a 'pondering booth' for agnostics.
- A pseudo-Georgian avatar exchange in Kettering, designed by Urban Jizz.
- The Hobbit Bar in Notting Hill, a fantasy landscape interior where all bottles, glasses, furniture and bar staff are twice normal size. Designed by Archiptextur.
- 'The house that turns into a car that turns into an office that turns into a bathroom that turns into a costume that turns into itself!' designed by Haus of Kar and currently parked in a lay-by near Coniston.

TUESDAY The Looks Nice Award is my first nomination of the year. Gratifying, of course, but also a bit embarrassing.

I mean obviously it's great that the judges like the Museum of Piracy's 'swashbuckling exterior, with its popular aerial plank-walk and rigged façade'. They admire the inside too. The Davy Jones' Hamper restaurant and Treasure Island gift shop are both highly commended. There's even wry approval for the unique visitor charging system, though that had nothing to do with me. Entrance is free but you have to pay a 'ransom' to get out.

It's embarrassing because the Looks Nice Award is sponsored by *Cutting Wedge* magazine, a trade publication aimed at the blatantly vulgar commercial sector. And the judges are my old friend Darcy the architecture critic and his border collie, Bess of Hardwick. I can already sense my enemies massing on Twitter like simpering starlings, devising some sarcastic hashtag about cronyism and swapping jokes about my weight.

Alas, the Looks Nice Award can't be fixed. It's dog-driven. Darcy simply takes Bess round to look at new architecture. If she likes the building, she barks. It's then 'short-sighted' along with half a dozen other buildings. Darcy and Bess go back to have a proper 'long look' at them all and the one that provokes the most tailwagging is the winner. Looks Nice Theory is incorruptible.

WEDNESDAY Or is it? I mean, if someone were to distract Bess with a chewy snack or jingling toy outside the Museum of Piracy, would that boost my chances? How unethical would it be?

I wonder if the same idea's now occurring to my fellow shortsighted auteurs. Yes, perhaps when Darcy and Bess go back for their long look I should, as a sort of moral imperative, be present. Encourage tail-wagging. Level the looking-nice playing field.

THURSDAY Irony on the high seas! A pirate version of my Museum of Piracy's being built in China!

Worse, this clone-sharking is being explicitly encouraged by *Cutting Wedge*. Their latest Special Pirate Issue has an editorial IN PRAISE of design piracy, which it says expresses the buccaneering spirit of the age. It's PROUD that the pirated piracy museum was featured in enough detail in the previous issue to make it easier to copy.

It is of very little consolation to think of those other imagineers of epic space, furiously discovering that Shanghai has a Hobbit Bar or Beijing's getting a giant virus petting zoo, but it is of some.

FRIDAY Frosty meeting with Darcy and Bess. Obviously I've withdrawn my Museum of Piracy from the Looks Nice Award. I have also engaged a cheap solicitor to copy someone else's legal strategy in pursuit of an infringement of intellectual copyright claim against the museum pirates. All that remains is to decide whose fault it was.

I blame Darcy. Darcy blames Bess. Bess remains inscrutable, but she's definitely avoiding eye contact with me. I swear to God I'm beginning to think – not for the first time – that the plastic arts are too important to be left to the pets of the practitioners of the plastic arts.

SATURDAY My fixer, Rock Steady Eddie, is actually pleased about my pirated piracy museum. 'What do they say? Imitation's the most flattering form following function, yeah?' I despair.

SUNDAY Become shadow of former self in recliner.

January 24, 2013

Five Versions of Me

MONDAY Tweaking the details of Moon Base Beta, the construction site for my lunar new town.

The first thing to do is to get basic regolith printing equipment up there. A module will land close to the Sea of Tranquillity and stay inert for a couple of days, adjusting to the space-time difference and 'settling in'.

Then a tubular module's remotely unpacked from mission control, inflating a dome-shaped Clerk of Works office in balloon form. This balloon is then overlaid with moon glue and dust tiles, as simply as you'd create a papier-mache globe. Once the lunar office has been built, we'll print a table and chair for the robot Clerk of Works and some humanising touches, such as a printed vase of flowers and a mug with 'You Don't Have to Be Lunar to Work Here but it Helps!'

Once that's signed off, the robot Clerk of Works can be printed and programmed to oversee the construction of the construction workers required to print out the lunar new town itself.

At this stage it's undecided whether the settlement will be a luxury destination for space tourists or an overspill camp for asylum seekers and those unable to afford affordable housing, so we're deferring any architectural decisions for as long as possible.

TUESDAY Another existential crisis looms. I entered a poorly regulated design competition several times using multiple identities in order to increase my chances of winning.

The competition was for a 'signalisation marker to re-stimulate interest in Tamworth's exclusive Millennium Quarter'. This former scrubland and municipal tip on the outskirts of the town was designated a 'corporate internet village' back in the late 1990s, when liberation from the twin tyrannies of social responsibility and the dial-up modem was a distant dream.

Despite new local authority infrastructure, some off-book lunches with exotic puddings and a brochure comparing Tamworth's Millennium Quarter to London's Docklands, nobody came. Now the feeling is that if the right marker can just be built it will attract business investment, as a bird feeder attracts sparrows.

I've entered the competition five times. As myself, as my friend Darcy's border collie, Bess of Hardwick, as my fictional twin brother, Ramone, as the metarchitectural dachshund, Bauhau, and as a design collective called Apptecture. God, I hope I win as myself. Otherwise the paperwork's going to be a nightmare. My marker variants are:

- A giant abandoned sofa in idealised form, apparently being lifted off the ground by a big balloon to symbolise the triumph of the human spirit over illegal fly-tipping, made from recycled, illegally fly-tipped materials.
- A 'geometric tower grid' of uncertain theme, calculated to act as a structural aperitif for anticipated investment in the area and incorporating spinning biscuits of light to help the observer 'visually digest' everything.
- A retro shuttered-concrete 'urban collar' overlayered with a necklace of trees, to stand as an exemplar of growth and renewal in both the abstract and vegetative senses.
- A half-scale *trompe l'oeil* office tower, with miniature people etched into the glass skin and looking hopefully out, with a sort of glowing bulb at the top to underline the importance of puzzled thinking.
- An elegant tapering tower of fondled steel with the word 'MARKER' written up the side in Helvetica.

WEDNESDAY Oh God, the five shortlisted schemes for the marker competition have all been designed by versions of me! Unfortunately in a situation like this, when the quality of entries is so high, there have to be losers. Four of them will be yours truly.

THURSDAY Phew. I've won the marker competition as the non-existent design collective. Spend the day inventing my team.

The boss will be the real me, obviously. I'll have a grouchy old-timer who once did prog-space council housing for the GLC. A sassy young graduate with crazy ideas about how we might live in a post-coherent world. A down-to-earth design technician who turns out to be a Scientologist. A bluff conservative who shmoozes all the deals but who has lost his soul.

FRIDAY Toying now with the idea of having someone who can 'get the job done'. Decide to make him a young, pitiable genius forced to work in an Indian draughting camp.

SATURDAY Five-a-zeitgeist theoretical football. Styled-Out Catas-trophism 1, Ironical Horrorism 1, after extra time and emotional deadlock.

SUNDAY Collect myselves in the recliner.

February 7, 2013

Kenny Axe-of-Wrath, Meet Julie Bloodbath

MONDAY It is with great solemnity that I take up my new role as the coalition government's temporary Common Sense Tsar.

I look forward to bringing my unique approach of lunch-based conciliation to several so-called 'intractable' problems facing the built environment in the next few days, after which my probationary performance will be reviewed and rewarded with a permanent post, I hope.

By mid-morning, my Common Sense Tsar inbox looks pretty full. I take a calm overview and award myself a long lunch.

TUESDAY If there's one thing history has taught us it's that peace is better than war. How ironic that some of the longest and bitterest battles between developers and conservationists have been fought over the future of historic battlegrounds themselves.

Even unwarlike historic sites have become battlegrounds. The bloody Battle of Stonehenge dragged on for generations and still nobody is entirely certain what the occult formation of 'visitor centre within car park' originally signified.

Today I have arranged a truce between some particularly entrenched battlefield opponents. On one side, high speed train enthusiasts who want to drive a railway through the ancient site of the Battle of Morsen Lewis in Oxfordshire. On the other, the powerful cultural guardians of Sponsored English Heritage, who definitely don't want that to happen.

After three courses and several armagnacs, both parties agree to cease hostilities, which have included very nasty physical threats and carefully orchestrated sulking. I feel a warm glow of achievement, which later turns out to be armagnac-inspired dyspepsia.

WEDNESDAY So yeah, my newest common sense solution is a high-speed English Battles Circle Line which instead of *accidentally* bisecting key battlefields does so *deliberately*.

The line would plough right through the middle of Bosworth Field in Leiestershire, through Yorkshire's Marston Moor and then on through all the major centres of historic carnage in England.

New transport and heritage interchanges would stimuate the creation of exciting new 'battle destination experiences' designed in a historically contemporary style with plenty of graphic scenes of violence, restaurants, etc.

This solution also allows the train people to stop worrying about being murdered by single men in their twenties who have full beards and big swords with girls' names.

THURSDAY Seek reconciliation between two hugely influential Mercian warlords. Kenny Axe-of-Wrath, direct descendant of Axe-of-Wrath the Baby-Eater who according to the Anglo-Saxon Chronicles 'did perish through consumption of tainted pudding'. And Julie Bloodbath, whose ancestor Bloodbath the Man-Butcher went on to become something of a cliché.

Both are claiming air rights for the proposed new Tamworth 'health service providers outlet centre' which will replace the existing NHS hospital's A&E, maternity and intensive care units. Their argument is that all air above the site was consecrated during the reign of Offa and therefore is one of the spoils of war.

After an eighth-century lunch (charred boar, trough of mead) everyone

114

agrees to call the Battle of Tamworth Infirmary a draw. Mr Axe-of-Wrath and Ms Bloodbath will split the equity stake in all retail, leisure and entertainment opportunities above the new community wellbeing and lifestyle hub.

FRIDAY Reconcile the North-South divide with an ornamental coast-to-coast ha-ha.

SATURDAY. I'm officially off duty today but such is my dedication to common sense that I act as a voluntary tsar at the pub.

Not just any pub. The Bride of Russia is located in a four-storey basement extension commissioned by my friend Dmitri the oligarch for his Kensington mansion. It's a great recreated pub. The Victorian fixtures were rescued by Dmitri's diligent team of salvage hunters following the break-up of basement pubs recreated in the 1960s from original features rescued from Victorian pubs bombed during the Blitz.

Dmitri argues that this makes The Bride of Russia 'double fucking historic' and he would very much like retrospective planning permission.

Dmitri's other guests include his architect, Django Liberace, and Colin Trout, the outsourced planner in charge of objecting to dangerous excavations in residential areas then inevitably agreeing to them. The evening begins predictably enough with the planner as a common enemy of the client and architect.

But by midnight everyone's gone all *in vino veritas* in the luxury solarium and it's clear that the planner isn't the architect's enemy. The client is. It's the client who through sheer force of wealth forces the architect to design exactly the kind of morally unsustainable, egomaniacal bullshit that same architect would vehemently oppose as a neighbour.

Or even abhor as a passer-by in a beret.

I seem to have caused more problems than I've solved here, but sometimes that's the nature of common sense.

SUNDAY Reconcile self with recliner.

February 14, 2013

Diana Princess of Wales Laying a Wreath at an Accident Blackspot Wearing Sunglasses Plus She's in a Wheelchair

MONDAY Redesign the Vatican, giving it a 'fallible pathos' Latin overmantle with a terra cotta bossa nova twist.

TUESDAY Spend the day looking at everything in the entire history of art and architecture with a quizzical gaze, then wondering what'll be next in little Twitter thought-fragments, then turning the quizzical gaze on myself, then settling on a pastiche of myself, then exploring the high-density interior of my fridge in an existential journey of snack-themed enablement.

WEDNESDAY Jamming out some contemporary beats for a bijou six-storey alpine apartment block, like a boss.

The alpine block is in Swiss Cottage, so is hugely contextual already. Obviously it will set new benchmarks in sustainability and innovative design, that goes without saying. I'm not an idiot.

Just as the humble alpine hut defies harsh weather conditions, so my exquisite inhabited crag will be sticking two fingers up at its environment. Asymmetrical profiling and iris-recognition software will minimise residents' exposure to the cold, harsh staring of passers-by and the heavy snowfall of fast food flyers that can make the Swiss Cottage climate so inhospitable.

Conserving Earth's Natural Resources is at the very top of my list. There'll be loads of ethical spruce and fir involved, for a start. Also, building materials will have to conform to some sort of 'green quotient' which will probably have its own sticky label and EU directive.

I will minimise wasted space simply by minimising space generally – indeed, restricting it to an almost unliveable standard – ensuring it definitely all gets used.

THURSDAY Lunch with my old mate Gutsy the graffiti artist. He seems remarkably sanguine about the recent removal of one of his works from the outside wall of Sound for a Pound, a discount variety shop in Tamworth.

'Diana Princess of Wales Laying a Wreath at an Accident Blackspot Wearing Sunglasses Plus She's in a Wheelchair' has mysteriously turned up for sale at a Moscow auction house. I think Gutsy may be in on it, for cash, ironically. 'Easy come, easy go, my lover. Plenty more where that came from...'

Another stencil – 'King Kong on Top of the Shard Swatting Away Architecture Critics in Microlights' – has already taken up the vacated space. Suddenly, works by Gutsy adorn every Sound for a Pound shop in the country, regularly disappearing into the international art market to be replaced by a stencil with approximately the same value.

Inside the shops you can buy blank Gutsy postcards with a red 'bought' sticker for a pound each. Gutsy's even considering a Sound for a Pound ad campaign in which he's seen breaking into one of the shops and stealing a selection of bargains.

In Wolverhampton somebody – and here Gutsy avoids eye contact – has stolen an entire Sound for a Pound shop, leaving only a vertical slab bearing the stencil 'George Osborne in a Onesie Decapitating a Tramp'. A more appropriate building is expected to appear behind it shortly.

FRIDAY In the morning, create a 'forgotten space'. In the afternoon, have to do it all over again.

SATURDAY Five-a-zeitgeist theoretical football. Radical Femgineering 8, Third Wave Memenism 0, after spatial regendering and own goals. Radical Femgineering now goes through to a quarter-final seminar at the Royal Institute of Patrician Arts, provisionally titled 'Ladyspace: how women are baking delicious epic spacecakes the whole family will find irresistible'.

SUNDAY It's the first Sunday of Lent and the cravings are becoming severe. This year I have given up GPS.

I have consequently rendered my familiar, knowable world a wilderness. By denying myself a verifiable location on the Earth's surface I hope to mortify the flesh and, come Easter Sunday, appreciate the higher power 'up there' that looks over us, and guides us.

It does mean I'm often late for meetings and daren't venture into the countryside. But it has allowed me to examine myself deeply, via the medium of watercolours, and has encouraged a 'rough and ready' non-GPS approach to site-specific design. For Lent, I am simply pointing vaguely at where my latest masterpiece should be built and handing over the detailed stuff to an intern who – I AM SHRILLY PROUD TO SAY – will be paid in due course and is allowed time off for lunch and the toilet.

Spend most of the day reclinered, suspended in spiritual horizontality and pointing sort of north.

February 28, 2013

The People's Centre for Cultural Transmution

MONDAY To Blingnang, China's fastest-growing urban megabulb, to push the professional development envelope.

Capitalists and communists alike have reservations about how this 'hybrid economy' works but I can honestly say the plasmic arts are much the same all over the world. You know, they have a saying in Blingnang: 'A stranger is just a contact you haven't bribed yet!'

TUESDAY Things have changed since my last visit. Most of the 'itinerant rurals' who gave Blingnang's historic quarter such character have disappeared, along with the historic quarter itself.

From this ashy rubble will rise a new People's Centre for Cultural Transmution. The client's being quite vague about what will actually occur there, and my Chinese agent's being quite vague about who the client is. Although, I discover during lunch, my Chinese agent seems otherwise alert.

'In Mandarin my name means One Who is Steadfast as Rock, but please call me Edward. Here, let me help you with that pan-fried shrimp and golden noodles. And should we tab another bottle of this excellent rice wine to your hotel room, which I believe is 1516, thank you, waiter'.

OK, I don't know what a centre for cultural transmution is. I do know, however, that the conceptual design fee is substantial, the building is to be fortified, the style guide is 'Queen Victoria goes to Swinging London' and the top two storeys will accommodate some kind of 'internet trace blocker'.

Obviously I have misgivings about this project. But come on. Moral certainties are a luxury these days and, like oysters, can actually CAUSE serious internal misgivings if they turn out to be 'bad' moral certainties.

Yeah, sod it. Resolve my misgivings by cladding the cultural transmution centre in a neo-Classical sheath, with faux-marble fluted pilasters and 'dolly bird' caryatids.

WEDNESDAY Edward and I are at Blingnang Freepitch. It's a weekly event held at a swanky digital tea house, where spatial artists and clients of discernment mingle without obligation in an atmosphere of mutual suspicion and venality.

I play the old 'Invisible Tower' manouevre. Tell a high-rolling client you have detailed schematics for the world's tallest luxury mixed-use tower. Two miles high, fashioned from materials so innovative nobody's heard of them. An articulated 'hard air' core with suspended floorplates of 'spectraluminum' and walls of translucent 'smart jelly'. Advanced light management plus magnetised atomic gap alignment equals 'building that blends seamlessly into its environment' and a new post-contextual global planning prototype.

Then you ask them if they'd like to see a rendering, they say yes and you slip them a blank sheet of paper. At this point it can go one of several ways but it usually helps if they have a sense of humour in the broadest sense, or if they're drunk.

Tonight I attract some interest. Edward is there to follow through and talk me up. Even I with my non-existent Mandarin can tell he's taking liberties. 'Executive designer' becomes 'he has overseen several executions already this year, each more ruthless than the last'. There are approving nods.

The evening ends with half a dozen potential clients exchanging details with Edward Who is Steadfast as a Rock, and some drunken architectural karaoke. One guy does a belting version of Frank Lloyd Wright's Guggenheim Museum before falling off the table.

THURSDAY A sophisticated Blingnang middle class is these days looking beyond traditional Chinese architecture. Already the city is fringed with an anthology of pastiche executive housing 'capitals' – a miniature Paris here, a dinky Berlin there. Now the jaded bourgoisie seeks something new, beyond the comforting exotica of Classical Europe's palette.

So I've come up with Blingnang Inner Citiburbia, a low-density upmarket gated community modelled on the sort of high-density, downmarket shithole that would theoretically exist in counterpoint to what's actually there.

The site visit's inconclusive. Everything looks a bit depressing but I can't tell which direction it's going in. That's a thumbs-up from Edward.

FRIDAY Get some brilliantly atmospheric shots of my Pea Souper Dickens apartment block (shaped like Big Ben) by waiting until the smog's really thick.

SATURDAY To the opening of my brand pavilion. The client's very pleased. It's full of tubular challenges and triangular fragments, and things 'punching through' other things.

SUNDAY. Reclining slightly in the plane home. Irritated. Can't for the life of me remember who the brand pavilion was for.

March 7, 2013

The K'buum el-K'buum Residuals Farm

MONDAY I've been whacking out some 'bonkers envisionments' for my bumbling homie Loaf, mayor of London.

He wants to create a Bi-Line across London, a segregated cycleway free from the hazards of hat-wearing motorists and the unions. My ideas so far:

- Elevated 'moral high ground' section over Labour boroughs.
- Business class lane offering premier access via executive gateways, uniformed bicycle minders and filtered air, oxygenated with notes of damask and chlorophyll.
- Ignorable red traffic lights at regular intervals.
- Every square inch of PFI tarmac slathered with smug bicycle-themed corporate bullshit glorifying the worst bastards on Earth.
- Hold a design competition for a 21st-century linear cycling environment. Then after a while announce a diverse shortlist with schemes featuring reclaimed Elizabethan brickwork, abstract fencing and assorted bollocks on stilts. Then after a while announce a controversial winner. Then faff about long enough for it to become

someone else's problem and just make do with existing de-pedestrianised surfaces. Then eventually see Loaf on the news, reluctantly standing for party leader.

TUESDAY Phone call from Loaf. He loves my Bi-Line conceptuals. As usual, he drifts into Latin.

I'm pretty rusty these days. Something about him being Achilles and David Cameron being Hector? And Hector's been slain and his body's being dragged behind a Boris Bike round and round Westminster Square? Is that right?

Loaf cackles in Latin. And they say it's a dead language.

WEDNESDAY I'm designing a luxury graffiti and urban skills pavilion in Brighton.

It will allow middle-class children to get involved in a 'street scene' that's vibrant, aspirational and doesn't smell of piss. My client, an entrepreneur specialising in youth leisure, reckons parents will pay a fortune to park their teenagers in an urban environment secured with adequate levels of insurance.

Only improving, experimental hip-hop will occur in the supervised stencil masterclasses. Beatboxing workshops will teach youngsters how to make a real difference with socially responsible saliva. In line with local council requirements there will be ample jamming provision and a counselling service.

THURSDAY To a desert far, far away with my old friend Dusty Penhaligon the conservactionist. He's helping with the restoration of a classic science fiction building – the K'buum el-K'buum Residuals Farm from *Star Clash Episode Four: The Beginning Again*.

I'm tagging along as his plus one, making notes and sketching enigmatic little asides in my special Unlined Overseas Moleskine.

In the fictional universe, the K'buum el-K'buum Residuals Farm exists on the planet Apostro V. It's where the character of Mark Staremaster (who becomes the leader of the Rebel Coalition that defeats the Royal Clone Army and saves the galaxy from voice-synthesised fascism and then does it again in the sequel) was born.

In reality, the badly deteriorating building is in a remote area of Tunisia where the climate is harsh and it's almost impossible to get planning permission.

Dusty's an expert witness for Omniversal Pictures, who want to make a pre-sequel prequel to the last sequel called *Return of the CGI*. A grizzled

Mark Staremaster will return to his home planet to squint mournfully at K'buum el-K'buum Residuals Farm and wonder where the last thirty years went.

It needs to be redone from scratch. Omniversal's problem is that Tunisia (Desert) Planning Authority have declared the site a historic ruin. Now nobody can touch it. Dusty's job is to convince them that a reconstructed residuals farm will generate more tourism revenue AND be 'more historic'.

But they stand firm. How can something rebuilt now be older than something built 30 years ago? Dusty's logic is impeccable. If he rebuilds this year and the movie is a pre-sequel prequel to the last sequel, it would have to be 58,377 years old to align narratively with the *Star Clash* story, whereas the one built 30 years ago is only 58,336 years old according to the official fan site.

The Tunisian planners all get headaches at the same time and give in.

FRIDAY In the morning, design a 'post-riot Hackney fashion hub'. In the afternoon, design a 'pre-revolution Whitechapel media vortex'.

Exciting times. That's one thing we DO have plenty of in this age of austerity. Nouns.

SATURDAY Five-a-zeitgeist theoretical football. Elongated Voidism 3, Compressed Absence 1. Compressed Absence wins on aggregate as it's worth more per square metre.

SUNDAY Me-space downtime in the recliner. Reflect on the starry blackness of infinity, then nod off.

March 14, 2013

If Only Time Will Tell, Should Architecture Really be a Narrative?

MONDAY Knocking out a luxury floating village for the Royal Docks. It's a difficult community to gate, so I'm trying to persuade a celebrity architect to design some stylish floating mines embedded with crystals.

TUESDAY Tweak masterplan for the Midlands, replacing Wolverhampton with a freestyle urban mix underpinned by fat basslines and a massive grid.

WEDNESDAY Oh shit. I agreed months ago to speak at a conference. It's today at the Institute of Plasmic Arts. I've turned up without a thought in my head.

The theme is *'Randomised Creativity: Turn Unwanted Luck into Cash!'* I promised, apparently, to present something after lunch on *The Question as Generator of Epic Space*. With images. I've got to fill half an hour.

Luckily I have a hat, bought in a panic on the way over. It doesn't quite fit properly, so it's perfect. I've brought my laptop, so I can plug that in and 'surf the net' like it's 1999. Good, yeah, think retro. I put my hat on backwards. Half an hour, say five minutes per question, open it up to the audience, sorted.

I quickly devise six meaningless questions guaranteed to pediment an audience of architects, artists, auteurs and we're not even on to the Bs yet. The first question I pose to my audience of serious-minded liberals: *Is Texture the New Fragrance?*

I repeat the question thoughtfully, the way vicars do. I throw the question out to the audience and they're on it like gulls on a discarded kebab. They think texture is definitely the new fragrance. Visitors to show homes are these days braced for the smell of baking bread or vanilla, and laugh at the estate agent for thinking punters are that suggestible. So estate agents now like to have textured stone and rough artisan brickwork for the visitors to caress. It works just as well. I show some pictures of sand, and rubble.

My next question: *How Fat is your Faceprint?* This is popular with bearded men and women with luminous grey hair. The audience tosses the question around playfully, as if passing a large beach ball one to another. Faceprint, we decide, is a great way to combine the notions of façade and footprint in a loose and non-prescriptive way, impressing clients who really like wind and straw. I show some pictures of bales, and lambs.

True or Magnetic North? That's my third question, and the audience dutifully goes all solemn about the disparity of wealth between where they live and anywhere north of Berkhamsted. It's a scandal, and almost certainly explains the question, which might have something to do with perception and prejudice, who gives a shit. I show some pictures of Halifax, and Carlisle.

Do Houses Dream of Electric Anxiety? I explain that this question is merely the point of departure for a journey of reflection. How useful is it, we wonder, to imagine that a building might be sentient? We agree it's quite an exciting thought but also possibly pointless, which makes it all somehow much more interesting. I don't show any pictures for this one, which makes everyone smile a bit and nod, wisely.

Is Modern Modernism Just Post-Modernism but with a Neo-Modernistic Coat on? This time, instead of throwing it out there, I keep it very much up here. It's just a passing thought. I don't know how THAT got in there! Everyone laughs. This is brilliant. I show some pictures of the South Bank, and a Shard pepper grinder.

If Only Time Will Tell, Should Architecture Really be a Narrative? Running out of time myself now, so have to hurry this one along. I ask for a show of hands. Roughly two-thirds of the audience think architecture should be a narrative, which is good enough for me. I show some pictures of books, and beach huts.

Standing ovation! This is money for old... oh, I see. They're doing it ironically.

THURSDAY Sketch out an idea for an affordable home. The client's parents have a house in Arundel, so I just stick a photo of that on a sheet of A4 and scribble 'They won't live for ever' above it.

FRIDAY Produce abstract painting in lieu of work.

SATURDAY Five-a-zeitgeist theoretical football. Working Classical 0, Brutalism as Plinth 3.

SUNDAY Question self in recliner. Get answers more or less correct.

March 21, 2013

Back to the Futurniture

Still a bit blurry after my annual tour of the Milan Furniture Fair's ultra-smart periphery. I never want to see another *amuse-bouche* in my life, even if it IS a latticed quail microtorte designed by eminent artist-engineer Santiago Calatrava.

Oh, and spare me the chippy jealousy. Like YOU wouldn't hang out behind the scenes with the world's top 'furnauteurs' looking at really good beta stuff that's not even on the internet yet.

Few people can afford a £4,000 chair. But some people can. That's why international salons are so tiresome and vulgar and why I prefer to stay far from the sodding crowd. Sitting, lolling, perching and collapsing with the industry's most mercurial furniture creators on their most mercurial furniture. Highlights included...

The Peepeldokker Not so much a 'sofa for living in' as an entirely new way of 'living in a sofa'. Crafted from a wood and textile melange devised by New Sofist wunderkind Shep Witters for high-end sofa wranglers DFS Lenin, the Peepeldokker pushes at the boundaries of extendable sedentary environments with notions such as 'proximal TV' and 'informally planal dining interventions'.

Where does sofa end and life begin? Perhaps it's easier to ask 'where does sofa begin?' It begins here. At either end.

Whimcloud Created by radical collective The Chaise Longuepigs for furnifacturer Bangi, this 'post-urban sitting opportunity' will be the talk of next season. The version I saw, though not entirely safe to sit on, was a marvel of theory, material and process. Moulded from ultralight opaque monosodium carbonate, it resembles a giant prawn cracker.

Most importantly – in contrast to traditional furniture – the Whimcloud encourages the user to question their surroundings. 'There doesn't seem to be much happening here, apart from this giant prawn cracker. Where am I? How is it even floating in the air? How do I get on it? Will it collapse?' And so on. Exquisite.

SitUation COMedy The thinking behind this reimagining of the chair, by legendary 'digital hermit' Klaus 72 for Hairy Father Spatials, is deceptively simple. Turn an ordinary chair upside down. Much more interesting, suddenly.

Now find a way of plausibly seating someone on it. Put the upside down chair on another chair the right way up and add a cushion. 'Yes, a solution, but a solipsistic one...' Klaus insists. 'One chair alone is a social abomination. Several upside-down chairs together, however, may form a nodular cluster, all facing in different directions...

'Twenty years ago people all stared into the corner of the room at the TV screen. Ha ha ha, idiots. These days everyone's doing something different, though admittedly probably all looking at a tiny screen in their hand, so with SitUation COMedy you could maybe have the chairs above and below one another to bring people more into one another's eyeline, or maybe a miniature ferris wheel, any of that cocaine left?'

Collabyrinth This is more of a project than a product, which makes it hugely desirable in the context of a furniture showcase.

If indeed the pure energy of furniture may theoretically be contained by ANY case, however accomplished the theoretical joinery. Collabyrinth brings together thirty of the industry's hottest young designers, each contributing a thought to the notional furnituristic narrative and then passing it on.

Thus a simple beanbag-with-a-twist mutates, evolving into a complex 'resting matrix'. As one of the very few non-furniturians to have been vouchsafed a glimpse of what animateur Bib Funnel is calling 'dialectic consequences in serial, stuffed form' I urge you to secure your own glimpse as soon as possible. Assuming you have, like me, VIP access to this kind of thing. Otherwise, I think there's a documentary on one of the Living channels later this year.

Rising Stair By MC Shroomblagger for upscale furniturologists Stannah & Sisters. Wow. This is so far beyond furniture, it's as if furniture has travelled through some kind of furniture wormhole, to emerge into another galaxy of possibilities. Welcome to a world of brutal taxonomy and meta-furnitural backspin. Imagine an environment where you're permanently going upstairs, yet stationary. Exactly. Wow.

Die Nachtrekleine Perhaps my favourite future furniture, caught in that inspirational gleam between thought and word. Although still very much at the pre-conceptual stage, I'm confident that someone somewhere will be about to think of an industrial form, digitally milled, with a soft overlay and organic colours. Here's to the futurniture!

April 18, 2013

Right Enough to be True, True Enough to be Trite

MONDAY Cash in on multiple cultural trends by patenting my new 'self-bake' affordable home protoype.

TUESDAY I just don't understand it. Over the last few days I've submitted four proposals and they've all been greeted with blank indifference.

A boutique urban picnic area. The conversion of an office block to a 'city hive' buzzing with inferred Mad Men chic and stylish space constraints. An artistic intervention in the roofspace of a Victorian railway station. A re-imagined Carlisle where, in my renderings at least, inhabitants enjoy sunshine and wi-fi and eye contact.

Why have these proposals not been welcomed by local politicians and planners with appropriate levels of enthusiasm? Why have I not, as is customary, been praised for my insight into the human condition and for my selfless generosity in showing how this could be ameliorated by the healing balm of epic space?

Not even a 'thank you'!

WEDNESDAY Wait. My fault. I don't know how it happened, but I sent out all four proposals without any references to a 'cloud' in the design. No wonder I've been getting the cold shoulder.

Everyone knows that – this quarter at least – 'it's the cloud, stupid'. For without 'the cloud' there can be no aspiration, no higher plane. THERE CAN BE NO NEBULISED FUTURE.

I ask the various recipients to destroy the proposals as they stand. To be honest I feel a bit guilty about blaming an unpaid intern for the cock-up but if you can't do that once in a while I'm struggling to see what the point of an unpaid intern is.

THURSDAY My revised urban picnic area now presents the swirl of humanity as a cloud of hopeful possibility. The residential tower block 'puts other lifeclouds in the shade'. My installation piece is now simply called RailCloud 2020. New Carlisle is reformulated along 'cloudsourcing principles of social stakeholding'.

Within an hour, everyone's sent me an email telling me how brilliant my proposals are, how these days the cloud is more crucial than ever. Of course, they're all idiots. Nevertheless we all need to be reading from the same weather chart when the cumulo-nimbies coalesce into their own inevitable clouds of poisonous gas.

FRIDAY In the morning, design a pop-up church. Sort of 'ecumenical rationalism'. I wouldn't want to offend any atheists, they're really touchy. Plus, it's made of laminated cardboard so you can't be having too many fiddly bits.

In the afternoon, struggle with the internal layout. A 'worship space' is obviously essential, but it's a non-specific church. I'm not entirely sure what or who will be glorified, or how. Likewise, toilets. Impossible to know how long people are going to be mumbling and bumbling about inside with the remembrance of sin pressing on their bladders.

In the evening, solve most of the architectural problems by creating a pop-up religion. Inclusive, welcoming, a range of deities to suit all members of the congregation and available in pill form for those who require their god within them.

I'm calling it Truism. 'Right enough to be true, true enough to be trite'. It's a credo I've borrowed from architecture, where trite is acceptable in a way that 'pastiche' can never be. In fact I think I'll make Truism an architectural movement AND a religion, it'll be much easier to determine an appropriate building style.

SATURDAY Lunch with my old friend Darcy the environmental correspondent and his muse Bess of Hardwick, the only border collie in the country to wear prescription Le Corbusier spectacles.

I explain the principles of Truism. Eclectic borrowing from the past without the irony of post-modernism. Dullness as a virtue. In due course, practitioners could become self-sanctified, etc.

Bess seems much more impressed than Darcy. She cocks her head and pants enthusiastically. Darcy just shrugs through another drink and says he's heard it all before. That's the WHOLE POINT, I tell him. Bess clearly shares my exasperation and gives him an old-fashioned look over her tortoiseshell frames.

Her cleverness is wasted on Darcy, whose outlook has been clouded by bitterness ever since he was ousted from the *Creative on Sunday* in favour of his former companion, the architectural dachshund Bauhau.

SUNDAY Eschew the recliner. Take Bess for a long architectural walk while Darcy skulks indoors. She really would make an excellent 'ambassadog' for Truism. I wonder...

April 25, 2013

Human Content Management

MONDAY As content manager for several high-profile architectural schemes, I'm looking at a pretty epic week of nipping and tucking, I can tell you.

Content management is a relatively new and lucrative concept in the world of epic space development. As the country's leading expert on the subject, I'm delighted to be hosting a pop-up workshop at the Institute of Plasmic Arts with guest speakers, high-production lighting and a nuanced buffet lunch suitable for vegetarians.

Those who can, do. Those who do, popshop.

TUESDAY I've always hated the phrase 'social engineering', with its sneery disdain for the science of compatibility.

Now we've finished with all that posturing social justice business, we can surely start an honest conversation about who should be in what. No longer can the Crouch End section of Twitter pretend an urban underclass would be comfortable living in Unesco-approved Georgian crescents.

It's as preposterous as saying that the super-rich, who could make this country great again with the proper incentives – would be happy living on capped benefits in Levenshulme.

As a content manager, it's my job to make sure a building is 'happy' with what's inside it. The Shard for instance is balanced and fulfilled because it contains the right people. Strivers. Havers. Goers. In a building's guts, the right people are like good bacteria.

And the wrong people in the wrong place are bad bacteria. All this fauxrage about 'cleansing' unaffordable people from our city centres just makes the splutterer seem ridiculous. In urbanism as in yoghurt adverts, a clean gut is a healthy gut.

WEDNESDAY To the Institute of Plasmic Arts. Quite a good turnout for my content management popshop. Obviously I've made sure they're the right people, otherwise it would look like I don't know what I'm talking about.

My keynote presentation is entitled 'Putting People in their Place'. For maximum effect I'm presenting it in a smoking jacket and military trousers. Summary: quality content management must be at the heart of any building remodelling process.

I glide haughtily through my slideshow, showing how crucial it is to match inhabited sculpture with what I wryly call 'sculpted inhabitants'. This draws a knowing chuckle from the audience. I show them one of my current jobs: rethought and upgraded content for the All England Lawn Tennis Club in Wimbledon, where a new architectural masterplan requires premium human fill.

The sketches of the improved crowd for Wimbledon Fortnight illustrate how content will be pushed further upmarket, with a new blazer plaza and retractable tax status. Of course spectators will remain brand-locked (slow handclapping, flag-wearing, petit-bourgeois hairdos) but more demonstrably 'All England'. It's a look I'm calling 'luxury Ukip'.

During the informal afternoon discussion, a relaxed-looking man in a safari suit suggests that perhaps in due course units of content might be subject to some kind of validation system, like that blue tick thing they have on Twitter. A young woman in a sort of business onesie, clearly at ease with herself, makes an excellent point about 'green' building.

'Why is there so much focus on static, passive building elements such as insulation material and glazing, and those lights that only come on in the dark?' she clangs, to appreciative nods all round.

'The most efficient environmental improvement you can make to a building is to tear out old content and install new, ecologically sound inhabitants. Green subsidies should go straight to where they have the greatest impact: hardworking property-owning taxpayers, via their accredited content manager'.

We all applaud Onesie Woman, the exciting future of our craft and mystery, and ourselves.

THURSDAY Content-manage the remodelling of BBC Television Centre. Out go the raggedy-arsed creative types with their 'rehearsals' and their serendipity and their Daleks and their nervous energy.

Into the swish new apartments and hotel rooms come emotionally continent grown-ups with a shrewd appreciation of iconic location and the buy-to-let market. The famous TVC 'inner circle' will be open to members of the public, and I am already planning auditions.

FRIDAY Remodel St Paul's cathedral, giving it a more inclusive façade. Content rethinking ideas: retain communal froideur, increase appearance of concern and civility. NB NO JUMPERS.

SATURDAY Five-a-zeitgeist theoretical football. Cascading Monetarism 3, Capillary Microfunding 0, after overnight bank recount.

SUNDAY Manage contents of recliner, decreasing self-awareness to the point where I'm self-content managing in my sleep.

May 2, 2013

A Critical Stream of Piss

MONDAY A mysterious cabal of leisure investors has asked me to 'remagine' the world of snooker.

Their briefing paper *Thinking Outside the Crucible* puts the case for a future snooker venue in general – and I have to say quite negative – terms. 'Something that doesn't look like an illegal boxing arena inside. And that doesn't remind you of municipal swimming baths when the camera follows the players back to their dressing rooms'.

Understood. Seriously, I'm all over this gig like a luminescent shroud. Yeah, I'm thinking powerful fusion: retro *Saturday Night Fever* dancefloor meets Tate Modern Turbine Hall. The spectators like puffins, lofted into balconies and boxes, kept well away from the interviews with past champions and any temptation to gurn and wave in the background.

That's another thing. As well as conceptualising a contemporary snooker colloseum, I'm also applying my content management skills to design a better audience to fill it.

OUT: bloated middle-aged men dressed in synthetics. IN: oligarchs, art geezers, Middleton types, tax swervers, all in natural fibres.

TUESDAY In the morning, watercolouring and soft-pencil scribbling. In the afternoon, 3-D abstract bronze printing and spatial software modelling. In the evening, conversion of synaptic energy into pure creative impulse, then an early night.

WEDNESDAY Rethink the notion of 'British artists', making them more conscious of their economic leverage and putting imaginary little red stickers on their chins.

THURSDAY Knock out proposals for the world's first self-aware Permanent Tallest Building.

Organic expansion packs would be stored in the top five storeys, their release triggered by a GPS alert of any encroaching second tallest building.

FRIDAY My friend Darcy the architecture critic is away for a few days, staying at a 'boytique hotel' in Bratislava. He insists it's fieldwork for an edgy new niche heritage show he's presenting on the Euro lifestyle cable channel Hefty Poppa.

'Stop looking so sceptical,' Darcy says, avoiding eye contact. 'Niche-ritage is totally a word. So is boytique. We're looking at the whole gay boutique ideology stroke phenomenon in a sort of shallow yet comprehensive way AND we're travelling across Europe in a pink Cortina Mark 2 and for your information the show's called *Boutiques Roadshow* so can you look after Bess or not?'

Bess of Hardwick, the architectural border collie and Darcy's muse, looks at me pleadingly through her tortoiseshell spectacles and gives a little bark. Of course I'll look after her. She's much better company these days than Darcy, with his passive-aggressive headwear and self-pitying blouson.

Darcy's mind is elsewhere, possibly Bratislava. 'They said Guide Dogs Only. I explained Bess was very MUCH a guide, helping me through the everyday socio-cultural labyrinth. They accused me of winding them up. Whatever, it's moot, the insurance is ridiculous...'

Bess and I leave him to it and go off to laugh at some gritty urban brasserie in Kensington she's reviewing for the *Guardian*. I'm her official scribe this week so I just scribble down what she's thinking to type up later.

We stand across the road to get a better look at the façade, all assymmetrical blobs of smoked glass and skeins of terracotta nova, apparently held together by oversized knuckles of butch steel clamping. Words have been puked randomly across everything. 'Eat' it gasps, weakly. 'Think. Live. Share.' It's as if the place is daring you to go somewhere else.

Bess looks at the brasserie quizzically through her weeny Corbusian lunettes, straining her leash in its direction. 'Arch!' she cries. 'Rough! Rough! Grrr! Arch! Crit! Crit! Rough!' I agree. This brasserie DOES look like it was designed by some wanker for a bet.

We cross the road to get a better look. Through the wibbly-wobbly glass we see people looking icily at their surroundings, predisposed to complain...oh no. Bess has taken her criticism to the next level by PISSING UP THE DAMIEN HIRST BIKERACK.

She pants conspiratorially at me. It's like we're sharing a joke. Ha ha ha! Is that what's happening here? I piss on the Damien Hirst bikerack too, then we leg it.

SATURDAY Take Bess to park with 'the bag' and 'the glove'. Like her, I disdain the mundane layout of much of our recreational spaces. But today I do not follow her critical lead in this matter.

SUNDAY Contentment in the recliner, reviewing the newspapers with Bess in her scaled-down Olympic 'bird's nest'. Nice to have a growling companion.

May 9, 2013

Obituary: T. Dan Hooker

T. Dan Hooker, the legendary blues modernist and last of the 'Thames Delta Brutalists' – has died at the age of 92 after a long battle with obscurity. He will be best remembered for his 1965 hit 'Proposed Mathematical New Town Near Greenwich'.

He leaves behind several women to whom he has done unspecified wrong, and countless brainchildren, including a mysterious unfinished sketch for a 'floating atheistic working-class city to be moored above Bath as both an idealised modern community and a lofted remonstrance'.

This theoretical project illustrated Hooker's status in the world of epic space as a doomed visionary. As he himself admitted many years later, getting planning permission for any floating city would be hard enough, let alone one above Bath. 'The sanitary arrangements were way sketchy, to say the least, man,' he is reported to have chuckled.

In 1958, much of Britain's new post-war architecture looked timid and provincial. With its snooks and tripery, its skiffled brickwork and New Elizabethan drapery-pokery, the built landscape seemed mired in nostalgia, a world away from exciting developments in Europe. There, architects were experimenting with Oxygenated Modernism: a new and shocking style, all backbeaten concrete and visceral walling.

Then came the Great British Brutes Explosion. Inspired by the global wave of raw petrified music, exciting new architectural combos appeared. The Kipling & Cavendish Modern Lookers. Sir Andrew de Montclerc & his Chartered Jelly Surveyors. The Fincher & Fincher Palladian Bluesdaddies. And in the vanguard, T. Dan Hooker & the Draught-busters.

Hooker and his fellow 'betonistas' ripped the scene apart with their flyovers and tower blocks and French cigarettes. Their plugged-in civic approach electrified a young generation of beatnik planners who'd seen nothing like it. Hooker's credo – 'Fight Squares with Squares' – later encouraged rebellious 60s students to tear up the hippie rulebook and design everything to a 12-bar grid instead.

'Think of an inhabited structure as a blues song…' he memorably told the audience at the 1967 Architectural Association Folk Building Festival. 'Make your first pencil line rough and honest, from the heart, maybe a little self-pitying. Unique, personal. Yet within the parameters of the style, so it's generic…' In the famous clip of his performance, Hooker's prowling intonation is brilliantly backgrounded by Marty 'Slim' Panatella on syncopated slideshow.

'So you want a unique, personal, generic first line. But also just the same as everyone else's first line. This is blues modernism, not bloody abstract painting. Something that sits nice on a four-beat system build plan, you dig? Of course you dig, ha ha, a foundation is absolutely vital for all art forms and nobody wants to see a good plan come tumbling down…' Here Hooker breaks off to wail on a harmonica for a couple of minutes, the audience riveted – indeed the front row laminated – with his audible, heartfelt saliva.

'Then you make your second line. Just repeat the first line. Exactly the same. Exactly the same. Then the third line, same length, make sure it rhymes, you're done. You be drawing the blues and no mistake, marvellous stuff and in the noblest of Vitruvian traditions.

'Say you're doing a council block, keep it simple. Repetition's the key. You can have your main riff on the ground floor, put in a lift and then you can keep the riff the same but move up to the fifth, back down again, up to the seventh and back. Repetition, basic riffs, solid structure, boom. *Nota bene*, no portable gas cylinders allowed ANYWHERE inside…'

But as soon as it had blossomed, blues modernism faded and died. A fickle popular culture had moved on from amplified Brutalism to so-called 'prog architecture' in the 70s. Now buildings were expected to walk, or squeak, and to be inhabited in drawings by men in flares and moustaches and severe women in weird costumes.

134

'I guess T saw the writing on the wall,' said former blues modernist colleague Manny Boyes in a 1989 interview with *Stomped Concrete Quarterly*. 'His built gigs always attracted a lot of graffiti. Then when the Tories got in it was all about the environmental determinism, man. Cats saying our riffs leading young people astray and whatnot. T quit the life. Moved down to Hastings, became a driving instructor. We lost touch. Man, I guess we all lost touch…'

A memorial service for T. Dan Hooker will be held next week at a South Bank undercroft.

May 16, 2013

Little Gatsby

MONDAY Finish the sketches for my latest reconciliation of architectural dynamism and 'found landscape' – a freshly-squeezed organic village.

Set in hundreds of acres of outstanding Hampshire beauty and recently liberated by the Coalition's common sense rural freedom fighters. Yes, freedom at last from the shackles of Stalinist town and country planners, with their suffocating spools of red tape and their case law and their dandruff.

It's bloody great, too, being able to write your own environmental impact assessment these days. Executive Summary: NO PROBLEM.

The proposed village, Little Gatsby, is an extended loose-fit cluster of double-specced 'resipads' in the grand tradition, i.e. the enlightened patronage of bourgeois futurism.

Each resipad is uniquely framed in locally sourced glass and steel. Each includes a signature open atrium tiled in a turf-and-sod mosaic. Each has its own thrillingly sinister roof of sliding Teutonic plates.

I have taken bourgeois futurism, piped in enough green electricity and wi-fi for a medium-size business park, drizzled over a bit of balsamic *et voila*: Connectivised Nouveau Ruralism. My clients are upmarket developers Flatwhite & Keenwagh, whose mission is 'to deliver quality homes set in exclusive countryside locations for people who deserve the best'.

153

Our masterplan deploys what I'm calling Luxury Settler Theory. Build an outpost of gated entitlement, sell the units off plan, build the next outpost with the deposits and so on. In ten years, there will be a necklace of outposts with an invitingly large void in the middle.

Once all the satellite organic villages have been established – Little Gatsby, Lower Gatsby, South Gatsby, Gatsby Dene, West Gatsby, Gatsby Meadows, New Gatsby, Gatsby Hollow and Gatsby Platinum – it would be absolutely unthinkable NOT to develop a rural new town at the vacant centre. Linking them all, like a benevolent spider's web.

The name of the great central settlement is still to be decided. Something swanky and opulent though, obviously.

TUESDAY Drinks with my old friend Dusty Penhaligon the conservactionist. It's a chance to catch up, and also to rehearse my lines for what I hope will be a rubberstamping public inquiry into Little Gatsby.

Dusty's a jihadist on the subject of building anything 'new' at all, anywhere. He's currently appearing as an expert witness for campaigners trying to sink what seems to me to be an utterly blameless gigantic enclosed international leisure destination, golf experience and retail nebulus ('Mega Scotia') in the Cairngorms.

'Very, very reactionary climate at the moment,' he drawls, quaffing real ale from a tankard with his name on it. 'And that suits us down to the ground. We're not blocking the proposals per se. In fact, we're arguing the site SHOULD be developed. But that all development should conform strictly to indigenous heritage guidelines and original use patterns. So we've drawn up plans for a scattering of sheep farmers' crofts. Not the modern pretend ones, with plumbing. Proper ancient smoke-clogged ones that give you TB . . .'

So if someone could prove that a certain area of Hampshire, say, used to be a largeish settlement with satellite villages . . . Dusty nods approvingly and takes another swig of Monk's Cock or whatever sad, bitter, signature brew it is he's drinking.

WEDNESDAY Strategy meeting with Flatwhite & Keenwagh. I mention Dusty's 'aboriginal precedent' argument, and suggest hiring the sort of archaeologist who might find traces of a neolithic settlement underneath the proposed Gatsbys.

THURSDAY They've duly appointed retired academic Sir Grenville Pumps, author of *Ye Fulle Olde Englishe Break-Fast, or Whatte Ye Wille.*

It's apparently a forgotten classic, this groaning four-volume treatise on how traces of Englishness can be found everywhere, even in neolithic settlements, and how traces of neolithic settlements can be found everywhere.

Unusually, and usefully, Sir Grenville is on a zero-hours contract with a mysterious guaranteed lump sum performance bonus.

FRIDAY Fuck me, that WAS quick. Pumps has found astonishing evidence of a thriving Stone Age community underneath our notional contemporary organic villages.

Excellent. Now we have a unique opportunity to correct the mistakes of history. Informal Stone Age live-work spaces most certainly did NOT have to comply with building regs.

SATURDAY Add little touches of specialness to the drawings. Compassionate weather. Classic car. Obedient dog. God, it could be a birthday card.

SUNDAY Cross-platform media research in the recliner. Little Gatsby's EVERYWHERE.

'This is not simply the rr-ruff restoration of an ancient community…' writes Bauhau the architectural dachshund in the *Creative on Sunday*. 'It is a moral woof woof and archaeological yip improvement'. Give that dog a bone.

May 30, 2013

Ha Ha Ha You Fucking Ants

MONDAY Excited to be curating this year's Tamworth Popupalooza.

It will be many things – an urban showcase, an indie artfest, a psychospatial experiment, a realtime craft fair, an intersectional delta, a global inreaching, a vertical thinkathon, a cultural boot sale, an actual boot sale, a celebration of biversity, a festival of affirmation, a carnival of tolerance, a network of beer-and-vinyl boutiques, the location of Britain's Biggest Conga, free all-day cycling and The Great Community Gurn-Off.

But Popupalooza is not just about fun. It has a grimmer purpose. It is about restoring Tamworth as the capital city of Britain. By bloody insurrection if necessary.

TUESDAY One of the features of our psychospatial experiment will be a specially created model village, 'Popuppingham'. All thatch and white-wash, smelling of cut grass and fresh laundry.

It has been designed to feel exactly like a Leicestershire superhamlet, the sort of place high-earning professional people retreat to at weekends. We tireless campaigners, we Friends of Mercia, are simply making a point. 'This is what we would have had within an hour's commute of Tamworth' we are saying, 'if only it had retained capital city status.

'Instead, the title Capital of England was wrenched from us by das-tardly Winchester in the ninth century, only to be snatched from THEM by suave, double-crossing London in the eleventh. As a consequence, nearly every wanker in a pink shirt lives in the South…' We are saying.

These days, Tamworth's notional commuter belt has one of the lowest densities of wankers in pink shirts in England. If there is anything posi-tive to be taken from this underperformance it is that such people belong in London, along with unpleasant wealthy foreigners, war criminals and charity beatboxers.

When Tamworth rises again (inevitable, given global warming and the success of *Game of Thrones*) we will develop an entirely new dress code for wankers. Let's draw a line under the pink shirt and move forward.

WEDNESDAY I'm with the rest of the judges in the secret judging marquee, shortlisting some architectural street food for Popupalooza.

As is customary we pause every now and then to pull a 'surprised' face. Or squint uncertainly over glasses. Or laugh, gaily. A local string quartet is in the corner, playing generic pizzicato passages to keep us 'in the mood'.

We like the look of the architectural kebabs. Mechanically retrieved animal plasma dyed emerald green, shaped into little Monopoly houses, then skewered into terraces. New York 'subways' have edible signage; French versions with Art Nouveau stylings at either end. Impossible-to-eat deconstructivist 'anti-pasties'. Ice cream cones in the shape of Shards. Exotic double-miniburgers with salad mezzanines.

Oh LOTS of salads of course, this food is architectural. Rewilded salads. Green roof salads. Salads like miniature rain forests. All great to look at but you wouldn't want to eat any of it. Never buy street food in Mercia, everyone knows that.

THURSDAY Finalise arrangements for our 'suburban beach', a strip of sand with herbaceous borders and a big sign prohibiting ball games.

FRIDAY A cloudmapped social happening such as Popupalooza would be incomplete without installations all over the place, challenging everyone's perceptions of what a cloudmapped social happening is.

There's some properly challenging stuff lined up. 'Ha Ha Ha You Fucking Ants' is a powerful installation by artists Con and Connie Connaught: 42 flags on the roof of the cider tent, 'each one a command to passers-by to think a bit more about things for a change'. Questions range from the provocative ('What are you looking at?') to the oblique ('How many pixels in a daydream?')

Let's hope it gets people thinking about how we can speed Mercian independence, crush the ancient kingdoms of Wessex and Anglia and reinstate Tamworth as the capital city, otherwise we risk getting a bit distracted.

SATURDAY Approve the planted wheelbarrow display. We're using only flowers, vegetables and weeds that flourished, along with Offa's Tamworth kingdom, in the eighth century. Hogstink. Deathpansy. Witchsnot. Arse-fennel. Gripeweed. Bloodturnip. Shitgrass. Bubbling Gashwort.

Happy days.

SUNDAY Leisurely afternoon, reviewing Popupalooza progress reports in my eighth century Mercian recliner. It's a reconstruction, fashioned from timber and clotted flax. Not very comfortable. But then the truth often hurts.

I smile grimly to myself and sketch out plans for a flooded Milton Keynes. In the era of New Mercian hegemony it will become a wet playground, the 'Venice of the Upper North-West South East'.

June 6, 2013

This Sorry Cabal of Pretension

MONDAY In the morning, go about things in a traditional and non-innovative way. Get absolutely epiphanied at lunchtime. In the afternoon, adopt a much more contemporary approach.

TUESDAY The secretary of state for entertainment, Tia Murrier, calls, asking me to help formulate guidelines for the arts community. I think.

'Ian – the days of putting all our arts eggs in one basket? They are SO over. We must cut our cloth to suit our eggs. And tighten our egg-belt. Too many omelettes of failure have occurred in the past. Broken eggs. Broken dreams. THIS is the egg legacy bequeathed to us by a soft-boiled Labour party!

'The times in which we find ourselves demand austerity egg management. The question we need to ask ourselves is not whether these eggs are nutritious, but whether we can afford eggs in the first place. Why should eggs even BE eggs? This is the age of toast, after all. Isn't it? Yes, the arts community needs to wake up and smell the toast. And then ask themselves how the toaster might add value to bread, or something.

'Forget the eggs for now, they're just confusing things. Listen, the car's waiting. Could you get something to me by close of business tomorrow? I'm giving a TED talk on Friday and to be honest I'm not sure eggs have got legs LOL. Bye. Byebyebye.'

WEDNESDAY Tia worries too much. The creative professions are so foetally defensive at the moment, they'll say whatever the government wants to hear even when the government isn't listening to them.

These days artists are so scared of making eye contact with potential patrons and possibly upsetting them that they've stopped going to parties and mostly just stay at home digitising themselves.

It's the same with architects. They're terrified of being bullied by the bigger, Tory kids. Being called 'gay' for revering beauty and harmony. So they lie. They lie through their teeth about how architecture's greatest gift is to push up equity yields. Or they quack impenetrable guff about 'meaning-making', or 'place-being' or whatever the fuck it is this week.

Every conversation that takes place within a creative profession – and I include 'writing' in this sorry cabal of pretension – is about money. It is predictable and profoundly depressing. Thank God my fixer, Rock Steady Eddie, takes care of all that stuff.

THURSDAY Dedicate the whole day (total eight hours excluding lunch but including comfort breaks and triangulated thinking) to helping Tia.

Firstly I send her an email telling her she's doing a great job in very challenging circumstances. People love being told that, especially those who are paying you a fee. I also tell her she's right to let go of the art/eggs analogy, it's run its course. People who are paying you a fee love being told they're right, too.

By mid-afternoon I've formulated a three-point plan. To make myself appear cleverer, I pretend it was a five-point plan that I've 'frugalised' down.

1. All arts – whether visual, plastic, performative or cross-platformed – must demonstrate how their deliverable artistic products will contribute to the economy. The geese of yesteryear, laying golden eggs of art everywhere, have been cooked. The days of ring-fenced funding for cultural development are over.
2. As a matter of urgency all remaining artistic ring-fences must be located and properly audited in a national initiative, perhaps with the help of Radio 4 listeners.
3. Following the audit, all artistic ring-fences to be broken up and used as cultural kindling, to fire the cultural boiler of our economic steam engine.

FRIDAY Watch a livestream of Tia presenting my three-point plan. It seems to go quite well, apart from her confusing ring-fencing with ornamental screens. And bringing up the eggs again.

Surprised to hear her say that this is a farewell address. She's standing down as secretary of state for entertainment to take up a new challenge in the private sector as lobbyist to the Arts Marketing Board. Apparently she'll be representing arts providers and their shareholders, so let's hope for a prosperous arts community in the future, one that builds on exisiting consultant contacts.

SATURDAY Five-a-zeitgeist theoretical football. Art As Economic Passenger 0, Art As Economic Driver 1.

SUNDAY Audit my artistic boundaries in the recliner. Summary: flexible, with scope for significant reshaping.

June 20, 2013

The Plagiarism Assizes

MONDAY Plagiarism is an ugly word. It suggests thievery, obviously. But it just *sounds* ugly.

'Plagiarism'. Like something nasty you catch from a stranger on the internet. Which is how it usually spreads, of course. Like a virulent, lucrative rumour.

They say troubles come in threes. No surprise then that my legal interns are currently dealing with a troika of bullshit from some of my bitterest rivals. The claims themselves are laughable. It is almost as if certain people have looked at my work, thought 'why didn't I think of that?' then forwarded that thought to some intellectual property busybollocks who has finessed it into 'Why! Didn't I think of that?'

And the next thing I know, I'm being sued up to the gallbladder by speccy chancers in buttoned, tieless shirts from here to fucking Addis Ababa.

TUESDAY Turn up to the Plagiarism Assizes, only to find someone's nicked my slot! Apparently this happens a lot.

WEDNESDAY Oh great. Court One. Justice Clone-Waugh. He has a fearsome reputation for getting to the bottom of things. We'll be here all week.

First up, some ludicrous ponce from an 'international urban design and space choreography studio' in California alleges I stole the 'crowd ambience' for my private prayer therapy centre in Tamworth from renderings of his stupid animal church in Santa Monica.

Note the SKY in my Auteur's Impression, m'lud. Does it look like Santa Monica to you? It's the colour of cigarette ash. Yes, I concede that the facial expressions of pedestrians in our renderings are identical. But these people are smugly anticipating entirely different outcomes.

Those heading for the animal church are expecting redemption for their pets. In my scenario, potential customers are converging for communionised self-pity and as a sidebar, there's nobody on a Segway in a bandanna traversing anything that could possibly be called a 'microplaza'. Plus the people in the Tamworth drawings are fatter.

Justice Clone-Waugh carefully weighs the body mass indices, inducts the integers *sana cum laude* and infers via hearing loop that it's – bang! CASE DISMISSED.

THURSDAY Next, a mischievous claim that I did, with foreknowledge and malice, base the design of my residential tower in Middlesbrough (hereafter known as the 'Value Sausage') on the design of a vertical community encasement in Moscow (literally, the 'Iberico Luxury Cylinder of Executive Meat and Gristle').

Some theatrically affronted dickhead is now demanding that either he gets a small fortune in compensation, or an assurance that the Value Sausage is demolished immediately. Luckily for me, he insists on wearing a little hat in court, 'in accordance with my atheist beliefs'. This infuriates Justice Clone-Waugh, who pronounces the claim null and void:

'All sausage-emulating architecture is defined only partially by its visual appearance. Of far greater importance is the common presence inside these built forms of humanity itself, the as it were connective tissue that inhabits and defines all nicknamed landmarks. In the context of a global skyline crowded with giant sausages, I find the plaintiff's assertion of *saucisson sui generis de facto profundis* to be frankly laughable and very poorly translated'.

Bang! CASE DISMISSED.

FRIDAY Last hurdle. Some posturing arsetrumpet in a bespoke frock has accused me of stealing her idea to create a completely new upper tier of London.

I was entirely ignorant of her proposals for 'Upper Jersey' – a very crude notion to confer tax exemption on anyone with a registered London address more than 200m above ground level.

My own suggestion – Aero Docklandsville – was much more nuanced and set at a slightly lower altitude. I accept that my client, a Qatari gentleman who wishes to remain anonymous, may have been influenced by 'Upper Jersey'. He definitely saw the initial drawings for this, shortly before commissioning me to map out Aero Docklandsville. What does this prove? Am I responsible for the amoral workings of my client's mind?

Bang! CASE UPHELD, FINED SIX MILLION EUROS.

SATURDAY So much for Qatari-owned British justice. I will be appealing against this harsh judgement, and making things as complicated as possible in order to avoid incurring interest on the six million euros.

I don't think the plagiarism industry realises whom they have pissed off here. We'll see who's laughing when that certain Qatari gentleman receives a very strongly worded letter from my friend the Prince of Wales!

SUNDAY Repeat of last Sunday's occurrence in the recliner.

June 27, 2013

Cross-Glaminated Poverty Style-Out

Four years after the Beige Building Awards replaced the Green Building Awards, the competition is fiercer than ever. It's always a shame that there has to be a winner. Depressing, in fact.

Feels like ancient history now, the pre-austerity world, with its 'green' this and its 'sustainable' that. And how wasteful it seems, with our New Frugalist hindsight. We squandered so much visual capital. Created buildings that were ecologically sound AND attractive. What a scandalous waste of neural and optical resources. Green. How laughably inappropriate for these joyless times we now trudge through.

Of course it takes a dazzlingly ordinary building to win a beige accolade. The stakes are lower than ever. 'Austerity Chic' is now merely the name of a pub tribute band.

As usual the judges were looking for that magic post-green combination of 'economically prim' and 'spectacularly dull'. As I say, it's a shame there has to be a winner and to be honest this year we just couldn't be arsed to pick one. Shortlisted Beige Projects of the Year were as follows.

Mumford-Lowry Centre, Salford Beige An ingenious combination of charity shop economics (pop-up clothes boutique) and vegetative retrofit (hanging baskets). The project's point of departure was a corner of Salford Beige Retail Centre, where a cluster of vacant units turned recession into opportunity.

A team of spatialology students from the University of Salford Beige Retail Centre experimented with notions of 'Lowry' and 'retail', translating sentences into French via a free online service. Soon a nondescript section of mall was renamed *Boulevard des Hommes Allumettes* and the faux-vintage clothing ironised as 'cross-glaminated poverty style-out'. Now fully up and running, energy levels remain impressively low.

A Beige Crossing For The Thames Magic arborealist Isis de Cambray was asked by the mayor of London to imagine 'something less than a bridge, something less than a garden'. She mapped out a zero-

144

carbon, zero-finance intervention along Blackfriars railway line featuring indigenous weedlife and inter-seasonal energy storage through the sustainable medium of urban litter. A very soft environmental landing indeed for the beige-fingered doyenne.

Beige Statting Hub, Haggerston Masterbeiged by Haggerston Plastiche Collective, this non-interfunctionalist remodelling of a derelict dry cleaner's features a secluded wildlife roof and an 'arm's-length' conservation of the building itself.

Existing form and mass are preserved separately behind blown-up pictures in the windows (stills from *Transformers* and *Carry On* films). A carbon-neutral website invites members of the Haggerston community to 'think of the kind of statistics the building might notionally be a hub for the collation of'. Particular attention was paid to achieving an airtight font pool, with targets of $5m^3/hr/m^2$ for imagined space and $7m^3/hr/m^2$ at weekends.

The Beigefield Initiative By proposing that huge areas of greenfield be redesignated 'brownfield' to encourage housebuilding and, further, that huge areas of brownfield be redesignated 'beigefield' to encourage speculation about what that might mean, young psychogeographers Osmo Kirkegrid and Poppy Cumbly-Prideaux hope to get a two-page spread in next Saturday's *Independent*.

Beigedale Retirement Home, Lancashire Designed and built by Beige Retirement Solutions, this offers residents a near-maximum flexibility of visual interpretation by being virtually featureless.

Quintuple-glazed 'merry windows' channel a) natural light into beige resi-pods and b) semi-skimmed light into beige communal areas. The beige cladding envelope, or 'cardigan', turns a pastel yellow on special occasions when photovoltaic microbes and algae come to visit.

Beige Office Village, Exeter Devised strictly within the matrix of healthier live-work reinforcement principles known as 'beige active design', this business park makeover by Herban Squelch shows a commendably narrow focus while languidly ticking all the beige boxes. Interior and exterior grassroots strategies. Human 'parklets'. Portable headspace. Communal trees. Networked walkthroughs. Repurposed sightlines. Connected 'playgrazing'. Leylandii.

Milkington Beigemarket, Ely Demountable structures assembled from milk crates in a church car park for the sale of allotment-grown produce, increasing both green and beige impacts through the presence of charmingly imperfect fruit and veg.

Beige Free School, Wimbledon Ingeniously formed by installing a primary school for the energy-efficient children of aspirational Conservative parents within the shell of a publicly owned building formerly occupied by wasteful, high-calorie state pupils, this centre of academic excellence was designed by education placemoulders Artshole & Batard.

An exterior of beige Serbian larch, heavy glazing, a deep sedum roof and planted 'beige barriers' help insulate the building from a) financial scrutiny and b) the rest of Wimbledon.

July 4, 2013

Eurafrica: A New Bivalve of Hope

MONDAY To Celebrity Space Slam. It's being held this year in a temporary bubble pavilion, or 'pavobubblion' as we must learn to call it.

The pavobubblion has been inflated, with some difficulty, inside the upstairs function room of a Shoreditch pub. As it's a charity event nobody's too critical of the celebrities' genuinely stupid ideas, barked into a fawning crowd of overdressed berks.

J K Rowling slams a monologue about a floating library without newspapers. Poet Laureate Carol Ann Duffy mumbles a sonnet to a nationalised food bank, where 'filo money and quince ingots lie'.

Benedict Cumberbatch declaims what might have been a moving little hymn to an imagined concrete poetry tower, but by then both the pavilion and the audience have partially collapsed.

TUESDAY Reconceptualise the Isle of Grain, giving it a contemporary slow-release energy vibe.

WEDNESDAY I find myself with a few days entirely free of work, so resolve to redesign the world.

It's worth thinking really big once in a while. It nourishes the ego AND earns valuable 'dreaming for humanity' points. That reminds me: must remember to hashtag any thoughts. And have the hashtag protected

146

as intellectual copyright. And have everything I've just said sealed up in a hyperinjunction.

THURSDAY In the morning, bring Europe and Africa closer together with a huge Photoshopped Bridge of Possibilities. Bang. Right across the Strait of Gibraltar.

This bridge is not just theoretical, it's inhabited. Lots of men in 21st-century clothes clutching 21st-century gadgets, but with fashionable 1950s haircuts. Which is ironic, as an utterly changed world full of men with 1950s haircuts is EXACTLY what the future looked like in the 1950s.

My Photoshopped Bridge of Possibilities will be teeming with women too. Women in cardigans and gender-irrelevant work clothes and suits of armour. Memo to Self: maybe put in little speech bubbles saying things like 'save the bees' and 'fuck the patriarchy'. That stuff goes down really well with the sort of third-wave liberal men who devise theoretical design competitions.

Any bridge though is more than simply an elevated road over an obstacle. A bridge linking Europe and Africa ought to transcend engineering itself. It should soar without hauteur, exploring common ground between culturally diverse continents. It must 'sing' without 'wobbling'.

I reckon the bridge would be about 10 miles long, so choosing an approprate material is top of my list. I'm going for adumbrated carbon, something I just made up which has the toughness of steel and the flexibility of a medium rare steak. The bridge will perform a shallow 'w' as I've now decided the central support will be built on top of an underwater mountain which, when squinted at, has more than a hint of Atlantis about it.

'Morocco to Spain and back again in a day'. That's one of the slogans for my Photoshopped Bridge of Possibilities. Others are 'Eurafrica: A New Bivalve of Hope' and 'Afro-European Leisure Investments®'.

FRIDAY Pushing on selflessly with my comprehensive global redesign. Still exhausted from the bridge, so I turn my mind to the more soothing non-material world.

Through the medium of drivelly pencil scratchings and images harvested from a search for 'tossers in coffee shops' I map out a New Geography. Land masses are divided not by archaic national boundaries but by download speed frontiers. Fast and Slow Korea have never seemed further apart.

I propose a Universal Cloud to enable some sort of Global Spring (details not important at this stage) and massive overscaled self-cooling routers marching across the Pyrenees like gormless silos (get some sig-nature architects to design them, they'll look brilliant, or grotesque, same thing really). Also, why not harness the natural social network of biology itself by infusing chlorophyll with wi-fi?

It's all about the connectivity, as E M Forster would have said if he'd had access to Wikipedia before the First World War.

SATURDAY Five-a-zeitgeist theoretical football. Incandescent Non-Contextualism 3, Compassionate Neo-Fabianism 0, after extra height.

SUNDAY Reflections in the recliner. Conclude that the world really is a shambolic mess. Maybe a retrofit just won't do it. Tear down and rebuild, or push on with my masterplan for a relocation to somewhere else in the galaxy?

Perhaps to create truly epic space we need to turn the Ascent of Us into some sort of space epic, I muse, before nodding off again.

July 18, 2013

Masked Grans Dancing on a Bungalow Roof

MONDAY Redefine asset-stripping as 'burlesque value removal'.

TUESDAY Sad news about the demise of one of the construction indus-try's true giants – my Vertical Pilchard tower in Benidorm. It was, briefly, Europe's tallest residential building, conceived in happier times when Spain's economy was booming and criminals were going on holiday a lot.

Then certain killjoys pointed out that the Vertical Pilchard was a 250m-tall high-density block permanently crammed with transient Brits on a packaged piss-up for a fortnight, so it couldn't really be called 'resi-dential'. I tried the whole 'what is life but a brief sojourn upon this earthly plane we call reality' bumjelly but the Tall Tower Verification Bureau was having none of it.

Cravenly, the Pilchard's new owners have reduced its height by 12 storeys to make it look less empty. It's not Europe's tallest anything now.

Bah, I yearn for the good old days when iconic non-residential towers were owned by East End gangsters.

As my fixer Rock Steady Eddie put it: 'Say what you like about their brutal taste in architecture, them so-called villains kept the leisure development sector safe for ordinary people. They had a zero tolerance policy towards slags and nonces and planning departments. Plus they wore proper suits, none of this Coalition Casual shit...'

He has a point. The 'financial concordium' now in possession of the ludicrously renamed El Crazy-Potato are just faceless, greedy buy-to-let crooks with no accountability whatsoever. Despite the fact that most of them sit in the House of Commons.

WEDNESDAY In the morning, design a 'customer-facing service centre' for a local authority. In the afternoon, design a 'victim-blaming social security abattoir' for a central government contractor.

In the evening, rough out a 'self-congratulating hyperbolic chamber' for my own amusement and gratification.

THURSDAY Lunch with Amy Blackwater, the extreme enviro-ecomentalist. Whatever you think of hyperactivist politics, you've got to admire anyone who insists on wearing a balaclava in a heatwave.

I expected Amy to be still glowing from her media coup a couple of weeks ago, when she led a plucky band of mischief-makers up the outside of the Shard to protest at the commercial exploitation of high space. She's glowing all right, but from a combination of stifling headwear and moral outrage.

'Twelve hours, that's all we had!' she barks through a mouthful of raw vegan tapas. 'Twelve shitty hours in the limelight, and then the newspapers discarded us like a ... whatever, a yesterday's newspaper. Twelve hours! It took us that long to climb UP the bloody thing!'

Still, I say. There were only eight of you. That's like an hour and a half's worth of national publicity each. Amy freezes with sudden inspiration. A clump of macerated veg falls from her fork onto her plate, a nut fragment falls from her balaclava into her drink, in an epiphanic boom-tish.

FRIDAY Amy calls, muffled but excited. 'Just to say thanks, dude. Totally following your advice for widening the campaign. I agree, if you can abseil down it, it's too high'.

I don't even remember saying that. I wonder if I'm now starting to tune MYSELF out during lunch with people, just to be on the safe side...

SATURDAY Incredible. The news is full of Amy's latest stunt in her ongoing campaign, People with Altitude.

She's formed an alliance with other activist groups for a Portfolio Day of Action to protest about the colonisation of public air, post-capital capitalism, men, the 'cartelisation of the media', non-sustainable buildings, the Royal Family, sexism in corner shops, Iain Duncan Smith, generically modified education, unchecked privilege and carbon.

Instead of a few angry, fit people climbing up a massive building, thousands of agreeable, ordinary people are instead climbing up very small buildings. News channels show protesters scaling thatched cottages and post-war prefabs. Slightly overweight urban guerillas risking bus shelter roofs. Wispy pro-polar bear types holding hands in a greengrocer's awning. A gaggle of masked grans dancing on a bungalow roof, chanting 'Weather, weather, weather! Out, out, out!'

The great thing about this demonstration is how representative it is. Very much a People's Protest. Lots of half-hearted protesters up a ladder for a bit, or just sitting in the attic.

It makes you vaguely proud to be British.

SUNDAY Conduct my own occupation, complaining about the way things are while suspended in the recliner.

July 25, 2013

From Fenestrated Parabola to Melty Fucklump

MONDAY I despair, I really do, again. Why can't people and stakeholders and consumers of the delivered environment just get along?

The key to civic harmony has always been the maintenance of 'good neighbourliness' between buildings. When basic politeness goes out of the window, well – urbanism may as well just pack its bags and migrate to a country where they DO appreciate architectural genius and public order. Kazhakstan, say.

Admittedly the construction of my landmark London office tower wasn't without incident. I acknowledge there were several on-site maimings, some casual racism in the scaffolders' shouted conversations, permanent traffic chaos and occasional rubble bouncing around.

But that doesn't excuse the latest bout of sheer bloody-mindedness from certain local businesses. Encouraged by the gutter press, they have RE-NICKNAMED my iconic tower.

It's completely unacceptable. The building was officially entitled the Fenestrated Parabola at a very early sketch stage, to reflect its curved façade of polished steel and glass. 'Oh, it certainly reflects all right,' said the manager of a nearby bespoke umbrella boutique, sarcastically, to online blog hub *Qubble*. 'I would say it positively dazzles.

'By late lunchtime there's like this fat bloody laser beam innit, penetrating the shop and – zzzp! – melting everything. We had this brilliant window display. An autumn scene with all different umbrellas and that, dancing through piles of artfully arranged crispy golden leaves. It took me and Darren bloody ages. It was, to be fair to myself, both "classic" and "classy" at the same time. I wish you could have seen it but – zzzp! – the whole scenario got totally fried by THAT flipping monstrosity.'

Cue synthetically outraged Umbrella Man pointing at the Fenestrated Parabola in a very poor picture, clearly taken without enthusiasm by the *Qubble* correspondent on his stupid phone.

First a meme did the rounds: Umbrella Man frying an egg on the pavement. Frying an egg on the bonnet of a Ford Focus. Frying an egg amid the macabre, blackened aftermath of the autumn umbrella inferno. Now, in an act of sheer malice, the Fenestrated Parabola has been 'dubbed' the Melty Fucklump by *Qubble*'s editorial team.

TUESDAY I consult my lawyers, who agree there's a prima facie case for disruption of intellectual purchase, application of false nickname with intent to wound emotionally, and calumny with aggravated disparagement via named third parties, to wit Umbrella Man and his business-owning mates.

WEDNESDAY Settle out of court. Luckily the Parabola's owners – Qatari Space Invaders Corporation – haven't been unduly upset by all this unpleasantness and have generously undertaken not to flounce out of the London buy-to-let market, a move which might have triggered an acute shortage of affordable homes.

Meanwhile, the 'offending' elevation has been covered by temporary sheeting bearing the message 'We would love to be able to show you our amazing façade for the Fenestrated Parabola that everyone's talking about but apparently certain people simply don't like sunshine! We hope you're HAPPY NOW.'

It'll only be up for a fortnight, after which the trajectory of the sun (the real culprit here, let's not forget) will render things non-controversial again.

THURSDAY Unbelieveable. *Qubble* has a follow-up piece, illustrated by a photo of Umbrella Man pointing at the temporary sheeting and laughing at the 'clumsy passive-aggressive tone' of our public apology.

I call Hisham from Qatari Space Invaders. Once I explain exactly how *Qubble* and Umbrella Man are disrespecting his honour, the honour of his kingdom and of his financial subsidiary, he too hits the roof.

'This will not stand,' he rasps. I can hear something snapping in the background.

FRIDAY I consult my lawyers, who agree there's a prima facie case for besmirchment of standing, articulated ridicule and vexatious libel (inferred, occasioning actual psychological harm).

Plus, Qatari Space Invaders have now announced they're mounting a hostile takeover bid for *Qubble*, with a view to moving operations overseas. The settlement fee is waived in lieu of *Qubble*'s mental capital.

Umbrella Man's been given his marching orders too. QSI are buying up the whole street as part of a ruthless and ingenious plan to excavate and then build an underground Dickens World. Obviously I'll be pitching some initial ideas, including a Fagin's Cellar silk handkerchieferie and an online merch cluster provisionally called The New Curiosity Shop.

SATURDAY Five-a-side theoretical football. Steroidal Parabolicism 5, Calibrated Hystericism 0, after extra legal advice.

SUNDAY Achieve inverted parabolic status in the recliner.

September 12, 2013

The Strategic Mentalising Unit

MONDAY Still cantilevered from last night's Comedy Architecture Awards afterparty.

Some great nominations this year. Lots to laugh at. But everyone agreed there was a worthy winner. Callbach and Peipwerk's 'Reveal House' explores a contemporary narrative of mistaken identity with a new twist on the spiral staircase, and an imposing neo-Classical double-entendre up the back end.

TUESDAY Bollocks. Just looked over my two big problem-solving gigs from yesterday and realised I got them completely mixed up. According to my notes we should be arming postal workers and privatising Syria. Oh, unless that's right.

WEDNESDAY Meeting of the government's Strategic Mentalising Unit, a freestyle think tank convened to posit the unknowable.

I've been co-opted to help with Operation Stitch-Up, an ambitious programme to reunite the north and south of England for the first time since the 1966 World Cup.

Of course it's all a bit of a pantomime. The Coalition thinks it can win the next general election by persuading everyone that the two halves of the country give a flying toss about one another, and that the best thing to do is award billions to a consortium of Tory donors to make the trains go faster.

This stuff is just for the punters. Behind the scenes, I've won tacit approval for my Reboot of the Seven Kingdoms masterplan – a return to traditional eighth-century values via a federalised UK.

Under the 7K2 Initiative, an economically cleansed London would be the centrepiece of New Anglia, a vast gated leisure and retail complex full of unsmiling people who look a bit like Jodie Foster. Meanwhile, cultural and administrative functions would move to a restored Tamworth, capital of New Mercia, where preparations are already well underway to create a Staffordshire version of Brasilia but with ale and pies.

And what shall be the destiny of New Wessex? That is a question of interest only to the four tribal leaders of The People of The West, whose beaded hair and timeless, loose-fitting garments are eloquent of an ancestral magic mediated these days through craft shop franchises, 'surfer-turfer' cuisine and hedgerow management. Nobody gives a fuck what happens to New Wessex, is what I'm saying.

Right now the priority is to make the north of England more attractive to the business community of London and the home counties. Remember, we're building a high-speed rail link. For that to be viable or sustainable or roll-outable or whatever it is this week we have to persuade the target group of 'BMWs' (bankers and media wankers) that it's worth their while travelling beyond Milton Keynes. A quick refresh of the north is required:

- Fully enclosed tram system in Redcar so nobody has to look at Redcar.
- Sheffield's public libraries converted into wine bars with retro-fitted 'book nooks' where young professionals with 'hairchitecture' can relax, shout at one another and mock the very ideas of books and silence.
- Jamie Oliver restaurant within a Tate within a Westfield shopping centre within an otherwise ignorable Carlisle.
- Enhanced weather with wifi connectivity in Warrington.
- High speed 'hotel trains' allowing passengers the opportunity to see the north 'safari style'.

THURSDAY Designing a new headquarters building for Google. Stuck for inspiration, so I do a wide-spectrum search on Wikipedia for 'compassionate fascism'.

Goldstrike. By lunchtime I've harvested a shitload of info on how to moderate monumentality with soft money and nursery colours. I chuck in a Spotify playlist of non-threatening hip-hop for good measure.

FRIDAY Designing a new headquarters for Wikipedia. Mind's a blank, so I do a wide-spectrum Google search for 'unverified provenance'.

Bingo. By lunchtime I've assembled enough crowdsourced architectural wisdom to bang out a prototype live-work hivemind in built form, with hundreds of interconnected cells and a big empty space in the middle. I articulate the spatial ambience with a Spotify list of easy-listening punk.

SATURDAY Five-a-zeitgeist theoretical football. Grand Theft Autonomic Urbanism 5, Teleological Meta-Identity Cloning 5, after reciprocal cross-platform shootout.

SUNDAY Trawl through the papers in the recliner. I try to avoid international news these days. There are only so many pictures of blighted neighbourhoods you can look at.

I mean, where's the community spirit? If on the way to the shops everyone picked up just one piece of rubble, the world would be on its way to being a better place. Selfishness and a wilful lack of understanding. That's what's killing us.

September 24, 2013

154

Supra-Heezy Ionised Piff

MONDAY Well, DUH. Doy-oy-oing. Of COURSE a new wave of Pre-Modernism is now rushing in to fill Post-Modernism's death vacuum. What ELSE was going to happen?

I predicted all this in the early 90s, along with Britpop, both Gulf wars, the demise of the classic phone box, and the whole internet shopping thing. We're in for another decade of bet-hedging, old-new melangey pragmatism before the proper stuff starts up again.

My advice now, as then, is to talk loudly about Baggy Urban Zoomorphism as a necessary counterpoint to Pre-Modernism, or risk sounding like a complete dick.

TUESDAY Sure, we can all sneer at an uneducated trillionaire gangster in exile, seeking reinvention by imposing himself and his fictionalised ancestry on the English countryside. But not all of us can design an inflatable pop-up castle for him, can we?

It's the size of Blenheim but we don't need planning permission because a) it's classed as a temporary tensile structure and b) as I say, trillionaire.

Obviously you have to be careful early on with inflatable pop-up castles – no swords indoors, etc. – but once it's been demonstrably inflated there's nothing stopping you from filling it in with cement, putting proper floorboards down and so on. The current rural development regime is in many ways very much LIKE an inflatable pop-up castle, in that it has lots of loopholes moulded into it.

Next on my inflatable pop-up to-do list: a new Heston Blumenthal restaurant in a zeppelin moored over St James's Park, called Blimp; a giant mobile gym modelled on a hamster ball; a cluster of bubble housing in a secluded, deluded part of Manchester, ironically named The Affordabubble.

WEDNESDAY Ach, I forgot to put design quality at the heart of the creative process. That's a whole morning up the fucking chimney. I start again, and put a note on the fridge to remind me next time.

THURSDAY Honoured that *Dope Gaff* magazine has voted my 'ambient urbipad' its Sick Crib of the Year.

The judges commended its 'top atmos…a classy finish delivers the perfect hang-work space…great for showing off to your mates at weekends or if you just be solo jamming yo'.

Tremendous. Very pleased with it, I must say. A series of four uncompromising container shed-like boxes piled up in an uncompromising heap, the urbipad was slipped into a gap in a North Finchey terrace, without any of the neighbours noticing.

The boxes, or 'environments', are sheathed in a variety of off-beat skins (living bark, digital lichen, vinyl albums, petrified halloumi) to give it an eclectic desirability and the neighbours, bless them, are now used to groups of admirers in skinny jeans and Edwardian tops hanging around outside to see who's going to emerge next.

Last week the owner, CEO of a 'grimefolk tonal logistics corporation', had Miley Cyrus round. And THREE of Frank Sinatra's grandchildren.

Let's not forget the eco stuff. You've got to shove that in or what's the point? So the whole unassuming stack of calmness is crowned with a sustainable 'sky meadow'. This blends urban context and nature's bombast with sheaves of coneflowers, echinacea, hellebore, wild strawberry, a banging sound system and a Brutalist barbeque modelled on Stockwell bus station.

The Sick Crib award is particularly gratifying as the building was designed to Vibe Code for Awesome Homes Level 8. It features 'chill piles' utilising a shiznit-assisted ground-source dench pump to deliver supraheezy ionised piff directly to a quality bliss bank slumped below ground level.

One can only envy the neighbours who bask within its vibal curtilage.

FRIDAY From vibal to tidal, as I sketch out some ideas to upgrade that mysterious stretch of the Thames – the bit that actually moves.

I've been asked to explore ways of getting people to acknowledge the river's existence – an important first step towards heightened awareness, increased interaction and ultimately, fond memories of a terrific day out on a mudbank including dinner in a squelching pontooned café and a trip to Gravesend and back in an amphibious bus.

Other thoughts: mysterious wiggly red line running along the length of the river. Some weird maps. A community project called 'Edible Biodiversity' to encourage local 'mud people' to nurture biodiversity by eating it, creating a perfect circle of 'sanctuary to sandwich'.

SATURDAY Five-a-zeitgeist theoretical football. Pre-Modernism 1, Pre-Modernism 2, after extra time and a pitch implosion.

SUNDAY Recharge batteries in the recliner by being asleep.

October 10, 2013

Insulational Rescue

MONDAY Lunch with my fixer, Rock Steady Eddie. He seems very – almost chemically – motivated. 'We should put MORE energy into LESS energy, wanna write that down, mate, you finishing them fancy nuts?' he gasps, excitedly.

There's a new report on the government's Right to Be Cosy initiative, which offers grants to hard-working householders who want to stay warm in the run-up to the next general election. It looks pretty convincing. There's a picture of a cheerful bloke in green overalls laughing like a donkey at a hole in someone's wall, with a bag of granular stuffing.

'It's not just lagging old gaffs,' says Eddie authoritatively through a mouthful of nuts. 'They wedge you up for like solar pumps and I don't know, warm air recycling bins, same again, I'm going to the toilet...' He slides his iPad over, its smeary, sneeze-freckled screen not quite managing to mask an Executive Summary.

It makes for pretty grim reading. Despite several relaunches of the scheme – variously badged 'Feel The Benefit', 'Turn that Light Off', 'Come On Britain Let's Save Some Energy, Yeah?' and 'Please Yourself DON'T Use a Passive-Aggressive Heat Exchanger Then' – people just aren't that interested in hooking up with private contractors trying to profit from the system.

The summary notes a 'surprising resistance' to cold calls from UK energy efficiency contractors mysteriously based in the Far East, offering a free home survey and also while they're on, noticing that your PC has been infected with a poisonous virus. I still don't see why any of this should interest me and my business associate, who has arrived at the bar sniffing loudly and zipping up his trousers.

'Scroll down, you doughnut,' he says, pointing me to the nub of his argument: 'At the current rate of 13,000 homes a month being assessed, it would take 160 years to survey all the homes in the UK.' So what?

'So what? Say we're energy efficiency contractors and we're pitching for the whole lot…' He pulls out the heavy Amstrad pocket calculator which has guided his thinking since the 1980s.

'Even allowing for fluctuations in interest rates, at say five hundred quid a home, you're looking at about…three billion pounds. Each.'

TUESDAY I offer up some possible snags to Eddie's masterplan. Neither of us is going to be around in 160 years, for a start.

Furthermore, the logistics of carrying out an energy efficiency survey of every home in Britain? Frankly, I've been inside some of them and they're horrible. Carpeted bathrooms. Weird fabrics thrown over furniture. Artificial log fires. People are idiots, their anecdotes are often long and tedious…

Eddie, however, is focused on the much bigger picture.

WEDNESDAY 'All they're worried about is take-up, right? Here's my five-point plan, I'll have a large one, cheers.' I have to admire his logic, which as usual takes a direct path from idea to payoff.

1. Go into department of whatever and tell them we can deliver 90 per cent take up for their hippie house-warming bullshit if they appoint us sole contractor from now on.
2. Put a notice in one of the good papers that it's all being done on an opt-out deal. If you don't tell us you don't want a free survey, you're taking it up.
3. Bosh.
4. Department of whatever announces a stonking 90 per cent take-up, looks like the government's doing something to stop heatwaves in Scotland and the sea going mental with polar bears floating tits up in it, cheers.
5. Invoice department of whatever for six billion. See 3 above.

THURSDAY Our initial approach to the department of energy and climate change is less than encouraging.

Their view is that an open market for energy efficiency contractors offers the best value for money for hard-warming householders, and also that six billion seems pretty steep.

FRIDAY Eddie refuses to be downhearted. 'Sod this, let's have a pop at overseas. Google "government in crisis, high energy cost, fix, sorted" and get us some cheese and onion.'

Search results: Iran, Greece and the Isle of Wight.

SATURDAY Greece and the Isle of Wight have blown us out but Iran is game. Eddie's formally requested the addresses of everyone in the republic, an estimate of how long it would take to survey everything, and 160 years' worth of fax rolls for an Amstrad Tonto 2000.

SUNDAY Form autonomous republic in the recliner.

October 17, 2013

An Inspector Calls

MONDAY My latest gift to the world is the invisible bedroom.

Internal walls are made of transparent 'hard air'* blocks. The space itself is saturated with ionised nanospheric optical glanceback 'gnobules' (patent applied for). These trick the human brain into wanting to go to the toilet urgently.

I'm hoping my invisible bedroom will hoodwink the portly new army of government bedroom tax inspectors. Bring it on, you fat bumptious jobsworths.

TUESDAY To semi-rural Essex, where a beta version of the invisible bedroom has been created in a local authority house occupied by my old friend Amy Blackwater, the ecomentalist and recently disabled activist.

She's been a bit down in the dumps lately, what with having to use a wheelchair, antagonising all her carers, being told she's fit for work and threatened with financial penalties for having too many rooms. The latest indignity is being threatened with the loss of social security benefits altogether unless she takes her balaclava off.

WEDNESDAY 'Those squares and breadheads can do one' she says firmly when I arrive. 'My bally is an expression of who I am. It's my turban, or burqa. I am sick of people telling me they can't see my face. This IS my face. And it's wearing a balaclava, OK?'

Great to see you too. She burbles on crossly while I check the invisible bedroom, giving it a final spritz of glanceback gnobules before the inspector arrives.

Oh, here he is now, pulling up outside in his silver saloon. A few muffled bars of 'Don't Stop Believin'' by Journey. Then the music dies, paperwork is gathered and a chubby, prematurely middle-aged G4S bedroom inspector beetles purposefully up to the front door. He seems completely at ease with his own cruel destiny, like an overweight Tarantino Nazi.

When Amy opens the door he simply holds his hand up and continues to huff into one of those ridiculous earpieces that look like a child's kazoo. 'Yeah, at first address now, over. Wheelie present. Roger that. Entering premises. Going offline, over. Right, love, I've come to count your bedrooms, yeah? What's going on with the mask then? Been in a fire, or you in a band or something? Who's this, your Dad?'

'Show us your ID,' demands Amy. 'For all I know you're just some fat knobhead with a clipboard.' There's an uneasy silence while he fishes out and flourishes his inspector card. 'OK, Pussy Riot? Now, let's count your fucking bedrooms.'

Man, it was worth every tedious second developing the hard air/gnobule prototypes with my nanotechnologist mate Beansy, just to see Fat Bedroom Cop's face wrinkled into a Martian landscape by unaccustomed brainwork. 'It says here this is two-bed...' 'Well how many bedrooms can you SEE?' I can hear Amy say. I'm inside the locked bathroom.

'Can I use your toilet?' 'No. It's engaged. You'll have to go down the pub'. 'I'm desperate!' 'Sorry love, that's the way the world is. You brought this on yourself...' I can hear Fatso ringing in to say Amy's house is one-bedroom and that he needs the toilet and he's going to the pub, over. Then a loud crack. Then silence. Then Amy humming 'Don't Stop Believin''.

THURSDAY This is the worst day out with Amy since that time I helped her with her animal laboratory thing. I was always against the fire-bombing, it was a late work by the Smithsons.

But burying a bedroom tax inspector in Epping Forest is worse. Dead people weigh a TON.

Yesterday's just a blur of gloves and fingerprint removal and driving the car to the pub and walking very quickly back, then heaving the body into the boot of Amy's car – 'don't look at me, I'm in a bloody wheelchair' – then discovering this is the THIRD inspector Amy's murdered since the legislation came into effect earlier this year.

And to think my invisible bedroom was conceived as a force for good.

FRIDAY Amy's interviewed by the police. Inspector Morose has been listed as a missing person and they're trying to trace his final movements. There's a faint smell in the hallway still from his last involuntary toilet break. Feel a bit sorry for Amy, who'll no doubt be blamed.

SATURDAY Moral dilemma. Maintain the invisible bedroom, or remove the incriminating invisible evidence?

SUNDAY Lie low in the recliner, waiting for a knock on the door.

November 8, 2013

Owning the Vagination

MONDAY Oh no, I've accidentally designed a sports stadium that looks like a vagina. In my defence, it was an experiment in parametric neuroscience. The facts are these.

1. A quarter-page ad appeared in the Qatari version of Exchange and Mart. Anonymous, box number. 'Looking for kick-ass parametric neuroscientist, into 3-D auteuring/procuring world-class soccer hub capable of delivering at the highest architectural level, men only, please send photograph.'

2. My fixer, Rock Steady Eddie, responded with a compelling Wikipedia-sourced pitch explaining that I specialised in 'curvitecture, which enters the brain via the eyes, stimulating the anterior cingulate cortex and making people all emotional, thereby enhancing the visitor experience and widening the whatever, aesthetic offer' and attached a photo of Michael Fassbender.

3. 'We' got the job, avoiding all contact with my client by submitting a forged doctor's note and a covering letter from Eddie explaining that I had 'a rare condition which has left him allergic to sunlight so he just lives and works in the dark like the Elephant Man or a French novelist, sorry for any inconvenience this may cause'.

4. I designed the stadium using the latest voice-to-space app, telling my laptop that I wanted the building to collate the latest building design trends in movie blockbusters and cough up an amalgam. It must be organic, futuristic, art nouvesque. Wavy. Curvy. Tough. But NB must NOT attract giant alien lifeforms or explode in a spectacular fireball of flame and matter.

5. The renderings were released in an upbeat press release and now

everyone thinks it looks like a vagina. Curse this voice-to-space app, I should have done it the old fashioned way with manually inputted data and aeronautical modelling software.

TUESDAY My Qatari clients make matters worse by refusing to acknowledge that the stadium looks like a vagina. 'Rather, the design reflects the smooth lines of a traditional pearl divers' dhow.'

WEDNESDAY Now 'pearl diving' has gone viral as a sexual euphemism, and there is a great clamour for me to speak on the issue. On the advice of my lawyer (Eddie's brother-in-law Legal Brian) I therefore issue a holding statement making it clear that I have no problem with a sports stadium looking like a vagina, feigning surprise that anyone else might.

THURSDAY The vaginal brouhaha is now at a critical level, so I decide to take it to the global media on my own terms.

I agree to be interviewed by the arts correspondent of Radio 4's *Today*. I was expecting an easy ride, as I have occasionally listened to the programme and formed the opinion that its arts correspondent was a simpering tosser.

Imagine my surprise when his first question concerns my nonresemblance to Michael Fassbender. It's clear that the Qataris are moving behind the scenes to shut me down. For all I know they have bought the BBC.

I have nothing to lose now, so I own the vagination. I say that it is a counter-patriarchal act at the very heart of the football industry (the World Cup or something is happening there at some point). A stadium that looks like a vagina is an act of reparation for all the phallic buildings throughout the world, oppressing our urban landscapes.

Of course, I get carried away with my own rhetoric and claim that vagitecture is going to be massive and there's nothing anyone can do to stop me designing everything in the shape of a vagina. I ignore the small voice in my anterior cingulate cortex telling me to shut the fuck up, and boast that I've now got a long waiting list of clients who want all sorts of buildings that look like fannies.

A vagina-shaped gated lido in Wandsworth. A pop-up vaginal cinema in Hackney. A magistrates court, the remodelling of a privatised local authority estate, a Great British Baking School. All shaped like vaginas. Up yours, patriarchitecture.

FRIDAY It took about seven minutes before the Twitter backlash started. I'm apparently now exploiting the female form and am no better than Hugh Bloody Hefner. Someone photoshopped my face into a vagina and it's everywhere.

SATURDAY The twitterstorm has moved on – they're demanding an apology from Russell Brand for something else now – but nobody wants their building to look like a vagina any more.

SUNDAY Spend the day moping in the recliner, like a dick.

November 22, 2013

A Bubble of Absence Enclosed by Sentient Retardant Foam

MONDAY Amazing. I've found a glitch in the Fibonacci Series.

You know the way those 'golden spirals' always looked so glamorously widescreen but sort of anal at the same time? Turns out there was a clerical error at Fn-2.

Yeah, apparently the sequence copier failed to put the 2 in italic when she was transferring it from papyrus to vellum. Nobody seems to know why. Perhaps she was an innately conservative mathematician who thought it was too dangerous to give forward-leaning emphasis to a number as it was about to hit one of several very difficult curves.

Maybe in her imagination she saw how an italicised 2 might set off a chain epiphany, rendering all subsequent drawn art 'formulaic'. Maybe she thought a perfectly beautiful Fibonacci series would instantly kill anyone who saw it.

Whatever, the result was that Fn-2 braked a little too suddenly and skidded slightly. I have now corrected the entire series, making sure everything's in italics, and it looks a bit like a Chelsea bun. I make no apologies. Truth is beauty. The world will be obliged to behold it.

TUESDAY Spend the morning in a nostalgic reverie for the International Style.

Experience a lunchtime transition to gloomy reality. Immerse myself for the afternoon in something called the New Global Fashion For High-

Yield Contemporaneity. It sounds similar to the International Style but instead it makes your heart sore.

WEDNESDAY The world of epic time and space is all a-quimble. No sooner had the latest redesign of *Doctor Who* detonated like an expensive firework across the digital media sky than an ideas competition for the NEXT redesign was immediately announced.

I think everyone's scared of *Doctor Who* fans not being in a permanent state of volatile expectation. As per the terms of the global licensing mandate, all *Doctor Who* interiors must 'undergo a refresh' once every five Earth years or once every 100 Whovian Nanobits if you're some weird adult with an improvised costume and a forum name.

My fixer Rock Steady Eddie and I are rock-steady ready. We spend the whole of an extended pub workshop mapping out the parameters. Time and space are an illusion. But are they the same illusion? Or are they separate but mutually dependent illusions? Or is it the illusion of space and time that is itself the illusion?

We exchange knowing, wonky looks and go our separate ways, Eddie to the bookmakers to put a monkey on What the Inside of the Next Tardis Will Look Like, and me to my studio to produce it.

THURSDAY A long, busy day locked into my own hyperdriven thoughts as I bang out *Doctor Who* interiors to a Delia Derbyshire soundtrack.

First the Tardis, which I have designed to Eddie's tight specification. 'Like being inside a lava lamp but them ones with glitter in, also a few weird sofas round the walls for chilling out between leaps through time and space, what about unisex toilets but get this they're uniSPECIES, a big fridge with everything like floating inside and it's only the size of a matchbox, all the Tardis controls in the air so you just wiggle your fingers about and bosh, weird bits of floor that you walk on and turn invisible or naked depending what side of the watershed we're talking about PS think glowing globules they're always good.'

Next, a selection of alien interiors. A bubble of absence enclosed by sentient retardant foam. Solid inhabitable wood, where the molecular essence of a character can move through the grain like rot. Crudely-drawn pink cube hovering above a strange landscape ready to be filled in by the viewer's imagination.

FRIDAY Submit my *Doctor Who* interiors just in time – the *Monty Python* lot want me to design a sustainable stage set capable of taking the live show 'beyond death itself'. Start working on a hilarious gilded cage containing ironic comfy chairs, only to be interrupted by a call asking me to design the Christmas party at the Finnish embassy and then there's a text seeking my resolution package for the Middle East, wait...

SATURDAY I'd nodded off in the pub with Eddie. All a dream. Wednesday to Friday was actually a dull trudge through invoices, accounts and design revisions for some buy-to-let arsehole in Cyprus.

SUNDAY Self-re-evaluation in the recliner. I've let *Doctor Who* down, I've let *Monty Python* down. Most importantly, I've let the Finns down. Will resolve Middle East next week.

November 29, 2013

Get a Grip, Munchniks

MONDAY I'm making Advent much more relevant this year by working for a client who's a ruthless giant internet retailer and who's paying me to redesign Advent.

Yeah, Advent's getting a sheeny, omnilayered fractal shakeover. I'm importing trans-global style narratives, incorporating supramorphic cultural push alerts and reworking the Christian calendar while I'm at it.

The First Day of Advent will begin on the Sunday after Black Friday, which follows Thanksgiving or Hannukah, whichever is closest to your credit limit.

From now on Advent will, I propose, be encased in a sparkling muslin sleeve, with windows along the side that open when you've collected enough reward points. All pets antlered. All snowflakes identical. Compliments of the season.

TUESDAY Once again I'm on the judging panel for the *Creative on Sunday*'s Hot Building Material of the Year Award.

The award is showcased in the newspaper's 'life and property' section *Equity,* so we need a building material that will look good *in situ.* And by *in situ* we mean preferably the light-drenched living room of an expanded London terraced house currently rising in value by seven per cent a month.

The Hot Building Material of the Year must be infuriatingly cheap, with a boho insouciance that makes the featured unsmiling couple who've installed it the envy of their social circle.

After rejecting 'a gorgeously ostentatious insulation' made from panels of flamingo feathers and gold leaf and a 'safely depleted' uranium dado rail, we decide on 'floorboards rescued from a neighbour's skip'. The new owners do indeed look very pleased with them, and with themselves.

WEDNESDAY It suddenly occurs to me that – bear with me here – if we design in the present with a respect for the past we will create better buildings for the future.

Deep, yeah? It sounds so clever and insightful, I can't believe nobody's thought of it before.

THURSDAY Certain people were 'shocked' to discover recently that as much land is occupied by golf courses in England as by homes.

Oh boo hoo. Stop doing your clumsy impersonation of *The Scream* and get a grip, Munchniks. A golf course is a much more efficient use of land than homes, for the following reasons which should be obvious to anyone in the epic space industry.

Firstly, as per the definition of a garden as 'an outside room', that's all a golf course is. One, admittedly massive, room.

Secondly, with that whole 'one outside room' thing still in your head, look at the number of people who use a typical golf course as opposed to, say, a typical living room. It's not like you've got quartets of people queueing up to tramp across your living room at five-minute intervals all day is it, Mr and Mrs Munch?

Thirdly, a golf course is a place for quiet contemplation, a place to find inspiration. People going on about how many executive homes you could fit on a golf course should pause for a moment and ask themselves where architects and planners might actually BE when they're mapping out that new development of luxury residential investment. That's right. On the GOLF COURSE. OK, maybe in the clubhouse. But you can't have a clubhouse without a golf course. Or maybe you don't WANT architects and planners to have somewhere civilised to chat and think, is that what you're saying?

Fourthly, and clinchingly, golf courses are green. They've even got the word 'green' in the…map thing. How many black redstarts or frogs or badgers have you got in your so-called ecological houses? None.

I rest my case, and by the way am definitely in the market for any golf course-related public inquiry work.

FRIDAY Boom. I've been appointed chief visionary for the Independent Scotland we all hope is just around the corner.

My new Scottish Design Guide will promote a rugged, swirling architecture, full of tartan grids and exquisite details with the word 'wee' in front. I want to nurture the 'soul' of Scotland, which is why I will be encouraging value growth and engineered well-being. Plus a land bridge to Scandinavia.

SATURDAY Five-a-zeitgeist theoretical football. Regenerational Colonialism 1, Resurgent Caledonialism 2, after penalty spellcheck and the discovery that theoretical football was actually invented in Caledonia.

SUNDAY Media review in the recliner. The Hot Building Material of the Year coverage in the *Creative on Sunday* looks good, but now the police are worried it might lead to a spate of floorboard burglaries.

December 6, 2013

Laughable Bear in a Frock

MONDAY 'Animals. Now that's a client base worth cracking you mark my words, can I have them chips, got any wi-fi on your mob?'

Rock Steady Eddie, my fixer, is explaining how the 'charity game' is changing the nature of client funding by jabbing at my phone with a sausage. 'Everybody loves a donkey sanctuary, I get that. But this is off the hook, son...'

This year's *Times* Animal Rich List is out. There's always something new. The richest animal in Britain this year is Caspia, a three-year-old Siberian bear owned by Iain Duncan Smith. She has her own apartment in Pimlico and a reading age of five.

I laugh cruelly. There's a photo of her arriving at the Royal Academy's Nativity Concert for Cancer Research in a gown designed by Daniel Libeskind. She looks fucking ridiculous. The gown's exquisitely tragic, cut on the bias but to little effect as she's mostly on all fours. And the shoes! Really, heels? Up those steps?

'Laugh all you like, mate, but it may interest you to know that this

Caspia has a disposable income of about three million sovs a year. Tax-deductible too, IDS knows how to play the system. It may ALSO interest you to know that this laughable bear in a frock has just been revealed as a leading affordable home provider working in partnership with Bristol City Council. This bear is a potential client now. Think about THAT while you're getting another round in.'

TUESDAY Oh my God, Eddie's right about the donkeys. People are giving so much money to this sanctuary in Dorset that even when admin and overheads are deducted each of the 14 donkeys is worth north of two mill per annum.

They've all got AGENTS now. None of this 'cameo on CBeebies for a scratch behind the ear and a bucketful of carrots' rubbish any more. They're pros. And they're planning a chain of sanctuaries called Nuzzle and someone's got the corporate design gig and it isn't me.

WEDNESDAY Eddie and I work our way through the Potential Animal Client list.

Mr Breezy, an oligarch's parrot, holds 51 per cent of the shares in a leisure development company.

A hedge fund ruthlessly buying up arable farmland in Gloucestershire has for the first time appointed a pair of swans – Tony and Carmela – as joint procurement managers.

A swarm of bees owned by former Coalition arts minister the Hon. Anaeas Upmother-Brown are now the collective head of innovation at Sainsbury's.

Eddie tells me he's not stupid. 'Some of these appointments are strategic. Some might even be a front, we don't know. I see that dog you used to knock about with is Number 87 on the list...'

Indeed. It gives me no pleasure to discover that my former acquaintance, the preposterous architectural dachshund Bauhau, is now head of the Bartlett school of architecture. AND running a hugely influential atelier in Shanghai.

Curse him and his ridiculous clothes... Eddie's snapping his fingers. 'Come on, son, focus. We need to concentrate on these gannets. And puffins.'

THURSDAY A quick day trip to Lister Craigs, a group of volcanic islands off the Ayrshire coast. Some nature conservation trust has just bought the lot – via a massively oversubscribed crowdsourcing initiative – to secure the future of Europe's largest gannet colony. The islands are also home to a shitload of puffins.

There's not much to see. A ruined castle here, some cottages there. It's mostly birds. 'We need to find out what they want and then take their demands to the new owners innit!' shouts Eddie, struggling to light a fag in the whooping gale.

FRIDAY The young people at Ornithol seem surprised when we turn up without an appointment and brandishing a client wishlist. Eddie is adamant.

'Can gannets and puffins get along? Do you care? Cos it's all a bit Sunni and Shia up there, mate. You need to get an income stream going, peace and prosperity, yeah?'

They seem less hostile to the ecological five-star gambling and hotel development than we'd expected, although of course we do propose preserving a lot of the landscape. Maybe for them securing the absence of Eddie is enough of a result for now.

SATURDAY Eddie calls. 'Fancy a quick one down the Gannet and Puffin? Wire transfer's come through...'

SUNDAY Conserve self in recliner.

December 13, 2013

Extended Prison Break

MONDAY It doesn't look like it'll be a brilliant Christmas, to be honest. I'm being done for accessory to murder.

My counsel, Legal Brian, is brutally candid. 'They got you bang to rights, mate. CCTV, witnesses, fingerprints, DNA, confession. I don't know if you play poker at all but as evidence goes, it's a full house.

'My advice? Plead guilty but sort of look innocent and hope the courtroom artist doesn't chalk you up like a kipper. Swear to God, half the time the judge is just checking Twitter on his phone, it could go either way, we did say cash, right?'

Legal Brian is the brother-in-law of Rock Steady Eddie, my fixer. Eddie has been anything but conspicuous lately. I'm getting Brian's Mates' Rates obviously. But it's still going to cost more than sixty quid for what now seems like pretty flimsy counsel, if I'm honest.

TUESDAY On the other hand of course he's dead right. All advice is irrelevant. My dear, reckless, stupid acquaintance Amy Blackwater has now cheerfully claimed responsibility for the deaths of 'at least' four ATOS assessors.

She hasn't always been such a handful. I remember her in the pre-balaclava days, before she embraced angry ecomentalism. An easy-going archivist at the Soot Association, chronicling the rise and fall of particulate carbon as a cultural signifier.

Then something happened, nobody knows what it was, and everything changed. Amy became a snarling avenger, passionate in her many animal- and vegetable-related campaigns, meticulous in the calibrated severity of vengeance she meted out to a hitlist of absolute tossers. She became an anarchivist.

I admit her latest campaign overstepped the mark. Her temper's got much worse since she became a wheelchair user, and I think the sheer indignity of being bullied by the DWP's thick, spiteful agency bouncers was too much. You can't excuse murder, even if the victims were horrible sadists trying to hit targets for witholding benefits from the most vulnerable people, you know what? Sod it, you CAN excuse it.

Obviously like all sane people I drew a line at her plan to shoot Iain Duncan Smith in the face, though I'm not saying which side I drew it on.

WEDNESDAY Text from Rock Steady Eddie: 'Best keep our distance til all this shit blows over dubais coming up again ill be staying at the burj whateverthefuck take it easy son yeah r s eddie.'

THURSDAY Amy's been sentenced to a long stretch in a private prison. I've heard it's pretty grim, despite being designed by chartered architects. She's been invited to upgrade for an extra grand a month, which would pay for someone to help her in and out of the wheelchair occasionally.

After lunch, my doctor's note – from Medical Sonia, another of Eddie's family finds – goes down badly. The judge sounded quite sarcastic, reading it out in a Radio 4 Cockerney drama voice.

'Please excuse Ian from prison. He had one of them Fugue States, I don't know if you've seen *Breaking Bad* but like what Walt had in that. Yours, Dr Sonia Kedgehog MDMA.'

I am sentenced to one year in an open prison, on condition that I don't become disabled.

FRIDAY Brilliant luck. HMP Archer is very middle class, stuffed with distinguished fraudsters, tax-dodgers and insider traders.

Quite a few of us from the epic space industry, too. My cellmate is Gav, a 'panterior designer' who's in for aggravated window dressing. By lunchtime we've formed a partnerhip with a view to rethinking the prison and maybe getting some time off our sentences.

One brainstorming session later, we've rebranded the whole place as a boutique kibbutz with scope for secure affordable housing, a permanent pop-up, or 'stay-up' craft fair and a civil partnership centre.

The governor's pretty receptive. As he says, in a hypermonetised private prison sector it's all about unlocking those doors to increased margin through innovation and outpush.

SATURDAY Five-a-side interdisciplinary prison football. Artistic Insularists 4, Professional Claustrophobes 5, after seasonal name-weighting and casual match-fixing.

SUNDAY Horizontal brainwork in the bunk. Am told unofficially I could be out by next spring if I behave myself, do the prison makeover with Gav on what the governor calls 'a pro bono shareholdico basis' and stop communicating satirically with the outside world. Fingers crossed.

December 20, 2013

Yesterday's News Is Tomorrow's Emergency Clothing

MONDAY They say that after a few months in prison you have to come out one way or another and here I am, about to rejoin the free world. I've been released early from HMP Archer for good behaviour. And by paying a one-off fee under the government's new Affordable Leniency scheme.

Thank God for the privatisation of everything. The seriousness of my crime – accessory to the murder of an ATOS assessor – diminished dramatically when ATOS announced they were 'getting out of the disabled benefits game'. This was also good news for my associate Amy Blackwater, the ecomentalist and murderer.

Despite bumping off four bedroom tax inspectors Amy will be released later this year, unrepentant and unrehabilitated. She's already planning another killing spree when she gets out, starting with private landlords and ending with people who call anything but a journey 'a journey'.

TUESDAY I am being discharged with the random clutter I went in with. About to bin a copy of a newspaper from December 2013 ('Good news at last as house prices surge beyond the reach of anyone who actually lives in Britain') but decide to hang on to it.

For all I know my gaff has been repossessed by auditors. Or squatted by creditors. If I DO end up sleeping on a bench tonight I'm buggered if I'm buying a newspaper.

WEDNESDAY God, it feels like I've been banged up for half a century. The world has changed beyond recognition.

Another 65 skyscrapers in London since Christmas! All designed by budget algorithm generators in India, then shat out in situ by Chinese 3-D printers for fictional Russian owners. Soulless, pointless husks of calcified ennui, precisely engineered for a market that requires them only to remain empty and silent. The world of plasmic arts shrugs and having shrugged moves on.

Yes, the world has become busier in the last few months but also spectacularly stupider too. The BBC's *Newsnight* had already turned into a parody of itself the last time I looked, but tonight's timely investigation into the capital's financial South Sea Bubble plumbed new depths of dumb.

Jeremy Paxman seemed very uncomfortable dressed as a Jolly Jack Tar in the nautically themed studio – 'Pirates of the Caribbean Tax Havens'. Even more uncomfortable when he had to leave his desk and dance a hornpipe, singing along to a vulgar sea shanty: 'What shall we do with the fucking Gherkin? What shall we do with the fucking Gherkin? What shall we do with the fucking Gherkin, it's back on the market…'

There followed several verses of suggestions, including the statutory jokey one about converting it into a huge tower of high-spec, low-rent apartments for key workers.

Memo to Self: dig out proposal for turning the Shard into a giant vertical urban farm.

THURSDAY Whoa. Theatrical agent Victoria Spong has died. I never liked her, to be honest. Someone who WILL miss her is the celebrated architectural dachshund Bauhau. Spong acquired him, then fashioned him into a media personality. I wonder if he'll now be auctioned off.

FRIDAY So much news to catch up with. I see the Royal Institute for the Pop-Uption of British Architects is in trouble for condemning the sequestration and development of Palestinian land for Jewish settlements in the West Bank.

I briefly consider applauding this moral stand. Just in time I remember that if I do, I MUST be anti-semitic. Clearly I don't want to be that, so decide to keep quiet. On reflection, I agree with the RIPBA's critics – you can't possibly condemn the Israeli government as long as the administrations of Saudi Arabia and Syria are more horrible.

I'd better shut up about architects working for demented arseholes anywhere at all, just to make sure. Then I worry about how the Twittermind of my subconscious might link the phrases 'Israeli settlers' and 'demented arseholes'. Resolve to stop thinking, in the interests of peace and justice.

SATURDAY Five-a-zeitgeist theoretical football. Macerated Relativism 1, Dynamic Nondeterminism 0.

SUNDAY Feels good to be back in the recliner after all those weeks in a prison bed. Although a little lonely, I have to say. I'd got used to the constant banter of my cellmate Gav, the ultra-butch panterior designer.

I realise I'm saying all this out loud to thin air. Sad. Idiot. Maybe I should get a dog...

May 9, 2014

The Emptiness Between All Particles

MONDAY Sketch out a protomeme for Expo Nano, the microbuilding and microdesign fair being held at a mirrored site on the Dark Internet.

Nanotypes are hoping the market improves soon. The average price of a bespoke nano-construction has fallen again, this time by 12 per cent in a year. To be honest, interest in the exciting new frontier territory of microscopic construction has pretty much been shoved aside by the whole 3-D printing business. Expo Nano's a desultory affair these days. A lot of exhibitors' avatars look unshaven and seem to be wearing the same outfits as last year.

Well prepare for an micro-earthquake, Expo Nano. Because my latest protomeme is about to bring sexy back to the under-underworld. How? By shifting focus AWAY from nerds in high-tech welding helmets fixing one tiny thing on to another tiny thing and waiting for a Nobel Prize, TOWARDS the exciting new world of nanofracking.

That's right. I've brilliantly combined the traditional world of nanotechnology with the exciting new world of detonating the fuck out of shit that's buried deep in the natural world. In partnership with my old friend Beansy the nanofuturologist, I have been exploring the possibilities inherent not just in 'stuff' but in the 'absence of stuff'.

Look at overcrowded-yet-empty-at-the-same-time-in-the-expensive-parts London. Nobody really gives a toss about quality architecture, it's raw space that's at a premium.

Well here's a fun fact: matter is not just particles, it's also the emptiness between. Simply by nanofracking all the spare space from the molecules in a Hammersmith bedsit, the canny nanodeveloper can create (theoretically) enough room to fill the O2.

Watch this expanded space.

TUESDAY Seminar on the Contemporary Lexicon of Epic Space. Lots of thirtysomethings here looking suspiciously like skateboarders.

One of the speakers is a London architect wearing a sort of rubber tube. He gets an appreciative snigger from the audience when talking about building occupants by using the acronym TMTs for 'trendy media types', despite demonstrably being one himself.

I resolve to have it out with him at the coffee break but things escalate quickly and I somehow manage to asphyxiate him with his own rubber tube. Oh bollocks, I CAN'T go back to prison. I've only just started an anger management course and they're aggressively strict about refunds.

WEDNESDAY Overnighter in the cells but my brief, Legal Brian, is upbeat. Apparently everyone hates the metropolitan elite now, including those newspapers responsible for sentencing guidelines.

THURSDAY Marvellous. Case dismissed. Ten minutes in and out. Pop-up magistrates court during the day, really nice Lebanese restaurant in the evening. Guilty of manslaughter, but only in the technical sense. Probation, with time off for the deceased's rubber tube clothing and generally elite demeanour.

Got a wink off the judge, too. Legal Brian was bang on about my wearing a suit and a Ukip rosette in court.

FRIDAY Lie low like a bungalow.

SATURDAY Fantastic vibe at Crouch End's World Squalidarity Day.

The Peter Mandelson Memorial Park looks splendid. Lots of local people have turned out in their most striking shabby chic clothes to articulate the plight of the world's poor. The children look adorable in 'cast-off' Euro 2004 T-shirts and ill-fitting camouflage trousers.

An educational favela has been set up at one end of the park, allowing visitors to explore the gritty urban reality of a Rio de Janeiro, or a Tottenham without the guns but very much with the delicious street food. Local actors – one of Crouch End's largest indigenous groups – are in exquisite favela costumes, interacting with members of the public as 'misunderstood drug gang members' and 'corrupt police'.

There's a bouncy Greek jail and a collection of Improvised Toilets of Asia, with local actors guiding visitors along the toilet spectrum through the medium of mime.

A Caribbean tin and plywood shanty house is presented as a 'show home', with a local actor playing the part of a shanty town estate agent but – very important, this – making the satire unmistakably clear. Throughout the park, casually arranged on the grass, are members of Crouch End's singer-songwriter community, the area's second largest social grouping: a fat Woody Guthrie here, a mumsy Pussy Riot there.

The sun sets. Local actors return to houses that have increased in value by two grand during the afternoon, wiser but guiltier.

SUNDAY Abandon recliner. Too much cynical reflux.

May 30, 2014

Fuck Shitter

MONDAY To Seaquest Detention Park, on a PFI stretch of the Lincolnshire coast. It's the flagship of the new 'free prison' fleet, run by secure accommodation provider Capitcha. I'm here to see my old friend, the ecomentalist Amy Blackwater.

Amy's getting out next month on semi-compassionate grounds. As a wheelchair user she's more expensive to keep banged up at Her Majesty's Indifference. The parole people have decided it's better for everyone if Amy's sent home, declared fit for work and has her benefits cut. Again.

She seems very cheerful when I meet her in the prison soft drinks bar. She's been guzzling Virgin Marys and they've left a lipsticky smile on her balaclava. I wonder briefly why she's wearing a headscarf as well. What's she planning to do when she's released? She points firmly to the ceiling. 'That is in the hands of ALLAH!' The nearby ox-faced teenage security guards move away a little.

TUESDAY Thank God, or Allah, for that. Amy's new religion is merely a ruse, another way of making herself indigestible. The privatised prison whale does not want a Muslim in a wheelchair roiling around in its guts. It wants to spit her out into the privatised sea of social services as quickly as possible.

Once the guards were out of earshot yesterday, she explained that for the past few months she's been corresponding with a billionaire anarchist. 'Calls himself the Angel of Death. Used to be a developer in the 80s. Patron of the arts or some shit. Apparently Prince Charles and that lot stopped him building a load of skyscrapers? Now he's watching all this bollocks go up in London and he is well bitter. Wants his revenge. Very interested in my past experience with explosives.'

I urge caution. People don't get out of prison and then just start blowing things up. 'He's dropped a mil in my account. Mate, I'm bringing down the SHARD. You in?' Oh God, I don't know.

WEDNESDAY The secretary of state for work and pensions wants me to 'rebadge the nanny state'. I'm wary.

The thing about Shitter is his capricious temperament. To his enemies he is a sneering Victorian melodrama of a man, an insufferable wanker, a sentimental yet spiteful bastard who greatly admires the work of Richard Curtis.

Friends, tenants, staff and employees all tell a very different, corroborated story. They say Shitter's a compassionate man, that Richard Curtis films make him CRY. Ha ha. Sure. I remember when Shitter pulled the wings off a wayward sparrow during the launch party for his book on Christian morality, *The Charitable Mind*.

He's a very quiet man. At meetings you can miss half the stuff he's mumbling. Or you suddenly realise you haven't heard him say anything for a while and there he is, hunkered down in a corner, finger to his lips, going 'shhhh…shhhh…'

Amy must never find out. As well as blowing up the Shard when she gets out she has also sworn to take Shitter's face off with a strimmer. I don't want to be collaterally strimmed. I'm not telling her.

THURSDAY Difficult to see what's left of the 'nanny state' TO rebadge. All benefits are now shame-tested. All non-free schoolchildren are demonised. All primary care patients are timewasters. All acute patients are bedblockers. With the help of the newspapers the Coalition's already recast food banks as political acts of aggression, and the smoking areas outside job centres as terrorist training camps.

My solution: redefine 'nanny'. Instead of being the sort of nanny who nurtures our most vulnerable people, let it be the other sort of nanny, who's just died, and we're selling off her bungalow and big back garden to a developer.

Shitter hits the roof, thinks I'm taking the piss. A row escalates. He says he knows people who could have me 'roughed up'. I tell him I know someone who could take his face off with a strimmer.

FRIDAY That's it. Fuck Shitter. And I am SO blowing up the Shard. Amy's given me some contacts to chase up while she's in clink. We're calling our-selves the Space Avengers. As those riot policemen always say: bring it on.

SATURDAY Fifty grand's appeared in my account, tagged 'THX-AoD'.

SUNDAY Moment of doubt in the recliner, dispelled by feeling of equilibrium. And a much better balance.

June 13, 2014

The Epic Space Foundation

MONDAY I've been commissioned by a spiritual project manager to redesign the mental landscape of Tony Blair.

It needs a total reset. Decide to tackle the overgrown, gloomy 'Mentalpotamia' of guilt and regret by ordering a full memory airstrike.

It's not an easy decision, mind-bombing, but look, doing the right thing rarely is.

After the rubble has been cleared, a multivalent plasma barrier will be activated around the conscience, accessed by the owner via a reconstructed Euston Arch guarded by armed clowns, in order to make everything seem 'less real'.

TUESDAY Idea: create London housing that's instantly 50 per cent more affordable by doubling the number of inhabitants.

WEDNESDAY Very excited. My plan to restore the legendary Epic Space Foundation has finally won approval from the provisional wing of the Liberal Metropolitan Elite. Alain de Botton and his mates held an extraordinary general meeting last night at Gymkhana and I've got the go-ahead as long as I change 'restore' to 'reboot'.

Oh, the Epic Space Foundation. This marvellous and erudite charitable institution, which did so much to keep alive the Festival of Britain in the fortnight after it closed, once dominated the world of architecture like a conversational Skylon of Excellence.

Indeed, many architectural conversationalists cite the absence of the foundation's guiding spirit as a key factor in the general shitness of buildings since April 27, 1963. That's when ESF chairman John Betjeman left its Charlotte Street headquarters to have lunch with Philip Larkin and never came back. The world of the built environment has effectively been in hibernation ever since.

I wanted to relaunch the foundation with fireworks, champagne, the lot. Plan A was to persuade the Royal Institute for the Pop-Uption of British Architects to move out of its grand home in Portland Place into something more befitting an admin centre for the processing of subscriptions – business park premises in Droitwich, say – so that the Epic Space Foundation could once again take up its rightful place at the heart of three-dimensionalised British auteurism.

Fat chance. The idea was firmly rejected by the very establishment squares and deadheads who have turned contemporary architecture into nothing more than a styling salon for developers. Curse them. Curse them all.

So I decided the relaunched foundation should 'do less, but better'. Plan B was a posh tent in Haggerston made from some kind of clever fabric. Just one permanent member of staff but with a huge reach thanks to television's insatiable appetite for petrified money. Alas, the TV people could not have been less interested if I'd proposed reviving the Monochromatic

Architectural Minstrel Show, that infamous Sunday night programme from half a century ago featuring Sir Kenneth Clark waffling on about big churches and country houses in blackface.

Plan C was to 'do much less but incredibly better' by setting up a virtual foundation on the internet with podcasts, live-streaming and uploaded images from Britain's artisans of the transcendental, but bandwidth requirements were too hefty.

Now, the perfect solution. I am officially relaunching the Epic Space Foundation IN THEORY ONLY. Our mission statement: 'do nothing, be superb'. Here's to the next half-century!

THURSDAY Off-grid, doing important work for the Epic Space Foundation.

FRIDAY Secret meeting for my latest clandestine project, an association of enthusiasts dedicated to 'rebalancing' the London skyline by destroying all buildings taller than the Gherkin.

We're reporting to Amy Blackwater, the ecomentalist. She's organising things from prison on behalf of a shadowy billionaire nihilist known only as the Angel of Death. Tonight, we discuss strategies for the Shard. Step One is to evacuate the building obviously, we're not heartless bastards.

Step Two's a bit of a toss-up. A few of us favour chopping it off at ground level, then using some sort of powerful supercopter to airlift it to the North Sea. Others want incremental contolled detonations from the top down, so it collapses in on itself like a jagged souffle.

Personally I'd like to see this disgusting stalagmite of congealed capital launched into the air by powerful explosives, then land upside down on the O2 during An Evening with Derek Acorah and Sting.

Whatever. One way or another, the Shard will be a breath of fresh air soon.

SATURDAY Five-a-zeitgeist theoretical football. The match between Defensive Architecture and Social Hierarchy was abandoned after a late tackle with anti-homeless floor studs.

SUNDAY Epic space suspension.

June 20, 2014

Oligarchitectural Capitalism Versus Patriarchitectural Sexism

MONDAY Honoured and delighted to be shortlisted in this year's Royal Institute for the Pop-Uption of British Architects Awards (London Housing category) for my innovative ventilated coal bunker.

TUESDAY Blue sky drinkathon down the pub with my fixer, Rock Steady Eddie. I really value these freestyle discussions where, unshackled from our usual business agenda, we can roam freely over a range of subjects and get pissed.

Items discussed today: if 'all design is redesign' does that mean that 'all payment is repayment'? In which case who's the creditor? And how can a building have 'fluid geometry' without risking collapse in a world of apparently arbitrary mathematics?

I say discussed, it's really me thinking aloud while Eddie reads a newspaper and talks through a mouthful of my chips. 'Stone me, you seen this? It says here China's used more cement in the last three years than the USA did in the whole of the 20th century! Do WHAT?'

That IS incredible, I have to admit. It's not just the sun that's setting on the American Empire, clearly. And once a cement race is started, there's no stopping it. Soon India will use more cement in an afternoon than China does in a week. Then Nigeria will use more cement in a minute than India does in a lunchtime. Israel will entirely concretise in the time it takes Nigeria to open a bag of Ordinary Portland...

'It's a mad world, chief, no question,' sighs Eddie, now fully carbohydrated. 'Cemental. Ha ha, your round, son.'

WEDNESDAY British Values Charts Day. Always exciting to hear David 'Fluff' Cameron counting down the Top 40 at Prime Minister's Question Time.

As expected, *Property Equity* remains the Number One British Value for the 8,662nd week. Up seven places this week at Number Two, it's

Shareholders' Dividend, while *Close Ties with Saudi Arabia* stays exactly where it is – frozen in fear at Number Three.

THURSDAY Lunch with Loaf, my old friend the mayor of London. As is customary, he wears his trademark privatised cycling helmet which this week is sponsored by an investment management company (slogan: Your Future, Head First).

As usual, we converse in Latin. At first of course I get the usual jowl-wobbling small talk. Branson's in on Mudbank Airport, as long as it's badged Boris Virgin International. The Ajerbaijani mafia want to buy the National Portrait Gallery. Heston's curating a 'scoffhub' on the South Bank this summer and the menu's just an anthology of atomised starters 'in those nitrous oxide balloon thingies you get at Henley Regatta...'

Then Loaf casually mentions that 'a spook pal' has got wind of some hare-brained scheme to remove the Shard from the London skyline. He doesn't make eye contact, but would like to think this is the sort of nonsense I'd run a mile from. 'Just casually enquiring whether anyone's invited you, let us say, to join some rag tag and bobtail anarchist group of total bloody nutters sworn to blow up everything bigger than the Gherkin...' It's at this point he fixes me with his famous 'Homerian baleful stare'.

I go extravagantly wide-eyed and express the sort of theatrical outrage and hurt you'd get from a senior policeman at a select committee meeting. 'I can't believe you asked me that, Loaf! Good God!' And with that I flounce from the restaurant. The only way I could look guiltier would be to accidentally drop a kilo of Semtex and a map of the Shard with all the stress points marked.

Memo to self: avoid Loaf for a while.

FRIDAY Extraordinary meeting of Space Invaders, the group convened by a mystery billionaire anarchist to destroy the Shard. Of which I'm plausibly not a member.

We need to get a wiggle on. This tottering excrescence of barren, sequestered wealth is actually up for a DESIGN AWARD. Once it wins formal acclaim from the humourless dickheads in brightly coloured trousers, it's within spitting distance of National Treasure status.

It must be destroyed before it becomes part of our cultural heritage. If Alan Bennett starts liking it we're stuffed.

SATURDAY Talking of cultural heritage, I bloody resent how our five-a-zeitgeist theoretical football has been Russianised. The final score was Oligarchitectural Capitalism 3, Patriarchitectural Sexism 2, but then the

Orthodox Church bounced in during extra time like Conchita Wurst and overturned it.

SUNDAY Longlistlessness in the recliner.

June 27, 2014

The Right to Let Die

MONDAY Today I am huffily informing the world that if it doesn't get a move on and provide the £463m necessary to start work on my brilliant Allotment Bridge over the river Tame I will be forced to withdraw my design input.

I have already completed at least two days thinking and sketching time on this prestigious project, which would elevate Tamworth to the premier-ship league of world cities with things growing on bridges. We can't hang around for ever.

Unless the world of world cities with things growing on bridges crowdfunds sharpish, I'm taking the Allotment Bridge somewhere it's going to be appreciated, like Sunderland or Mumbai.

TUESDAY To a conference, *Housing for Life and Death*. The organisers have tried to keep it upbeat but there's only so much you can do with a grim theme. Admittedly you can't call a conference *Disposing of Unwanted Pensioners in a Humane Way*.

Proceedings are conducted by a woman from 'proud sponsors Living With Dignity Residential Logistics'. Pixie cut, radio mic, demeanour of a vet who's telling you she'll have to put your dog to sleep. She introduces a succession of sinister guest speakers who bring us up to date with recent developments.

First on is a thin American designer wearing a tortoiseshell Google Glass. She talks animatedly about data-assisted living and how humane environments can 'smart-adapt' to the occupant.

Basically, old people are extracted from houses much too big for them and squeezed into 'supergreen personalised caraspaces'. Hundreds of caraspaces can then be 'con-modulated into beehives of collective care

182

with off-site supervision'. The deterioration of caraspace and old person is synced via the internet; when they pass away the unit can be composted with them inside and simply replaced with another.

Next, a tanned consultant who'd struggle to get served in a pub. He outlines a forthcoming government initiative, *Right to Let Die*. This will encourage the release of valuable habitable space by offering cash grants to lone pensioners in social housing.

'It would be wrong to call the elderly "spaceblockers" so I won't call them "spaceblockers", OK?' he says, indicating a slide of a baffled-looking old woman with 'NOT A SPACEBLOCKER?' stamped over her. 'This is about directing help where it's needed most, to senior citizens who are perhaps finding life a bit of a struggle – who can blame them, there's little profit for NHS contractors in treating old people – and who might welcome help with funeral expenses…'

Then some frothy yuppieccino on how everyone should be compelled to retire to Wales, and how this exodus of grandparents would suck many young families there with them for the childcare and how England could then be given over to the Childless Economy.

Then it's some demented beard with eyes, droning about a eugenically-modified planning system. Then it's lunch and I bolt for it, before I get any older.

WEDNESDAY Gig on the horizon. A high-rolling Crimean 'businessman' has bought a few hundred acres of beautiful ancient woodland in Kent and wants to develop it as a 'pleasure compound'.

I've suggested he applies for planning permission, not to develop it but to conserve it. Then do what Crimean 'businessmen' do in London – keep everything above ground level and excavate a five-storey underground extension.

THURSDAY Didn't get the gig. Apparently some smartarse had the better idea of elevating the ancient woodland on top of a five-storey overground extension, to deter ramblers.

FRIDAY Exciting times. Having seen bits of the Glastonbury festival on the TV, the mayor and corporation of Blingnang in China now want their own.

Except instead of a three-day smudge of mud, fancy dress and nitrous oxide, the brief is for a permanent Worthy Farm Traditional Big Dolly Music Tent Show (full, presumably, of half-timbered people) surrounded by a business park and a new town of 200,000.

SATURDAY Submit outline ideas for Blingnangstonbury. Have reversed the brief so that a business park is the hub of the whole thing, surrounded by an artificial ox-bow lake filled with endlessly circling drag acts, cider tents and temporary housing.

SUNDAY Didn't get Blingnangstonbury. Some smartarse has had the much better idea of just doing the business park and putting in a high-speed rail link to Shanghai.

Eschew recliner and call my fixer, Rock Steady Eddie. We must find and destroy this mysterious smartarse.

July 4, 2014

Evil in a Pork Pie Hat

MONDAY 'Seriously, mate. I can only apologise for any misunderstanding or inconvenience caused by this unfortunate turn of events,' mumbles Rock Steady Eddie humbly, through a mouthful of his own pie for a change.

We're in emergency session at The Parametric Tinker, a temporary craft pub in Dalston. I coolly note Eddie's contrition and suggest he gets another round in while I bitterly ponder the situation.

Summary: for the last month all my best ideas have been systematically stolen, to wit...

- The Breathe Block, a giant high-density dollop of mid-luxury housing shaped like a bath sponge, celebrating the triumph of rhetoric over science with huge structural 'air-confidence bags' that puff out a smart oxygen-caramel mix and suck in bad carbon, trapping it in sinister 'smoke lungs' and (who knows?) maybe compressing the bad carbon into ethical ivory in due course.
- An Iraqi parliament building designed as a deconstructivist hologram.
- The Shoreditch Shitscraper, an incremental pyramid partially built from the stylish recycled detritus of metropolitan life, e.g. itsu boxes, last year's tweed, late Britart.

- A trio of linked Brazilian supertowers affording panoramic views of the southern hemisphere.
- A heartbreaking 'premorial' commemorating the deaths of all those yet to perish in unknowable yet tragic circumstances, constructed from sad wood and stoical concrete.

All of these and more have been appropriated and talked about pretentiously in the *Creative on Sunday* by a business rival. None other than the legendary Tim Hedgespam.

Yeah, exactly. THAT Tim Hedgespam The can-doer from the 90s. Early Blair adopter. Proud owner of 365 subtly different pork pie hats. Developer, regenerator, OBE and arsehole.

It's not 'officially' him, of course. He's using a sockpuppet. A sockpuppet in the thick sausage-like shape of Bauhau, the celebrity architectural dachshund who has been 'writing' for the *CoS* for a while now. Hedgespam is Bauhau's latest owner, and by far the most unscrupulous. Not only has he been writing about 'his' ideas, he's been selling them to equally unscrupulous clients. Bastard.

Talking of bastards, Eddie's back from the bar. Chasers, too. No wonder he's penitent. The stupid idiot shared my ideas with his stupid idiot brother-in-law Legal Brian, who's in the same bring-your-dog Pilates class as Hedgespam.

'I don't blame you for having the right hump,' he says, generously. 'But right now we've got to focus on damage limitation, fucking the lad Hedgespam up good and proper, and making sure this never happens again ...'

I tell Eddie I'm way ahead of him, swallow my scotch, tell him he's fired as my fixer and walk out, a little unsteadily.

TUESDAY Revenge is a dinner best served in separate courses, each with a distinct and separate flavour. For starters, I intend to separate Hedgespam and Bauhau, thus depriving the intellectual copyright thief of his adorable barking mouthpiece.

WEDNESDAY Lunch with my old friend Darcy Farquear'say, the dandy socialite and freelance epic space commentator. He once owned Bauhau. I remember the delirious years of inseparability. The matchy-matchy, doggy-batchy, gaggy-waggy cloying sickness of it all. Darcy, like the flailing twat he is, still carries a photo of Bauhau in his wallet. A preposterous-looking quiver in a tulle fajita, with tiny biker boots.

Darcy's back in London, having sold his smallholding in Cumbria along with its architectural theorist-in-residence, a border collie called

Bess of Hardwick. The life of a rugged farmer/cultural chronicler was never really for Darcy. Apart from the lack of decent bars and his cow phobia, he couldn't ever grow a full beard.

THURSDAY Ha ha ha, oh dear. An anonymous tip-off seems to have scuppered Arsehole OBE's scheme to overhaul Tamworth's historic Entrails Market.

What a SHAME. Hedgespam had been quietly working up a scheme for some shadowy global investors, keeping the outside of 'Old Gutsy' as it's known locally but scooping out the good bits to make way for bag shops and semi-furnished equity.

Now it's been rejected by the secretary of state, conservationists are dancing on its grave and Rock Steady Eddie has partially, anonymously redeemed himself.

FRIDAY Darcy has lodged a suit against Hedgespam in the Chancery Court of Canine Paternity, alleging misappropriation of mastery over an architectural dachshund.

SATURDAY The *Creative on Sunday* are terminating the impenetrably arch *Woof over Your Head* column. Having Darcy and Bauhau back in my life suddenly seems a small price to pay for Hedgespam's downfall.

SUNDAY Plot-thickening in the recliner.

July 18, 2014

Rough Concrete and Mulleted Genitals

MONDAY The 'silly season'. An ideal opportunity to clear that irritating backlog of unfinished signature new towns from my tottering to-do pile.

They'll never get built, so I can make them as ambitious and deranged as I like. No cultural context. There hasn't been a genuine 'new town' since 1972, when the experimental Spumley in Hertfordshire was completed and immediately began to look old-fashioned.

Designed by radical naturists Alison and Dick Fabble in their trademark 'Arts and Crafts with a Heavy Groove' style, Spumley caused a sensation at the time. The bold combination of Corbusian grid and social nudity was dismissed as 'flapping, dangling gimmickry of the very worst kind' by influential style magazine *Architecturalisme et Couture Oui Oui*.

Urbanists now come from all over the world, disembarking at Spumley's 'park, disrobe and ride' stations to see for themselves how Perspex, Formica, rough concrete and mulleted genitals have survived four decades of indifference and gentle mockery.

Many of us remember this most emphatic of Britain's new towns from Michael Portillo's documentary *Shock of the Nude*, in which the broadcaster and former Tory minister strode authoritatively through Spumley's healthy and efficient streets, his probity blazoned by a comprehensive railway timetable and a quizzical expression.

TUESDAY When politicians moot a 21st-century new town it's either to distract us from something or to promote themselves. If you're a Liberal Democrat, both.

I've been asked to knock up a generic new garden city by LibDem Policy Hot Tank. 'Basically, we don't give a shit what it looks like,' says the refreshingly honest brief. 'What we're after is something that appeals to the affordable housing brigade, so could you put some rough-looking types in the pictures, with tattoos, holding carrier bags? Also something that appeals to homeowners so maybe also some semi-detached villas with Ocado vans and little girls in straw boaters?

'We just want to float it in general terms really so we can offer compensation to any Tories living next to it. That way everyone's happy when it doesn't get built and we're very much part of the next Coalition government, yes?'

Solution: Photoshop some Googled residents of Newcastle into cut-ups of Berkhamsted.

WEDNESDAY Controversial billionaire artist Dorian Gubb is a genius, of course he is. You can't argue with Charles Saatchi. Not in public, anyway.

The leading light of 'Britprop Art', Gubb revolutionised painting by getting other people to do it for him, then revolutionised installations by getting other people to do those too. He's made a fortune and for tax purposes wants to convert a sizeable lump of it into a new town.

That's where I come in, with my intuitive understanding of the artistic mind. I've sketched out an 'affordable settlement' where all the houses are cut in half, the community centre's full of flies swarming round cow carcasses, the roads are covered in dots and swirls and even a garden shed NOT encrusted with diamonds costs £750,000.

We'll submit this to planning, whip up scare stories in the press and get it rejected. Then Gubbo will shrug extravagantly somewhere in the Maldives, agree to have it redesigned in the style of a luxury starter home estate and bosh, job done.

THURSDAY The SCOTLAND AYE campaign wants me to design eight new towns to 'help avert a potential housing crisis'. Maybe they're expecting severe overcrowding when everyone on the mint-spectrum from 'oligarch' to 'benefits tourist' moves to the most fashionable region in New Europe. Or maybe they're being conjured up in order to be 'at risk' if the other lot wins the referendum.

Solution: a mixed eight-pack of new towns. Tartanauld, Cragaloof, Heatherloch, Peaty Edge, Glengrimmond Glen Ben, Polyunsaltire, Aarg and Ecklesprechenangettaefuchan.

FRIDAY Now I've told them about the SCOTLAND AYE new towns plan, the SCOTLAND RATHER NOT people suddenly want some new towns as well. Fine with me. Special rate for cash. Not those Scottish banknotes though thanks very much, people in parts of London don't 'believe' in them.

Solution: Hogwhim, Sahberdeen, Jacobeanory, Grecian Urbis, Upper Hackney, Type 2 Tablet, Kiltmist, Ooterienanny.

SATURDAY Develop the idea of 'new town' into the idea of 'newt-owned'. Curse the piddling megalomania of newts. Curse everything they stand for.

SUNDAY Imagine a new town called Newtone, and wonder if it might be time to change our whole attitude to 'housing' people, in the recliner.

August 15, 2014

The Henge

MONDAY Well thanks very much, 'public outcry'. I was just trying to bring a little magic to your shitty riverside park.

Fine. You don't want a visitor centre celebrating the Otherness of Royalty? I'll take it to Dubai or Mumbai or Shanghai or anywhere ending in -ai where they DO appreciate integrated genius.

The idea was to create a thrilling building first of all, which I obviously did WELL before imagining what might go inside. Angular roof, shingled pop-up fish tin overthrow, walls made of a smart hybrid of 'slow light' and 'treacly air', windows 'bouncing' slowly around within the rectangles like those logos on the old DVD screensavers.

It had AWARD-WINNING painted in dripping block capitals all over it, like a serial killer's chilling message to the cops.

Then an idea came to me in a dream. As I am an auteur, I quickly scribbled it down. Bingo – a concept outline. 'Something about Royals doing something else when historic events were taking place? Maybe lose the telepathic flying bears?'

Yes, a perfect fit for my riverside building. For example, while the Queen was on a barge sailing down the rainy Thames for her Diamond Jubilee celebrations, Prince Philip was in hospital with a urinary tract infection. Everybody knows what the Diamond Jubilee looked like, but who's familiar with UTI procedures?

Likewise the Prince of Wales – people would be astonished to learn what he was doing on that fateful night in 1997. And Princess Michael of Kent's 'Fergie wedding swerve' at the casino.

It's a sad day when this country no longer values tributes to the hidden contemporaneity of our own Royal Family.

TUESDAY Redesign the United States, giving it a wider, sedentary vibe.

Along the Canadian border I'm proposing a notional 'crown of specialness' made of powerful halogen beacons, visible from the International Space Station as whimsical, twinkling fairy lights emphasising the fragile grandeur of our world but also showing that grand, fragile world how the

US can still put together a kickass halogen light show, probably presented by some sun-dried cockpunnet shrieking 'Rock and Roooooooooll!'

Either side of the US: relaxed, post-imperial coastal borders. An enigmatic aquatic-territorial interface marked at regular intervals by Sea Nodes expressing comfortableness with our shifting self-perceptions and honouring America's fallen heroes.

Along the Mexican border, a spangled retaining wall.

WEDNESDAY Day off. Potter round in the stately home of my mind, or 'Downtime Abbey' as I humorously call it.

THURSDAY I'm finding that new BBC reality television documentary *The Henge* utterly inspiring.

It takes you behind the scenes at Stonehenge, following the day-to-day lives of ordinary members of staff. It underlines the humanity of routine situations with quirky incidental music, a device I admit was new to me.

We see the sun rise ('It is dawn…') over the iconic neolithic monument (pizzicato violins) as a pair of gorgeous, heritagey-looking ground staff arrive for another quirky day of quirky maintenance.

One, John, is nearing retirement and has the keys to the big maintenance shed. As he unlocks it ('First off us'll have to water 'em droy patches, BBC Weather bain't give 'em rain ber Froyday…') his companion, Cassie, who's on a placement year as part of her archaeology and wellbeing degree, stoops to fuss over a Golden Labrador (sprightly oboe).

Alas, when John and Cassie attach the hose to the standpipe as usual and set off to water them dry patches, gentle disaster strikes – in the multiform of a hose several metres too short, and a waddling tuba.

'Where's that producer's assistant?' demands John of the unit director. 'Someone's been [bleep] about with moy [bleep] hose, 'em bout twenny yards too short now, ert? Oi've had it with you lot. [bleep] the lot of 'em…' Here John looks directly at the camera and warns, as we hear minor chords on the piano. 'Don't think 'em can just stick sad-sounding piano over all this and call err heartwarming [bleep] drama, I call it a [bleep] cop-out mate.' Cut to Cassie, cheerfully watering the parts of Stonehenge she can reach with the hose, as the Labrador bounds around some Swedish tourists (dulcimer).

The point is, they realised the dry patches were where missing stones had once stood, making Stonehenge a proper circle (pizzicato violins). Result!

FRIDAY Bang out my masterplan for 'henge living'. A circular, traditional private housing development in the green belt.

SATURDAY Five-a-zeitgeist theoretical football: match abandoned 1, match 'unpacked' 0.

SUNDAY Circular thinking in the recliner.

September 19, 2014

Curse You, Buildings That Resemble Breasts Quarterly

MONDAY Spend the day in a mischievous mood, thanking people for their patience. I explain that I'm redesigning their interactive experience by elevating my level of indifference to them.

TUESDAY Ugh. Entrapment is the ugliest of all journalistic ploys and I condemn it unreservedly.

It is outrageous that I should have to resign my post as honorary chair of the Buildings That Look Like Penises Appreciation Society. I shall be writing to the Independent Press Standards Organisation about this affair, which has been maliciously timed to cause maximum embarrassment and loss of status.

The muckrakers and bastards of *Buildings That Resemble Breasts Quarterly* have much to answer for.

Summary: a reporter posing as an attractive young building restorer contacted me via the social epic space media platform *Wobble*. We exchanged innocent messages about Brunelleschi's early theories of linear perspective.

Then late one night 'Clemency', who said she'd had one too many proseccos, offered to send me explicit photographs of the Hagia Sophia. I agreed, and had to admit they were impressive. In a moment of recklessness I now bitterly regret, I sent her a picture of me in a sleepsuit holding a model of the Jean Nouvel-designed Torre Agbar, in the Barcelona area.

191

And so – snap! – the trap sprang shut. But what possible public interest is served by publishing such private folly?

WEDNESDAY I have informed *Buildings That Resemble Breasts Quarterly* that I am putting it in the hands of my lawyer. More sniggering. Insufferable.

THURSDAY A micro-exhibition has been curated by radical post-architectural thinkers Shayne and Molly Bellow, who are always impeccably dressed and taken very seriously.

The Bellows have transformed a flat in a condemned Glasgow tower block, built in 1969 and designed by celebrated Brutalist architect Ernie Beatles, using 'furniture, contents and decoration of the time'. The idea was to show how an ordinary Scottish working-class family might have lived when the flats were new and hadn't been not maintained properly yet.

In her 'Notes From A Curator', etched on responsibly sourced tie-dyed vinyl of the era, Molly Bellow writes: '1969 was a time of great cultural upheaval. The first Led Zeppelin album. The Austin Maxi. Much much more, just check out Wikipedia! What might a working class home of the time have looked like? We decided to find out by buying antique items on eBay marked "1969" and arranging them in the flat.

'But surely, critics will say, working-class families in 1969 did not have the wherewithal to simply go on eBay, search for items made "now" and decorate their flat from scratch? Fair point. Some things would not necessarily be "unique to 1969", which is why we have included in the exhibition a Tretchikoff print and a bottle of advocaat...'

I applaud this approach, and pay homage to the Bellows by 'visiting' the exhibition on the internet.

FRIDAY Lunch at the latest London restaurant you need to go to if you only visit one London restaurant before you die. It's so fashionable it hasn't even got traction on Twitter yet.

I say restaurant. Technically it's an 'experiential ingestion hub' called Denial. The premise is that consuming food, like consuming art, should be a struggle between what we think we know and who we think we are. Is this my lunch? Or AM I the lunch somehow? Is the lunch paying for ME? Am I to include starters and a pudding?

The menu lists all the items you're not allowed to have. You tell the waiter I DON'T want the chicken livers to start, etc. They pretend they won't bring you the food you've refused to order but then they do. Brilliant. Denial is run by a former architect. Of course it is.

I'm here to meet my old mate Loaf, the mayor of London. Hoping for some 'inside frack' on his latest scheme to help minorities in London, called OLIGARCHITECTURALOPOLIS.

The idea is to nurture the often misunderstood billionaire community. All Loaf will tell me is that a shortlist of imagineers will be selected on the basis of '1. Design, 2. Delivery and 3. Commercial drivers'.

SATURDAY Knock out my conceptuals for OLIGARCHITECTURAL-OPOLIS.

1. Half-scale central St Petersburg in Mayfair.
2. Delivery via de-unionised delivery system, e.g. Addison Lee.
3. Commercial drivers – as above.

SUNDAY Keep Gherkin, etc., to self, in recliner.

October 3, 2014

Yipster Gentrification

MONDAY Feeling relaxed and energised after the weekend, ready to create some life-affirming epic space. Then remember I have to do some conceptual prep for a genocide memorial, have a mood plunge and take the rest of the day off.

TUESDAY Bollocks, I've just spent the entire morning reconciling disparate elements to create – as per client instructions – 'a unified alliance of quality spatial components within a singular whole'.

Now I've found a disparate element on the floor. No idea where it's supposed to fit, and to be honest the singular whole seems to be working perfectly without it. Dilemma. Can I be arsed to take it all apart and work out where to insert this so-called 'affordable housing'?

In the end I decide to leave it as it is. If anyone notices I'll just rebadge one of the other disparate elements, or blame the economy.

WEDNESDAY Bang out a new holiday resort on the Italian Riviera. Yes, the luxury villas are high-spec but please don't lecture me on the moral ambiguities of 'exclusive place-making'. For all I know disabled kiddies will be staying there, and I have a headache.

THURSDAY Propose a regeneration scheme for Hartlepool via a process of 'gamification'. I've sketched in bouncy gaming platforms, giant gaming slides, a big bubble full of gaming possibilities, app-enabled wi-fi gameclouds, a rooftop gaming zone and an ongoing controversy about misogyny in the word of gaming.

The idea is that users can explore Hartlepool via gaming consoles and don't physically have to be in Hartlepool. This will enhance the town's status by getting it on Google without having to install any expensive landmark art pieces.

FRIDAY A landscape upgrading day. With one elegant drag-and-drop I secure 'additional seasonal solar shading' to the rear of the scheme by plopping a tree in. Bosh. Capability Me.

SATURDAY Five-a-zeitgeist theoretical football. Austerical Mockery 3, Void Cloning 3.

SUNDAY Media review in the recliner. Extraordinary piece in the *Creative on Sunday* in which Bauhau the architectural dachshund controversially suggests that hipster gentrification may actually be GOD'S WILL.

In 'his' latest *Woof over Your Head* column the extruded little bastard declares himself firmly on the side of those 'brave and intrepid settlers who made east London bloom'.

I'd never thought of haughty retro-normcore couples with their off-book opinions and parents' deposits as 'acts of God'. But acccording to Bauhau's ghost writer – my friend the flamboyant and controversial Darcy Farquear'say – gentrifiers are part of a divine plan.

'I cannot be the only dog living in the revitalised Chutney Meadows area to be grateful for its oft-derided "hipster culture", which has brought God's chosen dogs to a promised land to fulfil our destiny...' He barks on like this for some time. How hipster dogs are creating value. How they and their human associates have turned Chutney Meadows from an area of deprivation into a desirable postcode 'by displacing poverty and its associated pitbulls, Staffordshire terriers etc, with creative energy, cultured caninity and a genuine sense of purpose...'

There's a picture of Bauhau and friends enjoying the tasting menu at *Waggy Mama*, a fashionable brasserie for dogs on Chatsworth Road. Bauhau in prescription sunglasses and a little hat, quite the king of the salon.

His associates include a heavily tattooed chihuahua, a shitzu dyed platinum blonde, a Pomeranian in a crop top and hot pants and a miniature

194

Yorkshire Terrier sporting a fashionable short-back-and-sides. They look quite small and trembly in their skinny fit trouser suits and taffeta wraps.

Oh, hang on. Turns out the 'human carer' for the chihuahua with tats is millionaire cultural commentator and self-made pop-up Shayne Bellow. He's very keen to renotionalise 'hipsters and their stupid dogs' as 'mixed-species urban pioneers'.

So this is where Bauhau – I mean Darcy – is getting his inspiration from. He's even saying things like 'go see Chutney Meadows, discover what can be achieved with cheap property in a rising market when God's on your side. Virgin Atlantic are even talking about it in their in-flight magazine, bro!'

Bloody hipster dachshunds. Bauhau reckons he's part of a blessed canine project now and has, inevitably, baptised his neurotic tribe 'yipsters'.

You know, scientists reckon only an estimated 8.2 per cent of human DNA is useful. That's 8 per cent more than you'd find in an architectural dachshund, I reckon.

October 17, 2014

The Dalek Clusterfuck

MONDAY To a conference, *Where Next for the Branded Townscape?* Some amazing civic plans in the pipeline...

'Live, Work and Breathe Matlock'. An integrated 10-year plan for the Derbyshire county town includes more housing approvals, a new business park, and all air molecules to be wi-fi-imprinted with the word 'Matlock'.

'Hashtag Biggleswade'. A proposed development to the west of the town. Four long residential terraces arranged as an italicised noughts and crosses grid, creating a smart aerial branding presence.

'Brandford'. A multi-agency cross-stakeholder rebranding of Bradford to create a world-class centre of branding excellence. Every citizen of Brandford will be free to develop his or her personal brand, in the context of a growing urban superbrand, NB no 'Russell Brands' or other time-wasters.

TUESDAY Oh my God, I thought it was someone falling down the stairs. Just a voice on the radio saying, 'STARCHITECTS TEAM UP FOR OLYMPICOPOLIS BIDS.'

WEDNESDAY I'm redesigning Victorian England for television. Actually it's an adaptation of the Victorian England I redesigned for radio. This time round there'll be high production values and actors with multi-syllabic names.

The human element's easy enough – gritty but well-tailored, full of existential doubt about Empire and God. But it's vital to get the built environment spot-on or you get a torrent of abuse from influential *Telegraph* readers.

My note for the location manager could not be clearer. I want all churches to be Gothic and evil-looking. All working-class housing to be slummy but plucky; we're looking for gorgeous squalor. Railway stations – stick to interiors, everyone loves a steam train. General note for all locations: lashings of industrial hurly-burly, must look great with a knowing contemporary soundtrack gushing underneath. NB – follies!

All municipal buildings to be neo-Classical, foreshadowing perhaps the rise of totalitarianism, you never know, if this goes well we could be up to World War One by the third series.

THURSDAY Sketch out initial ideas for a radical feminist ideas hub and meeting space. Can't seem to get any further. Realise I've made it self-exclusionary. Go to pub.

FRIDAY My old friend Darcy, the well-dressed controversialist, has written a piece for a new online magazine called, appropriately, *The Well-Dressed Controversialist*.

It's the usual swooning mix of rehashed press releases, copyright images used with the permission of whoever's being written approvingly about, and clickbait. I wish this horrible aggregated sinkhole WAS actually 'full' of mischievously counterintuitive bullshit, but the sad fact is that websites can never be full. Gone are the days when you could look at the print version of the *Daily Mail* and think oh well, at least there it is – 'finite'.

I'm disappointed in Darcy. Times are tough, but this is a new low. A cursory glance at the latest additions to *The Well-Dressed Controversialist* gives you a pretty good idea of their editorial ethos. 'Let's Have More Shards'. 'Shut Up, the North – Nobody Cares'. 'Georgian Architecture Is Shit'.

Some Brussels-based visual artist has Photoshopped graffiti onto photos of Le Corbusier's Villa Savoye. Why? To 'question its primacy in Modernist historiography', you Brussels-based doughnut?

Darcy's own contribution is equally shameless: 'Three Cheers for the Dalek Clusterfuck'. This is how journalism works now. Because Darcy's pretending to like that appalling Dali-does-a-Rolex-ad 'high street' at poor old Battersea Power Station, they let the *Controversialist* use the pictures.

Darcy then imagines what he MIGHT say if he didn't like it, e.g. the unaffordable investment housing looks like a Dalek clusterfuck, the whole thing's an affront to the idea of a high street, it'll be full of wankers etc and then offers his own counter-argument.

Apparently he likes the boldness of the ideas, and the vision. And the money. 'The critics can carp and parp as much as they like – it'll still cost EIGHT BILLION POUNDS, so excuse me if I don't fawn over your frankly irrelevant little social housing refurb struggling to make it into seven fig-ures. London is all about glamour, and what could be more glamorous than an icon being forced into humiliating submission by anonymous international shareholders?'

Hang on, maybe Darcy's being sarcastic. If he is, and *The Well-Dressed Controversialist* hasn't noticed, he may have pushed forward the bounda-ries of online journalism another inch.

SATURDAY Reimagine Venice. No idea why.

SUNDAY Invent opposition to the idea of recliners, write piece 'In Defence of the Recliner', in the recliner.

October 24, 2014

Honeycombed Privatised Air

MONDAY The latest report from the Intergovernmental Panel on Climate Change has given us all a stark and final warning about carbon emissions.

As if that's not scary enough, I'm actually reading the report in a pub beer garden. It's uncomfortably warm in the November sunshine.

Butterflies and spring flowers everywhere. In the fields beyond, sheep and birds are on their third and fourth families of the year respectively.

Dilemma. Of course we must reduce our carbon emissions to zero. On the other hand economies such as China's and India's are driving new wealth the old-fashioned way, with coal and poisons. And with filth-powered wealth comes great responsibility but also quite a few lucrative gigs.

It is time we all faced up to the terrible reality. We have a moral obligation to take a stand on this, which is why I for one will be dismissing the IPCC report as racist at the earliest opportunity.

TUESDAY Redesign the North, giving it a new dynamic focus by reducing it to Manchester.

WEDNESDAY As part of the new government initiative to pretend it's doing anything useful at all to solve the housing crisis, the department for business solutions, delivery and skills is about to launch an appeal for construction specialists.

This is even less interesting than it sounds. My fixer Rock Steady Eddie has the heads-up. 'To be honest, son, I thought they were looking for consultants and contractors too. Turns out they just want someone to construct some specialist bullshit so it's ideal really, you finishing that sandwich?'

He hands me the draft release. 'The Department seeks the construction of a sloganised housing action plan. The proposed plan will exist as a temporary measure until the next General Election and must require neither resources nor complex thought...'

Eddie gives me one of his see-there-you-go looks. 'Yeah? Right up your Strasse. Just roll out a couple of yards of that smartarse guff that sounds as though it means something but it doesn't and nobody cares, whatever, hope follows hype, trope follows tripe, all that mincemeat – bosh, we're golden.'

THURSDAY So glad the Human Rights Act is still in place, because I intend to take Kensington & Chelsea to the cleaners if they carry out their threat to ban so-called 'mega-basement' development.

It is an assault on my basic freedom as an auteur. How dare these pettifoggers interfere with my bespoke subterranean visions for discerning, ultra-rich clients? Let's be clear. The planner's job is to accept my genius. Or at the very least, to nominate a sum of money that will render my genius acceptable. It should not concern a planner what potential misery may be caused to other ratepayers in the execution of an inverted mini-skyscraper underneath a modest garden. It is nobody's business but my client's.

And spare me the panic about replacing dense, heavy clay beneath our streets with honeycombed privatised air. These sunken mansions are creating value where none existed. They are residential equity mines. That makes me a HERO, surely.

What are planners planning 'for' these days anyway, if not their own redundancy?

FRIDAY Think I've cracked the government's zero-budget emergency housing action plan. As is customary, it's in five parts.

1. A serious-minded-sounding pledge to make 'decent housing' a 'genuine priority' after the next election.
2. A significantly extended Notional Mortgage Allowance so that first time buyers can borrow even more from parents or commercial lenders for a deposit, if they need to.
3. Tougher penalties for local authorities who falsely claim they can't afford to house their tenants in high-rent former council houses that they had to sell cheaply and which they now need as they can't build any new council housing, because there must be no return to the dark days of the 1970s.
4. Greater incentives for the private sector to do everything it can for hard-working people to get on the housing ladder, including knighthoods and redeemable 'tax miles'.
5. A new Reward for Innovation scheme to encourage impressive new housing construction targets through competitive thinking.

I'm calling the pop-up plan 'More Homes for Better People', which has a harmless yet inspirational ring to it.

SATURDAY Five-a-zeitgeist theoretical football. Promulgated Defabulism 4, Attenuated Flaneurism 58.3, after on-pitch anomalies and disquiet in the matrix.

SUNDAY Temporarily house self in recliner.

November 7, 2014

Twirly Atlantis

MONDAY Design a new agnostic contemplation space for a major retail destination centre, in a certain Arab state that wishes to remain anonymous.

I've gone for injection-moulded Gothic which OK is double the average person's retrovisionary intake, but if you can't comfort-gaze in a shopping centre, what's the point of life? Yes, that's certainly something to ponder, isn't it? And where better than in an injection-moulded Gothic space flooded with natural light and artificial air.

After it's built, half the contemplation space will be deliberately ruined by professional devastators. This will significantly enhance the visitor experience, as ruins are known to amplify musings about the human spirit triumphing over the melancholy of an unreachable past.

To be honest, the user experience isn't a major factor. My clients – it would be unprofessional to call them deeply religious debauched autocratic misogynist fucking scumbags – simply want the space to act as a human flytrap for agnostics, so they can arrest them and then lock them up.

And please don't tell me I have no business working for these people. One of them plays online polo with the Prince of Wales. Another's been on *Top Gear*.

TUESDAY All Soho is braced for a week of preening insufferability. The *Creative on Sunday* has been named Magazine of the Year by the Epic Spatialist Association.

Worse, Darcy Farquear'say and his appalling dachshund Bauhau have jointly won Architectural Writer of the Year for their stupid *Woof over Your Head* column, in which Darcy giggles about some new building, pretending to be Bauhau. All Bauhau has to do is remain continent while his picture's taken.

Just looking at them in their identical hip-hop lamé coatigans makes me want to heave. 'This award is really for the readers, who like us simply adore epic space…' 'Rrrak!' 'Thanks to everyone who voted, it's terribly humbling…' 'Yupyup!' 'I like to think we bring a new international style not only to architectural criticism but to the PRESENTATION of that criticism…' Oh ha ha whoops! Bauhau's style is suddenly incontinental.

WEDNESDAY What's the biggest problem faced by innovators and revolutionaries? Thieving bastard copycats. You've got a limited amount of time before someone nicks your idea and makes a fortune.

That's why I'm helping my mate Beansy the nanofuturologist to finalise some deals quickly to exploit neogen – the intelligent self-replicating supergas that's better than oxygen and can bend the laws of physics.

Neogen autosynthesises so fast, an asthma inhaler's worth can fill the Louvre in 20 minutes. It's an inspiring thought that neogen may serve the arts in this way. Our beta run at the Louvre demonstrably increased the alertness of the punters, who absorbed art 17 per cent more quickly and spent nearly 20 per cent above average in the gift shop. Neogen also sharpens the appetite. The Louvre canteen did a roaring trade, and ran out of baguettes by half past ten!

THURSDAY Beansy and I are a bit worried that a certain Japanese construction company could discover the formula for neogen and replicate it for their innovative Twirly Atlantis project.

Twirly Atlantis proposes bypassing spiralling housing costs by creating an alternative and actual housing spiral, fixed to the ocean floor, with individual affordable flatpods all joined up together like frogspawn. The one flaw in the Twirly Atlantis theory is this old-fashioned idea of creating power with 'methane-producing micro-organism factories'. What? Wake up, Japanese innovators. Where do you think you are, some trippy 1980s sci-fi cartoon?

Idiots. As ever, attack is the best form of defence, which is why we're nicking their inhabited spiral idea and filling it with neogen. It's the perfect gas, so much better than micro-organic methane. As well as being wi-fi-enabled, capable of producing clean electricity and self-aware without being completely 'up itself' it doesn't smell of amoeba farts.

FRIDAY Push skateboarding forward yet again by allowing the transgressive nature of 'street skating' to shape the municipal skate park I'm designing in full compliance with health and safety. That obviously makes it 'lamer' so I put in some landmines but that will mean it's STRICTLY NO ADMITTANCE so they'll have to break-and-enter in a 'streetwise' way, I hope everyone's happy now.

SATURDAY Five-a-zeitgeist theoretical football. Low Fidelity Cultural Reconciliation 0, High Linear Equity Boosterism 2.

SUNDAY Spatial contemplation in the recliner. Slightly disturbed at horizontal massing, so reconfigure entire form down the pub.

December 5, 2014

Austerity Christmas Human Turducken

MONDAY The *Creative on Sunday* have asked me to do something polemical for their Wise Howl spot.

Every week an influential cultural animateur throws down a sketch or a poem, a photographic composition, a micro-essay or whate'er-ye-will. It doesn't really matter as long as it chimes with some topical outrage, and the spectrum of howled liberalism is pretty wide these days.

I can't tell you what I've designed. There's an embargo until Sunday. But believe me it's as hard-hitting as anything else you'll see in the Wise Howl spot, which is on page 7 nestled between that snarky literary gossip column and an advert for some weird anthology of fairtrade chutneys.

TUESDAY To the Institute of Plasmic Arts. Fascinating lecture by Ross Kemp on environmental determinism, focusing on the link between late Modernism and gangsters, called *Bad Manors*.

WEDNESDAY Amazing TV documentary – *Schama Chameleon* – featuring an immersive Simon Schama on top form, exploring the evolution of social housing in period clothing and pissed on whatever they were having at the time.

Particularly moved by the animated account of slum clearances in Westminster and the advent of model Peabody estates, delivered by a gin-blitzed Schama in top hat and rakish trousers in one long shouted take before he lurched out of shot into what sounded like a pile of buckets.

THURSDAY My fixer Rock Steady Eddie and I are offering civic authorities a special deal on all rebrandings for 2015. We're calling it the '1+1 Affordable Masterplan Package'.

Eddie's copywriting has both vigour and economy. 'Attention all mayors, business development managers, urban custodians etc! Got the "inner shitty blues"? Struggling to secure that vital inward investment because your town centre's like the set of a zombie film? Need a professional team with the traditional know-how and contemporary expertise to unlock the romantic potential of wherever it is, no place too small, you've tried the rest now try the best?

'Then look no further! URBISTO has been delivering top quality solutions to the communities community since 2011. From as little as £20k, URBISTO can turn around perceptions of your urban location like THAT! Also, new for 2015! Rebrand one area no greater than 10 square kilometers, get another area no greater than 10 square kilometers rebranded HALF PRICE! Come on, these prices won't last for ever, we're not MENTAL OR ARE WE LOL!'

Surprisingly perhaps, we've already had a few enquiries. Not one person so far has asked us what the '1+1' in our affordable masterplan package means. Well, we recognise that a powerful visual narrative must be at the heart of every successful rebrand. That's why we always shoot the target location at night, from a £100 drone flying through £1,000 worth of fireworks.

Honestly, everywhere – anywhere – looks fucking great.

FRIDAY In the morning, embrace the self-employed festive spirit by sticking a bit of tinsel to my MacBook and calling it 'Lapland'.

In the afternoon, decorate my freelance subconscious with imaginary paper chains. Very dusty but there's no point in cleaning, I'm the only one who ever goes in there.

SATURDAY Five-a-zeitgeist horticultural blow football. Verdant Life-Affirming Bridge Full of Dark Woodland with Dense Undergrowth 6, Muggers' Paradise 0.

SUNDAY Lots of warm, gratifying feedback for my Wise Howl piece, which I've solemnly captioned 'Austerity Christmas Human Turducken'.

It's a stark portrait of retro-engineered misery. At the heart of my artisanal, hand-drawn exploded axonometric: a battery-farm manger containing a quivering dachshund wrapped in swaddling clothes. 'Perhaps he has been abandoned by some heartless buy-to-let landlord...' I have written above the bleak scene, in wobbly pencil.

We pull out to show the manger crammed into a food bank full of hapless people looking at tinned food. We pull out further to reveal that the food bank is itself crammed into a former public library, now a charity shop full of appalling old clothes and dead peoples' trinkets, staffed by tattooed women made to wear electronic tags by the Tories just because they're fat and they smoke.

We pull out further and discover that the charity shop is inside Yarl's Wood Detention Centre. Instead of a punchline, which would turn my Wise Howl into a joke rather than an excoriating satire on social policy, I have written the web address for Shelter in wobbly pencil at the bottom.

Peace. Goodwill. Have a great one.

December 12, 2014

The Worm Is Cast

MONDAY Redesign London's luxury housing bubble, giving it a tremulous, panoramic aspect.

I've created a 'rainbow effect' by breaking the white light into discreet bundles of graded luxury colour spectrum molecules. These can be monetised immediately or sold on the international bubble markets, creating stable and theoretically infinite bubble yield, year-on-year, no problem.

TUESDAY To a pop-up conference – The New Grotesque: Defeating Terrorism With Satirical Architecture.

For years, we designers of those buildings at risk of terrorist attack have been derided by liberal auteurs who are above this sort of thing, as well as by the bitter losers who didn't get the gigs. Oh yeah, our defensive, hyper-secure architecture was so 'funny' wasn't it, with its boring concrete berms, its tiny reinforced scaredy-cat windows, its dead buffer zones, its Stalinist landscaping.

Yes, everyone's had a right old laugh, haven't they? Well, who's laughing now? It's clear that a terrorist target can be anything – a railway station, magazine offices, a UN school, a coffee house. So apparently the laughter/architecture of liberal apologists/defenders of democracy must now be offensive/defiant. In the midst of all this cultural and intellectual chaos, one thing is clear. Architects are to blame. It is time to:

a) apologise to the world for the tiny percentage of architecture responsible for terrorism and

b) show the terrorists we cannot be cowed, by producing satirical and repellent architecture.

Quite how architecture might non-accidentally take the piss out of anything but itself is a conundrum, which is why this conference has been hastily arranged in an old snooker hall at £240 plus VAT, get your own lunch.

Plenary session ideas: when designing a mosque, put 'subtle jokes' in; terrorist entrances in museums, lined with deterrent art works; some kind of gun-jamming technology incorporated into all wi-fi; live Twitter feeds on exterior walls with hashtagged fenestration; pretend 'multi-secularism' is an architectural style; contextualise everything to the point where the building might 'externalise its self-loathing'.

Summary: oh for fuck's sake just put the word 'satirical' in front of everything, e.g. Classical, drainpipe, luxury, public space, fee, development, ethics, skyline, Islam, façade.

WEDNESDAY I'm reworking the concept of the beach hut. A design competition is looking for 'a wry take on the classic hut which also tells a story about mortality'. I've sketched out a series of disconnected huts to be erected several miles inland, each containing its own miniature beach. What does it mean? Who cares?

THURSDAY Those fickle bastards at the Royal Society for the Protection of Worms (RSPW) have withdrawn their backing for my brilliant yet apparently controversial Soil Tunnel underneath the Thames.

Up until yesterday the RSPW had been broadly supportive of the proposal to create a 'journey through earth and history'. The Soil Tunnel will allow bored Londoners and genuine people alike to immerse themselves in the mystery beneath our feet, interacting with the loam and clay of our shared geological narrative in an exciting and literally groundbreaking way.

But the bastard worm people have turned. The RSPW moans that 'the new, worm-positive habitat we had so fervently hoped for will clearly not occur'. As far as I can gather the stupid pillocks expected the tunnel to be filled with soil, users somehow wriggling their way from one end to the other. Perhaps in special 'worm suits', who knows? Idiots. Why would I have mentioned 'pedestrians' if people COULDN'T USE THEIR FEET?

The RSPW had 'assumed' the 544m-long tunnel would link existing 'worm hotspots' north and south of the river and would incorporate special worm hubs at intervals along the tunnel. Once these sanctimonious worm-lovers realised their preposterous fantasy would simply not be happening, they started putting it about that the Soil Tunnel was a 'folly', a shameful waste of resources.

'Frankly, if we were handed £1.03bn to help the worms, we could certainly find better ways of spending it. A few million on a courtesy campaign to respect worms in the garden. Maybe some worm hospitals, give us a minute, nobody has ever suggested throwing a billion pounds at worms before, wow.' Stupid worms.

FRIDAY In such a hurry to kickstart the delivery of something that I forget what it is, so have to kickstop myself.

SATURDAY Five-a-zeitgeist theoretical football. Triangulated Alternative 1, Cannulated Heritage 3, after a late collapse in linear time.

SUNDAY Tough thinking in the recliner.

January 16, 2015

This Feudopolitan Life

MONDAY Finish my sketches for a skyscraper that looks like an apple corer.

Nobody's done an apple corer before. Acknowledge my genius, yet feel a genuine sadness that the apple corer will be the last kitchen implement to be formalised in architecture.

Acknowledge my sadness, then acknowledge my genius again.

TUESDAY I'm giving Riyadh a 'solemn makeover'. It's all absolutely fine, ethics-wise. The competition brief, from the Office of the Half-Brother of the Guardian of the Two Holy Places, has been pre-approved by the Gulf chapter of the Royal Institute for the Pop-Uption of British Architects and believe me, those guys know their way around a moral conundrum, Allah be praised.

The brief stresses the need for 'stability and continuity, with a hint of cautious reform in the future'. Certainly, holding an open international design competition is very encouraging even if it does say in small print at the end 'Sorry – no ladies, Jews, Shi'ites, breadheads or haram piss-takers'.

Stability and continuity are easy enough to achieve architecturally. You just need to be heavy-handed on the conservation. Lots of restoration and maintenance, using ancient techniques and traditional slave labour. Lashings and lashings of respect for the old ways.

Of course Saudi Arabia is keen to show the West that it's a modern, forward-looking, civilised place. So I've put a parametric smart wall around that big public square, with a curvy glass-and-gold canopy over the bit where they behead people for witchcraft and sorcery.

WEDNESDAY Finished that Sagrada Familia at last! A dozen bottles of the shittest rioja I've ever ordered. Never again.

THURSDAY Honoured to be masterplanning one of the government's garden cities, in Oxfordshire.

It's nice and leafy here – an ideal spot for five thousand new homes with associated Netflix and sewerage system. Just don't call it an 'eco-town'. Nobody with any sense has said that for years. You might as well put 'green' in front and wear a Blur T-shirt.

Although my secret project is filed under Operation Garden Cities I concede that five thousand very similar looking homes isn't technically a city. It's not as if anyone's asked me to knock up a market square with municipal statues or a corn exchange or whatever.

On the other hand it's too big to be one of those awful pseudo-villages favoured by wealthy commuters. You know the sort. Extruded Georgian dormopiles laid out in a series of microcrescents and called something ending in –imley, –amley or Wood.

This is different. A social experiment drawing together the very best minds in environmental aesthetics (me) and historical reconstruction (my old friend Dusty Penhaligon the conservactionist).

We have gone beyond pseudo. To feudo. Wodwo Manor will be the first neo-medieval feudopolis in Western Europe. If things go well, it could double in size by 2030 and might even become a neo-medieval statelet in due course.

It addresses the problem of where to park all those cluttering London families on zero hours contracts and benefits who must be cleared out to make way for genuine earners. The solution, as with so many of this government's solutions, is stupidly simple. Stuff them well out of everyone else's way, in a feudopolis.

A sizeable portion of the public seem keen on 'tough love'. Wait until they hear about the harsh but fair realities of a strip-farming economic system.

In Wodwo Manor, the poor may ascend to 'electronically tagged but deserving' status by working in rows of mile-long 24/7 polytunnels run by a PFI contractor under the DWP's new rural community service system, Welfarm.

They will also be paying tithes (determined on a case-by-case basis) to lord of the manor Mr Zhu Peng, whose innovative sale and leaseback deal has enabled this part of Oxfordshire to become officially under new medieval management.

FRIDAY Design a new Greek order, creating a fluted, post-austere column with the weighty capital removed from the top and repurposed as a plinth from which an intoxicated non-loadbearing caryatid of progressive Greek democracy may rise and flourish, part of – yet separate from – the Classical European edifice, effortlessly eluding architectural analogy as usual, don't worry I'm sure another Greek joke will be along in a minute.

SATURDAY Five-a-zeitgeist client blow football. Impoverished Progressive Statists 0, Wealthy Fascistic Patrons 100, after a mysterious late buyout via cash bungs.

SUNDAY Feudally 'lie fallow' all day in the recliner.

January 30, 2015

Hello Kinky Pinky

MONDAY Reboot my franchise, by starting the week more or less as usual but wearing a little hat for a change.

TUESDAY Looks like the hat's working its serendipitous magic already. As my friend the great hip-hop architect Spandrell Mish puts it, 'rebooty be begetting rebooty'.

Amazing. Once he'd heard about my hat – actually more of a modest Tudor cap worn at a jaunty angle, in the style of Thomas Cromwell – Mish simply had to hire me on the spot as 'vibe acoustician' for his latest, very important, cultured do-over.

And what a gig. A major rebosh of London landmark Chequer Point, the stylish 1966 tower designed by king of the swinging architects, 'Colonel' Danny Shapiro. So honoured to be a part of this, its seventh incarnation. Fingers crossed this one works.

I was involved in two of the earlier revamps. There was that one in the 70s when we gave it all a stark counter-culture sort of 'squatty' feel, lots of improvised art and anarchist ballet and whatnot. Then there was that much less successful Tory hub phase that followed. Pinstriped captains of industry in a press conference for eight years, barking about the unions and reeking of lunch.

I'm optimistic about this reboot though. Back to basics. A return to the ethos of having a tall, beautiful Modernist slab in central London occupied by arseholes.

WEDNESDAY Of course I know Spandrell Mish by his pre-hip-hop name, Richard Audley-Bryce. Oh man, Dickie was the life and soul of every Georgian squat in Spitalfields in the 80s. Even spent a few months in the full get-up, wig and everything, talking like an antiquated pillock.

Eventually he took a weekend off, rejoined the actual world for a bit and never went back. Bowled over by hip-hop, he started wearing his Georgian wig backwards and working up a theory of architecture based on the principles of rap. Linear narrative. Street-focused. 'Authentic' and 'challenging' to the point where if you didn't like what he was designing you were basically racist or whatever.

First he lost his double-barrelled name – 'The hyphen be a siphon yo' – then changed it altogether. He moved to Brooklyn while it was still a bit rough and was one of the guiding lights during its resurgence as a gentrified auto-nostalgic version of itself. Then, BOOM. His brand of auto-nostalgic rebranding rebooted a score of major hipster shtetls throughout the world. Mish went platinum. Global. The absolute bastard.

But now we turn our attention to Chequer Point. Or rather Kinky Sexpads, as it's being rebadged. 'Yo, first phase of the action be getting that Asian traction,' says Mish and it occurs to me that this hugely successful architect has spoken in nothing but rhyme since before the internet.

I'm not happy with the frankly vulgar rebadging. If it gets out that we're calling it 'that' to attract creepy Asian investors we'll look ACTUALLY racist. I suggest the more conservative Hello Kinky Pinky. Mish looks thoughtful. It's certainly vacuous enough. 'Know what I think? Paint the motherfucker pink,' he says. We're off.

THURSDAY Hit our first major problem. At ground level, the walls are covered in exquisite mosaics. A thousand square metres of dancing, abstract, life-affirming mosaics by Kenneth Lamb, post-war Britain's most important sculptor and mosaicist.

Unfortunately they're right in the way of an entirely rethought ground level, with semi-public areas and 5,700 sqm of exciting shops and restaurants with sponsored linkage to Soho, London's exciting new premium residential investment district.

We'll have to smash the mosaic walls to pieces. It doesn't feel *quite* in the spirit of the original Chequer Point – correction, Hello Kinky Pinky – but luckily I've still got my jaunty Tudor cap on and I am thinking in it.

FRIDAY I propose we address any anxieties about the destruction of these irreplaceable mosaics by inviting leading historians, architects and artists to a special meeting about their future after we've destroyed them.

And while building works proceed we could swathe the site in expensive-looking prints featuring blown-up snatches of Kenneth Lamb mosaics. It seems only fair.

SATURDAY Mish and I review the Hello Kinky Pinky reboot. Looking good. Fetishised inside, with a pink wash exterior. Renderings are great. It could be Vegas London, or Chinese London, or a totally new London at the luxury end of the Middle East.

SUNDAY Deboot in the recliner.

February 6, 2015

Post-Ecological Re-Regeneration

MONDAY Redesign the historic quarter of a French seaport, giving it a much less historic feel, which will make it easier to redevelop.

I'm reassuring conservationists by putting *Plus ca change!* in a jaunty font at the top of the drawings.

TUESDAY Ethical quandary. My fixer, Rock Steady Eddie, has opened what he calls a 'moody channel' with certain Wahabbist clients. They're keen to use high-profile urbanism as a repositioning opportunity. What with all the oil they're selling on the Turkish black market, they can now afford some swish military headquarters.

Before I proceed, I ring the Royal Institute for the Pop-Uption of British Architects' ethical support line for guidance. 'Lauren' introduces herself and asks how I am today. I outline my ethical dilemma: my clients are demented, murdering, rapist scum.

Lauren asks if the outline brief puts quality design at the heart of the procurement process. I check: no, it puts the will of God there instead.

Lauren asks me to hold while she consults her supervisor. Three premium phoneline minutes of lounge jazz later, Lauren comes back and says OK that should be fine but remember to keep all receipts, was there anything else I could help you with today, no problem, have a good one.

WEDNESDAY My old friend Amy Blackwater the ecomentalist is staying for a few days. She's as bossy as ever. 'Just chill, squarebob. I need to retro-construct an alibi. So say I was here at your place asleep in front of *Wolf Hall* when the incident occurred, right?'

It's a bold move. The 'incident' was an eco-terrorist bombing that destroyed some partially-built luxury apartments. Apparently they were 'totemic', top of the scale investment pads designed by hot epic space-mistress Camilla Beak. A 'cascading waterfall of urgent, foaming style' apparently, overlooking a private section of the Thames. Now pulverised.

There's blurry phone footage all over the internet of a suspected eco-terrorist wearing a balaclava making her escape in a wheelchair. Amy's not saying it IS her (it is) but nor is she saying it isn't (it so definitely is). I tell her she'll have to tweak the alibi.

Nobody on Twitter will believe for a second that she'd fall asleep during *Wolf Hall*'s lingering examination of truly exquisite built heritage locations such as Stabbyguts House, Somerset, Shittabedde Hall in Kent and Popefucke Abbey in Wiltshire.

After some thought, we decide she was alibi-watching *The Real Housewives of Cheshire* on itvBe.

THURSDAY My latest niche service is 'post-ecological re-regeneration'.

The problem: a post-industrial landscape scarred with dozens of unsightly, decaying sustainable energy visitor centres. These once-mighty engines of social and cultural change now lie desolate and broken. The glory days of strawbale compounds full of educational guff about heat loss and compost are long gone.

Now if people want a lecture about how fat white carnivorous motorists are total bastards they can simply read the *Guardian*.

The solution: rejuvenate these defunct energy visitor centres as 1990s heritage parks, incorporating energy visitor centre museums, shops and retro restaurants serving Britpop vegetarian food.

FRIDAY Oh-oh. Visit from the cops, who clearly have their suspicions about Amy. Their balaclava-recognition software would obviously nail it, but a poker-faced Amy insists she's lost hers. True enough, it's been incinerated, there's no way it's coming back.

'So you are telling us that you were here on the Wednesday night with your...' the plod gives me a sceptical glance. 'Companion. And you are both watching *The Real Housewives of Cheshire* on itvBe...' Amy and I raise our eyebrows and nod in unison.

'Not *Wolf Hall*, then?' says Plod 2, eyes fixed on his notebook. Amy and I look at one another with exaggerated innocence. 'Only they are having some tasty buildings on, I hear...' Now they're both staring at us with focused disbelief. 'All that linen fold panelling. Beautiful stonework. Lovely tapestries...' 'Ooh yeah, and them lush Tudor landscapes, eh?'

Amy says she missed the first one and so wants to wait for the DVD. They shake their heads and read the caution.

SATURDAY That was a close one. Down the station they challenged us, separately, to name a single Real Housewife of Cheshire. I went safe with 'Sali'. Amy went hard with 'Wonga' and scored a bullseye. The alibi stands.

SUNDAY Sketch out my pitch for The Six Real Housewives of Hilary Mantel's Tudor England in the recliner.

February 27, 2015

If It Ain't Broke, Amend It

MONDAY 'Just a bit of fun' says Beansy the nanofuturologist, with a dismissive wave of his hand. 'Obviously it's not a serious design tool...'

He's talking about the beta version of Perlaastica, a 'real-life Photoshop' toy he invented at the weekend. Basically, you capture a lump of the built environment using a special 3-D laptop camera, then 'open it' in miniaturised real space, adding or changing whatever you fancy using 'a vast library of downloadable elements' – in other words, the internet.

Then you simply press DONE and Perlaastica spits the amended lump back into the real world, where it exists until the free trial expires.

I ask Beansy casually if I can borrow it for a week. No problem, he says, just don't do anything stupid. I return his dismissive hand wave.

TUESDAY In the morning, capture a smallish corner of a Canary Wharf office building, open it in Perlaastica then quickly remodel the miniaturised real space into a primitive 'oasis at night' with giant moths and robot camels, while security's attention is focused on his pie.

The robot camels are quite crude – I nicked them from a 1970s Israeli comedy – but let's face it they look a lot more entertaining than corporate polished concrete. It's thrilling to watch the reaction of passers-by, who seem cheered by the randomised temporary reality.

Also a relief to discover Perlaastica can't capture and amend bits of people. A weirded-out finance director staggers from the building, wondering why half her office space is now a surreal oasis. Everyone shrugs and assumes the building has been acquired by interests in the Middle East.

In the afternoon, I test Perlaastica's historical reach by causing an archived copy of the scissor arches from Wells Cathedral to appear in M&M's World, London. Not a flicker. People think it's just routine maintenance.

In the evening, try my hand at architectural busking on the South Bank, coughing up bits of the Festival of Britain from 1951 for delighted tourists, quickly reverse-modding back to the contemporary Festival of Aviva when the police swing by.

WEDNESDAY Drunk with power now. I'm in the *London Standard* at last! After months of trying to raise my profile with mad plans for elevated cycleways and stacked 'metrodorms' I finally make it into print as 'London's 3-D graffiti artist'.

My fixer Rock Steady Eddie is quoted as a source close to me. I'm called 'Urban2000', apparently I'm doing this to challenge perceptions of built reality and all commercial enquiries should go through him.

The article features pictures of my latest Perlaastica amends: a large section of Portsmouth's vanished Tricorn Centre repurposed as a new tower for Westminster Abbey; an ironic ring of Leylandii around Euston station; an Art Deco façade on Lewisham KFC; the Trajan Arch in the middle of Seven Dials; medieval stained glass enclosing a pod on the London Eye.

I wonder how long celebrity lasts these days.

THURSDAY Oh God, people are so gullible. Yes of COURSE there are 326 anonymous entries in the design competition for a new Thames crossing at Nine Elms, dummies. Just under 300 of them are mine.

I captured the air over the river and spent the day in a miniaturised real-space Perlaastica workshop, taking snapshots. I've got one that looks like a horizontal Niagara Falls, one that looks like a hairbrush, one that just looks like a redacted word in a confidential report... Wow, imagine if anonymous design compettions were actually like this.

FRIDAY Beansy calls. 'This you in the *Standard*, and all over the bloody world of epic space?'

Not happy. 'I told you not to do anything stupid...' I protest my innocence, extravagantly. 'Oh, really. So this isn't you then, using Perlaastica to create exciting new artist's impressions of an Arctic Metropolis.'

I tell him, honestly, that I haven't been to the Arctic recently, with or without his stupid gadget. He tells me, with impressive insight, that I clearly captured the interior of a freezer and used that as the notional Arctic site. Which apparently is an unforgiveable trespass against the sacred law of *genius loci* or whatever.

SATURDAY Perlaastica's back with Beansy – he sent a cab for it – and all my free trial creations have vanished in a huff, leaving a much more boring London and a massively diminished bridge competition.

SUNDAY Unchanged, in the recliner.

March 6, 2015

History Eats Itself

MONDAY Being an auteur of epic space isn't always easy. You have to take the rough with the smooth. And sometimes you have to bring together the very rough (my fixer Rock Steady Eddie) and the very smooth (my friend Darcy Farquear'say the architecture critic and his overdressed dachshund Bauhau).

Darcy and I have thought of a pop-up idea so exquisite it's a kind of mental torture. Post-Shoreditch. Just far enough ahead of the curve to be showing its arse to the hipster peloton.

This idea is SO good, we need to get it into development asafp, before another pair of slightly drunk acquaintances with a dog in a little hat come up with it too. If we're to succeed we need Eddie's fast-track mind, business acumen and underworld contacts.

TUESDAY 'Is it a bitch?' asks Eddie, squinting hard at Bauhau and helping himself to another of Darcy's offal-and-rhubarb nibbles.

Eddie's out of his comfort zone. We're in this week's most chictastic restaurant, an ephemeral dining experience created in a dilapidated Brighton drill hall, called SHOLDER. The twist is, the food's done by an ageing Young British Artist and the décor's by an aging TV chef. Also, Bauhau's wearing leopard print hotpants and salmon-pink bootees.

'A bitch?' Darcy gasps asthmatically. 'Bauhau's utterly a boy dog, thank you very much.' Eddie looks impressed. 'Well he's come to the right place innit. Brighton? Full of 'em. Waitress! Another go of them kidney phings and two more poofs' cocktails for my paedo friends. Get us a lager top, I'm spitting feathers here. Whoa. I'm not being offensive, love, but are you Asian? I know a lot of trannies are...'

I get Eddie off the premises while Darcy stays to be horrified for all of us.

WEDNESDAY Every cloud. Eddie blamed his disgusting rainbow of phobias on some bad gear he'd had, apologised to everyone and in his humility has pitched our project to Irish Connie, London's pop-up queenpin, who apparently will 'bite our hands off'. He feints a biting motion and barks at Bauhau, who reacts adorably by soiling his hotpants.

THURSDAY Send our outline proposal to Irish Connie. It's a pop-up restaurant combining the two things we secretly miss most about the 20th century: the Cold War and tinned food.

Imagine a basement diner done out like a 1980s nuclear bunker, with TINNED ITEMS ONLY on the menu. It's as if everything really DID go tits up after Frankie Goes To Hollywood's second single.

Staff in radiation suits and masks. Brutalist tables and chairs. Stencilled signage in Impact Bold. Rough concrete. Behind a long, heavy glass wall, a slow conveyer belt full of tinned food. You relay your dinner order via military walkie-talkie to anonymous 'lab assistants'. With massive gauntlets and long grippers they assemble your nuclear dinner for preparation in the Heating Area.

People will love this. Think about those immersive film nights, where they pay a fortune to dress as an extra on the set of *Fight Club* or *Shawshank Redemption*, queuing up for a beating or a difficult trip through a sewer. How much more stylish to be eating food from tins and pretending you're in a BBC Play For Today.

Eddie, Darcy and I are simultaneously excited and ravenous. Bauhau just barks excitedly, I suppose that's his job. 'Oh yes, darling, there'll be tinned dog food too!' coos Darcy.

I point out that as it's a nuclear bunker pets must be left outside to die. Eddie cackles. Darcy bristles. Bauhau remains enigmatically stupid.

FRIDAY Thumbs up from Irish Connie. Backing secured! More good news – another of those deeply cherished live music venues that make London so very special has just had its rent quintupled, so a tasty basement space has become available.

SATURDAY Irish Connie says our proposed restaurant name – Cool War – isn't mimsy enough for today's discerning wankers. She suggests TIN-TINS, which will chime but not infringe. Sorted.

And 'fun designers' East Algia are on board. Their recent underwater pop-up diner, Rejection, served food that had been partially digested and then regurgitated by dolphins, still warm.

SUNDAY Planning tasting menu in the recliner. Watney's Red Barrel. Tinned nuts, olives. Pre-mixed margarita. Little can of muscadet. Tinned Bismarck herring. Fray Bentos steak pie, giant marrowfat peas, big tin of gutsy claret...

Cor. Put on some Shostakovich. Have tinned lunch.

April 3, 2015

The Twelve Step Plan

MONDAY Open mic night at the Institute of Plasmic Arts. Here, brevity is gravity. And I am briefer, more plasmic and artier than any of those other epic space sucker MCs, even if I DO say so myself.

On the big screen side by side are projected images of a Modernist piloti and an iPad stylus. I shout 'GENRE SMASH!' The echo subsides. A silence. The audience considers. Does this mean anything? I remain on stage, implying that it most certainly does.

A sudden eruption of cheering and wild applause. I drop the mic, walk off stage. Boom. Done it again. Idiots.

TUESDAY Alas, genre smashes don't always work. Example: my visitor centre at a certain exquisite County Durham castle. Status: 'Especially Historic'. You can imagine the paperwork.

My clients decided to cut costs by squashing the energy centre and the faith garden into one single innovative landscape. Now the bindweed's gone mental and the place is full of religious windbags. Well done, 'holistic budgetary thinking'.

WEDNESDAY I'm reinvigorating a London 'tourist magnet' famous for its live music venue, ramshackle cafés, sprawling outdoor market and canal culture.

Tourists can always spend more. Land can always work harder. But it's of paramount importance that we preserve the area's character. Relax. That area character will be very carefully removed, lump by grimey lump, put carefully into a preservative skip marked FRAGILE – 'CHARACTER' and then whatever.

THURSDAY My fixer Rock Steady Eddie now has a lucrative sideline. He's a brownfield development planning consultant to philanthropist-developers keen to put something back into whatever community they've acquired a plot of land in.

The 'something' they usually want to 'put back' is high-density luxury apartment blocks aimed at either the overseas investment market or at domestic grim-faced dog owners in pastel jumpers who've just cashed in their pensions. The 'journey' of a brownfield development planning consultant has 12 billable stages:

1. The developer, having acquired a brownfield site with the intention of improving the neighbourhood for purely sentimental reasons, appoints a planning consultant to show everything's above board and totally legit.
2. Consultant conducts a thorough lunchtime site appraisal.
3. Developer astonished to learn there's a pub still operating in the middle of what he assumed was an abandoned car park, created in the wake of heavy German bombing in 1943, when plucky Brits defied the Nazi menace, etc.
4. Consultant's details appear at the bottom of a press release referencing the dark days of World War Two and the bravery of ordinary, aspirational people huddled in bomb shelters, dreaming of a future free from tyranny with access to high quality lifestyle signifiers in the heart of the sexy city with great wi-fi, transport links, the lot.
5. Developer applies to have historic pub removed from site, citing a report from the planning consultant warning that we live in uncertain times and that the building could literally fall down at any moment.
6. Planning authority refuses permission to demolish, thereby encouraging busybodies to have it listed for its special cultural interest as the only functioning public house left in a five-mile radius, all others having been erased or converted into 'luxury pubpartments'.
7. Planning consultant's supplementary application warns that neither the local authority nor the historic buildings people have seen the developer when he loses his temper; furthermore, they would really not like him when he's taken a drink.
8. Pub accidentally demolished by a coincidental anthology of heavy machinery in the early hours. Landlady narrowly escapes in her pyjamas.
9. Developer, as surprised as anyone else, promises to investigate and directs all enquiries to planning consultant.
10. Planning consultant unavailable for comment.
11. Developer, guilty of illegal destruction, is fined the equivalent of three months rent for one of the 42 luxury flats he's now developing.
12. Developer draws line under whole affair and moves on, having learned life lesson; all enquiries to planning consultant, who remains unavailable for comment.

FRIDAY Spend all day with Eddie in an undemolished pub, where he is unequivocally and relentlessly available for comment.

SATURDAY Jazz Architecture Huff Posts. 'Fuck You Man, I'm Not a Goddam Starchitect' by Frank Gehry's Middle Finger beats 'Iconicity' by Patrik Schumacher and his Identical Haircuts by 357,000 page impressions.

SUNDAY Self-pretentionise into a riddle, wrapped in a mystery, in a recliner.

April 17, 2015

Not Being Funny but Black People Don't Do Gardening, Do They?

MONDAY Democracy is broken. Our two-party system has silted up. A resigned sense of deadlock, torpor and inertia hangs over everything. Party strategists are utterly failing to reach a disengaged and apathetic electorate. There's panic at the top.

So that's PERFECT. One person's panic is someone else's built environment advisory gig at three grand a day plus VAT and a proper lunch.

TUESDAY To Spearmint Rhino, where a private room has been reserved in the name of 'Michael Green'.

Conservative party leader Grant Shapps is there in a wig and fake moustache, looking like a 70s footballer at ease with his sexuality. It's a clever disguise; Grant could easily be a Spearmint Rhino customer. 'Welcome to our thinking cell!' he squeaks. 'Let's scrum down and spank out some one-liners!' He keeps disappearing for half an hour at a time.

My cellmates are all about 80 years old and seem to be in a permanently bad mood. There's a medievalist scholar opposed to everything after Durham Cathedral, a weird Mussolini superfan smelling strongly of scotch, and some doddery architect who once converted Margaret Thatcher's pantry into a neo-Gothic CIA bedsit. Lunch is at Rules, where we scribble some coordinated Tory pledges on a spanking paddle.

Summary: dispose of all public assets including local authorities; incentivise housebuilders with subsidies and peerages; grant 'futurospective' planning permission for everything submitted after May 7; Beatrix Pottery design guidelines to attract overseas investors; get some hip-hop Tories to rap about our 'property-owning democracy'.

WEDNESDAY To a simple giant open-plan kitchen in Hampstead, where an unnamed, intensely relaxed billionaire is *in absentia* hosting a 'policy pitstop' for the Labour party.

Most of the people here seem to have very slight connections to the built environment. If I didn't know better, I'd say a lot of high-end development in central London was funded by laundered cash from gambling, petrochemicals, prostitution, tobacco and drugs.

My fellow 'policy possibilisers' (most are in their 30s, tiny radio mics attached to their contoured faces) seem in a terrible hurry to get back to whatever it is they do, so we've wrapped by lunchtime.

Summary: a new garden city for every actual city; simultaneously increase and reduce infrastructure spending; boost the affordability of everything by 20 per cent; declare hundreds of thousands of acres of scattered brownfield land to be a single entity, confer a personality upon it, then somehow publicly shame it into creating new housing.

THURSDAY The Liberal Democrats are holding their emergency thought-processing day in a converted Routemaster. Perhaps it's a metaphor. The mood's definitely depressed on the lower deck, a mood tinged perhaps with a nostalgia for antique relevance. They're smoking something upstairs, but nobody's laughing.

We all work in silence on our laptops, emailing our thoughts to an unsmiling 'conductor'. At the end of our shift he dings the bell and issues purchase order tickets.

Summary: network of 'allotment cities' with an engorged Cambridge concentrating mostly on vegetables; new network of housing suppliers to be encouraged through collaboration, partnership and shout-outs on social media; a Green Buildings Act to reverse climate change all the way back to the Renaissance, anything's possible, believe.

FRIDAY In the morning, I join an SNP 'brainhoolie' via videolink. Summary: a completely new built environment for the whole of Scotland, called something tabloid-friendly like 'The Great McOver'; Donald Trump to become National Design Laird; 21st-century building types, e.g. nanocrofts, microvillas, tinyments.

In the afternoon, a freestyle ideas jam on Google Hangout with the Greens. Summary: forge a spiritual consortium with the spirits of the wind and sun; an end to roads, airports and all unnecessary additives in building materials; new elvish space standards; more fibre in visual arts.

SATURDAY Ukip Policy Awayday. I say 'awayday', that's what Ukip's director of environmental policy (Alex 'Gyppo' Thompson) calls it. Conjures up the early days of team-building when you could smoke indoors, and homosexuality was just a phase people went through.

What today's actually about is a bunch of gung-ho Rotary Club types getting half-timbered all day in a Thanet pub. Every now and then 'Gyppo' scrawls someone's brainspurt on the 'I'm Not Racist But...' whiteboard. '...herbaceous borders make good neighbours...not being funny but black people don't do gardening, do they?'

Summary: Make sure everything's CAPPED. Immigration, social housing, golfers, cultural ambition, tweets.

SUNDAY Apolitically reclined.

May 1, 2015

The Bees Have It

MONDAY Recalibrate my optimism, bringing it into line with new five-year projections.

TUESDAY I've reconfigured Britain for foreign investors: Scottish Nationalist, Scottish Tearooms, Northern Powerhouse, Northern Shithouse, Worst Midlands, Eacist Midlands, Value Wales, Premium Wales, South West Land Bank, Non-Dormitory South East, First Class Coastal, Second Class Coastal, Help to Buy Home Counties, Qatar, All Rights Reserved.

WEDNESDAY Still, good news that the Hon. Aeneas Upmother-Brown has returned to government. His erudite and humane approach is in welcome contrast to the coarse and venal character of so many Conservative ministers. Also, he's a long-standing acquaintance of mine so if there ARE any low-hanging gigs I might be in with a shout.

Upmother-Brown is back in the department of entertainment, this time as Minister for Pop-Uption. Key role. Pop-ups represent the fastest-growing sector of British culture, according to the latest figures from 2011.

Pop-up is a framing mechanism for a wide range of monetisable cultural offshoots – architecture, niche dining, community dating, Brighton wankers selling gin cocktails from the boot of their classic Morris Minor. Its influence cannot be overmetastated.

THURSDAY Of course, whatever the Hon. Aeneas Upmother-Brown does, he'll always literally be overshadowed by his swarm of pet bees.

Bees have been his constant companions since the days of Cool Britannia, when people and bees could exchange cheeky banter at Number 10 parties in the company of luminaries such as Peter Mandelson, Ben Elton, the drummer from Elastica and Fat George the Namibian White Honeybee.

Today I'm at a Service of Remembrance and Hope organised by the Commonwealth Apicultural Association at Heathrow airport. Politicians, beekeepers and opinion-formers from across the world have gathered with their swarms to mourn those who have fallen and to resolve to build a better future. An optimistic requiem hum fills the prayer centre.

Later, everyone's buzzing as we shuffle and bank our way into the chartered plane. Milan – here we come!

FRIDAY Milan Expo. The UK's pop-up pavilion has so far been 'under the radar' because of the recent electoral unpleasantness.

It's a brilliant pop-up, but was kept quiet in case it was seen to be championing the values of Conservatives who were, after all, the clients. Technically so were the Lib Dems, but their extinction seems closer than even the bee community's so bollocks to them.

The Hon. Aeneas Upmother-Brown addresses an expectant crowd of media and business bastards. 'Ladies and gentlemen,' he says, the hovering commonwealth of bees behind him falling respectfully silent, 'we are here today to honour British pop-up ingenuity.

'This pavilion explores a series of landscapes travelled by the honey bee' – here the bees do adorable little jazz hands – 'showing how pollination is vital in feeding the planet. And how we must address this global challenge…' The sublest of movements within the bee-cloud suggests a corporate determination to improve things.

'The centrepiece of this marvellous creation is the Hive, a cuboid lattice structure inspired by the honeycomb's form…' Here Upmother-Brown unzips and steps out of his 'suit' to reveal a bee costume. The crowd murmurs. The bees softly sizzle. 'Yes, ladies and gentlemen, this incredible space comes alive through light and sound to mimic a beehive. But...have you ever witnessed thousands of bees mimicking an...incredible HUMAN space?'

The buzzing umma swirls into action. Specks of iron in the air, snap-magnetised – whoosh! They converge into an unmistakeable thicket of spires. 'Behold! The Sagrada Familia!' Gasps.

The winged mass dissolves and then resolves into a series of landmark buildings. The Freedom Tower (the bees hum a few bars of the 'Stars and Stripes'). Notre-Dame de Paris ('Frere Jacques'). The dizzying anthology continues, and there are tears when the bees create the vanished library at Rennie Mackintosh's Glasgow School of Art ('Auld Lang Syne').

Then, over a pounding Bee Gees medley, there's the obligatory upbeat urban waggle-dance routine. They've even got a little bee who climbs to the top of a massive bee pyramid and backflips off.

The crowd erupts. The bees embrace, awkwardly, and return to their respective handlers. Is it a metaphor for global unity? Possibly. Or a warning about the dangers of unions and collective action. The Hon. Aeneas Upmother-Brown should keep an eye on those bees. Only 37 per cent of them are Tories.

SATURDAY Return home with my Milan Expo business card pollen.

SUNDAY Non-industry in the recliner.

May 15, 2015

A Sense of Placenta

MONDAY The problem? A housing crisis in London, an urgent need to maximise brownfield and infill sites, affordable space at a premium. The solution? My new building conversion prototype, the SHEDSIT.

High-five self, take rest of day off.

TUESDAY God, I wish the high-pitched arty-farty Twitterati would give it a bloody rest for five minutes.

OK, so I designed one of the seven 'concentrated camps' they're setting up in Qatar to accommodate World Cup migrant labourers. What? You'd rather they were just sleeping rough? Spare me the finger-wagging.

My concentrated camp is called Conservative City and it has everything the contemporary indentured foreign labourer at the mercy of a powerful desert kingdom may desire. Roofs. Rentable mattresses. Buyable food. Generous discounts on all World Cup replica kits.

I've even included a discreet 'dormitory village', which is what my clients have thoughtfully renamed the mortuary.

WEDNESDAY I'm creating a potentially iconic profile for a city skyline. Doesn't matter which city to be honest, they're all more or less the same, aren't they?

I've started with the name, as this can really nail the spirit of a city, wherever it is. I'm calling whatever it is The Placenta. That gives it a literal sense of place, and also subliminally suggests that as a landmark entity it will be organic and full of transmittable urban nutrients.

Before I decide if my placenta landmark is actually a building of some sort, I decide that it will definitely be a) a gateway experience and b) the ultimate global branding vehicle. What's important these days is not 'how it looks' but 'what people see'. And with a 4,000 sqm LED urban placental meniscus completely covering whatever's underneath with arresting, effervescent 24/7 advertising, that whole boring problem of what to put underneath is literally 'overthrown'.

Expedience follows form follows function follows global branding. Yes, The Placenta will be delicious, whichever city it plops down in.

Oh, I know! I'll just stuff a generic office building underneath the LED meniscus, that's always a financially solid move. Everybody LOVES offices covered in adverts. Man alive, it's on days like this I feel proud to be whatever it is I am, doing whatever it is I do.

THURSDAY I was asked to carry out a survey of sexual orientation in the world of epic space. I'm afraid I can't tell you who the client was. Let's just say they're at the high end of online fashion retail.

It was a multiple-choice questionnaire. A lot of respondents put themselves down for more than one sexuality. Which is fine obviously although this may have tailoring implications for the client, I don't know. Which incidentally was itself a high-scoring sexual orientation. Percentage results as follows.

Actually Straight: 43. Straight for Clients: 87. Straight for Planners: 62. Simply Gay: 55. Minimalist Gay: 21. Baroque Gay: 17. Parametric Lesbian: 12. Right Angular Lesbian: 5. Generic Bi-Perpendicular: 29. Neither Know nor Care: 48. Polymorphic With Buffed Finish: 1. Cross-Dressed Mix of Folk Sexuality and High Architecture: 2. Open: 33. Ajar: 41.

FRIDAY Depressing day at Labour party headquarters. I've been asked over to give them an estimate for rebuilding. As is customary in this sort of extended metaphor I shake my head a lot and breathe in sharply through my teeth, which is more difficult to do with dignity than you'd imagine. I keep nearly choking.

The bad news I have to give them (and here I take the customary pencil stub from behind my ear and lick it, ugh, disgusting) is that even with the support of stylish professionals such as architects, ceramic artists, digital conceptualists and sound sculptors, Labour is extremely unstable and could collapse at any moment.

For now I'm recommending rhetorical underpinning and a temporary, disingenuous façade, but long term I think they need to demolish and start again on solid ground. Maybe a traditional community build next time, with nothing BUT 'poor doors'.

SATURDAY Five-a-zeitgeist reversible football. Pushme-Popup 2, Metrolympiad Olympicopopolis 2, after decompression, shirt removal and life-swapping.

SUNDAY Deep contemplation in the recliner. I think about where we are, and who we are, and it all seems a bit like one of those beautiful Grayson Perry pots. In many ways it's a funny old world, yet in a number of specific ways it's a tragic new one.

May 29, 2015

Acknowledgements

Firstly, massive thanks to everyone at *Architects' Journal*, where these columns originally appeared. The *AJ* has been incredibly supportive considering this is a cynical ploy to get paid twice for the same stuff. Cheers. I started writing a weekly sarcastic column for architects in 1990 and it has been at the core of my life ever since. Thanks, *AJ*, for just letting me get on with it. What a great magazine. What a brilliant gig.

I salute Emily Bryce-Perkins, who had the bright idea of taking this to Unbound.

Most of all I want to thank the British architectural profession. Architects are such a lovely bunch of people. Clever and resilient, game for a laugh. I have worked alongside you and mocked your world relentlessly. In return you have been stoical and forgiving. Thank you. It has genuinely been an honour and a privilege to have taken the piss out of you for three decades.

Let's all have a long, boozy lunch.

Supporters

Unbound is a new kind of publishing house. Our books are funded directly by readers. This was a very popular idea during the late eighteenth and nineteenth centuries. Now we have revived it for the internet age. It allows authors to write the books they really want to write and readers to support the books they would most like to see published.

The names listed below are of readers who have pledged their support and made this book happen. If you'd like to join them, visit www.unbound.com.

@tanjastweets

Martin Adams

Jo Addison

Keith Adsley

Ross Aitken

Ruth Alborough

Moose Allain

Robert Allan

Catherine Aman

Abigail Amey

Marija Andabak

Tom Anderson

Hanna Andrykowska

Roger Angus

David Aplin

Sandra Armor

Jamie Ashmore

Kindly Atcha

Mark Attmore

Nigel Auchterlounie (AKA Spleenal)

David Auerbach

Matthew Austin

Clare Axton

Matthew Ayres

Suzanne Azzopardi

Louish 'Opisbo' B

Adrian Bailey

Jo Baker

Joseph Baldwin

Jason Ballinger

Louis Barfe

Rhys Barter

John Bassett

Matthew Bate

John Batty

Adam Baylis-West

Alex Beasley

George Beasley

Lotte Beasley

Michael Beasley

Beaubodor Beaubodor

Jonathan Bell

Charlie Bennett

Jon Bennett

Noah Berman

Tania Berry

Brian Bilston

Julie Bindel

Lewis Blackwell

David Blair

Eddie Blake

Tony Blow

Simon Booth

Jon Bounds

Steve Bowbrick

Richard Bower

Matthew Bowers

Jonathan Bown

John Boxall

Frankie Boyle

Maria Boyle

Ben 'not your average horticulturist' Brace

Richard W H Bray

Ian Brice

MC Brown

Tamara Brummer

Bunny Brunnhilde

Nick Bryan

Emily Bryce-Perkins

Zuul Bubulj

Liz Buckley

Sarah Buczynski

Ainslie Bulmer

Julia Burden

Mark Burford

Andrea Burgess

Alison Burns

Holly Burns

Chris Busby

Duncan Campbell

Kelley Campbell

Martin Carr

Ali Carron

Barry Caruth

Daragh Carville

Steven Cassidy

Daniel Castellá

David Catherall

Alison Cawley

Kevin Cecil

Rick Challener

Marnie Chesterton

Jake Child

George Chinnery

Terry Clague

James Clark

Jude Clarke

Elliott Clarkson

Mathew Clayton

Dave Cohen

Richard Cohen

Andrew Colclough

James Cole

Nigel Cole

Jenny Colgan

Stevyn Colgan

Paul Collins

John Cooke

Colin C. Cooper

Corrie Corfield

Tracey Cormack

Thomas Corrie

crapstone_villas

Alejandro Crivellari

Andrew Croker

Ingrid Curl

Rod Dale

Baker Danny

Gillian Darley

Paul Bassett Davies

Stephen Davies

Tom Dawkins

Michelle De Larrabeiti

Alex Dennis

Anthony Dhanendran

Safety Diagnostics

Sarah Ditum

Nick Dixon

Anne Doherty

Steve Doherty

Jason Douglas

Tiernan Douieb

James Dowding

Asmat Downey

Andrew Driver

Angela Duggan

Lee Duncan

Ceri Dunstan

Cameron Eccles

Eden and Amanda

Justin Edwards

Paula Edwards

EdWilbur EdWilbur

Håvar Ellingsen

Sam Ellis

Susan Emmens

Soulla Tantouri Eriksen

Neil Erskine

David Evans

Gareth Evans

Matthew Evans

Simon Evans

Emmet Farragher

Jennifer Faulconbridge

Chris Fay

Dawn Fearon

Peter Fellows

Simon Ferguson

Loz Fillmore

Toby Finlay

Lauren Fisher

Iain Fleming

Peter Fletcher

Sue Flymptoms

Adam Foster

Isobel Frankish

Peter Fraser

Curtis Frye

Martin Gardner

Tony Garland

Keily Geary

Amro Gebreel

Lauren Geisler

Rose George

Andrea Gibb

Abi Gilmore

Mark Ginns

Chris Gittner

Helen Goddard

John Goddard

Clare Gogerty

Pippa Goldfinger

Christopher Goldie

Alan Gordon

Alex Gordon

Kenneth Gordon

Jeremy Gostick

Charlie Gould

Christopher Gower

David Graham

Stuart Graham

Clive Gray

Sean Gray

Zachary Gray

Lucien Green

Phil Greenland

Geoff Griffiths

Jonathan Griffiths

Mike Griffiths

Ray Griffiths

Charlie Guymer

Jake Haggmark

John Halton

Thomas Hamid

Jana Hannon

Orla Hannon

Simon Harper

Lauran Harris

Sophie Hay

Jason Hazeley

David Heath

Eric Heath

Luke Hebblethwaite

Keith Hector

Simon Henry

Charlotte Henwood

Stuart Heritage

Lorenzo Hermoso

Sean Hewitt

Sam Higgins

James Higgott

Dan Hill

Marcus Hirst

Niall Hobhouse

Paul Hodges

Clark Hogan-Taylor

Nico Hogg

Sophie Holborow

Lisa Holdsworth

Jonathan Hope

Alex Housden

Catherine Howard-Dobson

Bob Howell

Sali Hughes

James Hunt

Cait Hurley

Elisabeth Hutchinson

Sara Huws

Paul Huxley

Ben Ingram

Dale Ingram

Michael Islip

Dan Jackson

Ollie Jacob

Sam Jacob

Chris James

Gareth James

David Janes

Greg Jenner

Ric Jerrom

Colin Jones

Neil Jones

Nick Jones

Angus Jordan

Jack Jordan

Martin Joyce

Shirley Judd

Joanne K

Cory Kamholz

Ian Oddfodder Kavanagh

Steven Kealey

Dave Kelly

Matti Keltanen and
Amanda Thurman

Rory Kennedy

Vicky Kett

Dan Kieran

John Kiernan

Rachel Killeen

Jessica Killingley

John King

David Knight

Jon Knight

Jonathan Knowles

David & Rebecca Kong

Mark Kozakiewicz

Paul Labbett

Jenny Landreth

Robert Langley

Per Larsson

Jimmy Leach

David Lewis

Justin Lewis

Oliver Lewis

Rhodri Lewis

Jenny Littlewood

Greatbig Lizard

Paul Lobban

Clare Long

Stephen Longstaffe

Cat Lort

Sean & Callie Love

Malcolm Lowe

Graham Lowell

DeAndra Lupu

Tim Lusher

James Lynch

Patrick Lynch

Dorian Lynskey

Neil Macehiter

Murdoch MacPhee

Megan and Edie Macqueen

Jennifer Maidman

Daniel Maier

Joanne Mariner

Linda Marric

Rhodri Marsden

Jammyful Martian

Becky Martin

Betsy Martin

Daniel Martin

Daryl Martin

Eileen Martin

Ian Masterson

Richard McConnell

Helen McCorry

Sam McDermott

Mhairi McFarlane

Jamie McKelvie

Dom McKenzie

Shirley Mcmillan

David McParland

Ryan McRostie

Malik Meer

Ian Meikle

Kirsty Merryfield

Saul Metzstein

Maureen Millar

Adam Miller

Chris Miller

Phil Miller

Margo Milne

James Milner

Tracie Misiewicz

John Mitchinson

Gordon Moar

Caitlin Moran

Sarah Morgan

Stuart Moss

Jojo Moyes

Jon Mundy

Jane Murison

Peter Murray

Peter Natural

Rebecca Naughten

Carlo Navato

Gee Neale

Richard Neville

David Newsome

Jeanette Nicholas

Simon Nicholls

Al Nicholson

John Niven

Greg Norman

Iain Norton

Lorraine Nutt

Rory O'Donoghue

Robert O'Neil

Mark O'Neill

Shane O'Toole

Lauren Oakey

Georgia Odd

Ben Oliver

Richard Osman

Alan Outten

Sali Owen

Ian Page

Ian Painter

Alex Paknadel

Anya Palmer

Pradumn Pamidighantam

Ol Parker

Richard Parker

Steven Parker

Mark Parmenter

David Pasquesi

Sarah Patmore

Debbie Patton

Martin Pearce

Hugh Pearman

John Pendlebury

Lori Perlman

Elizabeth Perry

Ivor Phillips

Tom Phillips

Debra Pickering

Basil Pieroni

Jeremy Pike

John Pluthero

Justin Pollard

Daniel Potter aka
@legobookworm

Mandy Powell

Sunand Prasad

Lawrence Pretty

Neil Pretty

Georgia Pritchett

David Quantick

Neil Quinn

Julia Raeside

Andy Randle

Dan Rebellato

Claire Redmond

Margaret Reeves

Gail Renard

Ben Reynolds

Christopher Rhodes

Paul Rhodes

Simon Ricketts

Hugo Rifkind

Mike Rigby

Andy Riley

Liam Riley

Wyn Roberts

Josy Roberts-Pay

Craig Robertson

Rachael Robinson

Eddie Robson

Tony Roche

Stian Rødland

Jenny Rollo

Seb Rose

Charlie Rowlands

Keith Ryan

Peter Sach

Ben Sansum

Darren Savage

Rob Sawkins

Ian Saxby

Neil Sayer

Penny Schenk

Siobhan Scott

Jack Seale

Matthew Searle

Dale Shaw

Jodi Shields

Nadia Shireen

Barry Short

Steve Simms-Luddington

Andrew Simpson

Julian Simpson

Robert Skilbeck

Catherine Slessor

Bob Smith

Brian Smith

Michael Smith

Will Smith

Rachel Sommerville

Tom Southerden

Andrew Spencer

Truda Spruyt

Thom Stanbury

Murray Steele

Robin Stephenson

Esther Steward

Daniel Stilwell

Martin Stockley

Helen Stone

Brendan Strong

Susan Surface

Graeme Swanson

Cat & Owen Taylor

Justine Taylor

Mark Taylor

Neil Taylor

Tot Taylor

James Taylor-Foster

Ben Thacker

Advent the318

Joe Thorley

Tracey Thorn

Amanda Triccas

Julia Trocme-Latter

Jeremy Truslove

Hannah Tucker

Christopher Turnbull-Grimes

Adam Turtle

Rita Tweeter

P H Ukwit

Paul Unett

Gus Unger-Hamilton

Shaun Usher

Chris Van Tulleken

Ian Vince

Elizabeth Walker

Stephen Walker

Ian Wall

Susan Wall

Mick Walsh

Christian Ward

James Ward

Tim Warneford

Joe Wass

Simon Watkins

Rose Watt

Sean Watters

Ximena Waudby

Neil Weatherall

Nathan Webb

David Webster

Kate Webster

Scott Weddell

Rosie Weeks

David Welsh

Peter Welsh

Roy White

Stephen White

Ben Whitehouse

Andrew Wilcox @unclewilco

Will Wiles

Ben Willbond

Gruffudd Williams

Martyn Williams

Mike Williams

Robin Williams

Alan Wilson

Alexa Wilson

Gregg Wilson

Sam Wilson

Anna Wood

Matthew Wood

Francesca Woodhouse

Steve Woodward

Emma Woolerton

Nick Wray

Paul Wray

Alex Wright

Lauren Yeates

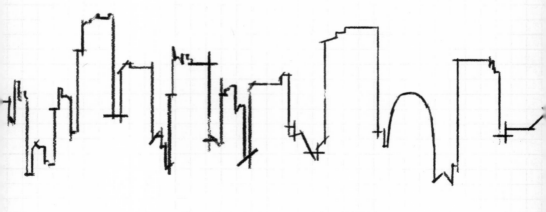